TRIUMPH
A BUCKHEAD TALE

ETIENNE

Published by
Dreamspinner Press
382 NE 191st Street #88329
Miami, FL 33179-3899, USA
http://www.dreamspinnerpress.com/

This is a work of fiction. Names, characters, places, and incidents either are the product of the author's imagination or are used fictitiously, and any resemblance to actual persons, living or dead, business establishments, events, or locales is entirely coincidental.

Triumph
Copyright © 2012 by Etienne

Cover Art by Reese Dante   http://www.reesedante.com

All rights reserved. No part of this book may be reproduced or transmitted in any form or by any means, electronic or mechanical, including photocopying, recording, or by any information storage and retrieval system without the written permission of the Publisher, except where permitted by law. To request permission and all other inquiries, contact Dreamspinner Press, 382 NE 191st Street #88329, Miami, FL 33179-3899, USA
http://www.dreamspinnerpress.com/

ISBN: 978-1-61372-454-5

Printed in the United States of America
First Edition
April 2012

eBook edition available
eBook ISBN: 978-1-61372-455-2

Praise for ETIENNE

Bodies of Work
"It had me hooked and I didn't want to put it down. The characters are so real."

—Night Owl Reviews

Drag and Drop
"Etienne is a terrific story teller and it is his skill that makes the reader continue to read. His prose is well written and his plot is literate and well thought out."

—Reviews by Amos Lassen

The Burdens of Truth
"The characters and mystery surrounding them are sure to hold the readers' attention."

—Top 2 Bottom Reviews

Birds of a Feather
"Quentin and Nate have what it takes to make a fantastic addition to the Avondale series. They are loving, considerate, and have a subtly sexy vibe that cannot be beat. The telepathic abilities they share keep things interesting, and it ramps up their adventures to a whole new level."

—Coffee Time Romance & More

The Path to Forever
"The concept of longevity as it is presented here, with all its details and consequences, is fascinating…"

—Queer Magazine Online

NOVELS BY ETIENNE

THE AVONDALE STORIES

Bodies of Work
Drag and Drop
Break and Enter
Sleuth LLC: Birds of a Feather
Magic Fingers
The Burdens of Truth
Love Turns the Page
Curiosity Satisfied

THE FOREVER SERIES

The Path to Forever
Prognosis: Forever

THE APPEARANCES TRILOGY
Trial
Tribulation
Triumph

A word of thanks to the fans of this story, who kept asking for more, long after I was certain that the idea well had run dry. Which prompts me to thank Charles and Philip for leading such interesting lives.

To Jim Kennedy, my patient editor, who does his best to keep me on the straight and narrow comma path.

To my partner of sixteen years, for his support and encouragement.

1

Charles

PHILIP and I dealt with a growing list of social obligations after the Christening, and we hosted a Christmas party for my office about a week before Christmas. I was pleased that Andrew and Emily could attend, as they'd been out of the country at the time of the Christening. Andrew and I had kept in contact by telephone every ten days or so, so he was up to speed on what was happening in our lives, as well as what was going on at the office. We told both him and Emily to consider themselves to be honorary grandparents to the boys, and the pleasure on their faces at that announcement was obvious.

We had, by comparison, a fairly quiet Christmas celebration at home for Gran, Philip, and myself. The gang came over Christmas Eve, and we exchanged gifts before we all attended midnight mass at St. Philip's. The next morning, we carried the boys downstairs to see the Christmas tree, and they seemed to be fascinated by all the bright lights, although at less than two months of age, we weren't sure how much they could actually see.

We celebrated New Year's Eve with the gang, and we all drank a little too much Champagne, so much so that we insisted that the four of them use two of the guest rooms, which they did. True to his promise, Philip's nephew Steve kept in regular touch with his uncle Philip, calling him at least once a week. Occasionally, he would ask to speak to Uncle Charles as well, which pleased me very much.

January and February flew by, and we were now well into March, looking forward to spring and warmer weather.

A little after six o'clock one Saturday morning in mid-March, Philip's cell phone rang. We'd just gotten up but were not yet showered and dressed. He looked at the display, said, "It's Steve," and continued, "Hi, Steve, how's my favorite nephew? This is kind of early for you, isn't it?"

His expression changed to one of surprise and then shock, and he said, "I see." Then he listened for a while before he continued, "Do you know how to find the house? Good. Thank God for MapQuest. We'll have the gate open and the lights on out front."

He snapped the phone shut and said, "That wasn't Steve, it was a friend of his. To make a long story short, my sister Marie, her husband, Frank, and their two daughters are out of town, visiting my brother Jack down in Alexandria, which is almost one hundred miles further south in Louisiana than Monroe, where they live. My nephew Steve stayed home and had a friend over. Frank came home unexpectedly by himself last night and caught Steve and his friend in flagrante. The friend says that Frank beat the shit out of Steve. Steve insisted on being brought here, so the friend and an older brother are doing just that. They've been driving all night and will be here in twenty minutes or so." He'd been pulling on clothes while he told me all of this, and I'd automatically followed suit.

We hurried downstairs to turn on lights and open the gate; then I went to the kitchen and started the coffeemaker. Philip and I stood anxiously in the foyer, watching through the cut glass panels on either side of the front door. Finally, we saw headlights turn off the street into the driveway, and we went outside to wait.

The car stopped in front of the house, and two boys got out. The driver appeared to be at least eighteen or so, and I guessed the passenger to be Steve's age, which was a couple of years younger. The younger one came up to us and introduced himself as Jeff Smith and his older brother as Rob. Then he said, "Steve is in the backseat. He finally passed out a couple of hours ago."

"Okay, guys," I said. "Let's get him upstairs and into bed."

The four of us managed to get Steve up the stairs and into our old room. The two boys and I held him while Philip turned the covers back;

then we laid him on the bed and stripped him down to his shorts. His torso was a mass of bruises, as was his face, and Philip said, "Son of a bitch. I could kill my brother-in-law for this."

"We'll deal with him later, babe," I said. "Right now we need to take care of Steve. You stay here while I call a doctor."

I left the three of them with Steve and hurried to our little office. Then I found Dr. Butcher's home number and called him. Luckily, he hadn't left home yet to make his morning hospital rounds, so he agreed to come at once.

I went back to the bedroom, where Philip and the two boys were hovering around the bed, and said, "The doctor's on his way. Philip, while we're waiting for him, go get the digital camera. We need to photograph those bruises while they're still fairly fresh."

I went down to wait for Dr. Butcher, who arrived about twenty minutes later, black bag in hand. When he and I entered the room upstairs, Philip was busily taking photos of Steve's injuries and said, "I'm going to have my brother-in-law's ass in jail for a very long time over this."

Dr. Butcher directed the two of us to turn Steve over on his side so that he could examine his back, which was also a mass of bruises, and Philip took pictures of Steve's back, as well. After a few minutes spent taking vital signs and listening with his stethoscope, the doctor pulled Steve's shorts down to check the rest of him.

We all stared in shock at Steve's groin. One of his testicles had swollen to the size of a small orange, and the other one was almost as bad. Philip said, "Damn, he's going to pay for this." He began snapping picture after picture while the examination continued. Finally, the doctor seemed satisfied and directed us to slip Steve's shorts the rest of the way off and pull the covers back up over him.

He looked at Jeff and Rob and said, "You two brought him here?"

"Yes, Sir," they said.

"When did this happen?"

"About ten o'clock last night, Louisiana time," Jeff said. "Steve's parents were out of town, and I was staying with him. His dad came back unexpectedly and caught us fooling around. He went into a rage, hitting and kicking Steve, and you don't want to know the awful names he called Steve. I think he would have killed him if I hadn't hit him over the head with a brass bookend hard enough to knock him out for a bit. While he was out cold, I dressed and got Steve's clothes back on him and took him out to my car. I wanted to take him to the hospital, but he wouldn't let me. He just kept saying over and over, 'Take me to Atlanta, I'll be safe with Uncle Philip and Uncle Charles,' so I called my brother Rob, and he printed out the directions on MapQuest. Then I drove Steve to my house, Rob got in the car, and we hauled ass for Atlanta."

"How long has he been out of it?" Dr. Butcher said.

"He was moaning and sort of babbling for a couple of hours. We stopped at a truck stop and got him some Tylenol for the pain, and he finally passed out a couple of hours ago or maybe a little longer. I don't know whether he passed out from the pain or what. We don't fool around with drugs or alcohol or anything like that."

Dr. Butcher said, "He probably has a mild concussion, but I need to examine him when he wakes up. In the meantime, don't give him anything else for pain. I need him to be conscious and relatively alert before I can make a final diagnosis." He paused, then added, "Charles, do you have an ice pack?"

"Yes, we do," I said.

"Good. Get it and fill it with ice and put it on his genitals. It will help the swelling in his testicles go down."

Jeff said, "Doctor, is he going to be all right?"

"I don't see why not. He's young and appears to be healthy. However, I'll withhold final judgment until he comes to and I can talk to him."

I said, "Jeff, Rob, is there anyone that you need to call right now?"

"No, Sir," Rob said. "Our folks are out of town, and we keep in touch by cell phone."

"Good. You both look like you could use some sleep, so let me show you to a couple of guest rooms. Then I'll get going on the ice pack. I'm a lawyer, and I'll want to get a recorded statement from both of you later today when you're awake and rested, okay?"

"Yes, Sir," they chorused. I took them down the hall and got them settled in two of the unused bedrooms, then went back to Steve's room.

Dr. Butcher was just closing his bag when I got there, so I said, "Is he going to be all right, do you think? You weren't just saying that for the boys' benefit, I hope."

"Subject to an examination when he's conscious, I should think so. These things nearly always look worse than they are, although I don't mean to minimize the seriousness of his injuries. You wouldn't believe how much of this sort of thing we see."

I walked back downstairs with him. As he turned to go, he said, "Charles, call me the minute he wakes up, and I'll come back and check him over again. And Charles—get the son of a bitch that did this."

"You can count on that," I said.

After he left, I found an ice pack, went to the kitchen, filled it, and went back upstairs. Gran was just coming out of the nursery when I got to the head of the stairs.

"I've heard a lot of comings and goings this morning," she said. "What's going on?"

"We have guests. Come with me and see."

She followed me back to Steve's room, where Philip was sitting patiently by the bed.

"Why, it's Steve," she said.

"Yes, it is, but that's not all."

I lifted up the blanket and placed the ice pack gently on his testicles. Gran looked at the body on the bed and said, "Merciful God, what happened?"

"His father happened to him," I said.

"His own father did this to him?" She stared at me, incredulous.

"In a word, yes. I'll tell you about it in just a minute. Philip, where's your cell phone?"

"I put it back on the nightstand by our bed. Why?"

"Because while you stay here with Steve, I'm going to use your phone to call his mother—you do have her in the phone's memory, don't you?"

"Yes, she's the only listing under M."

"I'll handle it. Keep an eye on him and make sure that ice pack stays in place. Dr. Butcher wants us to call him as soon as Steve is conscious."

I took Gran's arm, and we walked back to the study and sat down. I told her as much as we knew of the story, and she said, "Dear God, what kind of man would do that to his own child?"

"A twisted and sick son of a bitch, to put it bluntly. Philip and I will make damn sure that he goes to jail for a very long time for this."

"I certainly hope so. What are you going to do now?"

"First, I'm going to call Marie and fill her in. Then I'll invite her here for the duration. If she has any sense, she'll divorce the bastard. Then I'm going to call the detective who handled our shooting and get him over here to start building a case that can be turned over to the police in Louisiana. After that, I'll see what happens. By the way, when you go downstairs, you might want to tell Mrs. Goodman that there are three teenage boys in the house who will most likely wake up hungry in a few hours. Two of them drove all night to get Steve here, and I know they'll need feeding. Steve will probably be hungry as well."

"I'll take care of it. You go on about doing what you have to do."

She went to the elevator, and I returned to our bedroom and located Philip's cell phone. After carrying it back into the office, I went online, searched for flight schedules from Alexandria to Atlanta, and printed out some information. I also retrieved a minicassette recorder that I used for dictation and slipped it into my pocket.

I picked up Philip's phone and selected the appropriate speed-dial code. The phone at the other end rang for a long time before a sleepy voice answered, "Philip, is that you?" It was Marie.

"No, Marie," I said, "it's Charles. Are you alone?"

"Yes, I am. Frank went back home last night. Why?"

"Marie, there's no easy way to say this, so I'll just say it. Frank walked in on Steve and his friend Jeff fooling around in bed last night and beat the crap out of Steve." I filled her in on the rest of what had happened, including the nature of Steve's injuries. There was a minute of stunned silence at her end, so I continued, "Did you follow all of that?"

"Yes, I believe so. I was thinking for a minute."

"If you can leave the girls with your brother, I can get you on a flight from Alexandria to Atlanta at eleven. The flight takes about three hours, with a change of planes in Memphis. If you agree, I'll make the reservation and call you back with particulars."

"Oh yes, please. Please do that."

"And Marie," I said, "one more thing."

"What?"

"Philip and I are going to see to it that your husband goes to jail over this. Whether you agree to that or not, this will become a police matter and out of your hands."

"Charles, on that you have my blessing," she said with a great deal of firmness.

"Good. Philip would talk to you, but I left him in Steve's bedroom keeping watch while I set things in motion."

"Okay," she said.

"Do you know the boys that brought Steve to us? Jeff and Rob?"

"Yes. Their parents are friends of ours. They're good kids," she said.

"Rob said that their parents are out of town, but they keep in touch by cell phone, so we'll let them hang around here as long as they want to."

"Thanks. It's an hour earlier here, but I guess I'd better go and wake up my brother and sister-in-law."

"Fine. I'll call you back in a bit with your ticket information," I said, and we hung up.

I rummaged around in the desk, found Detective Howard's card, and dialed the number, and for the second time that morning, I woke someone up. I identified myself and apologized before explaining the reason for the call. He agreed to come by the house around noon, and I thanked him.

I returned to the Internet and made an airline reservation for Marie. Then I called her and gave her the particulars. It was an electronic ticket, so all she would need was a photo ID. I told her that someone would meet her at the airport.

Having gotten all that under way, I went down to the kitchen and poured two cups of coffee and took them up to Steve's room. I handed one to Philip and said, "Has there been any change?"

"He stirs and moans once in a while, but I don't see any indication that he's going to wake up for a while."

I filled him in on what I'd done and said, "Why don't you go and take a shower. I'll keep an eye on him for a while."

"Okay," he said, and he got up and kissed me before taking his coffee cup and heading down the hall.

After a while, Philip returned and I went to shave, shower, and dress. When I'd finished, I picked up my phone and called John and Joe, the two nurses who'd taken care of me when I was home, recovering from having been shot in the leg. I asked them if they had plans for the afternoon, and they said no, so I told them what had happened and asked them to come and stay with Steve while I took Philip to the airport to meet his sister. They readily agreed. Then I went down to the kitchen and asked Mrs. Goodman to prepare a breakfast tray for Philip. While she was doing so, I joined Gran in the sunroom.

"Is everything all right?" she said as I sat down at the table.

"It's getting there," I said, and I went on to tell her of the various wheels I had set in motion for the day.

Mrs. Goodman brought me some toast and juice, and told me that she'd taken a tray up to Philip. "Thanks," I said. "I would have done that shortly."

"It was my pleasure. I saw that poor boy in the bed, and Philip showed me some of the bruises. It's hard to believe there are parents out there who would do such a thing to their own children."

"I know, but sadly, it's all too common."

I finished my breakfast, went back upstairs to Steve's room, and said, "Has there been any change?"

"Maybe. It's hard to tell for certain, but I think he might be coming around."

I pulled a chair up beside Philip's chair, put my arm around him, and said, "I have to believe that Steve is going to come out of this just fine."

"I know, that's what I keep telling myself. Thank you, babe, for taking charge of things this morning."

"What else could I have done?"

"I know, but I just want you to know how much I appreciate it."

"I love you, babe. Your problems are my problems and vice versa. That's the way it is, and that's the way that it's always going to be." I leaned over and began to kiss him thoroughly until we were interrupted by a groan from Steve.

We looked at Steve. His eyes opened slowly and focused on us, and he said, "Uncle Philip, Uncle Charles, is it really you guys?"

"It's really us," Philip said. "You're safe with us in Atlanta."

I pulled the recorder from my pocket, turned it on, and said, "Steve, do you remember what happened?"

"I think so. Mom and Dad took the girls down to Alexandria on Thursday for a long weekend visit with Uncle Julien and his family. I didn't want to go, so they let me stay home. My friend Jeff was sleeping over, and we were kind of fooling around in my bedroom. Then Dad burst into the room and started yelling at me and beating on me. I don't remember much else."

"Your friend Jeff hit your dad on the head with a bookend or something and knocked him out long enough to get you out of the house. Evidently you demanded to be brought here to Atlanta, so he got his brother Rob, and they did just that," I said.

I pulled my phone out and called Dr. Butcher. He answered on the second ring, and I said, "Hi, Terry, this is Charles Barnett. Our boy just woke up, and he seems pretty coherent."

"I'm only a few minutes away. See you shortly."

I said, "Steve, the doctor wanted to see you again as soon as you woke up, and he's on his way over here. I talked to your mom earlier and got her a flight to Atlanta from Alexandria. She'll be here later this afternoon."

Steve looked frightened and said, "I don't want to go back home. I don't ever want to go back there again." He started crying as he said it.

"Don't worry, kiddo," Philip said. "It would take an army to get you out of this house right now. You're here for as long as you want to be here, no matter what anyone else says."

"Where are Jeff and Rob?" Steve said.

"Asleep just across the hall," I said.

"Are you in a lot of pain?" Philip said.

"I hurt everywhere. Especially down there," he added, gazing toward his groin.

"That's because the bastard evidently kicked you in the balls. Both of them are swollen pretty badly, and there's an ice pack down there to help with the swelling," I said.

Philip said, "Steve, you lie back and concentrate on getting better. Charles and I will take care of everything. We'll take care of your mom, and we'll see to it that Frank goes to jail. Okay?"

"Okay," he said, and he closed his eyes.

There was a knock on the door, and Goodman said, "Dr. Butcher is here."

Dr. Butcher came into the room and said, "How's the patient?"

"Awake and talking," I said.

"Good. Let's have a look."

He sat down beside the bed and began checking Steve over once again. Steve opened his eyes, and I introduced Dr. Butcher as our doctor, thinking that the fact that Terry was a pediatrician might bother Steve.

Terry was busy doing doctor-type things, looking in Steve's eyes and ears with his whatchamacallits, testing his reflexes, poking and prodding here and there, asking if it hurt when he did this or that. Finally, Terry sat back and said, "I don't think anything is broken, but in a couple of days, when he feels up to it, why don't you bring him in for some X-rays just to be certain?"

We promised to do that, and Terry continued, "What he needs more than anything right now is bed rest. He can get up and use the bathroom when he needs to, but other than that, I want him to remain horizontal for at least two or three days until we see how he begins to heal. You also want to keep the ice pack on his groin. His testicles will begin to shrink back to their normal size over the next few days, and the ice will help that process. I'll write a prescription for a mild painkiller, but use it sparingly, okay?"

"Sure," I said. "Instead of writing it, can you telephone the Buckhead Pharmacy? They'll deliver it."

"Certainly," he said.

"Can he have some Tylenol or Aleve now?" I asked.

"By all means," he said.

"Terry, we're setting the wheels in motion to have his father arrested for this, so I'll need a full write-up from you in a few days as part of that process."

"That won't be a problem, Charles. Any man who would do this to his own son or, for that matter, anyone's son, needs to be behind bars for a long time."

Once again there was a knock on the door, and Goodman announced Detective Howard.

I introduced him to Dr. Butcher and to Steve, saying, "This is Detective Howard of the Atlanta Police Department. He's a friend of ours who's going to make sure that we dot all of the Is and cross all of the Ts when we send the paperwork to Louisiana to have Frank arrested for this."

Detective Howard spoke to Dr. Butcher for a few minutes, and they exchanged business cards. Then Detective Howard focused on Steve and said, "Feel like answering a few questions?"

Steve said he didn't mind, and Detective Howard went through the process of asking him the particulars of what had happened to him. When he'd finished, he asked me, "Where's the other boy?"

"Down the hall in a guest room, sleeping," I said. "We can probably get him up in a bit, and I'm sure he'll answer any questions you have."

"Fine. Let's go down the hall and talk about this."

He and I left the room and went down to the study. As soon as we were there, I said, "I want Steve's father in jail ASAP. Will that be a problem?"

"No. I'll write up a complete report, fax it to Louisiana, and follow it up with a phone call. If they don't drag their feet, the guy could be in jail before dinner."

"Good. The boy's mother will be here this afternoon. She's flying in from Alexandria. Will you need her signature on any paperwork?"

"I doubt it. When abuse of a minor child is concerned, the process takes on a life of its own, as long as the accused doesn't have connections."

"I don't know the answer to that question, but I can certainly find out. Philip and I want his brother-in-law behind bars, and we'll do whatever it takes to make that happen. Do you want to interview the other boy now?"

"That wouldn't be a bad idea," he said.

"Good. Make yourself comfortable while I go wake him."

I went down the hall to Jeff's door and knocked softly before I entered the room. Jeff was sound asleep, so I shook him gently by the shoulder and said, "Jeff, it's time to wake up."

I waited for a minute or two while he pulled himself together, and he said, "What's happening?"

"Steve is awake, for one thing, and there's a detective here who would like to take a statement from you that will help us get Steve's father behind bars, where he belongs."

"Good. Give me a minute to splash some water on my face."

"The bathroom is across the hall, and I'll be just down the hall near the stairs," I said, and I left him to pull himself together.

A few minutes later, he emerged from the bathroom, and we walked down to the study. I introduced him to Detective Howard, and he gave a complete statement of what had happened. I'd already given the detective copies of the photographs of Steve's injuries, and he left to set things in motion.

"Jeff, would you like to see Steve?" I said.

"You bet," he said, and he followed me down the hall.

When we entered Steve's room, Philip was holding a glass of water and handing him a Tylenol capsule. Steve swallowed the pill, drank some water, and sank back on the pillow.

"Hi, Jeff," he said. "Thanks for everything you did last night. You probably saved my life."

"Not a problem, buddy. You'd have done the same for me."

"Jeff," I said.

"Yes, Sir?"

"Are your parents going to give you a hard time about all this? I mean, when they find out what happened to Steve, they'll surely find out what you two were doing before he was beaten up."

"No, Sir. My folks know I'm gay. They aren't exactly thrilled about it, but they've pretty much learned to deal with it."

"Good. That's one less thing for Steve to worry about."

Philip said, "Steve wants to stay here with us permanently, and I'm pretty sure my sister will allow it. Will that be a big problem for you, Jeff?"

Jeff thought about it for a moment and said, "If he stays here, I'll certainly miss him, we've been best friends for years, but we're not exactly boyfriends. We just sort of take care of each other, if you know what I mean."

"In other words, the two of you are what we would refer to as 'fuck buddies' rather than boyfriends," Philip said.

Both Jeff and Steve laughed at that, and Steve said, "That pretty much sums it up."

"I hope you took our advice and have been playing safe," Philip said.

"We haven't done anything that requires a condom, Uncle Philip," Steve said. "We both want to save that for someone special."

"Good for you," Philip said.

Someone's stomach grumbled loudly, and we all smiled, so I said, "I don't know who that was, but somebody in this room is hungry. Jeff, why don't you go wake your brother up, and by the time the two of you have had a shower, I'll have lunch brought up here so you can keep Steve company for a while."

"You'll have to show me which room he's in," Jeff said. "All I remember from earlier this morning is a lot of doors."

"Not a problem," I said. "Follow me."

I led him down the hallway, tapped on Rob's door, and opened it. I turned back to Jeff and said, "You know where the bathroom is." Then I went downstairs to the kitchen and asked Mrs. Goodman to send lunch for the three boys upstairs when it was ready.

I went to the sunroom and found Gran having an early and solitary lunch. She looked up at me and said, "How is he?"

"Awake and hurting. Also, he's adamant that he doesn't want to go back home ever. Philip and I have assured him that he doesn't have to, and we're hoping that Marie won't make an issue of it. The boy feels safe here with us."

"Good for the both of you. In his present state he certainly needs to feel safe."

"I just asked Mrs. Goodman to take lunch up to Steve's room for all three boys. John and Joe are coming over later to stay with him while Philip and I go to the airport to pick up Marie."

She looked at me with an expression that I couldn't quite figure out, so I said, "What are you thinking?"

"I just had a memory flashback, so to speak. You are so much like your grandfather. In any crisis, large or small, he took charge and made things happen."

"I guess it's an inherited tendency," I said, and I excused myself to go back upstairs, where I found Jeff and Rob sitting beside Steve's bed.

"Guys," I said, "lunch will be brought up here shortly, and none too soon, because someone's stomach was rumbling earlier. Steve, is there anything you need before Philip and I go downstairs to eat?"

"Yes, Uncle Charles, there is," he said. "I need to pee."

"Hold on for just a minute," Philip said, and he went into the bathroom. He returned a minute later with a urinal. "I bought this last year when Charles was laid up in this room with his leg in a cast," he said.

"I can get up if you guys will help me."

"Maybe next time. Right now you need to rest, and this will be a lot easier for you." He lifted one corner of the covers and inserted Steve's penis into the device. "Now, let's hear water running."

Nothing happened for a bit, so I said, "It's not as easy as you think it is to pee lying down. I had a hard time using one of those things when I was in the hospital." Finally, we heard the unmistakable sounds of water flowing.

Philip looked at me and said, "Babe, go get me a hand towel."

I did as instructed and brought a small towel back to the bed. Philip used it to dry Steve's penis and handed me the urinal and the ice pack. "We need more ice," he said.

I went to the intercom and asked Mrs. Goodman to send some crushed ice up with lunch so that we could refill the ice pack. Before Philip and I could go downstairs to have our own lunch, Goodman pushed a rolling cart containing lunch, Cokes, and ice into the room. Philip filled the ice pack and put it back in place on Steve's groin, and we told the three boys to help themselves to the food.

I said, "Jeff, one of you can help Steve prop up on some more pillows, but don't let him get out of bed just yet, okay?"

"No problem," Jeff said.

We went downstairs, ate lunch quickly, then checked up on things in the nursery. Grace, our resident nanny, was feeding Mark when we got there, so we filled her in on all the comings and goings that she must have been wondering about since early morning. We took over after Grace had finished feeding the boys and rocked them to sleep.

We placed them carefully in their cribs and stood for a while just watching them. When we were back in the study, Philip said, "If anyone ever hurt one of those two kids, I think I could commit murder without a qualm."

"I know, babe. I feel the same way."

2.

Philip

WE WENT to Steve's room and found that the boys had devoured all the food. All three boys appeared to be totally worn out, so I said, "Jeff, why don't you and Rob go back to your rooms and hit the sack? You look exhausted."

They thanked us for the lunch and went back to their rooms as instructed. I could tell that Steve, too, was sinking rapidly, so I asked him if he needed another Tylenol, but he declined. I suggested that he should close his eyes and take a nap, and he eagerly complied.

We sat in the room for a while until his steady breathing told us that he was sound asleep. Then I took the lunch cart and rolled it out into the hall and pulled the door part of the way closed. Then we went downstairs and talked to Gran while we waited for John and Joe to arrive. A little while later, Goodman escorted the two of them to where we were sitting. After they'd said hello to Gran, Charles and I took them up to the study and filled them in on the events of the day. When I showed them the pictures of Steve's injuries, their reactions were explosive.

Charles told them what the doctor had recommended, and they nodded in agreement. "Who's the doctor?" John said.

"The babies' pediatrician, Dr. Terry Butcher," he said.

"We know him," Joe said. "When John and I were working pediatrics a couple of months ago, we saw him at work regularly. He's very good."

John asked, "What do you want us to do?"

"Hang around and keep an eye on the patient while we go to the airport and pick up his mother," I said. "You can use the computers in here, go to our room and watch television, or whatever. We just want someone to keep watch."

Thirty minutes later, Charles and I were on the way to the airport. He dropped me off at the arrivals area and went to park the car, saying, "I'll stay with the car. When you and Marie are ready to be picked up, give me a call and I'll circle around and get you."

I went to the security area to wait for Marie. About ten minutes after I got there, she came through with a group of passengers that I presumed had all been on her flight. The first words out of her mouth were, predictably, "How is he?"

"He was asleep when we left the house. Do you remember John and Joe, two of the godfathers?"

"Yes, why?"

"They're both registered nurses, and they came over to the house to keep watch while Charles and I came to pick you up."

I took out my phone, called Charles, and told him we'd be at the entrance in a few minutes. Marie didn't have any checked luggage, so there was no further delay and Charles pulled up to the head of the line of cars as we came through the doors. I got into the backseat with Marie so we could talk, and Charles pulled away from the curb.

Before Marie and I could begin a conversation, Charles said, "I just got a phone call from Detective Howard here in Atlanta. Frank was arrested in Monroe about half an hour ago, and because of the nature of the case, he won't be allowed to post bail until he's arraigned on Monday."

"Good," I said.

"Marie," Charles said, "does your husband have any contacts in the police or courts down there that he could use to defeat the system?"

"Not as far as I know."

"Are you going to divorce him?" Charles said.

"Indeed I am."

"In that case, you ought to arrange to clean out any joint bank accounts first thing Monday morning."

"I'm way ahead of you there. I don't know if Philip has told you, but our brother Julien, who I was visiting in Alexandria, is a lawyer. He'll be at our bank first thing Monday morning with a power of attorney to take care of that little matter. He's also going to drain the company bank account down to zero."

"Good," Charles said.

"Marie," I said, "I have some pictures to show you. They're of Steve's injuries, and I want you to look at them now, so you won't be so upset when you see him, okay?"

I took out the digital camera and displayed the pictures one by one. When I'd finished, she was sobbing, and when she finally regained control of herself, she said, "That bastard. That no-good fucking bastard. To do that to his only son. It defies comprehension."

"If Steve's friend Jeff hadn't hit Frank over the head with a heavy bookend and knocked him out, Steve might have been killed," I said. "From Jeff's account, Frank was totally berserk and out of control."

I waited a few minutes for her to regain her composure and said, "Sis, one more thing."

"What?"

"Don't say anything to Steve about taking him home right now. He starts crying and gets hysterical at the mere mention of going home. He feels safe with us, and we've told him he can stay as long as he wants to, if you'll let him. Frankly, you'll be going through your own trauma with the divorce and taking care of the girls, not to mention running the business, and you really don't need a somewhat troubled son to handle as well."

Charles interrupted, saying, "Marie, do you remember Lydia Brannon from the Christening?"

"Yes, I thought she was a nice woman."

"She is that. She's also a clinical psychologist who specializes in dealing with abused children. We want to have her come over and talk to Steve a few times to help him deal with what happened. She'll do it unofficially, so there'll be nothing in any medical history to indicate that Steve ever saw a shrink."

"The bottom line, sis, is that we have Steve and his care well in hand. You can go home when you're ready and deal with everything else knowing that he is both loved and well cared for."

She let out a sigh of relief and said, "You're both absolutely right, and even though it's a hard thing to contemplate, he can stay in Atlanta. Thank you both."

"By the way," I said, "we ought to call Jeff and Rob's folks and let them know what's going on. Do you have a cell phone number for them?"

"Been there, done that. I talked to the boys' mother before I went to the airport. She said that Jeff and Rob can stay with Steve for a few days if they want to. She asked me to buy some clothes for them, and she'll reimburse me later."

"Good," I said, "because they're part of Steve's support group right now."

We pulled up in front of the house, and I led Marie upstairs. John and Joe came out of the study and met us at the top of the stairs, and I said, "Is everything under control?"

"He's still asleep," John said. "We've checked him every fifteen minutes or so, and he's fine. I think he's simply exhausted, both physically and emotionally, right now. We just refilled the ice pack a few minutes ago."

"Thanks, guys," I said. "We really appreciate that you interrupted your day off to do this for us."

Marie thanked them as well and they said good-bye and left; then I led her to Steve's room. He was still asleep when we entered the room but woke up when Marie kissed him on the forehead. Then he said, "Mom, I hope you didn't come to take me back home, because I don't want to go there. I'm not sure I ever want to go back into that house again." He started crying. "Please don't make me go back there," he repeated, openly sobbing.

She bent over, hugged him, and said, "It's okay, sweetie, you don't have to go back to Monroe if you don't want to. I've already told

Philip and Charles that you can stay here as long as you like."

Charles had come into the room during this exchange and was standing by the door, listening.

Steve got himself under control and said, "Thanks, Mom. You know I'll miss you and the girls, but I don't think I'll ever feel safe anywhere near where that bastard is."

"Well, the bastard's in jail right now," Charles said, "if that makes you feel any safer."

"Not much. Mom, Jeff and Rob said that they'd drive back to Monroe and get my stuff from the house."

"Baby, that's over seven hours each way. That's a lot," she said.

I spoke up and said, "I think Charles can handle that. He just happens to fly his own airplane."

That was Charles's cue to say, "If we leave very early tomorrow morning, we can be back by late afternoon. We can even stop by their house so they can get a couple of changes of clothing."

Jeff and Rob chose that moment to walk through the door. Marie got up and hugged Jeff tightly. He said, "I'm sorry, Mrs. Cox. I'm so sorry."

"Sorry for what?" she said. "As I understand it, you probably kept Steve from getting killed by his father, so there's absolutely nothing to be sorry for. I'm so grateful to the both of you for all you did for Steve. By the way, I spoke to your mother this morning, and she said you two can stay here in Atlanta with Steve for a few days if you want to."

Their faces brightened at that, and Rob said, "We don't have any clothes."

"She asked me to buy some for you, but we've just had a better idea," Marie said.

Steve spoke up. "Uncle Charles is going to fly you guys down to Monroe early tomorrow morning in his airplane. You can get my stuff from the house, and you can go by your house and pick up enough clothes for a few days."

Jeff looked at Charles and said, "Your own plane! Cool."

"You two must be more than ready for a change of clothes," I said. "I think I can find a couple of warm-up suits you can wear while we run your clothes through the washer and dryer downstairs."

Charles said, "I'll go get them." He left the room and came back after a while with two complete warm-up suits and a couple of T-shirts, and he handed them to the brothers. "Here you go, guys. These outfits will probably swallow you whole, but they'll do for a couple of hours while your clothes are being washed and dried."

Jeff and Rob thanked him and left to go change clothes.

"Steve, do you need to go to the bathroom or anything?" I said.

"Yes, I do," he said. "I need to do number two. Can you help me to the bathroom?"

"Sure," I said. "Charles and I can help you get there."

Marie said, "I can help."

"Mom, I'm naked under these covers."

"So? I've seen you naked before."

"Not since I was ten."

"Okay, I give up," Marie said. "I'll go quietly."

"Thanks, Mom."

She left and closed the door behind her. I turned the covers back and helped Steve slide around sideways on the bed. Charles and I walked him to the bathroom and got him seated. "Holler when you're ready to go back to bed," I said, and we went back into the bedroom to wait.

Eventually, we heard flushing sounds, followed by Steve saying, "I'm ready."

We helped him back to the bed and got him settled in place. He looked up at us and said, "I can't thank you guys enough."

"For helping you to the bathroom? Puhleeze," I said.

"No, I mean for talking Mom into letting me stay here. I know the two of you had to have worked on her a bit."

"I confess," I said. "We did do a bit of persuading, but really we just pointed out the obvious, which is that she's going to have her hands full divorcing your father, taking care of your sisters, and keeping the business going. She really wouldn't have time to devote to take care of you properly."

Charles said, "Understand this, Steve. Your mother wasn't happy about leaving you here, but in the end she saw the wisdom of doing so."

"Thanks," Steve said.

"Now, we want you to do something for us," Charles said.

"What?"

"Do you remember Lydia from the Christening? She's the boys' godmother."

"Sure," he said.

"Lydia is a psychologist, and she just happens to spend her entire working week helping kids who've been abused. I want to have her come by and see you a few times. She is a pro at this kind of thing, and she can help you deal with what happened to you," he said.

"I'm okay," Steve said.

"No, you're not okay. If you were okay, you wouldn't start crying at the mere thought of going back to Monroe for any reason. That's definitely not a symptom of 'okay'. I'm not saying that we think you should ever go back there if you don't want to, but Lydia can help you get over being afraid of it. So will you do this one thing for us and help yourself in the process?"

"I guess so," Steve said.

"Good. I'll call her and set it up. We need to get you enrolled in school as well. I'm going to call my old school on Monday and see if we can't get you in there. I think you'll like it, especially because it's a school for boys only."

Steve smiled at that and said, "Cool."

There was a knock on the door, and Steve said, "Come on in."

Marie came into the room, followed by Jeff and Rob. They were wearing the warm-up pants and the T-shirts, all of which were several sizes too large for them. They handed me their dirty clothing, and I picked up the clothes Steve had been wearing when they'd arrived.

Charles said, "Dinner should be ready downstairs just about now. Why don't we guys go downstairs and leave Marie with Steve. They probably have a lot to talk about, and I'll have their dinner sent up to them."

We arrived in the sunroom while Mrs. Goodman was placing dishes of food on the table, which was set for five. Charles made the introductions and explained why the two boys were dressed in oversized clothing.

Mrs. Goodman took the dirty clothes from Charles and said she'd attend to them.

"Thanks," he said. "And when you have that in hand, will you send a tray up to Steve and his mother?"

She nodded in understanding and returned to the kitchen.

I said, "Gran, as you know, Jeff and his brother drove all night to bring Steve to us, and it's safe to say that Jeff probably saved Steve's life last night. They'll be staying with us for a few days."

Charles proceeded to tell her where he was flying to tomorrow and why. Then he excused himself to make a couple of phone calls. Gran, as always, was the consummate hostess, and she very quickly had the boys feeling at ease in what were, for them, strange surroundings. Charles returned to the table, sat down, and said, "Okay, guys, the plane will be serviced and ready at seven in the morning, which means we have to leave the house by six thirty, so we need to be downstairs at breakfast no later than six.

"Philip," he said, "I just spoke to Lydia, and she'll come by after lunch tomorrow to talk to Steve. Detective Howard will be coming by later this evening with a bundle of paperwork for me to take to the police in Monroe. He didn't want some things, such as the photographs of Steve's injuries, sent over the Internet. He's going to have the Monroe detective who's handling the case meet me at Steve's house. I also spoke to Dr. Butcher, and he's going to check in on his patient sometime tomorrow morning. Have I forgotten anything?"

"Yes, you've forgotten to eat. Now please do so."

While Charles and I ate, Gran managed to extract a mountain of information from the two brothers about life in Monroe and their school and other activities. She never ceased to amaze me with her ability to draw information out of people.

After we'd finished with our food, Charles stretched and said, "I need to work the kinks out. Come on, guys, we'll show you the pool and Jacuzzi. If I'm not mistaken, I think some friends of ours are using it right now."

We walked across the yard to the pool enclosure, and when we entered it, we saw that the gang was busily engaged in playing their version of water polo. The game stopped when our presence was noted, so I said, "Hi, guys, I'm sure you remember my nephew Steve. This is Steve's best friend, Jeff, and Jeff's brother Rob. We'll be with you in a minute."

We went back to the changing area, and Charles said, "I'm sure Steve must have told you we don't wear swimsuits around here." He retrieved a couple of towels for the brothers, then began to remove his clothes and place them in a basket. I did likewise, found our goggles and earplugs, and followed him from the room.

While we were getting our gear in place, the two brothers emerged from the changing area with their towels over their shoulders, and I immediately understood why. As the saying goes, "when you've got it, flaunt it." They jumped in the pool and began to play water polo with the gang while Charles and I swam some serious laps.

We'd just passed the mile and a half mark when I sensed that the other activity in the pool had pretty much ceased, so I pulled up in the shallow end of the pool, and while I waited for Charles to join me, I said, "What are you guys doing?"

"Watching you two swim like a couple of fish," Joe said. "I don't know how you do it."

Charles smiled and said, "Practice makes perfect. Did you guys remember to turn the Jacuzzi on?"

"You bet," John said.

"Then what are we waiting for?" Charles said as he grabbed hold of the nearest ladder and pulled himself out of the water. I followed him into the Jacuzzi, and we settled down on the tiled bench. Soon eight naked guys were soaking in the hot water.

Jeff and Rob were clearly comfortable with the gang and didn't hesitate to participate in any discussion that took place. I think they probably appreciated being treated as equals by a bunch of older guys, so I said, "Jeff, you and Rob seem to be enjoying yourselves."

"You bet," Jeff said. "This is awesome."

Rob added, "I could get used to doing this every day."

Charles said, "All you have to do is persuade your parents to move to Atlanta. Then you can come visit Steve every evening and use the facilities."

Jeff said, "I wish."

Later, when we'd all cooled down in the pool and showered and everyone was drying themselves vigorously, John, who was watching the two brothers, said, "It must be something in the water."

"Say what?" Joe said.

"I was just noticing that they grow them big in Louisiana and I thought that there must be something in the water down there."

Jeff and Rob blushed, and Joe said, "Size queen," and he popped John on the butt with a perfect snap of his towel.

"I'll get you for that," John said.

"I certainly hope so," Joe said.

Everyone laughed at that, and we all finished dressing and went back into the house.

3

Charles

SUNDAY morning, Philip went to the kitchen and prepared breakfast while I made sure that both Jeff and Rob were awake and on their way to the shower. I quickly took care of my own morning routine, dressed, then went down to the sunroom. A few minutes after I'd begun to eat my breakfast, the two brothers arrived in a state of excitement, which led me to say, "Let me guess: you guys have never flown in a small plane before, right?"

"We've never flown in any plane before," Jeff said.

"This is going to be so cool," Rob added.

We finished breakfast and drove to the airport, where they followed me into the hangar and helped me remove all of the passenger seats in the plane but one, thus creating a great deal of additional cargo space for Steve's belongings. We were in the air in short order, and after we were safely out of the busy Atlanta area and on autopilot, I allowed them to take turns sitting in the copilot's seat. Needless to say, they spent the entire flight glued to the windows.

We picked up a generous tailwind and landed in Monroe a little under three hours after takeoff. I'd arranged for a rental minivan to be waiting for us at the Monroe airport, and we were on our way into town in short order. The boys directed me to their house first, and when we got there, they hurried inside and returned a few minutes later carrying overnight bags.

In the basement at home, I'd found some disassembled U-Haul

moving boxes left over from when Philip and I had moved the contents of the townhouse to Buckhead. When we arrived at Steve's house, I gave each of the brothers a roll of tape, and they started assembling the boxes. As they were doing so, an unmarked police car pulled into the driveway and the driver got out and walked over to us. For a middle-aged detective he looked fairly fit; evidently they don't all live at Dunkin' Donuts. His passenger also exited the car.

The detective introduced himself as Detective Robichaux, and we exchanged business cards. His companion was a deputy district attorney named Simon Woods, and we also exchanged cards.

I gave the brothers the keys to Marie's house so they could start loading, and the detective, the DDA, and I discussed the case. I handed Detective Robichaux the pictures of Steve's injuries. He looked at them and said, "Goddamn," as he passed the pictures over to Mr. Woods. "The son of a bitch did this to his kid because he was fooling around with his best friend?"

"That about sums it up," I said. "There's no chance that he'll get away with it, is there?"

"Not in this jurisdiction," the detective said. "We take this sort of thing very seriously."

"I was thinking about judges and/or juries whose religious views might tend to make them believe that the kid deserved to be beaten up because he's gay."

"That won't happen," Mr. Woods said. "All child abuse cases go before Hanging Hannah, and she takes a very dim view of abuse of any kind."

"Hanging Hannah?"

"Judge Hannah McDaniel. All child abuse cases are referred to her courtroom. We call her Hanging Hannah because she's tough as nails. If you have a redneck on the jury who thinks the kid deserved it, she'll put the fear of God in him. If you have a bleeding heart juror who wants to be lenient toward the father, she'll put the fear of God in him, as well. With this kind of evidence, there's no doubt of the outcome—the kid's father is going to do hard time."

"Good," I said. Then I continued, "Mr. Woods?"

"Please, call me Simon."

"Fine, I'm Charles. Simon, can you get a conviction without the victim having to testify in open court?"

"Probably, but testimony in person would be better. Is there a problem?"

"Yes. Right now, Steve gets hysterical at the mere mention of coming back to Monroe for any reason. We're arranging for him to have some counseling, but I don't know how long it will take for him to feel comfortable coming back here. The family has more than its share of problems, what with his father cheating on his mother."

"That's certainly understandable. We could arrange for a videotaped deposition. What about the other boy?"

"You can ask him yourself. He's one of the two boys loading the van."

"Mr. Barnett, do you have children?" Detective Robichaux said.

"My partner and I have two four-month-old sons, and he happens to be the victim's uncle."

"Well, I have one this age," he said, pointing at the file folder containing the photos, "and if anyone ever did that to him, I'm not at all certain that I could stand by and let justice take its course. I think I could cheerfully track the guy down and shoot him myself—and save the state a lot of money."

"Believe me, I understand the urge," I said. "Would you guys like to see the scene of the crime and interview the other boy before we leave?"

"Yes, we would," Simon said, "but I wouldn't want you to miss your flight."

"That won't be a problem—the airplane can't take off without me. I'm the pilot."

Jeff and Rob had just come back to the van, each carrying a large box, so I called Jeff over.

"Jeff," I said, "this is Detective Robichaux and Mr. Woods from the district attorney's office. They'll be handling the case here in

Monroe and would like to ask you a few questions, then see Steve's room, where it happened."

"Sure," Jeff said. "Anything to help keep Mr. Cox in jail."

I helped Rob finish loading the van while Simon Woods and Detective Robichaux interviewed Jeff. As Rob was carrying the last box and I was removing the last armload of clothes from Steve's closet, Jeff and the two men came in the room. When I returned to the room, Jeff was showing them the bookend, and the detective handed it to me, saying, "This is solid brass and heavy. No wonder the guy was knocked out."

I hefted the bookend and said, "That was really quick thinking, Jeff."

"I didn't know what else to do," Jeff said. "I tried pulling Mr. Cox off Steve, but he was too strong for me."

"Well, son, you did good," Detective Robichaux said. "Too bad you didn't hit him a lot harder and solve the problem permanently."

Both Detective Robichaux and Simon Woods promised to keep me posted as to any developments with the case, and returned to their car.

The boys and I had carried all of Steve's belongings to the van, so I asked them to secure the house. We grabbed some fast food on the way to the airport, and in less than an hour, we were back in the air. I called Richard to give him our ETA, as he was meeting us at the airport with a van—there was no way all of those boxes would fit in my car. When we landed, Richard was waiting with the requested van and a helper, and we had the boxes loaded in no time.

When we arrived at the house, I instructed the guys to stack the boxes and the clothes in the hallway outside Steve's room so that the boxes could be emptied and their contents put away in an orderly manner. After the crew left, I looked in on Steve.

Marie was sitting beside the bed, talking to him. As I entered the room, I said, "Steve, all your stuff is in boxes out in the hallway."

Marie said, "Thanks. I'll start unpacking for him."

This drew a protest from Steve. "Mom, you don't have to do that."

"Of course I do," she said, and she went out into the hall to survey the boxes.

I closed the door behind her, walked over to the bed, and said, "Steve, let your mom set up your room for you. You can rearrange everything to suit yourself as soon as she goes home, but right now she needs to feel useful."

Steve nodded and said, "Okay."

Jeff and Rob opened the door and came in with their arms full of clothing on hangers, followed by Marie, who had clearly taken charge. She had them place the clothes in the closet and arrange things to her satisfaction. She orchestrated the movement of half of the boxes from the hallway into the bedroom; then she started unpacking them. When a woman goes into high gear in the housekeeping arena, it's time for the men to withdraw, so I took Jeff and Rob with me and went in search of the rest of the family. We found Philip and Gran in the sunroom, having tea.

Philip looked up when we entered the room, and said, "What's up?"

"Your sister has taken charge of unpacking all of Steve's belongings and arranging his room. He protested at first, but when she was out of earshot, I told him that she needed to feel useful right now and he should play along with her. I also told him that he could rearrange everything to suit himself later."

"Good for you," Gran said. "Are you boys hungry?"

"I'm not particularly hungry," I said, "but I imagine these two guys are."

Mrs. Goodman chose that moment to appear with a tray of sandwiches and soft drinks. The woman must have some form of radar that can detect hungry teenagers from two rooms away. I said, "Mrs. Goodman, how do you do that?"

"Do what?"

"You always seem to know when there are hungry boys around. Are you clairvoyant?"

She smiled at that and said, "Not at all. I heard noises and investigated. When I saw people running up and down the stairs carrying boxes, I started making sandwiches."

The boys thanked her and, in short order, devoured a fair number of the sandwiches. When they'd finished, they excused themselves to go upstairs and check on Steve.

When they were well on their way upstairs, I said, "Philip, do you have any ideas with respect to entertaining the brothers for the next few days?"

"Well, for a start, I thought I'd give them some cash and suggest they might enjoy going to Six Flags tomorrow. I've also thought about taking them out to Stone Mountain on Tuesday or Wednesday."

"Good. They'll get tired of hanging around Steve's room all day long, and that will give them some things to do."

And so the week went. On Monday, while the brothers were at Six Flags, Marie said a tearful good-bye to Steve, and Philip took her to the airport. While she was in the air, we learned that her husband had managed to post bail, one of the terms of which included a restraining order barring him from coming anywhere near his son. That would take care of the situation in Louisiana, and I'd already filed a petition for a restraining order that would be effective in Georgia.

Tuesday afternoon, Philip took the brothers out to Stone Mountain, and they came back suitably impressed with the place. On Wednesday, Philip received an overnight envelope from Marie containing transcripts of Steve's school records, along with some documents authorizing Philip to make medical decisions for Steve should he become ill. Documents in hand, we made a Thursday appointment with the headmaster of my old school, Exeter Academy. Ostensibly, we were there to enroll the two babies, but we hoped to slip Steve into the school during the process. The fact that one of the buildings on the school's campus had the name Barnett associated with it would probably be a major factor in his acceptance.

I gave Philip a brief tour of the campus before we went to the administration building to keep our appointment with Dean Lloyd. We were in his reception area almost exactly on time and were kept waiting only a few minutes before being ushered into his office.

Dean Ralph Waldo Lloyd turned out to be balding, fiftysomething, and more than a bit pompous. I introduced Philip as my partner and explained that we were there to enroll yet another generation of the Barnett family in Exeter Academy. He produced the necessary forms, and in short order, Mark and Steven were signed up for fourteen years of Exeter—from K-4 through grade twelve.

That having been taken care of, I explained that Philip's nephew had recently come to live with us and that we wished to have him transfer from his school in Louisiana to Exeter Academy. Philip handed over the transcripts, and the dean studied them carefully. He finally looked up from the documents and said, "Well, the boy certainly has an impressive academic record, and I see that he's active on the swim team as well."

"That's true," Philip said. "He's also started taking advanced placement courses."

"Yes, I see that. The problem is that we don't normally accept transfers in midterm, even when the student is obviously so well prepared."

"That's too bad," I said. "I took Philip on a brief tour of the campus before we came to your office. The computers in the Barnett Library seem to be somewhat outdated, and the building itself is looking kind of shabby. I'm sure I could persuade my grandmother to do something to rectify both situations."

Dean Lloyd instantly turned into a poster boy for "unctuous" and said, "Of course, there are always exceptions." He made this statement sound as though it were a continuation of his last sentence. Then he continued, "I am curious, however, to know why he would suddenly move away from home in the middle of a term."

We were ready for that question. Philip handed him a couple of the photographs of Steve's injuries and said, "Because of this."

The dean looked the photographs, and his complexion grew pale before he said, "This is terrible, but I still don't understand."

"To put it simply, his father is abusive," Philip said. "His father did that to him, and the boy took refuge with us. He's terrified of going home, with good reason. My sister is in the process of divorcing her husband and has signed all the necessary paperwork to make me his guardian until he's eighteen." This was a slight exaggeration. Marie was going to sign the paperwork, but the process wasn't quite complete, and there was the issue of her husband, who could be expected to fight it.

"When will he be able to resume classes?" the dean said.

"The doctor says he can start back to school on Monday," Philip said. "However, he may not be able to participate in sports for a while longer. His father kicked him rather savagely in the groin, so his testicles are badly swollen, and he's still quite sore in that area."

Dean Lloyd produced another set of forms, filled them out, and gave them to Philip to sign. In turn, Philip wrote a check for tuition for the balance of the school year. Steve now had an appointment to go over his schedule as soon as school began on Monday.

I told the dean that I would have a computer company contact him within a few days to survey the library's needs and make some recommendations. We also arranged to walk through the library in the near future to discuss improvements to the facility. We shook hands on it, and Philip and I left.

When we were safely in the car and on the way home, Philip grinned and said, "That's how deals are made."

"I know. Greed is a powerful motivator, isn't it?"

"Too true. Who did Dean Lloyd remind you of?"

"I don't know."

"He reminded me of the actor Fred Clark playing a similar type in a sitcom," he said.

"Now that you mention it, I agree."

"When it comes to paying for the computers and renovations to the library, I'll take care of it. We don't need to bother Gran with the details."

"If that's the way you want to handle it, fine. But we might as well tell her what you're doing. Someone from the school is bound to call her."

"You're right, of course. I hadn't thought of that."

"We'll need to get Steve outfitted for school this weekend. Somewhere in that paperwork there should be information on the school uniforms and where to purchase them."

"I'll handle it. He should be up to a trip to the mall by tomorrow."

When we got back to the house, we went straight up to Steve's room to tell him the good news. We found him dressed in a warm-up suit, lying on top of the covers, with Jeff and Rob sitting nearby. The three of them were engrossed in the latest Batman movie. Steve hit the pause button on the remote control when we entered the room, and Philip said, "We got you enrolled in Charles's old school. You're all set to start classes on Monday."

"Cool," he said. "When can I see the campus?"

"If you feel up to it, I'll drive you over there tomorrow and show it to you. Then we have to stop by the mall and purchase your uniforms," Philip said.

"Uniforms?"

"You bet. This is a college preparatory school, and you'll have to wear the school blazer and tie, along with pants of an appropriate color."

Steve's face told us that he wasn't thrilled at the prospect of uniforms. I picked up on that and said, "Look at it this way, Steve. You won't have to worry about what to wear every day, and you won't have to worry about dressing to impress anybody."

"Sounds good to me," Jeff said.

Steve still looked uncertain and said, "I won't know how to act around a bunch of rich kids."

"Steve," Philip said, "those rich kids pull their pants on one leg at a time just like you do, and I know that my sister has raised you to have basic manners."

I added, "Besides, now that you're a member of this household, you more than qualify as one of those 'rich kids' yourself. If one of your classmates turns out to be a little snob, just remind them that the Barnett Library on campus is named after your Uncle Charles's great-grandfather. That should shut him up."

"As soon as Dr. Butcher okays it, you can try out for the swim team," Philip said. "You can invite some or all of them over here once in a while. That should impress them just a bit. I doubt if very many of them have enclosed pools that large in their backyards."

"Kiddo," I said, "meeting new people in new situations is always a little weird. Just be yourself and you'll fit right in."

4

Philip

AN HOUR or so after Charles left for work on Friday, the three teenagers came downstairs for breakfast. I was still in the sunroom enjoying a cup of tea with Gran when they appeared in the doorway. I said, "Good morning, guys. Are you sure you're ready to be up and about, Steve?"

"Yes, Uncle Philip. I'm tired of lying around doing nothing."

"How are you feeling?"

"Pretty good. I'm still a little sore down...." He paused as he registered Gran's presence and added, "You know."

"Okay," I said. "After we get you guys fed, I'll show you the school. Then we can go to the mall."

Mrs. Goodman appeared as if on cue and laid out a small breakfast feast for the three of them. Lance, our resident Irish Setter, sensing the arrival of potential handouts, moved from his spot beside me to a spot nearer to the three boys. They consumed their breakfast rapidly, as only teenagers can do, and by ten we were in my car and on our way.

When we arrived at the school, I drove slowly along the street that made a large circuit of the campus. At about the halfway mark, we heard a bell ring and the area between the buildings was suddenly filled with boys of all ages, all of them dressed uniformly in dark-blue blazers and khaki pants.

"Wow, they look pretty cool," Jeff said.

"Yeah, they look pretty much like the guys back home, except they're dressed better," Rob said.

Thank you, guys, I thought, *for bolstering the argument in favor of uniforms.* Then I said, "So, Steve, what do you think?"

"I hate to admit it, Uncle Philip, but I guess I'm impressed."

"And well you should be. Those boys' parents pay a lot of money to have them in this school, and the boys get a superb education in return. By the time they're seniors, they'll have the best colleges in the country begging them to enroll."

We left the campus and drove over to Lenox Square. Once we were inside the mall, I pointed the brothers in the direction of the video arcade, and Steve and I went to the department store that carried the necessary blazers. In the men's department, we purchased three blazers, several pairs of pants, half a dozen shirts, and a couple of ties.

I asked the salesclerk about socks, and Steve said, "Uncle Philip, I've got plenty of socks."

"No, you don't, kiddo. I've looked in your sock drawer, and you only have three pairs of suitable dress socks. All the rest are white."

"What's wrong with white socks?"

"White socks are for tennis shoes or work boots. You don't wear white socks with dress clothes," I said.

"What happens if I do?"

"The Fashion Police will get you," I said, trying to keep a poker face.

"You're kidding, right?"

"Of course. However, you need to remember that you're not in rural Louisiana anymore, and even if you were, I'll bet you wouldn't see your Uncle Julien going to his law office wearing white socks with his suit."

The salesclerk backed me up on that, and Steve grudgingly acquiesced. Fortunately, he was pretty much "off the rack" as far as sizes went, so there were no alterations necessary on the blazers or the pants.

As we walked down the concourse of the mall toward the video arcade to meet the brothers, I said, "Steve, are you doing okay? This is the most exercise you've had in days."

"I'm okay, just a bit sore here and there."

"Good. Just take it easy and you'll be over this in no time."

"Uncle Philip, Jeff and Rob are going home tomorrow. Do you think it would be okay if Jeff and I... you know?"

"Fooled around tonight?"

"Yeah."

"I don't know why not, as long as he doesn't squeeze your testicles. You'd probably be more comfortable lying flat on your back with him on top. Doing a sixty-nine shouldn't place any stress on your bruises."

"God! I can't believe I'm talking to you about this stuff."

"Why not? We're both guys and we're both gay. What's the problem?"

"I don't know. It's just weird talking to anybody that's so much older than me about sex."

"Steve, I think you'll soon come to understand that there isn't anything that you can't discuss with Charles or me."

"Yeah, I sort of realize that now, but realizing it and doing it are two different things."

We located the brothers and went to the food court for lunch. The guys wanted to have dessert in the food court, but I persuaded them to hold off a bit on that. On the way back to the house, we stopped at a little restaurant in Buckhead, and they soon understood why.

"Wow, Uncle Philip, I've never seen a restaurant that only sold dessert," Steve said.

"Awesome" and "totally cool" were the responses of Jeff and Rob, respectively.

All three of them selected huge pieces of cake or pie, and I settled for a small dish of custard. When we arrived at the house, I noticed a car in the driveway and said, "Looks like we have company."

The three boys carried Steve's new clothes up to his room, and I headed to the back of the house, where I found Gran and Lydia in the sunroom. I said, "Lydia, did Steve have an appointment with you today? If so, I apologize for his not being here—he didn't say anything to me about it."

"No, he didn't have an actual appointment. I was driving through the neighborhood on the way from one place to another and decided to check in on him. How's he doing?"

"He's mending physically, but I can't vouch for the rest of it. Right now he has the distraction of having his two friends from home here with him. I suspect the test will come sometime tomorrow after they leave."

Mrs. Goodman appeared with a pitcher of iced tea in her hands, which she poured for us, and said, "Did the boys have an adequate lunch?"

"I think so. They stuffed themselves in the food court at Lenox Square. Then we stopped by a dessert place on the way home. I think they will be all right for a few hours, at least."

She left the room, and Lydia said, "How are things in Louisiana?"

"As far as I know, everything is under control. Steve's father is out on bail and under a restraining order not to get within a certain distance of his son. Charles is working on a similar restraining order for this area. My sister has filed for divorce and should have no trouble getting control of the business, particularly in light of the fact that her husband will most likely be in jail for a very long time."

"Charles told me that the prosecutor in Louisiana would prefer to have Steve testify in person against his father, but is willing to accept a taped deposition if Steve isn't ready to attend the trial in person when it begins," she said.

"Do you think he'll be ready for that?"

"That depends upon how long it'll be before the trial begins. As I understand it, a preliminary hearing is scheduled in a couple of weeks. The trial date will be set at that hearing."

"Well, I'm no psychologist, but it seems to me that it would be good for Steve if he was able to face his father in court and testify."

"I tend to agree with that sentiment," Lydia said, "but it's going to take a little time to bring him to that point."

Then my cell phone rang. I noted the originating area code and said, "This is a business call, and I need to run upstairs to the office." I answered the call as I hurried down the hall and up the stairs.

By the time I reached my desk, I'd made a decision, passed it along to the caller, and made a few hasty notes on a yellow pad. As I concluded the call, Steve stuck his head into the office.

"Uncle Philip, we're going out to the pool for a while," he said.

"Enjoy yourselves. See you later."

The fax machine began to hum, and I waited patiently for all four pages of the document to land in the tray before I picked them up and scanned them carefully. I signed the document in the appropriate spots and faxed it back to the sender. When it had gone through, I sent it out again, this time to Randolph Forney, my tax attorney, for his records.

He must have been hovering over his fax machine, because my cell phone rang two minutes later, and Randolph was on the line. He was ecstatic.

I talked to him for a few minutes, then went back downstairs to rejoin Gran and Lydia. Gran looked up when I entered the room, and said, "You look like the proverbial cat that just swallowed the canary. I take it that your call was good news."

"Indeed it was. I've been negotiating back and forth for weeks with a Realtor in Boston. The seller has finally agreed to my terms, and this has every appearance of being the biggest and most lucrative project I've ever undertaken."

"Are you referring to the apartment building that you looked at while we were in Boston?" Gran said.

"Indeed I am. This will be a multimillion-dollar project, and I'm purchasing it with income that I received tax-free from the court settlements. When the project is completed and fully rented, I'm going to donate the building to the foundation. My tax attorney is salivating over the prospect of taking a huge write-off from funds that were never taxable income in the first place. More importantly, the foundation will have a steady source of cash flow that will be more than sufficient for its day-to-day operations."

"That's very clever," Lydia said.

"Yes, it is, but I can't take credit for it. Charles is the one who came up with the idea of the tax advantages."

"He has the devious mind of a lawyer," Gran said.

Before anything else could be said, my cell phone rang again. A name came up on the display, and because I suspected the nature of the call, I took it without leaving the room.

When the call was over, I said, "Gran, this *is* a day for good news. That was our publisher. The publication date for your book is set for about six weeks from now."

Before Gran could respond to that, Lydia had to be brought up to date on the book project. She was amazed and impressed and said that she would certainly want an autographed copy. This gave me a germ of an idea, and I said, "You know, Gran, they'll probably want you to do a book-signing tour when the book is published."

She gave me a look and said, "I have no intention of flying around the country visiting bookstores. You know I don't like airports and long lines."

"You could certainly manage some of the bookstores in greater Atlanta, and Charles could fly you to some of the other cities in the Southeast."

"We'll see," she said, and she changed the subject.

A bit later, I excused myself to go upstairs to work. I'd been setting aside two or three hours every afternoon for writing and was getting into a new project. I was deep in concentration when I heard the boys come barreling back upstairs. There was a knock on the office door, and I looked up.

Steve stuck his head in the room, and I said, "How was the pool?"

"Fine. The Jacuzzi made my balls a bit uncomfortable, but the cool water in the pool felt great."

"What's up?"

"Do you mind if we go back to the mall?"

"Not as long as you don't overdo it. Remember to be back in time for dinner—Mrs. Goodman is planning a going-away feast for Jeff and Rob."

"We'll be back in plenty of time."

"Do you need any money?" Charles and I had already discussed the need for Steve to have a regular allowance, and Steve had eagerly agreed to take on the role of gardener and groundskeeper by way of chores.

"No thanks, I'm okay for now," he said.

"Then run along and have a good time."

He left the office and closed the door behind him, and I got back to work. I'd just gotten into the story when Grace knocked on the door. She was taking off for the weekend and handed me the wireless monitor so I could listen out for the babies. I wished her a pleasant weekend, clipped the wireless device to my belt, and resumed my writing. I was still at it when Charles came home. He entered the room so quietly that I didn't know he was there until his arms slipped around me from behind.

"You're hard at it," he said.

"I've had a very good day in a lot of ways."

"Tell me about it?"

"Let's go to the bedroom and get naked first," I said as I saved, then closed the document I was working with.

Instead of answering me, he grabbed my hand, pulled me up from the desk, and led me down the hall to the master bedroom. Without releasing his grip on my hand, he closed the door behind us, locked it, and maneuvered me onto the bed. In no time I was flat on my back and naked. Charles paused as he began to kiss his way down my torso and said, "Now, tell me about your day."

I proceeded to do so between gasps of pleasure as he located one sensitive spot after another. By the time I'd finished my report of the day, his mouth had found its target, so I said, "That pretty much sums it up. Now move your body 180 degrees so I can reciprocate."

He did just that, and I quickly lost myself in the giving and receiving of pleasure. Half an hour later we were showered, dressed, and sitting in the study when the boys returned from the mall. They came into the study and said hello to us, and we visited with them until the intercom rang and Mrs. Goodman announced that dinner would be served in fifteen minutes.

The boys excused themselves to go wash up. I followed them down the hall and asked Rob and Jeff to stop by the office for a minute while Steve was in his bathroom.

When the three of us were in the office, I closed the door, walked to the desk, retrieved two envelopes, and said, "What time are you guys planning to leave in the morning?"

"Pretty early," Rob said. "Our folks will be home tomorrow evening, and we want to get home in time to have the house straightened up before they get there."

"Yeah, we left in sort of a hurry that night," Jeff added.

"I know, and I can't thank the two of you enough for all you did for Steve. You probably saved his life and certainly saved him a lot of grief by bringing him here."

I handed an envelope to each of them, saying, "This is to reimburse you for your gas and give you some cash for the trip back."

As I expected, they protested, but in the end, they pocketed the envelopes and thanked me. "You're both very welcome," I said, "and remember, you're always welcome to come and visit anytime."

They went to wash up, then I rejoined Charles in the study, and we went into the nursery to look in on the babies before we went down to dinner. They were sound asleep, so we quietly closed the door and headed downstairs.

Dinner was great, even if the atmosphere was somewhat gloomy, the impending departure of the brothers having had a dampening effect on Steve's spirits. We'd just finished our main course when the wireless monitor at my belt started making noises, so Charles and I excused ourselves to go up to the nursery and take care of business.

The babies were both wet, so we changed them and took them into the study, where we set them down in a playpen that had been set up in one corner of the room. They were a few months from being able to crawl and lay happily on their backs, trying to reach the colorful mobile that was suspended from the edge of the playpen.

Charles turned on the stereo system and selected some Mozart and Vivaldi, and we were settled back on the sofa, listening to the music and watching the babies, when Steve and the brothers came back upstairs. The three of them had decided to go to the movies and were seeking directions to the theater they'd selected. Charles told them the theater wasn't too far away, and suggested that they go into the office and use MapQuest, which they did.

Gran arrived in the study just as the babies were beginning to get restless and show signs of needing to be fed, so we took them back into the nursery, where she fed Mark and rocked him to sleep while Charles and I took turns doing the same with Steve. When both babies were sound asleep, we transferred them to their cribs and returned to the study. Charles poured a nightcap for each of us, and we sat and discussed the events of the week.

Gran said, "Philip, how do you think Steve will do once his friends leave?"

"It's hard to say. I suspect he'll be a bit lonely Saturday and Sunday, but as soon as he gets caught up in the routine of school, he should be all right."

"You and I should make a concerted effort to keep him distracted over the weekend," Charles said.

"No problem, but it'll have to be home-based activity. Remember, we're on duty this weekend."

"I know," he said. "We'll have to take turns. I'll think of something to do with him tomorrow, and you can do so on Sunday, or vice versa."

"The gang will be over for pizza by the pool tomorrow evening. That will help," I said.

"That sounds like a plan," he said.

Gran said goodnight and went to her room, and Charles went to the sound system and selected some more music. He walked back to the sofa and sat down next to me as soft piano music began to come from the speakers.

"What's that?"

"Satie. More specifically, the Gymnopédies."

"I don't know him at all."

"He was a contemporary of Ravel and Poulenc and considered to be a forerunner of the minimalist movement."

"I don't usually like the so-called minimalist music, but this is charming."

"Yes, isn't it?"

"Are we going to wait up for the boys?"

"You know we are. We might as well get some practice with Steve until he goes off to college. That should prepare us for fifteen or twenty years of waiting up for Mark and Steve."

"Too true. We need to think of a way to differentiate between the two Steves now in residence."

"How about Big Steve and Little Steve?"

"I was thinking more along the lines of Steve, which my nephew already goes by, and Steven for my son."

"That'll work just as well."

"Good. I'm still getting used to the concept of being able to say 'my son'."

"I know what you mean."

We each settled down with a book, and I'd dozed off on the sofa by the time the boys came trooping up the stairs and into the study. Their chatter woke me up, and I snapped out of it when Steve said, "You guys didn't have to wait up for us, Uncle Philip."

"Of course we did. We couldn't possibly go to sleep knowing that the three of you were on the loose in the big bad wicked city."

"How was the movie?" Charles said.

"It was good," Jeff answered for the three of them.

"Do you guys need a wake-up call tomorrow morning?" I said.

"Yes, please," Jeff said. "If we aren't already up by seven."

"You've got it," Charles said.

They said goodnight and left for their rooms. Charles went downstairs to secure the house, and I went into the nursery to check on the babies. He joined me in our room a few minutes later, and we crawled into bed.

5

Charles

PHILIP and I were awakened the next morning by sounds of distress coming from the nursery monitor. We got up, pulled on shorts, and went next door to take care of things. Both babies were soiled and hungry, and I got Mark changed, fed, and back to sleep before Philip had finished taking care of Steven.

"It's almost six thirty," I said. "I'll go wake up the guys while you finish here."

He nodded in agreement, and I went down the hall. I looked into our old room, now Steve's room. Steve and Jeff were snuggled up together in the middle of the bed, so I went in the room and tapped Steve on the shoulder. Then I said, "Steve, it's six thirty. If you guys wake up now, you have time for a quickie before you get dressed. Breakfast will be ready by seven."

I heard a groggy "Thanks" in response, and I left the room. I walked across the hall, opened Rob's door slightly, and knocked lightly as I looked into the room.

"It's a little after six thirty," I said. "Breakfast will be ready by seven."

Rob said, "Thanks," and I closed the door and went back to the nursery.

Philip was closing the nursery door as I arrived. "All quiet," he said. "Both of them are out cold."

"Good. We have time to shower and dress before breakfast."

Philip and I were downstairs at the breakfast table sipping coffee when Rob came down and immediately said, "Where's Jeff? I just looked in his room, and he wasn't there."

"Jeff bunked with Steve last night," Philip said.

Before Rob could respond, Steve and Jeff entered the room, and I said, "Speaking of the devil."

"Did you two get any sleep last night?" Philip said.

"Yes, but not enough," Steve said, yawning.

At that moment, Mrs. Goodman appeared with a tray of food, and all conversation ceased. Half an hour later, we were standing in the driveway saying good-bye to our guests.

I said, "Guys, I'm sure Philip has told you this, but I want to reinforce what he said. The two of you are welcome to come visit Steve anytime."

"Be sure and call Steve to let him know when you get home," Philip said.

The boys promised to do that, and after hugs all around, they got in their car and drove away. When we were back in the house, Steve yawned and said, "If you guys don't mind, I'm going back to bed."

"Go get some rest," Philip said. "If you aren't downstairs by lunchtime, we'll come looking for you."

Philip and I followed Steve up the stairs. Steve headed toward his room, and we went to the nursery to check on the boys. They were still sound asleep, so we went back to the study and were engrossed in the morning papers when Gran appeared and said, "Did the boys get off all right?"

"About thirty minutes ago," I said.

"Where's Steve?"

"He went back to bed, and we don't really expect him to surface for a couple of hours," I said.

"Good. After what he's been through, he needs rest. By the way, you might want to add the Cyclorama to your mental checklist of things with which to distract Steve today."

"Thanks," Philip said. "I hadn't even thought about that."

"Have you ever been there?" I said.

"Years ago."

"Me too," I said. "In fact, I was probably still in high school at the time."

Further conversation was halted by sounds from the nursery, and I said, "Duty calls." Philip and I went to check on the boys while Gran went downstairs to breakfast.

Both babies were awake and mercifully dry, so we carried them into the study and placed them in their playpen. I went to the computer, called up our calendar for the coming week, and said, "Guess what?"

"What?"

"We have our first tasting with the Atlanta Wine and Food Society next Friday evening."

"Good. You haven't met with the tasting committee yet, have you?"

"Not yet. As you know, it's been postponed a couple of times for various reasons, mostly because everyone involved has a busy schedule and all of us have multiple involvements and commitments."

"Do you know what we'll be tasting on Friday?"

"Yes, I do. It will be a vertical tasting of Baby Jesus."

"Say what?"

"You mean you don't know what a vertical tasting is?"

"Of course I do. It's a sampling of several different vintages of the same wine. The 'say what' was in reference to Baby Jesus."

"The proper name is Vigne de l'Enfant Jésus, or Baby Jesus for short. It's a fine Burgundy. There's a story behind the name, but I'd have to look it up to give you an accurate version."

"That's okay. I'll look it up between now and Friday."

"While you're at it, look up the history of Burgundy as it pertains to wines. You'll find it to be an interesting story."

"How so?"

"It's a long story, but in a nutshell, until the eighteenth century, most of the Burgundy wine region was owned by the church. After the French Revolution, most of the church's properties were given to the peasants in small parcels. Today the majority of the small growers each own little more than a hectare or two of vines."

"It just hit me," he said. "We never took Steve to get X-rays."

"Add it to the list of things to do this weekend to keep him occupied."

"The boys are getting restless, so I think it's time to feed them," he said.

I went to the nursery, rounded up bottles and formula, and returned to the study. As soon as both of them were satisfied, we put them back to bed and returned to the study. Then we went down the hall to our office and spent the rest of the morning reviewing the details of the new Boston project, along with a couple of smaller projects that Philip had been investigating. As we were putting the files away, Steve stuck his head in the room and said, "Is lunch ready?"

Philip looked at his watch. "I should think so. Let's go downstairs and see."

As we walked down the stairs, I said, "Did you have a good time last night, Steve?"

I turned my head just in time to see a grin spread across his face as he said, "You know I did."

"There's nothing like a night of wild sex to lift your spirits," Philip said.

We were approaching the entrance to the sunroom, so I changed the subject and said, "Philip needs to take you to get an X-ray this afternoon. We promised the doctor that we would, and he isn't going to release you to try for the swim team until he sees one."

I took over nursery duty for the weekend so Philip could entertain Steve. Getting the X-rays taken care of and a trip to a mall for school supplies and some casual clothing occupied the rest of Saturday. Most of Sunday was dedicated to showing Atlanta to Steve, including the Cyclorama and a brief visit to Stone Mountain.

Early Monday morning I had the digital camera ready when Steve emerged wearing his school uniform and took a number of photos for Philip to send to Marie. Philip took Steve to school, leaving just before I went to work. That evening, I arrived home anxious to hear Steve's reaction to his first day at the Academy.

Philip had already given me a private briefing in our room, but at the dinner table, I said, "So, Steve, how was your first day at the new school?"

"It was fine. I sort of liked it."

"That's good to hear," I said. "Did you meet any guys who you think might become friends?"

"Maybe. There were a couple of guys who seemed okay. One of them, Roger Cartwright, says he lives nearby. Uncle Philip is going to call Mrs. Cartwright and offer to take turns driving Roger and me to and from school. He's on the swim team."

"I know the family," Gran said. "The boy's grandparents moved to Florida a few years ago, and his parents moved into the grandparents' home."

We settled into a steady routine, and Steve seemed to be adapting very well to the school. A week later, Dr. Butcher having given the green light, Steve tried out for and was accepted on the swim team. He was in a high state of excitement that evening, as he'd really missed that aspect of school.

Later that evening, after Steve had retired to his room, Philip and I were downstairs in the library enjoying a glass of wine with Gran. I said, "We're going to have to think carefully about Steve and the swim team."

"Why?" said Philip.

"Because he'll inevitably want to invite some or all of his teammates over to use the pool."

"So?" Philip said.

"For one thing, we need to obtain a signed release from any parent whose son uses the pool with Steve and others. We don't have a lifeguard, and people sue at the drop of a hat these days. I don't think it'll be necessary if he invites one or two friends over, but if it's most or all of the team, then it's a must."

"That seems to be a no-brainer," Gran said.

"And so it is," I said, "but that's not what I'm really concerned about."

"What, then?" Philip said.

"From time to time, we'll surely have occasion to join Steve and his friends."

"So?"

"Think about it. Two gay men, naked or nearly naked, in a pool and/or Jacuzzi with a bunch of teenagers. All it would take is for one greedy or disgruntled kid to make a false accusation, and we'd have a mess on our hands."

"Surely no student at Exeter Academy would do something like that," Gran said.

"I wouldn't like to think so, but there's too much at stake, and we have to consider the possibility."

"What's your worst-case scenario?" Philip said.

"Worst-case would be a kid making an accusation. They'd be after money, of course. I have the legal firepower to successfully defend anything that might be thrown at us, but even when you win a case like that, the odium attached to it never goes away entirely. You remember the guy I successfully defended in just such a case—despite being proven innocent, he finally had to relocate to escape the stigma."

"Have you a suggestion?" Philip said.

"Simply this: you and I need to make sure that we're never alone with any of these kids. If Steve wants to have a pool party with some teammates, we might also consider always having at least one other parent present."

"I guess that's a good idea, but it seems like overkill," he said.

"Not when you've defended as many high-profile people as I have against frivolous lawsuits. And thanks to your trial, we're both very much high profile in that sense of the word."

"Okay," he said, throwing up his hands. "I bow to the voice of experience, and we'll be extremely careful in dealing with Steve's friends."

"Steve seems to be doing all right in his new environment," I said.

"Yes, he does, doesn't he? I was afraid he'd have a hard time making the adjustment from rural Louisiana to urban Atlanta."

"Lydia says that she thinks he'll be able to testify by the time his father goes on trial," I said.

"Good," Gran said. "Facing his father in court and testifying should do wonders for his self-esteem. Speaking of wonders, he's already doing wonders for the grounds."

"True," I said. "He seems to have a natural talent for plants."

"He's also extremely eager to earn his keep, as the saying goes," Philip said.

"His sixteenth birthday is just a few weeks away," I said, "and you know what that means."

"What?" Philip said.

"It's time for a driver's license, of course."

"Oh. I hadn't thought about that."

"Well, you'd better start thinking about it, because I can assure you Steve is."

"Why? Has he said something?"

"Of course not, but what kid doesn't yearn for the perceived freedom that a driver's license promises? I certainly remember that, don't you?"

"Now that you mention it, yes. I guess I'll have to think about getting him a car, as well."

"I'd hold off on that. Encourage him to save enough money over the summer to make a down payment on a used car. Despite the trauma he's been through, he doesn't need to be handed everything on a platter, so to speak."

"That's true," Gran said. "He'll appreciate a car and take better care of it if he feels that he's earned it."

The next evening at the dinner table, Steve provided his own solution to the subject of transportation when he said, "Uncle Philip?"

"Yes."

"I'll be sixteen soon, and I want to get my driver's license."

"No problem."

"I've been thinking about a way to earn money so I can buy a used car."

"Have you?" Philip said.

"Yes. I'd like to go after some lawn care business in the neighborhood. You know, houses that are in bicycle range."

"You don't have a bicycle," Philip said.

"I have one back in Louisiana. Mom's coming to Atlanta on the weekend after my birthday. She can bring it with her."

"That works for me," Philip said.

"Do you plan to go around knocking on doors?" I said.

"There's no need to do that. Roger and I have been talking about doing lawns together, and he knows everybody around here."

"Well, a little hard work never hurt anybody," Philip said. "As long as it doesn't interfere with your schoolwork, I think it's a good idea."

"Why don't you invite Roger over for dinner some evening or for lunch Saturday or Sunday?" I said. "Philip has met him because he drives the two of you to and from school every other day, but I haven't."

"The last time I saw him, he was just a baby. By all means, invite him over," Gran said.

In point of fact, Philip had told me privately that Roger was blond, cute, and almost certainly gay. He had by now driven the boys to and from school a number of times.

"Thanks, I will," Steve said.

Steve asked to be excused, but before he went upstairs to do his homework, he circled the table, giving Philip, Gran, and me each a hug and saying, "Thank you," after each hug.

"For what?" Philip asked for all of us.

"For taking me in. For making me feel at home. Maybe for just being here."

Before we could respond, he slipped quietly out of the room.

Gran broke the silence and said, "My, my, life with his father must have been rougher than we thought."

"Apparently," Philip said.

"By the way," she said, "I recently received a letter from Exeter Academy thanking me for my generous donation. I send them a check once a year, but it could hardly be called generous enough to warrant a personal letter, and that was months ago. Can either of you enlighten me?"

"Oops," Philip said. "I was going to fill you in on that, but it slipped my mind."

"Gran," I said, "Dean Lloyd seemed reluctant to take a new student in midterm until I pointed out that the Barnett Library needed new computers and some refurbishing. I hinted that I might be able to persuade you to do something about it. Philip paid for it, of course. We'd planned to tell you about it the day we enrolled Steve, but with all that was going on, we simply forgot."

"I thought that pompous twit had been put out to pasture by now," she said.

"I didn't know you were acquainted with him," I said.

"I met him at a fundraiser or two while you were at Harvard. He positively salivates at the prospect of donations. Your father and your grandfather were on the board of trustees of the school, and I'm frequently invited to such functions. I haven't been to one in several years, but I still receive the invitations. The next time I receive one, you can escort me. It's inevitable that you'll be asked to join the board at some point, particularly now that you have a child enrolled, so you might as well become acquainted with the members."

"Just what I need," I said. "Yet another commitment."

"Charles Marks Barnett," Gran said. "Shame on you. You have a position to maintain and a responsibility to serve where you can."

"Sorry, Gran. I sit rebuked."

"And well you should. I happen to know that two of the board members are getting up in years. One or both of them is likely to die or retire at any time, and you are a logical candidate."

On that note, we said goodnight and climbed the well-worn stairs.

The days rolled by, and Friday evening found us at the wine tasting, which was held in a meeting room at the Ritz-Carlton. Long banquet tables were set with eleven-inch by fourteen-inch sheets of white paper at each place setting. The papers each had circular outlines the size of a wine glass numbered from one through seven, arranged in a semicircle, surrounding a small plate.

An empty wine glass was placed precisely in each circle, and each glass was embossed with the logo of the Atlanta Wine and Food Society. In addition, the glasses had lines on one side, which marked the appropriate level to which they should be filled. These markings were carefully calibrated (we learned) to allow the people pouring the wine to gauge the amount poured. At most of the tastings, each bottle was divided equally between ten glasses (a ten-pour), but there were markings that indicated eight, ten, twelve, and fourteen pours per bottle. With extremely expensive wines, the society utilized a twelve- or fourteen-pour. In addition to the seven wines that were being formally tasted, we were handed a glass of wine at the door, which served as an apéritif.

The tables also contained plates of fruit and cheese and baskets of bread. Because we were the newest members present, Philip and I were publicly welcomed into the group. While volunteers poured the wines, the presenter gave us a detailed and most interesting history of Burgundy as it pertained to wine growing, along with a rundown of weather and climate for each of the vintages we were sampling. The differences between each vintage of the same wine were interesting.

Needless to say, Philip and I thoroughly enjoyed the evening. After the tasting was over, we met with the tasting committee and tentatively approved three dates in the fall for tastings from our cellar, as well as a date in early summer for a private tasting for the committee, to be held at the house.

As we were driving home, I said, "That was a great evening, wasn't it?"

"It sure was. I'm already looking forward to the next one."

"Are you feeling any effects from all that wine?"

"Well, we each consumed about four-fifths of a bottle of wine, offset by the bread, cheese, and fruit, not to mention the dinner we had afterward in the hotel dining room. That being said, I'm feeling warm and fuzzy but not particularly impaired."

"Me too. I was just wondering if we ought to take a taxi next time?"

"Maybe. On the other hand, when Steve gets his license, he can act as chauffeur."

"Works for me."

As soon as we were home, we checked on Steve and the boys and went straight to bed. We had both just drifted off when my cell phone rang. I answered and listened for a moment to the caller. Then I said, "We'll be right down."

"Who was that?" Philip said.

"Security. It seems that they've apprehended someone prowling around the front gates."

We dressed hastily, went downstairs, turned on the outside lights, and opened the gate. Two of the security people came up the driveway with a third man sandwiched between them. They each had a firm grip on the intruder and sort of frog-marched him up the drive.

Before I could say anything, Philip said, "Well, well, Frank. What brings you to Atlanta?"

"I want to see my son," the man said sullenly.

"Why? So you can beat him up again?" Philip said.

I turned to Philip and said, "Let me guess, this is your brother-in-law."

"In the flesh," Philip said.

I addressed the security people. "Gentlemen, please call the police. This man is out on bond for beating his teenage son within an inch of his life. He's also under a restraining order, which prohibits him from coming anywhere near his son, and the Louisiana police will be happy to have him back in custody." I didn't have to explain who the son was—the security people had been fully briefed when Steve had moved in.

Philip added, "Detective Howard of the Atlanta Police Department has a file on the case."

"I still want to see my son," Frank said.

"I can assure you that my nephew doesn't want to see you," Philip said. "However, you'll see him at your trial when he testifies concerning the beating you gave him. You damn near killed him."

The man withered visibly at Philip's words, and the security people marched him back down the driveway. We waited until they'd cleared the gate, then went back inside and secured the premises, and Philip said, "I guess I'd better call Marie and let her know about this."

"Agreed, but what about Steve? Does he need to know?"

"Much as I dislike upsetting him, I think we'd better tell him. He probably needs to be a little more vigilant than he has been—just in case Frank manages to weasel his way out on bond again."

"You're right, of course, but it can wait until morning. And I think perhaps we ought to run it by Lydia first."

We went upstairs to our room, and Philip called Marie while I checked on the boys. When I returned from the nursery, Philip said, "Marie is going to alert the local police to expect a call from Atlanta."

"Good. Now can we go to sleep?"

I called Lydia the next morning and brought her up to date on the events of Friday night. She thought a moment, then said that Steve was sufficiently recovered from his experience that he could and should be told.

Philip and I knocked on Steve's door just before lunch and broke the news to him. I don't really know what was going on in his head, but on the surface he took it well.

"Steve," I said, "the bottom line is that as of now, your father is on his way back to jail and will probably stay there until his trial. He not only violated the restraining order, but he violated his bail bond agreement as well. That being said, Philip and I think that you need to be very aware of your surroundings when you're out and about."

"Charles and I have someone keeping tabs on things in Louisiana," Philip said. "If Frank manages to weasel his way out of jail before the trial, we'll know about it immediately."

"All we're saying is go about your normal routines, but maybe you should stay out of dark alleys," I said.

Steve managed to smile at that and said, "I'm okay."

"Are you sure?" Philip said.

"You bet I am. He caught me off guard last time. That won't happen again."

"Good for you," I said. "Ready for lunch?"

"You know I am," Steve said, and the three of us headed downstairs.

"What do you and Roger have planned for this evening?" Philip said.

"Nothing much," Steve said. "After dinner, we'll probably use the pool and the Jacuzzi. He's bringing a couple of DVDs with him."

"Sounds like a late night," I said. "Is he going to sleep over?"

"Probably, if that's all right with you guys."

"No problem, kiddo," Philip said, "as long as his parents are okay with it."

"They are. His folks are pretty strict when it comes to where he can go, what he can do, and how late he can stay out."

"Nothing wrong with that," I said. "I would call that being responsible parents."

"Is the gang coming over tonight?" Steve said.

"I don't think so," I said. "They were over last night, and as far as I know, you and Roger will have the pool area to yourselves."

"Charles and I will probably swim a few laps at some point in the evening," Philip said.

Philip and I spent the afternoon running errands, including visits to the cleaner's, the mall, and a couple of other places. We invited Steve to join us, but he declined, pleading homework. We were sitting in our study when Goodman escorted Roger upstairs, and Philip made the introductions before he led Roger down the hall to Steve's room.

When he returned, I said, "You were right on the money about Roger. Blond, cute, and certainly gay."

"I wonder if Steve has figured out that last bit?"

"I don't know, but you know what they say—like attracts like."

"True, and he certainly needs someone to replace Jeff at the moment."

We were already seated at the dining room table when Steve and Roger appeared. Grace joined us a few minutes later. I was impressed by the fact that both Steve and Roger joined in the general conversation at dinner. So many teenagers these days seemed to go out of their way to affect an attitude of being both sullen and uncommunicative. The two boys were both intelligent and articulate, and their participation in our conversations added immensely to our enjoyment of the meal.

Later, when Philip and I emerged from the dressing room in the pool enclosure, we noted that the boys were horsing around at the shallow end of the pool. As we entered the pool, they headed for the Jacuzzi. Half an hour or so later, when Philip and I settled into the Jacuzzi, the boys excused themselves to go shower, change, and head back to the house.

When they were out of sight and hearing range, I said, "I have two observations."

"Yes?"

"One, Roger is a real blond, and two, both boys have trimmed their pubes."

"I noticed the former. As for the latter, I noticed it as well. It probably has something to do with being on the swim team. Trimming, and for that matter shaving, is all the rage with swim teams these days."

"Really?"

"Yes. I've been reading up on such things in an attempt to hone my parenting skills, so to speak."

"Good for you. This will give us some practice for dealing with Mark, Steven, and the rest."

"Speaking of 'the rest', have we had an update from Boston lately?"

"If we had, babe, you'd already know it. You know what they say: 'No news is good news.'"

We soaked in silence for twenty minutes or so, then showered and went back to the house. Steve and Roger were at the table in the sunroom, consuming enormous bowls of ice cream, and I said, "Did you guys save any for us?"

Steve's mouth was clearly full, so he merely nodded and pointed toward the kitchen. Philip and I checked the freezer, scooped out some ice cream for ourselves, and carried small dishes of it to where the boys were sitting. We chatted easily with the boys while consuming the ice cream. After a few minutes, I said, "We couldn't help but notice, Steve, that you seem to be doing a little trimming."

Steve blushed slightly and said, "Everyone on the team does that to one degree or another. Some of them even go all the way, like you and Uncle Philip."

Philip gave me an "I told you so" look.

"What's stopped you from going 'all the way', as you put it?" I said.

"I told him that I would if he would," Roger said, "but neither one of us has the nerve to do it."

"We'll get around to it," Steve said.

We finished our ice cream, and the boys went upstairs. Philip and I rinsed out the dishes, left them in the sink, and headed upstairs as well.

Sunday morning we went to St. Philip's, taking the two young men with us. After the service, we were introduced to Mason and Angela Cartwright, Roger's parents, and his two younger brothers, all of whom were communicants. Mason Cartwright was tall and dark-haired and appeared to be in his early forties. The two younger sons closely resembled him. Roger, on the other hand, derived his blond good looks from his mother.

While Angela visited with Philip and the two boys, her husband and I played a game of "who do you know" and discovered in the process that we had a number of mutual acquaintances in the Atlanta business world. He'd met Gran on a number of occasions with his parents, mostly during the years that I was at Harvard. We promised to have Roger home before ten, Sunday being a school night, and went our separate ways.

My cell phone rang Monday morning as we were finishing breakfast. When I'd finished the call, I said, "Gran, do we have a history of twins in the family?"

"As far as I know, there have never been any on either side of the family," she said. "Why?"

"That was our Boston contact on the phone. It seems that I'm going to have two babies instead of one this time. Unfortunately, it wasn't all good news, as there appear to be some complications with the pregnancy."

Philip

MOMENTARILY taken aback, I sat for a moment until I finally found my voice and said, "Complications? What complications?"

"I don't pretend to understand the medical details," Charles said. "All I know is that a seemingly normal pregnancy has turned into one that is high risk. They're going to keep us posted. By the way, everything is going well with the other pregnancy."

Charles said good-bye to Gran and me and left the room. I walked him to the door, kissed him, and returned to the breakfast table.

When I was seated, Gran said, "Is he all right?"

"You know our boy as well as I do. If he wasn't, neither of us would know about it, at least not until he wants us to."

"Too true," she said as she handed a small piece of bacon to an eager Lance, who took it gingerly from her fingers. "All we can do is hope and pray for the best. Medical science performs miracles every day."

Roger spent the following weekend with us. Charles and I were beginning to wonder if the two boys were becoming boyfriends, but had decided to wait and see rather than inquire.

Saturday afternoon we ran laps around the pool house, and when we went inside to the pool to cool off, we found the boys relaxing in the Jacuzzi. They had cans of Coke on the ledge next to them, along with a large bag of chips. Lance, as usual, was lounging nearby, waiting for handouts.

We swam a few laps to cool off, then settled in the Jacuzzi with the boys. Charles looked at Lancelot's damp fur and said, "Was Lance in the pool with you guys?"

"Yes, Sir," Steve said.

"Be sure you give him a good bath when you shower. It takes a lot of soap and water to get the chlorine out of all that fur. He'll need a good rubdown with towels before he goes back to the house."

"We'll take care of it," Steve said.

"If this is going to happen regularly," I said, "we should probably add a supplement to his food—all that shampooing can cause problems with his coat."

The days turned into weeks, and the time came to celebrate Steve's sixteenth birthday. He invited all of the team members over for the occasion, and we held the party around the pool with ten out of the twelve members present.

In addition to Charles, myself, and Mason Cartwright, three other fathers were present. There were hamburgers, hot dogs, and the usual side dishes, followed by birthday cake and ice cream, followed by a great deal of horseplay in the pool. The adults sat around with glasses of wine or cans of beer, watching the boys have a good time. It was, incidentally, the first time that bathing suits had been worn in our pool.

After school the next day, I took Steve to get his driver's license, and he passed the test with flying colors. He had, of course, been studying the Georgia Driver's Manual for some time.

Marie and the girls arrived late Friday afternoon. I hadn't seen my nieces for several years, and I noted that at ages ten and twelve, they were turning into carbon copies of their mother. I was also struck by the change in my sister. As I escorted her upstairs, I said, "What did you do, Marie, find the fountain of youth?"

"Not exactly. The strain I was living under is going away, and I'm beginning to feel like my old self again."

"Good."

"Frank is still in jail, my divorce will be final next week, and I'm really enjoying running the business. Speaking of changes, I can't believe how my son has blossomed in such a short time."

Steve had already escorted his sisters upstairs, and we were able to talk freely, so I said, "Steve was living in fear all the time you were living with his father's infidelity. Removing Frank from the picture has done you both a world of good."

"It's more than that. From his e-mails and telephone calls, it's quite clear that both you and Charles have done more to parent him in a couple of months than Frank did in fifteen years."

"We're enjoying having him here. We also sort of see it as practice for what we'll face in a few years with our own sons."

"Speaking of the babies, how are they doing?"

"Just fine and growing like weeds, as you'll see."

We reached the upstairs landing, and I said, "You're in the same room you were before, the girls are next door to you, and you have plenty of time to freshen up before dinner."

I left her to her own devices and went down the hall to the office to complete the paperwork I'd been in the middle of when they arrived. Steve had planned a full itinerary of things to do with his mother and sisters, starting with a visit to his school and then on to Stone Mountain. At dinner he outlined his plans in some detail, and both Marie and the girls were looking forward to the next day. They were also very tired from the long drive and retired fairly early.

They left shortly after breakfast Saturday morning. Charles had allowed Steve to take the Jag, and he was a bit overwhelmed with the responsibility, but Charles said as he walked to the car with them, "Just be your usual careful self and you'll be fine."

"But what if I scratch the car?" Steve said.

"That's what insurance is for," I said. "Now go, take care of your guests."

We waited until the car had disappeared through the gate, and returned to the house.

At lunch, Gran said, "Your sister has certainly changed a great deal since the last time I saw her."

"She was under a terrible strain dealing with her husband's infidelities. The source of the strain has been removed from the picture, and she's bouncing back."

"Good for her. Do you have anything planned for tomorrow?"

"I don't, but Steve does. However, if he manages to take them to half of the places on today's list, they'll need tomorrow to rest. He wanted to go out to Stone Mountain straight from the school, but I talked him into postponing that outing by one day. I gave him some cash, and he's going to take them to Phipps Plaza. They have lunch reservations at the Uptown Grill; then they can go to Stone Mountain and walk off their lunch."

"Good for him," she said. "He's come a long way in the short time he's been with us."

"He has done that," Charles said. "Lydia tells me that he's very nearly over his terror of going back to face his father in court. If he can look his father in the eye and talk about what happened, it will go a long way toward completing the healing process."

Steve and his charges returned around four. Marie went to her room to take a nap, and Steve took his sisters out to the pool, where they stayed until we called them to the house for dinner.

After dinner, Roger came over, and he and Steve took the girls to a movie. When they'd departed, we took our wine glasses and settled on the sofas in the sunroom to visit. Marie had been suitably impressed by the tour of Exeter Academy and said so.

"I don't think he really knows what he wants to do yet," I said, "but with his grades and a diploma from that school, he can go to any college in the country. In point of fact, many of them will be approaching him during his senior year. The better colleges recruit heavily at schools like Exeter."

"He has such an affinity for plants," Gran said, "that I sometimes wonder if he ought to consider landscape design."

"Now that you mention it, I think he may be," Marie said. "He said something to that effect this afternoon. There was so much to see and do that it didn't register at the time."

"Now that Steve has his bicycle, he and Roger can go ahead with their plans to earn money doing lawns this summer," I said.

"He told me about that," Marie said. "He wants to buy a used car with his earnings."

"What sixteen-year-old doesn't?" Charles said.

"It was his idea," I said. "Right out of the blue, in fact."

"How are things back home, Marie?" Charles said.

"Getting better all the time. I've discovered that Frank had been skimming money out of the business for some time to pay for his affairs."

"How can you tell?" I said.

"Because the volume of business remains fairly steady, but the cash flow has increased considerably since he's been in jail, among other things."

"I don't suppose it's worth a complete audit of the books so you can lower the boom on Frank with that fact as well," I said.

"No, I don't think so. I thought about it, but full-blown audits are horribly expensive, and there isn't that much money involved. Basically, it appears that instead of allowing his family the occasional luxury, Frank was funding his affairs. I've been reviewing old credit card bills for the business, and there are charges from restaurants and motels that I've never visited. There were also several charges from a jewelry store, and he never bought me jewelry. Need I say more?"

"How despicable," Gran said.

"Yes, it's all of that and more," Marie said, "but I'm determined to put it all behind me and get on with my life."

"Good for you," Gran said.

Marie excused herself to go to bed, as she was still a bit tired from the drive up. We assured her that we'd wait up until the kids were safely home.

Sunday morning, Steve and Roger took Marie and the girls to Six Flags. Then we spent most of Sunday afternoon around the pool, winding up the day having a picnic and watching the kids play in the pool.

Marie and the girls left for Louisiana very early Monday morning. A few days later, one of the members of the Board of Trustees of Exeter Academy resigned, citing health reasons, and Charles accepted a post on the board. The call had come just before dinner, and during dinner, Charles asked Gran if she'd been working behind the scenes to achieve that.

She said, "I thought about it, but before I pursued the matter, two of the board members called me to inquire about you."

After many delays, Gran's book had finally been published, and she'd reluctantly agreed to participate in a few book-signing events. She limited them to places that were no more than two hours from Atlanta by car, but after she'd exhausted the possibilities in suburban Atlanta, Macon, Athens, and Chattanooga, Charles persuaded her to let him fly her to Savannah and a few other places in the Southeast. The book did very well regionally and was extremely successful in greater Atlanta, as it dealt with Atlanta history from a personal perspective.

By the time the school year ended, Steve and Roger had already obtained grounds maintenance commitments from a dozen or so residents of the neighborhood, all of which were referrals from their existing customer base. Most, if not all, of the new customers had had existing arrangements in place, and they had all been canceled effective the end of the school term.

We hosted a pool party for the entire swim team on the day after the term ended. By this time, we'd met their coach, Ethan Forbes, who was a good-looking blond about our age. He was present, along with Mason and the fathers of four other team members. The boys ate first, then went back into the pool to enjoy it, leaving the adults to their meal.

As we were finishing our lunch, Steve, Roger, and three other members of the team came up to the table, and Steve said, "Uncle Philip, we need some ideas on how to raise money for the team over the summer."

"Why do you need money?" I said.

"There's an empty room next to our locker room that we'd like to turn into a steam room, but there's no budget for it."

"True enough," Ethan said. "The room is just the right size and could be converted into a very nice steam room, but the athletic department doesn't have the funds for it right now."

"We know we could hit up some of the parents for the money," Roger said, "but we want to do this ourselves."

"I have an idea," Charles said. "Why don't you offer car washes every weekend during the summer?"

Steve let out a groan and said, "Uncle Charles, every student group in every town does that."

"That's true, but you could give it a new twist," Charles said. "Try this on for size—get permission from Lenox or one of the other malls and set up a car wash tent in their parking lot. Call it the Speedos Car Wash, because all the guys will be washing cars wearing their Speedos."

"I love it," I said. "You'll have matrons from the Junior League there every weekend." *And half of the gay community*, I thought.

"That would work," Ethan said. "You could offer to wash their cars while they waited or while they shopped."

"Also, you could charge a premium price and announce that a portion of the proceeds was going to charity, say the Aflac Cancer Center for children, and the rest for your team," Charles said.

"You also need to have a couple of parents around to keep an eye on things," I added.

"Will the school have a problem with this, Ethan?" Charles said.

Ethan said, "Not with the newest member of the board of trustees involved. Exeter Academy isn't quite as stuffy as it was when you attended."

"It wasn't that many years ago, but your point is taken," Charles said.

Steve excused himself and ran back to the house, returning a few minutes later with pens and yellow pads. He and Roger polled the team and got their enthusiastic agreement. A steering committee was nominated, and he and Roger found themselves jointly in charge of planning.

When the boys had all gotten back into the pool, Mason said, "Is there somewhere that the three of us can talk privately?"

"Sure," I said. "We can go up to our study. There are enough adults here to keep an eye on things."

We led Mason up to the study and offered him a seat, and I said, "What's on your mind?"

"Steve and Roger have gotten very close," he said.

"True."

"I'm glad, because Roger has never had a close friend before."

"And?" Charles said.

"Do either of you think that the two of them are fooling around?"

"It wouldn't surprise me," I said. "They're both sixteen, and you know how the hormones rage at that age. Steve is definitely gay, and I'm certain that Roger is also."

"How can you tell?"

"I have a highly developed, almost infallible, sixth sense about such things," I said.

"Would it bother you to learn that your son is gay?" Charles said.

"I've suspected it for some time now, and it certainly isn't the most wonderful thing I've ever had to deal with. On the other hand, I know enough about such things to understand that it's not something he chose to be." He paused for a moment before continuing. "Actually, when I was a little younger than Roger, my best friend and I fooled around a bit. Then I discovered girls."

"Most boys fool around with friends at that age. Then most of them discover girls and move on, but a few of them don't," Charles said.

"Excuse me for a minute," I said. I went down the hall to our office, unlocked a file cabinet, and returned with some pictures.

"This is what Steve's father did to him the night he caught Steve fooling around with his best friend in Louisiana," I said, and I handed Mason the pictures. "It's also why he's living with us."

Mason looked at each picture carefully. I'd given him all of them, including the groin shots.

"Jesus H. Christ," he said. "How could a man do that to his own child?"

"My brother-in-law isn't a man," I said. "He's a sick and twisted son of a bitch. Sadly, he's far from unique in that respect. This is one of the reasons my sister divorced him, and it's also the reason that I now have legal custody of Steve."

"We were told that Steve was here with you because his father was abusive," Mason said, "but this defies comprehension."

"I know," I said. "Steve's friend Jeff tried to pull my brother-in-law off him and failed. Finally, he hit him over the head with a brass bookend and knocked him out. Steve was hysterical and wouldn't let Jeff take him to a local doctor. He begged to be brought here, so Jeff and his older brother drove all night, arriving here early the next morning."

"Steve was unconscious when they arrived, so we put him in bed and I called our pediatrician," Charles said. "While I waited downstairs for the doctor, Philip took those pictures as evidence."

"Philip and I had a long conversation with Steve a day or so later," Charles said. "He and his friend hadn't gone beyond mutual masturbation at that point."

"We told him two things," I said. "Never let anyone talk him into doing anything he wasn't totally comfortable with, and never practice unsafe sex."

"If Roger were to talk to us about sex, we'd tell him the same thing," I said.

"All of us in this household are very protective of Steve, and that concern extends to Roger, as well," Charles said. "Steve was very fragile when he came to us. He needed a friend, and Roger has been good for him. From what you've just told us, it appears to be a two-way street."

Mason looked at us for a moment. You could see that he was choosing his words carefully. Then he said, "If I'd met either of you in a business setting before all that publicity two years ago, I would never have pegged either of you as gay. You seem so normal. Frankly, I thought all gay men were like those people who march in the parades."

"Think of an iceberg," Charles said. "Ten percent of its mass is above the surface and highly visible. The other 90 percent is unseen. The flamboyant people you see marching in parades represent the tip of the iceberg, and, frankly, they're an embarrassment to the rest of us—the unseen 90 percent."

"You probably come into contact with a great many gay men and women during the course of a typical week," I said, "but you don't know it because they look and act like everyone else."

"Mason," Charles said, "it's obvious that you and Roger have a good relationship. The time may come when he'll want to talk to you about his sexuality. There is no way to predict when, but it will surely happen. All you have to do is be ready for the conversation."

"What about your wife?" I said. "Does she share your concerns?"

"We've talked about it at length, and all she wants is for Roger to be happy," he said.

"What more could you ask?" I said.

"Would you like me to ask Steve anything about Roger?" I said. "Or perhaps suggest to Steve that Roger ought to talk to you?"

"Thanks for the offer," he said. "I'll have to think about that for a bit."

I returned the pictures to the filing cabinet, and the three of us went back to the pool. Some of the boys were still in the water, but it was obvious that the steering committee was in session.

We walked up to the table where the boys were in deep discussion. When Roger saw us, he said, "Dad, don't you know some people at Lenox Square?"

"I sit on the board of directors of the parent company," Mason said, "and, yes, I can probably get permission for the team to use the parking lot."

"Thanks," Roger said, and he turned back to the group. One of the boys was making copious notes on a yellow pad. Before the meeting ended, the boys had a full-blown plan of action in place, and Steve, Roger, and two other boys went up to the house to type it up and print copies.

While they were gone, Charles said, "Listening to those guys talk about the money they're going to make and how they're going to do it makes me think we have a bunch of budding capitalists on our hands."

"You've got that right," Mason said.

"Ethan, are you certain about the school's reaction to all of this?" Charles said. "I may be on the board, but only as a very junior member, and I certainly don't have any clout."

"A very junior member whose father and grandfather before him were also on the board, not to mention a very junior member whose family name just happens to be on one of the buildings on campus," Ethan said. "If I were you, I wouldn't waste any sleep worrying about my lack of clout."

The boys returned with a copy of their plan for each of us to review, and gave each of us a pencil to make any changes or suggestions. We all studied the document carefully, and a few changes were suggested and agreed upon. The boys made another trip to the computer and returned with corrected copies, and the party broke up.

By the following weekend, the Speedos Car Wash had become a reality. The boys staged a preview on Thursday afternoon. The local media had been alerted, and the project managed to make the five o'clock news on most of the local television stations. Friday morning, cars began arriving, and there was a steady stream of customers all weekend long.

The boys had scheduled two parents to be on hand at all times, and as the various parents changed shifts, they kept the boys supplied with food and bottled water. The boys had a ball. As they hosed cars off, they frequently hosed each other down as well. They also managed to maintain enough self-control that they didn't hose down their customers in the process.

Three of the boys had opted to wear swim caps and goggles just for the heck of it, and a couple of them had brought swim fins, occasionally putting them on for show, especially when there were cameras around. The media was again present on Friday afternoon, and by Sunday, one television station had put together a full-blown piece on Exeter Academy, as well. It was scheduled to be aired late Sunday evening.

In addition, a local Baptist preacher had publicly railed against what he referred to as the immorality of young boys washing cars while immodestly dressed. Charles's position as the newest and youngest board member made him fair game, and he was interviewed at length about the school and his family's long association with it. The reporter asked Charles about the Baptist preacher's statements, and he laughed, telling her that perhaps she should go interview Dean Mangrum at St. Philip's Cathedral and ask him how he felt about his son participating in the car wash.

The reporter did so and taped an interview with the dean, who was dressed in full canonicals, as it was just after a Sunday service. With a few well-chosen words, he put the Bible-thumper in his narrow-minded place.

The reporter had also asked Charles why rich kids from a private school needed to raise funds, and Charles said, "First of all, not all of them are, as you say, rich kids. There are slightly more than two thousand students at the school, and 10 percent of them are there on full scholarships. Just over half of the rest are from middle-class or upper-middle-class families. These families pay huge amounts in real estate taxes to fund government schools that have clearly failed their children. Because of that failure, they're willing to sacrifice whatever they must to ensure that their children receive a decent education. The rest of the students do come from more affluent backgrounds, but so what? Do you equate affluence with indolence? The boys came to us with a genuine desire to do something for themselves and, not incidentally, something for a good cause rather than asking for a handout. I think it's commendable and speaks very highly of them."

After the mall closed on Sunday evening, we had the entire team over to our pool, along with many of the parents. Before everyone was fed, the steering committee conducted a full-blown postmortem of the weekend's operation. Everyone was delighted with the event, and the boys had raised a great deal of money. In fact, the final tally was more than four hundred cars washed at ten dollars apiece. The boys had also split a substantial amount of tips amongst themselves.

The committee held a brief meeting and agreed to continue the same schedule for the rest of the summer. There was no dissent from anyone, parents included. Charles had been given a rough cut of the television piece and interviews to preview, and we'd set up a flat screen television set on the pool bar and played the preview DVD for the group. At the end of the interview, everyone applauded, and Charles said, "As far as we know, this will be aired late this evening and perhaps some time next week, as well. I have no idea how much of it will be cut in the interest of time. My answer to the reporter's last question clearly wasn't what she wanted to hear, so it'll probably wind up on the cutting room floor."

Everyone said that they planned to watch and record the report.

Monday morning I took Steve to a local credit union so that he could open a savings account. He used his share of the tips as an opening deposit. That afternoon, he and Roger began doing lawns in earnest.

Just after lunch on Tuesday, my cell phone rang. It was Charles, and he said, "Babe, I know this is short notice, but can you pack an overnight bag for each of us? We have to fly to Boston."

"Why? What's happened?" I said.

"Good news and bad news. I'm on the way home, and I'll tell you about it when I get there. If you can find Steve, you might ask him to stand by so he can drive us to the airport around four."

7

Charles

AFTER my call to Philip, I hurried home in record time. As soon as I walked in the door, I located both Steve and Grace and asked them to join Philip and me in the sunroom with Gran. When everyone was present, I said, "I got a call from the clinic in Boston just before lunch."

"And?" Philip said.

"Twin boys were delivered prematurely around midmorning. One of them is underweight but otherwise okay, but the other one was stillborn."

"Oh, Charles," Gran said. "How sad. I'm so sorry."

"I know, but I don't have time to worry about that. What we have to do is go to Boston and deal with it. The question is, will you and Steve be okay while we're gone?"

"You know we will," Gran said. "Grace has the babies in hand, and Steve and I will look out for each other."

"Good," I said, looking at my watch. "I have just enough time for a quick shower and a change of clothes."

"Do I need to call a hotel?" Philip said.

"Rosemary took care of that when she booked our flight. I thought about staying with William and Henry but decided that we might prefer to be alone until we assess the situation and decide how long we need to stay in Boston."

Then I turned my attention to Grace and said, "Grace, we need to start thinking about rearranging things upstairs."

"Mark and Steven are sleeping through the night now," she said. "Maybe we should move them to another room so the new baby won't disturb them."

"Good idea," I said. "When we get back, we'll move the two of them into the bedroom next to yours."

"We'll also need to talk about your salary and/or some more help for you," Philip said.

Philip followed me upstairs and double-checked our overnight bags, as well as the contents of the travel cases for our laptops, while I showered and changed. Steve was waiting for us in the foyer when we came downstairs, bags in hand, and Gran was seated in a chair nearby.

We each gave Gran a hug, and I said, "We'll be at the Taj. If you can't reach us there or by cell phone, call Rosemary. She and I will be in more or less regular contact."

Philip and I got into the backseat of the Jag. As we headed for the airport with Steve at the wheel, I said, "It's kind of nice to have our own chauffeur, isn't it?"

"True," Philip said. "Maybe we should get him a uniform."

I was sitting behind the driver and noted the grin on Steve's face reflected in the rearview mirror, so I said, "Steve, would you like me to call Mason and ask him if Roger can keep you company while we're gone?"

"Sure. That would be cool."

"I don't know for sure if we'll be back in time to fill our slots at the car wash this weekend, so you might want to have substitutes standing by," I said.

"I'll handle it," Steve said.

"I'm sure you will."

By this time, both Philip and I had Mason's private number in our cell phone directories, so I made the call and spoke to Mason. When I ended the call, I said, "Okay, kiddo, you've got a roommate for the next few nights. You can use the car to drive the two of you to school while we're gone."

"Thanks," Steve said.

"Do you have enough cash for the rest of the week?" Philip said.

"I'm okay. Roger and I usually get paid on the spot for the yard work, and we did two large jobs yesterday, and we've got two more today."

Steve dropped us off at the airport and promised to call as soon as he got home safely. We checked our bags at the curb and began the increasingly tedious process of going through security. For once the lines were moving rapidly, and we wound up in the Delta Sky Club with nearly an hour in which to relax. When we were settled on a corner sofa, glasses of wine in hand, Philip said, "How are you holding up?"

"I'm okay. It's a very sad situation, of course, but I'm not going to get all angst-ridden."

"You'll have to make some arrangements. Have you thought about that?"

"Been there, done that. I called the funeral director who handled Robert's funeral and left it to Rosemary to handle the details. I'm going to have the baby buried next to Robert and name him after Robert."

"That's sweet."

"I haven't thought about the rest of it. It seems a bit much to have a funeral mass for a baby that never lived, and I honestly don't know what's customary."

"Perhaps just a simple graveside ceremony would be adequate."

"That sounds good."

"Anything else happening that I ought to know about?"

"Not really," I said. "I did get a call from the headmaster of Exeter today."

"Indeed?"

"Yes. It seems that all the publicity about the car wash has resulted in a much larger than usual volume of inquiries about the school."

"I take it he was pleased?"

"Ecstatic would be a more apt description." I leaned back on the sofa, closed my eyes, and said, "This is the longest I've sat quietly in one place all day."

"Rough day?" he said.

"Hectic."

"Are we expected at the clinic tonight?"

"First thing in the morning," I said.

"Good. Then you can get a good night's sleep."

"You know what would be even better?"

"What?"

"A full-body massage, followed by sex, followed by a good night's sleep," I said.

Philip booted his laptop and found several massage listings for Boston. The second therapist he telephoned was available and agreed to be at the Taj later that evening.

"I'm glad we did that," I said. "We sort of got out of the habit after my convalescence, and I've missed the regular massages."

"Yeah, me too," he said.

"You know, babe, there's something else we need to talk about."

"What?"

"Mark and Steven will be walking in a few months, and we can't keep them confined to the nursery all the time. Sooner or later they'll figure out how to climb out of their cribs, and from there it won't be too long before they figure out how to circumvent those childproof doorknobs."

"I know. What are you driving at?"

"We need to figure out some way to childproof the upstairs. That is, some way to keep toddlers from falling down the stairs."

"Well, they make all kinds of barriers and gates."

"True, but if we put a gate across the head of the stairs, how will Sir Lancelot get downstairs to use his doggie door?"

"I hadn't thought about that."

"We could designate one or two of the bedrooms in Gran's wing as guest rooms. Then we could knock out a wall between two rooms in the other wing and make a large playroom out of them."

"I like it," Philip said.

"I just thought of something else," I said.

"What?"

"I don't know if you've been up there, but there's a huge unfinished attic running the length of the house. It would make one heck of a play area for little boys."

"I like that even better. It sounds like there would be room for a train table and all kinds of things."

"That's what we'll do, then. Of course, we'll have to widen the stairs to the attic, as they're kind of narrow."

"Why?"

"So we can install one of those chair lifts for Gran. You know how much she enjoys the kids. It wouldn't be right to effectively deny her access to them."

"Works for me," Philip said.

Steve called to say that he'd gotten home safely, and eventually, the Sky Club attendant told us it was time to go to the gate for boarding.

We arrived in Boston without delay and were settled in our hotel room with just enough time to grab a light snack before our massage appointment.

Rudy, the therapist, was both good-looking and well built. I undressed and climbed on the table while Philip retired to the living room of our suite to read the local papers. An hour later, he looked into the bedroom as I was heading to the shower.

Rudy motioned Philip to the table and said, "Next."

Later, we were both totally relaxed and in a slight state of euphoria—Rudy had amazing hands. After we'd consumed our room service dinner and the better part of a bottle of Bordeaux, we were naked in the middle of the huge bed. We were so comfortable and relaxed we skipped the sex, said, "I love you" to each other, and drifted off to sleep.

The next morning we were at the clinic just before nine, waiting to see Dr. Blinn, and we were ushered into his office promptly. He greeted us and immediately launched into a lengthy explanation of what he felt had gone wrong with the pregnancy, but the bottom line was that I had a healthy but underweight son and a stillborn one.

"How long will he have to stay in the incubator?" I said.

"A week or ten days, I should think. He can be released as soon as he gains some weight."

"May we see him?"

"Of course," Dr. Blinn said. "Follow me." He led us down the hallway to a room that held a variety of medical equipment, including two incubators.

We stood in front of the machine, looking at the incredibly small body inside it, which prompted me to say, "My God, he's so tiny."

"A little over half the weight of a full-term baby," Dr. Blinn said.

"And everything else is okay?"

"Yes, it is just the weight that's a problem. We've thoroughly tested him over the last twenty-four hours, and there are no other identifiable problems."

"You're sure?"

"Yes, I am. Premature twins are regularly born in this weight range with no problems. Once they attain normal birth weight, they progress like any other infant and catch up very quickly."

"There's no possibility of holding and/or interacting with this baby as we did the other two, is there?" I said.

"Not until he's out of the incubator, and by then he'll be ready to go home."

"Would there be any possibility of transferring him to Atlanta by air so we can be close by?" I said.

"It's unusual but neither impossible nor, for that matter, contraindicated. As long as he stays in an incubator, even on the plane, I don't see a problem."

"We'll have a plane, complete with the necessary equipment and a qualified pediatric nurse, here in Boston by tomorrow morning," I said.

We returned to the office and completed the paperwork, and I wrote a check. When we were back in the hotel, I opened my cell phone and began to make calls.

When I'd completed my calls to Atlanta, I called Dr. Blinn and told him that a private jet, complete with portable incubator and qualified medical personnel, would be arriving in the morning. *Thank God for friends and extremely grateful clients*, I thought.

Then I made a call to the local mortuary people to arrange for the body of the other twin to be transported to the airport as well. After all of the necessary arrangements had been made, I called Gran and brought her up to date. Then Philip and I took a nap, followed by an intense session of lovemaking. Earlier, we'd called William and Henry and arranged to go to dinner with them that evening.

The Lanes were slightly miffed that we hadn't opted to stay with them. I told them that had our stay extended beyond two nights, we would have called them, and they accepted my apology. We went to Mama Leone's, of course, and had the usual wonderful meal. Mama Leone was ecstatic in her praise of the pictures we showed her of the two boys.

While we consumed several courses of wonderful Italian cuisine, William and Henry brought us up to date on themselves, and we reciprocated. On the way back to the hotel, we promised faithfully to stay with the Lanes on our next visit to Boston.

The next morning we were waiting at the airport when the plane arrived. Dr. Frank Edwards, one of Terry Butcher's young associates, exited the plane, followed by both John and Joe, who were in uniform and carrying a portable incubator between them.

We'd arranged for an ambulance to transport us to the clinic, where Frank examined the medical records, then the baby, and pronounced him fit to travel. John and Joe transferred him to the portable incubator, and the ambulance took us back to the airport.

While we'd been at the clinic, the local mortuary had delivered a tiny box containing the other twin, and it had been carefully stowed away in the cargo area of the plane. The funeral home in Atlanta was to take delivery of the body after we'd deplaned.

All of the necessary arrangements had been made, and when we landed in Marietta, an ambulance was waiting to take the patient to a pediatric hospital. The medical team followed the ambulance. A car from the funeral home was also waiting to take charge of the tiny body in the cargo area.

Steve pulled up as we were stepping out of the plane. Roger had come along, and on the trip to the house, the boys brought us up to date on events in Atlanta. The boys reported that the entire team was still excited about the car wash project. Several of their teammates had brothers who felt they were missing all the fun and wanted to participate. The committee had agreed, but had limited the extended participation to boys aged fourteen and older. They'd set a goal of six hundred cars for the coming weekend and were adding a wax and polish service to the list of services offered.

The boys were also excited about their business. They were working from dawn to dusk every day and earning very good money for their efforts. They were also becoming deeply tanned in the process. We had a quick lunch at the house; then I headed downtown to the office.

That evening we had the gang over to dinner so we could bring everyone up to date. Before we'd finished dinner, Richard asked the question that we'd been waiting for someone to ask. "What are you going to name this one?" he said.

"This one will be christened Richard Bruce," I said, "and Philip's new heir, when he arrives, will be John Joseph. To avoid confusion, we'll probably call them R. B. and J. J."

The guys were all genuinely touched and said so.

"What's the latest word from the hospital?" Bruce said.

"Everything is fine," I said. "Your namesake can come home just as soon as he gains a little weight. I stopped by the hospital on the way home from work, and things are well in hand."

"I just remembered something," Philip said.

"What?"

"We need to buy new furniture for Mark and Steven so their furniture can stay in the nursery. We also need to set up monitors in their new bedroom."

"Handle it, babe," I said.

Charles

THURSDAY evening, Roger and his dad came over because the boys had requested a meeting with us. We went upstairs to the study and got comfortable, and I said, "Okay, guys, what's on your mind?"

"As you know," Roger said, "business is going great. We have so many referrals from satisfied customers that we're going to have to hire some help."

"But?" Mason said.

"We need to buy some equipment," Steve said. "We have the mowers that you and Uncle Philip let us have, but it's just not enough. Also, it takes too long to get them from one customer to the next pulling the mowers behind bicycles. A lot of our customers don't have any equipment of their own, so we have to provide everything."

Roger said, "We want to purchase a used pickup truck, a trailer, and a couple of used riding mowers that have a wider cutting diameter, along with edgers, hedge trimmers, and leaf blowers."

"We have a list of what we need and what it will cost, and we were hoping you guys might consider lending us the money," Steve said.

"You know we'll pay it back as quickly as possible out of our earnings," Roger said.

We studied the paperwork the boys had given us, and Mason said, "You've certainly been thorough. You've even figured in the cost of insurance for the truck along with everything else."

"Yes, Sir," Steve said. "We tried to think of everything."

"Also, we're thinking about offering actual landscaping services to plant flowers and shrubs for our customers, as needed," Roger said.

"Right," Steve said. "The last time I borrowed Uncle Philip's car, Roger and I located a small mom-and-pop nursery out in the country that will sell plants to us wholesale."

"I see that you have income projections based upon your current contracts," Philip said.

"Steve, why don't you take Roger downstairs and check out the supply of ice cream in the freezer while we talk about this," I said.

When the boys had gone downstairs, I said, "What do you guys think about this?"

"I think the two of them are very serious," Mason said. "Serious enough to put together a thorough presentation."

"They're both hard workers," Philip said. "However, I have one thought about their list."

"What?" I said.

"I think it would be better if they were to buy new equipment rather than used," he said. "New equipment will last longer and require less maintenance than used."

"Even the truck?" I said.

"Not new, but perhaps a year-old model with low mileage—one that would still be under warranty," he said.

Mason said, "I like it, and that won't increase the capital outlay by too much."

"We need to make it clear that the truck might have to replace their urge to purchase used cars," I said. "At least this year."

"Why do they need two vehicles anyway?" Philip said. "They're virtually inseparable. As far as I know, it's been weeks since either of them went anywhere without the other."

"Not to mention they don't have much free time anyhow," Mason said.

"If they hire help, we need to help them get some kind of workmen's compensation insurance," I said.

"Just for doing lawns?" Philip said.

"This is your attorney talking," I said. "Think about it—two boys hiring other boys to operate equipment that can, if carelessly used, cause injury. Even if they're careful, accidents happen. As their guardian and parent, respectively, you and Mason would be held liable for any accident that happened."

"Since you put it that way," Mason said, "I concur."

Philip and Mason agreed to split the investment, each providing half, and we outlined an interest-free repayment schedule that was well within the boys' budget.

I went to the intercom and called the kitchen. When Steve answered, I told him that we were ready to talk about the proposal. "Bring three dishes of ice cream with you," I said.

"What flavor?"

"One each of three different flavors," I said. "We'll figure out who gets what when you get here."

The boys came back upstairs, one of them carrying a tray containing dishes of ice cream. When they were settled on a sofa, we laid it out for them. They were a little overwhelmed at what we proposed and didn't understand the need for insurance at all.

"Guys," I said, "you're under eighteen. That makes your parents or guardians responsible for anything you do. If you hire someone to work for you and he gets hurt, Mason and Philip will be held responsible. Trust me on this. I sue and defend people every day. The fact that both families are well-to-do makes them that much more vulnerable."

"As for buying new instead of used equipment," Mason said, "you won't have so much downtime with repairs. You'll still have everything but the truck paid for by the end of summer."

The boys agreed to our terms, and I went to the computer and quickly drafted a contract, which everyone signed. R and S Landscaping and Lawn Maintenance became a reality, at least on paper.

We returned to our normal schedule. I stopped by the hospital on the way to and from work every day, and Philip handled the task of getting the nursery and new bedroom ready. He also took the boys shopping and helped them locate a low-mileage Ranger pickup that was a little more than a year old. It came with an extended cab and an extended warranty. I'd insisted that the boys either fulfill the legal requirements to obtain a fictitious name or form a corporation, and Philip helped them open a checking account in the name of the business. He also saw to it that they obtained the necessary city and county occupational licenses.

Philip also purchased another copy of the accounting software that he used to track his projects and our finances and installed it on Steve's computer. Then he set up a set of books for the boys' business and showed them how to record their income and expenses.

Once they had a small trailer with a ramp at the rear, they were able to quickly load and haul their gear anywhere as needed. The two of them began working like Trojans, and they acquired first two helpers, and later, two more, so that they could accommodate all their existing customers as well as additional clients. The little truck was washed, waxed, and maintained rigorously.

Steve and Roger arranged for their helpers to do the lawn maintenance on the weekends so they could continue to participate in the car wash project. As good managers, they always checked behind their helpers to ensure that all jobs were up to their standards.

The car wash resumed Friday morning with the twelve team members and eight of their siblings hard at work washing cars. By the time the mall closed Sunday evening, they'd surpassed their goal of washing six hundred cars. In addition, they'd polished over fifty vehicles. There had also been incidents when one woman and two men had wanted to tuck tips inside one of the boys' Speedos. The boys handled themselves well in each instance, and the parents on duty stepped in and quietly steered the customers away to defuse the situation. The committee decided that in the future, the actual washing and waxing of the cars would take place in a roped-off area to minimize unnecessary contact.

That Sunday afternoon, we had a very private graveside service, and little Robert was interred in the Barnett plot at Westview Cemetery, next to big Robert.

On Tuesday, we learned that a high school swim team in one of the outlying counties had run its own Speedos Car Wash over the weekend, and the committee held an emergency meeting to discuss their options.

"When you succeed at something," I said, "you've got to expect to be copied."

The boys decided to make a new banner, which proclaimed that they were the Original Speedos Car Wash.

Wednesday afternoon, Philip and I went to the pediatric hospital and brought Richard Bruce Barnett home. We'd increased Grace's salary to compensate for her additional duties and responsibilities. In addition, we'd engaged a young woman to help her on a part-time basis.

R. B., as we were calling him, was still a couple of pounds shy of what would be considered normal birth weight, but he was otherwise healthy and normal in every respect.

Philip and I had yet to visit either the beach house or the Keep that summer, with all that was going on in our lives. We decided to postpone both and take a week or ten days off in early September after school was back in session. We did, however, arrange for the gang to use the beach house a couple of times.

The team had extended the car wash to a four-day event for the Fourth of July weekend. As that weekend coincided with the Peachtree Road Race, which began at Lenox Square, thousands of people were in the area, and business was better than ever.

The four-day weekend was so successful that the committee decided to extend the car wash hours to Thursday, Friday, Saturday, and Sunday for the rest of the summer.

Several of the team members' families had planned to take their sons on vacation over the summer, so the committee worked out a schedule that would permit two boys to take off each weekend. A few of the boys took advantage of that, but most of them were having so much fun with the car wash that they persuaded their parents to leave them behind with friends or relatives while the rest of their family was away.

On the Tuesday after the Fourth of July weekend, Philip and I were in the study catching up on our respective days when he said, "Guess who I got a call from today."

"I give up."

"My brother Julien called to tell me that he'll be in Atlanta on business tomorrow and Thursday and would like to come see us."

"He's your oldest sibling, isn't he?"

"Yes, he is. Julien is fifteen years older than me."

"Has he visited you before?" I said.

"This is a first. I suspect he's checking up on the situation with Steve."

"So what did you do?"

"I invited him to spend the weekend, of course."

"Good for you," I said.

Julien d'Autremont arrived at the house about two minutes after I got home on Wednesday. In fact, I'd just gotten out of my car when I spotted a strange car coming up the driveway. It pulled up beside mine, and when the driver got out, I saw the family resemblance immediately because Julien was an older, slightly heavier version of Philip. I introduced myself, and he followed me into the house and upstairs to the study.

Philip got up from his chair when he saw us, and I said, "Guess who I found loitering around the driveway."

"He's certainly more welcome than our last loiterer," Philip said.

"As you may have heard, our security people caught Steve's father prowling around the fence some time back," I explained to Julien.

"Marie told me about that," Julien said.

Philip and Julien greeted each other warmly enough, but I sensed that there was a bit of distance between them, so I said, "If you guys will excuse me, I need to go shower and change."

I took a long and refreshing shower. When I emerged from the bedroom, Philip was back in the study, so I said, "Where's Julien?"

"Showering and changing," he said.

Julien was walking back down the hallway when Steve bounded up the stairs and said, "Do we have company? There's a strange car in the driveway."

Philip pointed, and Steve looked to his right and saw our visitor. "Uncle Julien," he said, and he gave his uncle a hug.

Steve was dirty and sweaty and said, "Excuse me, but Roger and I have been doing lawns all day, and I need a shower." He scooted down the hall to his room without waiting for permission.

I laughed and said, "He's been working hard all day and still has energy."

"He and his friend Roger have just about cornered the market on lawn and grounds maintenance in the area," Philip said.

"The two of them are turning into little businessmen," I said. "They've already had to hire employees to help them."

"Good for them," Julien said.

We gave Julien the fifty-cent tour of the house, winding up at the pool. Steve caught up with us as we were leaving the pool house. Lance, as usual, was following Steve.

"Do I have time to use the pool a while before dinner?" Steve said. "The shower wasn't cold enough."

"Knock yourself out," Philip said. "If Lancelot jumps in the pool with you, you know the drill."

"Lots of soap and water to get the chlorine out of his fur, followed by a rubdown with plenty of towels," he said.

"That's the one," I said.

Because we had company, dinner was served in the dining room. Earlier small talk had revealed that Julien was fond of good wine, so I'd selected something special to serve with dinner. We had a very pleasant evening. Julien had told us that he would be finished with his appointments by midafternoon on Thursday, so I came home from the office a few hours early myself. When Julien returned from downtown,

Philip and I took him over to Lenox to see the car wash in progress.

Steve spotted us as we drove up, and hurried over to the car. "Are you guys here for a wash?" he said.

"Why should we pay you to do it here when you do it for free at home?" Philip said.

"Go ahead, Steve," I said, handing him the keys. "Run it through the process. It's for a good cause."

Steve retrieved a sheet of clear plastic and placed it carefully on the driver's seat. The boys had learned on the first weekend that they got a bit too wet to move the cars around without protecting the seats. The usual practice was to let the customer pull the car into position and drive it away, but those customers who merely dropped cars off while shopping required a different procedure. He drove the car over to the tent, and it was quickly covered in soap.

"They are really having fun with this, aren't they?" Julien said.

"True," Philip said, "and you wouldn't believe how much money they've already raised."

"It's refreshing to see kids working for something worthwhile," Julien said.

Philip introduced Julien to the parents who were on duty, and we stood watching the activity for a while. Finally, Steve announced that the car was ready, and as I paid the fee, I said, "The gang is coming over tonight with pizza, so get home as early as you can."

"I will," he said.

"Is Roger coming?" Philip said.

"No, Sir. His paternal grandparents are in town, and he has to go out to dinner with his family."

When we were back in the car and on our way, Julien said, "The gang?"

"Four friends of ours," Philip said. "Actually two couples. Richard, who has been Charles's best friend since junior high school, owns and runs one of the largest detective agencies in the area. His partner, Bruce, is in charge of the computer networks for the local district attorney's office, and John and Joe are both registered nurses."

"They come over almost every Thursday, Friday, or Saturday, depending on their schedules. They usually bring pizza, and we all use the pool and Jacuzzi," I said.

"I don't have a suit," Julien said.

"No problem," I said. "We don't use them."

"So, brother," Philip said, "are you man enough to get naked with six gay men and a gay teenager?"

"How could I resist a challenge like that?" Julien said, smiling.

We went to the pool enclosure just before seven and encountered the gang as they were arriving. Introductions were made, and we were all in the pool in short order. Steve showed up a few minutes later and did a running cannonball into the water.

Instead of their usual free-form water sports, the guys actually swam laps this time. When we were all in the Jacuzzi with pizza and cold drinks, I commented on this, and Bruce said, "You guys set a good example. Besides, our medical team"—he indicated John and Joe—"has assured us that swimming is the best aerobic exercise, second only to rowing."

I sensed that Julien was dying to ask the usual question, so I told him about the pubic hair defense and all that had followed. John said, "I took care of Charles in the hospital while his leg was in a cast. I was just an orderly then and had to give him a sponge bath."

"John came home and told me about the shaving thing, and we tried it," Joe said.

"You have no idea how good it was," John said.

"Sex is intimate," Joe said, "but shaving someone's balls is really intimate."

"Not to mention the fact that you have to really trust someone to let them that close to the family jewels with a razor," John said.

The gang left after the pizza was exhausted, and we went up to the study. I poured glasses of wine for Philip, Julien, and myself, and handed Steve a Coke. We sat for a while talking about nothing in particular until Philip said, "Okay, Julien, have you seen what you came to see?"

"What do you mean?"

"How many times a year does your law practice bring you to Atlanta?" Philip said.

"Two, sometimes three."

"I've lived in Atlanta for a dozen years. That means you've missed somewhere between twenty and thirty opportunities to drop by, so, I asked myself, why now?"

"Okay," Julien said. "You're right. I wanted to assess the situation with Steve for myself."

"Did you think that Charles and I had turned Steve into some sort of sex slave?" Philip said.

"That sounds like fun," Steve said, grinning.

"Steven Randall Cox." The words spat out of Philip's mouth. "That isn't even remotely amusing."

"What did I say?" Steve said.

"Just sit there quietly and think about it while the adults talk," Philip said. "So, Julien, am I on target?"

"I'll have to admit," Julien said, "that I've always had a lot of preconceived notions about gay men, and I wanted to see for myself how things were."

"And how were they?" Philip said.

"Exactly as Marie described them to me," Julien said.

"And how was that?" Philip said.

"I see a teenager who is happier and more at ease than I've ever known him to be," Julien said, "and two men who look at each other in a way that would put most married couples to shame. I saw the same thing in your friends earlier this evening."

Philip turned to his nephew and said, "Steve, do you have any idea how serious what you said could have been if you said it in front of the wrong people?"

"No, Sir," Steve said.

"Let me do this," Julien said. Then he continued, "Steve, right here in Atlanta, there are thousands of people who, if they'd heard you say that, would *not* have taken it as a joke. Most likely, the authorities would have been called to investigate, and you would have been removed from this house by force within a day or so and turned over to the juvenile authorities."

"You're kidding!" Steve said.

"No, I'm not," Julien said. "And it wouldn't stop with you. The three babies in this house would very likely have been taken away as well. Charles and Philip would surely have gotten them and you back, but it would have been one hell of a mess."

"I'm sorry," Steve said.

"Learn from it," Philip said. "There are some things that you simply cannot joke about, at least when you don't know who might be listening."

"Steve," I said, "all the fundamentalist preachers in town believe gay men are sexual predators, as do most of their congregations. They would automatically assume that what you joked about was actually happening. You have no idea how deeply the hatred runs."

The point having been made, I decided to change the subject and said, "Julien, can you bring us up to date on your brother-in-law's trial?"

"There's not a lot to tell at this point. The trial is set for early October."

"The local assistant prosecutor told me that the judge is strictly no-nonsense," I said.

"We know all about Hanging Hannah, even down in Alexandria," Julien said. "There's no way Frank will get out of this, especially if Steve is able to testify."

"Are you ready for that, Steve?" I said.

"Yes, Sir, I am. Anything to keep the bastard behind bars."

"Good for you," Philip said.

Roger spent Friday and Saturday nights with us, and after dinner on Friday, the two boys drove Julien out to see the school campus. Before he left for the airport Sunday morning, Julien told Philip and me privately that after having observed the two boys together, he thought they were good for each other.

In mid-July, we got the expected call from Boston, and Philip and I flew up the next day. We stayed with William and Henry and carried John Joseph home with us two days later. A week or so after that, we were sitting in the upstairs study listening to music and generally relaxing when Steve and Roger came into the room.

Steve said, "I've never heard you guys listening to modern music before."

"It's not modern, kiddo," I said. "Not even close."

"It sure sounds modern, almost like jazz," Roger said.

"Want to bet?" I said.

"Oh no," Steve said. "We know better than to bet with you guys."

"Go over to the sound system controls," I said. "The current album's jewel case is on top of the CD changer."

Steve did as instructed and inspected the label on the album. "Glenn Gould playing Bach Partitas," he read out loud.

"Right you are," I said. "That music was written over three hundred years ago."

"But it's so modern sounding," Roger said.

"The man was a genius and way ahead of his time. What can I say?" I said.

The boys sat down on a sofa next to us, and I used the remote to turn the volume down a bit.

"Guys," Philip said, "there's a whole world out there of really satisfying and exciting music. Music to which you haven't even begun to be exposed."

"That's true," I added. "I guess we need to expand your horizons a bit."

"We'll have to take them to the symphony with us a few times this season," Philip said.

I decided that the time was ripe for a serious discussion of another matter, so I said, "Steve, I need to ask you and Roger something."

"What?"

"Are the two of you actually boyfriends or just fooling around?"

There was a long moment or three of silence before Roger said, "Yes to the last thing. We're not sure about the first part."

Steve nodded in agreement. "Why do you ask?" Steve said.

"We've been wondering, and for that matter, so has Mason," I said.

"My dad has been wondering about Steve and me?" Roger said.

"He asked us some time back if we thought that the two of you were fooling around," I said.

"We told him we didn't know but wouldn't be surprised," Philip said.

"Roger," I said, "your folks have already pretty much figured you out, and while they don't think it's the most wonderful thing in the world, they're dealing with it and they aren't going to give you any grief."

"Wow," Roger said. "This is too much. I'd been worried sick that they'd find out, and you're telling me that they know."

"That's about the size of it," I said. "All they lack is confirmation."

"The bottom line here," Philip said, "is that you can talk to them if and when you want to."

"Steve," I said, "you do realize that at least half of your teammates are gay."

"We suspected that," Steve said, "but nobody talks about it."

"There's no need to go around blabbing about private things," Philip said. "The point of it is the two of you are not alone, and there are people to whom you can turn should the need arise."

"The two of us, for example," I said, "and Roger's parents, as well."

"On the other hand," Philip said, "I wouldn't exactly recommend going to any of your friends and making any announcements unless you're very sure how that announcement will be received. What you do behind closed doors is nobody's business."

"Anyhow," Philip said, "Charles and I will tell both of you the same thing we told Steve early on. Don't ever let anyone talk you into doing anything that makes you uncomfortable, and don't ever practice unsafe sex."

"Do you guys practice unsafe sex?" Roger said. "I can't believe I said that," he quickly added.

"Yes, we do," I said, "but we didn't do so until we knew for certain that we were in a committed, monogamous, and long-term relationship, and even then not until we'd been tested for HIV."

"In point of fact," Philip said, "there's really no such thing as safe sex. Some activity, however, is significantly safer than others. Oral sex, for example, is generally believed to be fairly but not 100 percent safe. Anal sex, on the other hand, is definitely not safe."

"The awful reality today is when you have sex with someone, you're not only having sex with them but with everyone with whom they might have had sex for the past ten years," I said. "That's how long the HIV virus can lurk in the human body without manifesting itself."

"That's scary," Steve said.

"Indeed it is," I said. "You won't believe how many fools there are, straight and gay, who truly believe that it can't happen to them or that doing it once won't matter."

"I can't believe we're having this conversation," Roger said.

"I told you we could talk to them about anything," Steve said.

"I know, but I guess I didn't really believe it."

"Believe it," Philip said.

Somehow the subject got changed, and the boys said goodnight and retired to Steve's room. We turned off the music and went first to Steven and Mark's room, then to the nursery. "It's hard to believe," Philip said, looking at the two newest arrivals, "that we have four children."

"That was the plan."

"I know, but the reality is so much more real than the plan."

We went to our bedroom, and after we were in bed, I said, "You know, babe, the clinic has enough semen left from each of us to produce at least one more baby."

"I think we need to give that some thought," he said, "but not right now."

"Works for me," I said as I snuggled up against him.

The two new arrivals were christened in late July, followed by a gathering at the house for family and friends. The gang had, of course, once again been named as godparents. Andrew and Emily were in town on this occasion, and we spent some time catching up. Although he and I had managed to have occasional telephone conversations, they'd been few and far between—such was their travel schedule. Emily was still somewhat wound up over the traveling she still wanted to do, but I got the impression that Andrew was ready to stay home for a while.

July and August passed, and the team had their final car wash over the Labor Day weekend. They shut things down around six o'clock Monday, and we hosted a final party for the project the following Saturday afternoon. The group's treasurer read the final report, which revealed that the team had averaged almost a thousand cars each weekend for thirteen weeks. Along with the wax and polish services, they'd raised well over $100,000.

The weather had played a large part in their success, as it had only rained on two or three of their car wash days. Each time, the rainfall was brief enough that it didn't force them to shut down. The group voted to donate $50,000 to the children's cancer center, and after the new steam room was completed, any remaining funds were to be used to fund as many scholarships for promising swimmers as possible. We held a highly public ceremony at the school, where the entire swim team and their siblings, all proudly wearing their Speedos, complete with caps and goggles, presented one of those huge blown-up checks to the chairman of the hospital board.

The media loved it and ran with it. Fortunately, there were no national or international incidents that weekend, and the team and, for that matter, the school were all over the news. Mason reported that the mall officials had been doing some random surveying of people visiting the mall during the weekends of the car wash, and had noted a significant number of shoppers who made it clear that they were only there because of the car wash. Participation by the mall next summer was thus assured.

Steve and Roger began their junior year at Exeter, and I attended my first board meeting right before Philip and I went on vacation. Enrollment was up by 10 percent, and the headmaster was effusive in his appreciation of the team's efforts.

Philip and I spent a few days at the beach house, followed by a few more days at the Keep, and we returned to Atlanta well rested and up to any challenge.

The next big challenge, of course, was to be Steve's testimony at his father's trial. It was set for the first Monday in October, and both Philip and I were planning to be at Steve's side to lend him support.

9

Philip

AS THE first Monday in October drew closer, Steve began to show a few signs of nervousness, but he seemed to be handling it well. Charles was all set to fly the three of us down to Louisiana for the trial, and we planned to arrive just in time for Steve to testify, and then fly out again that same day. None of us, least of all Steve, had any particular desire to linger in Monroe.

Dr. Butcher had been deposed on videotape concerning Steve's physical condition on the morning after the beating. Because of the distance involved, the deposition was handled through the technology of a teleconference, which gave the prosecutor in Louisiana ample opportunity to ask questions.

Marie was waiting for us at the airport when we landed. She greeted Steve with a hug, gave him a worried look, and said, "Are you all right?"

"To tell the truth, Mom, I'd rather not be here, but I've gotta do this."

We arrived at the courthouse around nine and were seated in the rear of the courtroom just before the proceedings began. Jury selection was finished, and after a few preliminaries, during which Simon laid out the details of the crime, he called Detective Robichaux, who testified that he'd taken the call from Atlanta and about his search of Steve's room. That led to the playing of Dr. Butcher's recorded deposition. After the video had finished, Simon entered pictures of

Steve's injuries into evidence and passed copies to the jurors.

I was then called to the stand, and Simon led me through the preliminaries. Then he asked me about Steve. "Have you had a lot of contact with your nephew over the years?"

"I'm closer to my sister than my other siblings, so I saw her family regularly until I moved to Atlanta, but less frequently after that. Steve was, in fact, named after me, and Marie and I have always kept in close touch by telephone and e-mail. She brought Steve with her to Atlanta last year when my son was christened, and they spent the weekend with us."

"Us?"

"I live with my partner. Our household also consists of his grandmother, our children, a married couple who serve as cook and handyman, and a resident nanny. During the course of the weekend, Steve confided in me that he was gay and terrified that his father would find out."

"What else did he say to you that weekend?"

"That his father had made it clear to him that there would be no money made available for college when the time came. I told him that when he turned eighteen, he should come to Atlanta and I would see to his education."

"What happened on the day in question?"

"My cell phone rang around six that morning. The caller was Steve's friend Jeff. He was calling to let me know that Steve had been badly beaten, that he and his brother were less than thirty minutes away, and they had Steve with them. When the boys arrived, we carried Steve to one of the guest bedrooms and called our pediatrician to come and examine him."

"Why did you call a pediatrician for a teenager?"

"Because we knew him and we knew that he made house calls. Besides, it isn't unusual for children to see pediatricians all the way through their teens."

"What else can you tell the court about that morning?"

"Steve was unconscious when he arrived. Later, when he woke up, I told him that his mother was flying in to see him. He assumed she was coming to take him home, and became hysterical at the prospect."

"What did you say to him about that?"

"That he could stay with us as long as he wished, provided his mother agreed, which is what ultimately happened."

During cross-examination, the defense attorney honed in on the gay thing, but Simon managed to deflect all of the attacks as irrelevant.

Finally, Steve was called to the stand. He stated his name and age and took the oath. Simon led him gently through the examination with a few general questions about himself. He asked about Steve's life, school, and other things—questions which were designed to place Steve at ease, if such a thing were possible under the circumstances.

Finally, Simon said, "Tell the court what happened on the night in question."

"My folks had gone down to Alexandria to visit my aunt and uncle. My sisters went with them, but I didn't really feel like going, so I stayed home. My best friend Jeff came over to spend the weekend with me."

"Tell us about Friday evening?" Simon said.

"We ordered pizza and spent the evening watching a couple of movies. After the movies were over, we went to my room and were fooling around when my father came home unexpectedly."

"Fooling around?" Simon said.

"We were on my bed fooling around," Steve said.

"You mean you were engaging in mutual masturbation, an activity in which many teenage boys engage at one time or another."

"Yes, Sir."

"What happened next?"

"My father came into the room and shouted and screamed ugly things, and started hitting me."

"And then what happened?"

"I really don't remember much else until I woke up at Uncle Philip's house in Atlanta the next day."

"Why Atlanta?"

"Like I said, I don't really remember. Jeff told me that I refused to let him take me to a local hospital and kept insisting that he take me to Atlanta."

"Looking back, Steve, why do you think you begged to be taken to Atlanta?" Simon said.

"I guess because I knew that Uncle Philip was gay and he wouldn't let anybody else hurt me just because I'm gay."

"You've been in Atlanta ever since, haven't you?"

"Yes, Sir. As part of my mom's divorce, Uncle Philip was made my guardian."

"Why?"

"Because I was scared to come back home, even with my father in jail."

"Scared?"

"I don't want to be anywhere near him. He tried to get to me in Atlanta while he was out on bail, but the security people caught him."

"Why do you think he did that?"

"He told the security people who caught him that he wanted to see me," Steve said, "but I think maybe he wanted to finish the job. Otherwise he wouldn't have been sneaking around in the middle of the night."

The defense attorney objected to this answer, and the jury was told to disregard it.

"But you're here today," Simon said.

"Yes, Sir. I was too scared to come back here a few months ago, but I've been seeing a psychologist, and she's helped me learn to deal with all of this."

"And how do you feel about your father today?" Simon asked.

"I came here today," Steve said, staring at his father, "so that I could look him in the eye and tell him that I hope they keep him in jail forever and throw away the keys."

The defense attorney ran Steve through the story again and tried to shake him up. Steve, however, was resolute. The attorney also attempted to bring up gay issues, but every time he did so, Simon objected that they were not relevant, and the objections were all sustained.

The defense attorney also made a serious mistake. After his last exchange with Steve, he said, "Steve, aren't you being a little hard on your father?"

Steve sat up straight, once again looked straight at the table where Frank was sitting, and said, "He's not a father, he's just a sperm donor."

At that point, the defense attorney gave up.

Jeff was then called to the stand, and after being sworn in, he confirmed Steve's story and walked the court through the events of that evening of which Steve had no memory.

Simon asked him why he didn't call 911 or simply take Steve to a local emergency room.

Jeff said, "I wanted to, but Steve got hysterical when I mentioned it. He kept saying, over and over, 'Take me to Uncle Philip's in Atlanta, I'll be safe there.' Besides, I knew that Mr. Cox would wake up sooner or later, and I didn't think it was a good idea to be anywhere nearby."

"So driving to Atlanta sounded like the best course of action?"

"Yes, Sir," Jeff said. "I called my older brother, drove over to our house, then he and I took Steve to Atlanta."

Once again, the attorney for the defense tried to shake and/or undermine the witness's story, but Jeff was just as resolute as Steve had been.

Simon also called Rob to the stand to confirm Jeff's story about the trip to Atlanta. After that, there wasn't a whole lot left to talk about, and the defense had no witnesses to call. Both sides had made their closing arguments before the one o'clock recess. Judge McDaniel, in her instructions to the jury, managed to make it clear that she expected to hear a guilty verdict without actually directing the verdict. The jury was sent out to have lunch and begin deliberations, and Marie drove us to a local restaurant.

Jeff, Rob, and their parents joined us at lunch, and we lingered for a couple of hours, allowing the boys to catch up with each other's lives.

They had, of course, been in regular contact by cell phone and e-mail, but this was the first time they'd been in the same place since Jeff and his brother had returned to Louisiana.

Over lunch, I asked Charles if this sort of case was always so brief, and he said, "Not always. However, in this instance, there are no points of contention. That is, there's no disagreement as to what happened. Basically, all that was done this morning was to establish an official record of what happened. The defense attorney was doing little more than going through the motions. He knew he had a losing case, and I don't think his heart was really in it."

"It sort of makes you wonder why Frank didn't plead guilty," Jeff's father said.

"That's true," I said, "but I'm glad he didn't. I think it was important for Steve to face his father in court today and tell his story."

"In any case," Charles said, "Jeff is the hero of the hour. He probably saved Steve's life that night, and he was certainly instrumental in nailing Frank today."

We were interrupted by Charles's cell phone ringing. He answered, listened for a minute, and then said, "The jury is coming back."

We hurried back to the courthouse and were seated in the back row when the jury returned. The judge asked them if they had a verdict, and the foreman said yes. He then read the verdict. Frank was found guilty of assault and all of the related charges, with sentencing to take place two weeks later.

After court was adjourned, Simon came back to talk to us and said, "I knew this would be a slam dunk, but I didn't expect it to be this quick."

Steve asked the question that was on everyone's mind. "What sentence will my father receive?"

"At least twenty years. This judge doesn't allow crimes like this to go unpunished."

"Good," Steve said.

"Steve, you have to be prepared for one thing," Simon said.

"What's that?"

"Simply this," Simon said. "Men who abuse children frequently don't survive prison. Other inmates find out about it and exact their own punishment."

"You mean he might be killed while in prison," Steve said.

"Yes."

"I don't have a problem with that," Steve said.

"Steve," Jeff's father said, "he's still your father."

"No, he's not," Steve said. "I meant what I said in there. As far as I'm concerned, Uncle Philip and Uncle Charles are the only dads I have."

"These two men have done more parenting in the past six months than Frank ever did in fifteen years," Marie said.

"Good for them," Simon said. "I merely brought the subject up so you would all be made aware of the possibility."

"Actually, I had thought about that," Charles said, "but I wasn't going to say anything about it for a while."

A bailiff came up to us and spoke to Simon for a moment, and he said, "The judge wants to talk to Steve privately."

"Why?" I said.

"It's not unusual, during the presentence investigation, for victims to be questioned. She knows that Steve is headed back home to Atlanta, and doesn't want him to miss any more school because of the trial."

"What do I say to her?" Steve said.

"Just answer her questions fully and truthfully," Charles said. "You'll be fine."

We settled down in the rear of the courtroom to wait. After about ten minutes, the bailiff brought Steve back to us and said that the judge wanted to speak to Marie.

Shortly thereafter, Marie returned and Charles and I were summoned to the judge's chambers.

Judge McDaniel was a large and formidable black woman who appeared to be in her fifties, and she greeted us warmly and asked us to sit down. She wasn't at her desk, and the three of us sat informally in comfortable chairs in one corner of her chambers.

"I wanted to meet the two of you for a number of reasons," she said. "I followed your murder trial two years ago with a great deal of interest, and I must say that you had a brilliant win, counselor."

Charles said, "As I said at the time, Your Honor, that case was won because a great many people spent a great amount of time and an even greater amount of my client's money putting it all together."

"Perhaps, but it takes a good conductor to keep the orchestra members on the same page."

"Thank you, Your Honor, but you didn't call us back here to tell me that I'm a good lawyer."

"No, Sir, I did not. As you know, I've talked to the boy and his mother. Mrs. Cox tells me how much the two of you have done for her son, and the boy clearly thinks that both of you walk on water."

"Your Honor," I said, "my sister and her son are the only two members of my family that I really cared for at the time Steve came to us, although others have become closer since then. In any case, I simply did what had to be done. As Steve began to recover from his injuries, we suggested that he might want to come back home to be with his mother, and he invariably became hysterical to the point of tears at the prospect."

"A very good friend of mine just happens to be a clinical psychologist who specializes in abused children," Charles said. "We had her talking to Steve before he was fully recovered. Were it not for her, it would have required sedation to get him into the same room as his father."

"I know," she said. "I've read her report."

"We don't think we've done anything special," I said. "Taking care of your family is what you are supposed to do, isn't it?"

"Between us, Philip and I have four sons of our own, all less than a year old," Charles said. "Parenting Steve is giving us practice for the four of them."

"Four boys, all under a year?" she said.

"It was arranged through a clinic in Boston with surrogate mothers," Charles said.

"The two of you must have wanted children very badly. I have a pretty good idea how much that must have cost, not to mention what an impact four small children will have on your lives."

"As you may recall from my trial, I lost an unborn child when my wife was murdered. When Charles and I were shot last year, we gave a lot of thought to the future and our desire for posterity. In the end, we decided that we needed to have a family of our own."

"We could both have been killed, and that gave us a sense of urgency, so we sort of speeded up the process," Charles said. "Besides, having decided to have children, we decided that we wanted to see them grown and out of college before we retired."

"How do you folks feel about the chance that the defendant might get out of prison early?" she said.

"I don't want my nephew to spend the rest of his life looking over his shoulder," I said. "As you know, we've already had one incident."

"I should think not, but I wanted to ask for the record."

We talked about Steve and his schooling at some length, including the Speedos Car Wash of the summer just past.

"I saw something about that in the news," she said. "Those boys gave a huge amount to the children's cancer hospital."

"They raised well over $100,000, all on their own initiative," I said. "They gave $50,000 to the hospital, paid for the steam room at their school, and designated the remaining funds for scholarships."

"They're already planning to raise even more money next summer," Charles said.

"Your Honor," I said, "after he came to us, Steve was very fragile for quite a while, but he's begun to blossom and become his own person. He wants to put this sordid business behind him, as do we all."

"I realize that," she said. "I'm not causing you to miss a flight, am I?"

"No, Your Honor," Charles said. "I flew us down here in my plane. We don't have a timetable to worry about, other than the fact that I don't particularly like to fly at night."

"I won't keep you that long," she said with a smile. Then she added, "The boy's mother has had a rough time of it, hasn't she?"

"Your Honor," I said, "when Marie and Steve came to the

Christening of our boys last year, I hadn't seen her in five years or so, although we've kept in regular contact by telephone. In that time, she'd aged at least ten years. She eventually told me that her husband had been serially unfaithful, and more recently she learned that he'd been skimming money from their business to fund his affairs."

"She's getting her life back together," Charles said. "Leaving Steve with us where he feels both safe and comfortable has made her life easier, despite the pain of being separated from her only son."

We talked for a bit more with the judge, and a few minutes later we were back in the rear of the courtroom with Steve and Marie. Charles said, "I think we're ready for a ride to the airport."

We thanked Simon for all of his help, and he promised to keep us posted. Steve and Jeff said good-bye and hugged each other, and we were off. On the way to the airport, the four of us compared notes on our various conferences with Judge McDaniel.

"I thought she was nice, but I sure wouldn't want her to be mad at me, because she is one tough lady," Steve said.

"Did you invite Jeff to come visit you in Atlanta?" I said.

"Yes, Sir, but I doubt that he will."

"Why not?" Marie said.

"Because he has a boyfriend now, and I have Roger," Steve said. "Jeff and I will always be friends, but that's all."

"So," Marie said, seizing the opening, "does that mean that Roger is your boyfriend?"

"Not officially, but we like each other a lot, and I think he will be pretty soon."

"By the way, Philip," Marie said, "I talked to Julien last night, and at the end of the conversation, he told me to tell you that he'd bought his wife a razor. He said that you and Charles would understand."

Charles and I smiled at that, and Steve tried and failed to suppress a giggle.

Marie said, "What was that all about?"

"Private joke," I said.

"It's a guy thing," Charles said.

Steve giggled again.

"You're not going to tell me, are you?" she said.

"In a word, no."

During the flight back to Atlanta, I sat in the copilot's seat, and Steve dozed in one of the back seats. We got home just in time for dinner, and the three of us made an early night of it.

10

Philip

FRANK was eventually sentenced to twenty years without any chance for parole, with credit for time served. On the last Friday in October, we were relaxing around the pool. Steve and Roger were in the pool with Sammy Mangrum. Mason Cartwright and his wife were there, as were Dean Mangrum and his wife. Gran had even made a rare appearance.

The three boys got out of the water and came over to where we were sitting, and Roger said, "Dad, you know the team went on a field trip to the children's cancer hospital recently."

"Yes, I do," Mason said.

"Some of us would like to go out there and help once in a while," Roger said.

"Help how?" his mother said.

"We were talking to one of the hospital administrators, and she said they were always looking for kids who were willing to read to the patients that were confined to bed. She said that it's good for the patients to interact with kids who aren't sick. Also, they have a pool, and some of the kids are encouraged to use it for physical therapy. We can give them swimming lessons if they don't already know how."

"Anyway," Steve said, "we decided that we want to help."

"So, can we?" Roger said.

"I don't see why not," Mason said. He looked at the dean and me, and we both added our agreement.

Gran said, "I think that's commendable, and I'm proud of all of you."

Mrs. Mangrum expressed a desire to see the babies, and Gran said, "If you don't mind walking an old lady back to the house, I'll take you up to see them."

The ladies left, and a few minutes later, the dean said that he needed to round up his wife so they could leave. He and Sammy left, leaving us alone with Mason, while Roger and Steve returned to the pool to swim laps. They were both facedown in the water, so I wasn't worried about being overheard. I leaned across the table and said, in a soft enough voice that it wouldn't carry around the pool enclosure, "Mason, do you remember the question you asked us a few months ago up in our study?"

"Yes, I do," he said.

"We have the answer. One evening while Charles and I were listening to music, Steve and Roger joined us in the study. During the conversation, Charles asked them point-blank if they were boyfriends or just fooling around."

"What did they say?"

"Roger answered and said yes to the last part, but they weren't sure about the first part," I said.

"Charles and I told him that you and your wife suspected he was gay," Philip said.

"How did he react to that?" Mason said.

"He was relieved. He'd been very worried about your reaction."

"We told him that when he finally decided to talk to you, you wouldn't be judgmental," Charles said.

"We don't know when that will happen, but it will happen," I said.

"I don't know how to thank you," Mason said.

"Don't thank us," I said. "Just go easy on the boy. When he finally decides to come out to you, it will be the most difficult thing he has ever had to do."

"I understand."

Further conversation was precluded when the boys came out of the water and announced that they were going to shower and change.

We already had season tickets for the Atlanta Symphony, and when the new season began, we acquired season tickets for Steve and Roger, and they seemed to enjoy the various events. In November we had a first birthday celebration for Mark and Steven, who were beginning to walk a great deal of the time. We also began serving most of their meals in high chairs at the table with us.

We'd been attending the monthly functions of the Atlanta Wine and Food Society, and the November tasting was from our cellar. It had been decided that the group would sample all of the first growth Bordeaux wines year by year, starting with the earliest year available in the cellar. So many vintages were available in the cellar that the schedule stretched out for quite a while into the future. The wines were wonderful.

We also began the renovation of the attic in November, having decided to wait until the working conditions wouldn't be so hot for the carpenters. When I inspected it for the first time, I was amazed at its size—as Charles had told me, the attic ran the length of the house. The roof was high enough that there was almost ten feet of clearance in the center, tapering down to nothing at the sides. A series of dormers ran along both sides of the attic.

We had walls constructed at a point where the roof was about three feet from floor level, and each dormer wound up with a built-in window seat. Although we'd have preferred hardwood floors, we elected to have heavily padded carpeting installed so that sound penetrating to the floor below would be kept to a minimum. Widening the stairs involved knocking out a wall and making one of the spare bedrooms about three feet narrower than it had been. We also added a couple of security cameras, placed such that we could monitor the kids from the study.

We hosted a party for Charles's office in early December. Steve, Roger, and Sammy had been going to the children's hospital almost every Saturday since they'd asked permission to help, and they appeared to be genuinely touched by the plight of all the kids who were fighting cancer. They were particularly fond of an eleven-year-old named Jimmy, whom they were teaching to swim.

At thirteen months, Mark and Steven were too little to really appreciate Christmas, so we decided to take a Christmas trip, knowing that it would be our last until the boys were old enough to enjoy travel. Charles persuaded Gran to go along by dangling the prospect of a private compartment on the train in lieu of an airplane seat. We booked three bedrooms: one for us, one for Gran, and one for Steve and Roger.

Steve and Roger were beside themselves with excitement on the train. They couldn't get over having a private room with two bunks and a tiny bathroom that included a shower.

We arrived in Penn Station nearly on time, and got Gran settled in our suite at the St. Regis. Then we took the boys sightseeing. They were overwhelmed, especially by the crowds around Rockefeller Center, not to mention the window displays along Fifth Avenue.

By the time Christmas Day arrived, we'd seen two performances at the Metropolitan Opera and one Broadway play. We'd also sampled a number of very nice restaurants and had walked endlessly up and down the streets of Manhattan. We'd also visited the Metropolitan Museum of Art and the Guggenheim Museum of Modern Art, and we had one more surprise in store for the boys.

We arrived at the restaurant we'd selected in plenty of time for our one o'clock Christmas brunch reservation. When we were seated, Steve said, "Why are there three extra places at the table, Uncle Philip?"

"Some friends of ours are joining us," I said.

"Who?"

"Just wait and see."

"No need to wait," Charles said. "Simply turn around and look behind you."

The boys did as instructed and jumped up from their places to greet Mason, Angela, and Marie, who were being escorted to our table. We'd arranged for Marie to fly to Atlanta and then on to New York with the Cartwrights. We lingered over our brunch for a couple of hours, during which time the boys could hardly stop talking as they related their various adventures in New York.

They'd particularly enjoyed *The Marriage of Figaro* and

Madama Butterfly at the Met. They'd also enjoyed a performance of *Arsenic and Old Lace*, which featured two or three actors that the boys recognized from television.

The two of them wound down for a moment; then Steve said, "We went to Midnight Mass last night at Smokey Mary's."

"Smokey Mary's?" Marie said.

"The Episcopal Church of St. Mary the Virgin," I said. "It's on 46th Street, just off Times Square, and is commonly referred to as Smokey Mary's because they use a lot of incense."

"Right," Charles said. "If you Google the term 'Smokey Mary's', you'll get a hit on their website."

"Tomorrow night we were going to see *Miss Saigon*," Roger said, "but now that you guys are here, maybe we ought to cancel."

"We already have tickets for everyone," I said.

"Cool," Roger said.

The next day, Charles and I stayed in the hotel with Gran while the two boys went out and about with their parents. That night, after the performance of *Miss Saigon*, we had dinner at Sardi's, having stopped by the hotel to pick up Gran for the occasion. She'd attended the Met performances with us but had declined the play.

"How did you like the play?" Gran asked the boys.

"It was great," Steve said.

"Right," Roger said. "They even had a helicopter on stage."

"I noticed something else about the play," Steve said.

"What would that be?" Gran said.

"*Miss Saigon* is sort of the same story as *Madama Butterfly*, isn't it?"

"Pretty much," I said.

"What are we doing tomorrow?" Roger said.

"I think you guys might enjoy going out to The Cloisters," Charles said.

"What's that?" Steve said.

"It's a museum of medieval art, and it's at the extreme northern tip of Manhattan Island," Charles said.

"Why don't you make it a guy thing?" Angela said. "We ladies want to check out the post-Christmas sales on Fifth Avenue."

"That's too much walking for this lady," Gran said, "but you young folks go right ahead."

The next morning we took a taxi to The Cloisters. The boys seemed quite taken by the artifacts on display, and we were back at the hotel in time to have a late lunch with Gran in the hotel restaurant.

When we'd finished our lunch, Angela and Marie appeared at our table, and they were both carrying several shopping bags bearing a number of famous logos. That evening we had a wonderful dinner at the Cornelia Street Café in the Village, and the next day we went our separate ways home.

11

Philip

SHORTLY after New Year's, we invited Mason and Angela Cartwright to dinner. Their younger sons were with their grandparents, and Steve and Roger were expected back from their weekly hospital visit just in time for dinner. We sat down to dinner, and the boys appeared a few minutes later. They were both somewhat subdued, and when we suggested that they should sit down at the table with us, they said they weren't hungry.

"Did you pick up something to eat on the way home?" I said.

"No, Sir, we're just not hungry," Steve said.

"Okay, guys," Charles said, "what's the matter?"

"Do you remember us talking about the little kid we were teaching to swim?" Roger said.

"Yes," Mason said. "Isn't his name Jimmy?"

"Yes, Sir," Steve said.

"We were going to give him another swimming lesson this afternoon after we spent some time with the other kids," Roger said, "but...."

Steve finished the sentence. "They told us that he died last night."

It was clear that both boys were on the verge of tears. Angela got up from the table, hugged her son, and said, "I'm sorry, sweetie, but these things do happen."

"But they told us he was getting better," Roger said.

I got up, gave Steve a hug, and said, "Cancer isn't all that predictable."

"But it isn't fair, Uncle Philip," he said. "Jimmy was such a neat little guy, and he was fighting so hard to get better."

"Of course it's not fair," I said. "Life isn't always fair."

At this point, Gran intervened and said, "I think both of you are being very brave, but why don't you go up to Steve's room and have a good cry in private. Get it out of your systems, then come back down to dinner."

"Yes, Ma'am," they chorused, and they left the room.

When they were well out of earshot, Charles said, "I wonder if it was a mistake allowing them to do that hospital work?"

"No," Gran said. "You can't protect children from all of life's realities. It just isn't possible. Besides, both of them have the moral fiber to learn from this tragic experience and be strengthened by it."

"I agree," Mason said.

Angela said, "So do I."

By the time we'd finished our dessert, the boys had come back downstairs and joined us at the table. It was evident that they'd taken Gran's advice, for their eyes were red and puffy. They ate quietly for a while, and finally Mason said, "Do you guys want to talk about what happened?"

"Not now, Dad," Roger said. "Maybe later."

"I know what the two of you ought to do as soon as possible," Gran said.

"What's that?" Steve said.

"I think that you should write a letter to Jimmy's mother and tell her what you thought of Jimmy and how much you enjoyed working with him. It will do you both good to write your feelings down on paper, and I'm sure it will mean a lot to his parents."

"Was Jimmy from Atlanta?" I said, knowing that the patients at the hospital came from all over the country.

"His family has lived here for a couple of years," Steve said, "but they're originally from Valdosta."

"Then I think the two of you need to go to his funeral," I said.

"Will you guys come with us?" Roger said.

"You bet we will," his father said.

The boys, having eaten all they wanted, excused themselves to go back upstairs.

"I think we have two very fine young men there," Gran said.

"No argument here," Mason said.

Gran excused herself to retire for the night, and Mason and Angela came up to the study to have a nightcap with us. When they were ready to leave, we walked down the hall with them to collect Roger.

I tapped lightly on Steve's door, but there was no answer, so I opened the door and looked in. The television was on with the volume turned down low, and the two of them were out cold on the bed, still fully dressed. Steve was flat on his back, Roger was snuggled up against him, and Lance was curled up in a ball at their feet.

Lance looked up at us, and Charles pointed to the door and said softly, "Lance, bed." The dog gave him a "who, me?" look of reproach, hopped off the bed, and left the room.

"I guess there's no point in disturbing them," Mason said quietly. He and Angela moved around the bed, pulling the boys' shoes off and spreading a comforter over them. Charles went to the television to turn it off, and I elected to turn off Steve's computer.

The screen saver was running, so I brought the monitor to life before I shut the system down. There was a WordPerfect document up on the screen, and I glanced at it. The first few words caught my eye, so I quickly read the entire document. When I'd finished, I sent four copies to the printer, saved the document, and shut the system down.

When we were back in the hallway, Charles said, "What did you print?"

I motioned them into our office, turned on the light, and said, "Before they went to sleep, the boys were writing a letter to Jimmy's mother." I handed the copies around.

Angela finished perusing the document and said, "They weren't just writing a letter, they were pouring their hearts out."

"So they were," Mason said. Then he added, "This is extremely well written."

"We'll see to it that they finish it tomorrow and get it to the boy's family," Charles said. "Surely someone at the hospital will give us the address, not to mention the boy's last name."

We saw the Cartwrights out, closed up the house, and went upstairs to check on our children. All was peaceful and quiet, so we went to bed. The next morning, we encouraged the boys to finish and sign the letter, which they did. Charles obtained the name and address and arranged for the letter to be delivered to the family by courier.

Two days later, we accompanied the boys to Jimmy's funeral. Mercifully, the casket was closed, but there was a framed picture of Jimmy resting on it. The minister was Dr. Albert Kissling from the First Presbyterian Church. After the religious portion of the service was over, he said that he had something very special to read to us.

"You may not be aware of this," he said, "but members of the swim team at a local private school have been working with the patients at the cancer center for some time now. Two of them were teaching Jimmy to swim as part of his physical therapy. When they learned of his passing, these two boys wrote a letter to Mrs. Anderson, and I want to read a portion of it to you today."

He proceeded to read excerpts from the letter that Roger and Steve had written, which focused on how they felt about Jimmy, his struggle, and how upset they'd been when they learned of his death.

He went on to say, "These two young men have said it all, and I cannot think of a more fitting tribute to the deceased."

After the service, we went up to pay our respects. Angela had picked up the boys from school, and they were, of course, wearing their Exeter blazers. Mrs. Anderson recognized Steve and Roger, having met them at the hospital, and she gave them each a hug and thanked them for all that they'd done for her son. She told them that the letter they'd written was the most beautiful thing she'd ever read.

Everyone got a little teary-eyed at that.

The graveside service was scheduled for later that day down in Valdosta, where the Andersons had a family plot, so we left and took the boys to lunch. When we were very nearly finished with our lunch, both boys excused themselves to go to the restroom, giving the adults an opportunity for private conversation.

Mason told us that Roger had finally told them that he was gay.

"That took a great deal of courage," I said.

"We know," Angela said, "and we told him so."

"The two of them seem to be holding up well after what happened," Mason said.

"Yes, they are," Charles said. "I think they're putting the whole thing in perspective."

The boys returned to the table, and I asked the question that was on everyone's mind. "So, are you guys going back to the hospital this Saturday?"

"You bet," Roger said.

"We went over to St. Philip's yesterday after school and talked to Sammy's dad," Steve said.

"He told us that there are lots of other kids in the hospital who need our help and that we shouldn't give up," Roger said.

"He said that although most of them go to the cancer center hoping to be cured, many of them go there to die, and they deserve whatever comfort we're able to give them," Steve said.

"Good for you," Mason said. "We're all very proud of you two."

Angela fished in her purse, produced a key ring, removed a key, and said, "Roger, why don't you and Steve go back to school in my car. Someone will take me home."

"Okay, Mom," he said. Then he and Steve excused themselves and left the restaurant.

"What was that about?" Mason said.

"We need to tell Charles and Philip the rest of it," she said.

"I guess you're right," he said.

Charles and I looked at the Cartwrights with raised eyebrows.

Angela looked at her husband and said, "You start."

Mason sat for a minute, then said, "When Roger told us he was gay, he also told Jack and Harry, his younger brothers."

"The two of them have been making Roger's life miserable ever since," Angela said.

"In what way?" I said.

"For one thing, until we caught them at it and put a stop to it, the two of them never missed a chance to tell Roger that he was going to Hell for being gay," Mason said.

"They weren't raised to believe things like that," Angela said, "and they certainly didn't hear it in Sunday school classes at St. Philip's, so we started looking for the source of the contagion."

"And we certainly found it," Mason said.

"There's a family a couple of streets over from us who have two boys the same ages as Jack and Harry," Angela said. "The four boys have played together most of their lives. The other two are frequently guests in our house, and Jack and Harry are regularly at their house."

"The other boys' father, Robert Wilson, is an associate pastor at one of the big Baptist churches," Mason said. "Apparently, he's a major Bible-thumper, and he never misses an opportunity to brainwash and/or indoctrinate anybody who happens to spend any time in his house."

"He's turned our two younger sons into raging homophobes," Angela said.

"That's not all," Mason said. "Angela surveyed some other parents in the neighborhood, those who have sons who we know interact with that family. These parents started questioning their sons and found that they, too, had been fed a great deal of hellfire and brimstone and a number of outlandish beliefs."

"We found out that any time there are one or two kids visiting, if Mr. Wilson is around, he always has an impromptu prayer meeting with the kids," Angela said. "The boys mentioned it to us once or twice, but we thought it sounded harmless. After all, how could prayer be harmful?"

"It turns out that those little prayer meetings were regular indoctrination sessions," Mason said.

"That's the most despicable thing I've ever heard," Charles said.

"Yes, it is," Mason said.

"What have you done about it?" I said.

"For one thing, we've banned those two boys from our home and absolutely forbidden Jack and Harry to have any further contact with that family," Angela said.

"The other fathers and I paid a call on the Reverend Mr. Wilson one evening," Mason said, "and we told him in no uncertain terms that we thought he was a totally despicable person. Since then, we and the other families have made things just unpleasant enough for them that the Wilsons have put their house up for sale," Mason said.

"Naturally, Jack and Harry are blaming Roger for the loss of their two friends, which of course has made things that much worse for Roger," Angela said.

"Dean Mangrum has put us in contact with a group that has some expertise working with children who have fallen in with cults," Mason said, "but it will take months, perhaps even a couple of years, to undo the damage."

"We haven't heard even a hint of all this," Charles said.

"We asked Roger not to say anything, even to Steve, until we had a handle on it," Mason said.

"Would it help defuse the situation if Roger came to stay with us for a few months, or as long as necessary?" I said.

"Yes, it would," Angela said.

"Frankly, if you hadn't offered, we were going to ask," Mason said.

"Consider it done," Charles said.

"The affected families ought to sue this bastard," I said.

"Is that possible?" Mason said.

"You could sue, and you might collect some damages," Charles said. "You would certainly make a very public point, but I don't know if it would have any long-term effect. On the other hand, it might let other parents know that they need to be wary of just who their children spend time with."

"It sounds like something the Integrity Foundation ought to take up," I said.

Charles gave the two of them a quick rundown on the foundation, and I promised to put them in touch with its attorney.

"I want to make that bastard pay for what he's done to this family," Mason said.

"I think I can assure you that we can do just that," I said.

Charles and Mason returned to their respective offices, and I drove Angela home. She decided to take the two younger boys with her to visit her parents that evening so Mason and Roger could move Roger's things out without distraction.

I was waiting in the study when Steve got home from school that afternoon, and I asked him to come sit beside me on the sofa. When he was seated, I said, "Has Roger given you any hint of problems at home lately?"

"He told me that he'd come out to his parents and his brothers," Steve said.

"And?"

"His parents were fine. However, I think his brothers have been giving him a hard time, but he won't talk about it."

"His brothers have been giving him more than a hard time," I said, "but his parents made him promise not to talk about it for a while."

"They talked to you?"

"That's why Angela gave Roger her car keys at lunch. She wanted to tell us what was going on."

"What did she tell you?"

"I'll let Roger fill you in on that when he gets here."

"He's coming over?"

"He's doing more than that—he's going to come live with us for a few months—maybe longer."

"Cool."

"Follow me," I said, and I led him down the hall to the bedroom next to his. I did a quick inspection of the room and the closet.

"You need to clean out this closet," I said, "and any of the extra stuff in this bedroom. Mr. Goodman will show you the storage areas in the basement."

"We don't need to do that," he said. "Roger can share my room."

"I know he can, and I'm sure he'll spend most of his time, day and night, in your room. However, he still needs his own space, even if it's mostly for show and never used."

I gave the room a once-over, pointing out things that could be stored in the basement downstairs, and left Steve to handle things. I went down to the sunroom and found Gran in one of the easy chairs with a book in her lap and a cup of tea nearby. I'd already told her what was happening, and her reaction, as always, was "The more young people around, the merrier."

She looked up from her book as I approached, so I said, "I just told Steve the news."

"I take it he was pleased."

"You can say that. He's busily cleaning up the room next to his right now."

"I'm surprised that he didn't offer to share his room."

"He did, but I told him that Roger needed a space that was uniquely his, even if he seldom used it."

"That makes sense."

"Did you ever think you would see six boys in residence in this house at one time?"

"Not in my wildest dreams, but I think it's wonderful."

"I don't know if Charles has told you, but we still have the option of producing two more babies."

"Are you going to do so?"

"It's on our schedule."

"Good. The two of you have such a lot to offer."

"Are you certain that you don't relish some peace and quiet?"

"My dear boy," she said, "at my age, I can expect to have eternal peace and quiet soon enough. You and Charles both know that I'm enjoying all the sounds of life in this house."

We were still talking when Steve came down to ask me to inspect Roger's new room. I followed him upstairs, looked the room over, and pronounced it ready for occupancy. Mason and Roger arrived about an hour later, and we began carrying Roger's belongings upstairs. We stacked the clothing and other items in the hallway, just as we had done when Steve had moved in. I opened the door and said, "Roger, this will be your room."

"I thought I'd be sharing Steve's room," he said.

"That's what Steve said, and I have no doubt that you'll probably spend most of your time in Steve's room. But as I told Steve, everyone needs his own space, so this will be yours, even if you hardly ever use it."

"Okay," he said.

"Why don't you and Steve start organizing the room while Philip and I go back for another load?" Mason said.

The boys started doing just that, and Mason and I went back down to the driveway.

"You handled that one very well," he said.

"You and I both know that the two of them will spend every minute together, but as I told Roger, everyone needs his own space. In a week's time, I'll bet that most of Roger's everyday clothes are in Steve's closet, but that's up to the two of them."

"This whole business has really pissed me off," Mason said. "As soon as I hear from your foundation guy, I'm going to the other parents—I know they'll agree to go full tilt with a lawsuit."

"I'll make the call first thing in the morning. By the way, Steve was clueless about all of this. He told me that he sensed there was a problem with Roger's brothers, but Roger wouldn't talk about it."

"It's good to know that Roger kept his promise," Mason said.

"They're both good kids," I said.

"Yes, they are, and now that Roger is safe and out of the line of fire, Angela and I can focus on making good kids out of Jack and Harry."

Charles drove up as we were heading back into the house, loaded down with clothing. He hurried upstairs to change and quickly joined us. With a third pair of hands available, it only required one more trip to finish emptying Mason's car. We joined Gran for a late dinner, after which Mason and the two boys went to the Cartwright house to retrieve the rest of Roger's things.

When Roger's room was set up to everyone's satisfaction, we walked Roger and Mason to the door. Roger hugged his dad fiercely. Mason returned the hug and said, "You behave yourself and be good."

"I will, Dad," Roger said. "I love you."

"I love you too, son," Mason said.

Mason left, and we closed up the house. I gave Roger a set of keys and asked Steve to show him how to operate the gates and set the alarm. The two boys sat with us in the study for a while. They each hugged and thanked Charles and me before they went down the hall to go to bed.

We checked on our offspring and went to bed as well.

12

Charles

HAVING a second teenage boy in residence didn't really change things all that much, as Roger had been a fairly constant visitor since he and Steve had become friends. Philip had a long conversation with Roger's parents, and it was decided that the two boys would be allowed to drive their little business truck to and from school.

Both of the boys took home trophies for their individual performances in regional swim meets early in the year, and the team had collectively done very well.

Marie and the girls came for a visit during the girls' spring break, which preceded that of Exeter by almost two weeks. While they were visiting, we had the Cartwrights over to dinner a couple of times. The second time they came to dinner, they brought their younger sons with them. The two younger boys treated Roger with a cool indifference that stopped just short of hostility, and we took that to be an indication of progress. Angela's parents picked up the two boys after dinner, and Steve's sisters retired to their room to watch television, leaving the adults, along with Steve and Roger, in the upstairs study.

Conversation eventually turned to the boys' plans for the future, and Mason asked them if they'd decided about college.

"Yes, Sir, we have," Roger said. "I want to be an architect, and Steve wants to be a landscape architect. We'll probably go into business together after we graduate."

"Georgia Tech has good programs in both fields, and we want to go there, if it's all right," Steve said.

"Of course it is," Philip said. Marie, Mason, and Angela nodded in agreement.

"Do you want to live on campus?" Mason said.

"No, Sir," Roger said. "We'd just as soon stay right here, if it's okay."

"You know it is," Gran said. "You boys are welcome in this house as long as you need or want a place to stay."

Steve excused himself for a minute and left the study. When he returned he was carrying two envelopes, and he handed one of them to Mason and the other one to Philip.

"What's this?" Angela said as her husband opened his envelope and scanned its contents.

"A profit and loss statement for the boys' business," Mason said. "Attached to it is a check, which pays off my half of the loan on their truck and equipment."

Philip had been studying his copy of the document and said, "I see you've added a separate category for the landscaping portion of the business."

"Yes, Sir," Steve said.

"You wouldn't believe how many people want lots of shrubs and seasonal blooming plants but don't have the time or ability to do it themselves," Roger said.

"Steve, why don't you show this to your mother?" Philip said, and he handed the document back to Steve with the attached check.

"You didn't have to pay off the loan in a lump sum," Mason said.

"We know that, but we need to buy another truck and some more equipment," Roger said.

"And we wanted to make the point that the money is rolling in," Steve said.

Marie had been studying the document Steve had handed her, and said, "I didn't know that there was this much money to be made in lawn care."

Steve said, "Mom, you have no idea. The majority of our

customers don't just have lawns, they have estates. There's a lot of acreage to maintain and miles of hedges to trim, not to mention a bunch of edging with each one of them."

Roger said, "Dad, one of our customers is a real estate developer out in Gwinnett County who's willing to give us a contract to landscape some of his model homes. He says many of his customers want their homes to be landscaped before closing so they can finance the whole package."

"He wants us to do the model homes at our cost for materials and labor. In exchange for that, we get to place an advertising sign on the grounds, and he'll refer his customers to us," Steve said.

"Who is this customer?" Mason said.

"Scott Reynolds," Roger said. "He has three new subdivisions in various stages of development off I-85."

"Do you know this guy, Mason?" I said.

"Only by reputation, but he has a good one."

"A couple of his developments include strip shopping centers, and we may get some of that business also," Steve said.

"But not at cost," Roger said.

"As you know, I develop mostly shopping centers and commercial property, all of which require landscaping," Mason said. "Why didn't you boys approach me?"

"We thought about it, but we wanted to prove ourselves first," Steve said.

"We thought it would seem too much like charity coming from you," Roger said.

"Can you guys keep another truck and crew busy?" Philip said.

"Absolutely," Steve said.

"We even have the help lined up," Roger said.

"Right," Steve said. "There are a lot of guys our age who are willing to work hard, even for what we pay."

"What do you pay your crews?" Marie said.

"We start them at ten dollars an hour, including travel time from job to job," Steve said.

"After sixty days, if we're satisfied with their performance, we raise them to twelve. If they stay with us and are worth it, they'll start the next season at fourteen. Our crew chief gets a couple of dollars more," Roger said.

"That's more than they can make in a lot of places," Steve said.

"After these checks clear, will you have any working capital left?" Philip said.

"Yes, Sir," Steve said. "We always keep enough cash in the checking account to operate for a full week, and we put the rest in savings."

"How much money do you need this time?" Mason said.

"About the same amount as last time," Roger said. "Enough for a used truck, a trailer, and some equipment."

"We'd like to pay interest this time to keep it more businesslike," Steve said.

"Also, we have so much equipment and stuff now that we want to rent one of those little self-storage places just off of I-75," Roger said.

"Yeah," Steve said. "It's getting a little crowded in the shed behind the garage."

"What do you think, Mason?" Philip said.

"Based on their track record, I say go for it."

"We think we can make enough money this summer to pay off the new equipment and set aside some money for college as well," Steve said.

Philip said, "That's admirable, but you don't have to do that. I told you the first time you visited here that I would take care of your education."

"You and Uncle Charles have done a lot for me, and I appreciate it, but I want to feel like I'm contributing too."

"I feel the same way," Roger said. "I know all that counseling my brothers have been going through because of me must be expensive, and I want to help any way I can."

Mason said, "Roger, your brothers aren't going through counseling because of you or anything you did. They're going through it because that bastard spent several years indoctrinating them. Get it through your head... it wasn't your fault."

"Besides," Angela said, "if you hadn't come out to the family, we would never have known that Jack and Harry had been manipulated—at least not in time to do anything about it."

When Roger had moved in, Philip had brought Marie up to date as to the underlying reason, and she said, "I'm still somewhat flabbergasted that a preacher would try to indoctrinate someone else's children."

"It's just too bad that people have to be like that," Gran said. "I've lived in the South for seventy-odd years, and I can truthfully say that in all that time, I've only ever known one Southern Baptist who had enough integrity that he could be fully trusted, and I know for a fact that the man in question was a closet Presbyterian."

"By the way, Mason, how's the lawsuit coming?" I said.

"The attorneys for the foundation will be filing suit against the Reverend Wilson in a few weeks," Mason said. "They're planning on naming the church as well."

"How do you think it will play out, Charles?" Philip said.

"There are too many variables to make an accurate call right now," I said. "A lot depends on how many fundamentalists the foundation's attorney can keep off the jury. Ask me that question after a jury has been selected and opening arguments have begun and I might be able to make an educated guess."

The boys excused themselves to go to their room, and Gran said goodnight shortly thereafter.

Philip asked Marie if she'd thought about dating since her divorce, and she said, "I've thought about it, but I'm not ready for that yet. It's too soon."

"You know what they say about falling off a horse," Philip said.

"I know, and I'll admit that I get lonely at times. On the other hand, I got married right out of college, and until now, I've never had a chance to be my own person. Give me another year of running the business and getting my life back, then ask me that question."

"How are Jack and Harry doing, Mason?" I said. "I noticed that they were polite but cool toward Roger at dinner."

"Getting them past all of that indoctrination is going to be a long, slow process. The counselors say that if we're lucky, they'll have it behind them before they're ready for college."

"It takes a long time to undo that kind of damage," Angela said. "Most of what was done to them was both subtle and subliminal. We can't thank you enough for allowing Roger to stay here; it's made an extremely difficult time just a bit easier for us."

"That's right," Mason said. "The tension level at our house is significantly lower with Roger in residence over here."

"We're happy to have him," I said, "and it certainly hasn't imposed any hardship. He and Steve are just about as close as any two boys can be."

"Do you think the two of them have become boyfriends?" Marie said.

"I think that's fairly obvious, but they haven't made any formal announcement," Philip said.

"They'll let us know when they're ready to do so," I said.

"How does Mrs. Barnett feel about having so many young people around?" Angela said.

"I asked her that same question the night Roger came to stay with us," Philip said. "Rather, I asked her if she didn't yearn for peace and quiet."

"I can well imagine what Gran said," I said.

"She said that at her age she could expect to have eternal peace and quiet soon enough, and in the meantime, she was quite happy to have sounds of life all around the house," Philip said.

"Speaking of sounds of life," I said, "I think our presence is required in the nursery." After dinner, Grace had gone out for the evening.

"You two keep your seat," Marie said. "I like taking care of babies."

"I'll join you," Angela said, and the two women went to the nursery.

"What is it about women and babies?" Mason said after the two women were out of the room.

"I guess it's the mothering instinct," I said. "It's never far below the surface."

Mason had been following our progress on the Boston project, and he asked how it was going.

"The agent is actually signing leases as we speak," Philip said. "We expect to be fully leased by the time the renovations are complete."

"Are you still planning to donate the building to the foundation?"

"You bet," Philip said. "My tax attorney is getting orgasmic over the possibilities, and we'll time the donation such that it will have the maximum positive impact tax-wise."

"Who's your tax man?" Mason said.

"Randolph Forney."

"I've heard good things about him."

"If you need to make a change, he's top-notch," I said. "He walked me through withdrawing the principal from two trusts with very little impact on my tax liability."

"We have trusts and other things set up for Steve and the kids," Philip said. "If both of us died tomorrow, the IRS wouldn't get a dime."

"That's something that I need to do but keep putting off," Mason said.

"Well, if you feel good about sending more money to Washington to finance more waste, the politicians will love you for it," I said.

"You know I don't feel good about paying taxes," Mason said. "Can you get me an appointment with Forney?"

"He isn't officially taking new clients right now, but I think I can arrange to have someone from his office call you," Philip said.

The women returned from the nursery, each carrying a small body and a bottle. They settled down on one of the sofas and watched their charges greedily sucking away.

"You two have quite a little family," Angela said.

"Yes, we do, and it's not through growing," I said.

"We haven't told anyone yet, but we're planning two more arrivals for sometime next year," Philip said. "By the way, Marie, you need to put a cloth over your shoulder when you burp J. J. He doesn't simply burp, he erupts like a little volcano and spits all over you."

"I know how to deal with spitters. One of the girls was like that."

"Two more," Angela said. "That's quite a load of responsibility you're taking on."

"Well," I said, "I never was one to do anything halfway."

Philip said, "By the way, did you know that the boys have been buying plants and shrubs wholesale out in the country for the landscaping portion of their business?"

"We know," Mason said.

"I rode out there with Steve the other day, and while he was making their purchases, I looked the place over."

"What's it like?" Mason said.

"The nursery is run by an elderly couple. They have about twenty acres surrounding their house. It's quite a nice operation, actually. They have three or four large greenhouses, and a little more than half of their acreage is dedicated to rows and rows of shrubs and trees that they're growing for eventual sale. They raise the shrubs from cuttings, but they buy the trees as seedlings. The rest of their land is cleared but not currently in use, so they have room for expansion."

"What else?" I said.

"It's a good piece of land in a prime location, and I think the old couple is going to want to sell out in a couple of years. I had a lengthy conversation with Mrs. Johnson while her husband rounded up Steve's purchases. She likes the boys and dropped a hint or two. My instinct tells me that she and her husband are eventually going to make the boys an offer they won't want to refuse."

"So what did you do about it?" Mason said.

"Nothing specific, but I made it clear that I would back them if the opportunity came up."

"Not by yourself, I hope," Mason said. "Count us in for half of whatever you do."

"No problem," Philip said. "The property would be a good

investment at the right price. They get a break on real estate taxes because they're agricultural. If the boys are serious about this landscaping business, having a source of supply they can control will be good for their business."

"That's all well and good," I said, "but I think you need to wait and let them come to us with their own ideas."

"No argument there," Mason said, and Philip nodded.

"It's a good thing we had them form a corporation shortly after they started the business," I said. "That way, they'll be ready to take title to real estate when the time comes."

I noticed a strange expression on Marie's face, so I said, "Marie, are you all right?"

"I'm okay. I was just thinking about how much you and Philip have done for my son, and I started to feel a little inadequate as a mother."

Philip got up, walked to Marie's chair, bent down, hugged her as best he could without squeezing J. J., and said, "I keep telling you, sis, that we enjoy having him here."

"I know. I just don't know how to thank you all."

"No thanks are necessary. You need to concentrate on the girls and making a life for yourself," he said. "As for being inadequate, if you hadn't given Steve the basics in terms of character and upbringing, among other things, he wouldn't have had what it takes to take advantage of the opportunities that have come his way."

"I agree," Angela said. "Roger was always a rather quiet boy and not particularly outgoing. Since he and Steve became friends, he's changed dramatically, and for the better."

I decided it was time to change the subject and said to no one in particular, "Exeter's spring break is week after next, and Philip and I are planning to take the boys down to the beach house for that week and the preceding weekend."

"Right," Philip said. "They've been working very hard and had absolutely no time off last summer, so they haven't had a lot of time to just be boys. We thought it would be good for them to get away."

"We're sending Jack and Harry to a special camp that week,"

Mason said, "one that was recommended by Dean Mangrum."

"Then why don't the two of you join us for as much of that week as you can?" I said.

"That's a great idea," Philip said. "It would give you a chance to spend some time with Roger."

"Where's your house?" Angela said.

"Fort Walton Beach," I said. "It's right on the beach, and there are three bedrooms, so there's plenty of room."

"Actually, we were planning to visit relatives down in Mobile," Mason said, "but I think we can work around that."

Both of the babies went right back to sleep after their feeding, and the women took them back to the nursery. After they returned, conversation began to wind down, and the Cartwrights left. Marie helped us check up on all the boys; then we retired for the evening.

Over the course of the next two days, Philip once again took the boys truck shopping, and they acquired a second truck, which was almost a twin of the first, along with another trailer and the needed equipment. By Saturday, the boys had the new crew hard at work.

13

Charles

THE game plan that evolved for the beach trip was to leave on Friday afternoon. Mason and Angela were expected the following Tuesday, at which time we would fly home, leaving the boys with the Cartwrights. Steve and Roger were adamant about not being away from their business on two successive weekends, so I agreed to fly down and pick them up Friday afternoon. Mason and Angela would close up the house and drive home on Sunday.

Armed with a favorable weather report, we flew out on Friday afternoon as scheduled. Since only two of the four passenger seats were occupied, Lance accompanied us, and instead of using his crate, I allowed him to curl up in one of the unoccupied seats.

On the way from the airport to the house, we stopped by Publix and stocked up for the week. At the house, Philip began putting the groceries away while I showed the boys their room. The boys took Lance down to the water's edge to sample the surf, and Philip and I stripped, then settled on the deck. There wasn't enough sun left to worry about protecting our genitals with socks.

When the boys emerged from the shower room, towels wrapped around their waists, we were in the kitchen, behind the counter, still naked, in the final stages of preparing dinner.

"I hope you were careful to get all the salt and sand out of Lance's fur," I said.

"Yes, Sir," Roger said. "Just like we do for chlorine from the pool at home."

The boys rounded the counter and stopped dead, and Steve said, "Whoa! You guys aren't wearing any clothes."

"That's my nephew," Philip said. "Sharp as a tack. He doesn't miss much."

"Pay no attention to him," I said. "Actually, we've gotten into the habit of not wearing clothes in this house."

"Can we go naked too?" Roger said.

"You bet," I said.

The towels came off in a flash and were tossed into the laundry basket. Then the boys retrieved a couple of cans of Coke from the refrigerator.

"Steve," I said.

"Yes, Sir?"

"Remember when your Uncle Julien visited us and you made a careless comment?"

"I remember."

"Well, this is another one of those things that it would definitely not be wise to talk about, even to your friends."

"I understand."

There was a puzzled look on Roger's face, so I told him what Steve had said that night and about the discussion that had ensued, adding, "Think about what someone like Reverend Wilson would do if he heard that two sixteen-year-old boys spent a weekend naked with two gay men."

"He could cause a lot of trouble, couldn't he?" Roger said.

"He would certainly try," I said.

"Okay, guys," Philip said. "Dinner's ready, and it's totally self-service. Also, we have to clean up after ourselves around here, since we don't have a Mrs. Goodman in residence."

Philip and I had already carried a table and chairs out onto the deck, and we took our plates and beverages outside to eat.

When we were settled, Roger said, "This is so cool, eating outside naked."

"Are you sure nobody can see us?" Steve said.

"Not unless you walk over to the deck railing and flash them," I said.

The boys were seated at the table playing cards when we went upstairs to bed, so I said, "Be sure to close and lock all of the doors to the deck before you go to bed."

The next morning, Philip and I were sitting at the kitchen counter with toast and coffee when the boys came downstairs. I said, "I see that you guys have decided to join the club." I was looking at their bare pubic areas.

"Yes, Sir," Steve said. "We've been talking about it for a long time, and last night we decided to go for it."

"Breakfast is strictly DIY," Philip said.

"DIY?" Roger said.

"Do it yourself," I said.

Philip and I spent most of the day stretched out on the deck, soaking up the sun. The boys joined us in between trips to the surf to play with Lance. We had a late dinner and sat around the table for a while watching the sunset.

"Anybody want to go skinny-dipping after we clean up the kitchen?" I said.

"Can you do that here?" Steve said.

"All the neighbors are pretty open-minded," I said, "and we all sort of look the other way when necessary. Nobody minds as long as it's very early in the morning or late in the evening and you aren't too noisy late at night."

The kitchen was cleaned in record time, and the boys followed us down to the beach, where we had a good time in the surf. Later, just before we went upstairs, the boys turned off the television and moved to a sofa opposite us, and Steve said, "Uncle Philip?"

"Yes?"

"What's the best way to go about having anal sex? I mean, how do you do it without it hurting so much?"

"Have you two tried it?"

"Yes, Sir, but it didn't really work out too well, and it hurt."

"Okay, guys," Philip said, "here's what you do. Have your partner lie flat on his back with his knees bent. Then you lubricate your middle finger and slowly, very slowly, insert it into his anus...."

"Don't forget to use a condom," I said.

"We don't want to do that," Steve said.

"Are you sure that you're in a long-term, committed relationship?" Philip said.

"Yes, Sir," both boys said.

"When you get to Tech, how do you know that some stud on the swim team won't wiggle his ass at you and sweep you off your feet?" I said.

"That isn't going to happen," Roger said. "We love each other, and we're not interested in anybody else."

Steve was nodding his head vigorously in agreement.

Philip finished his Anal 101 instructions, and we said goodnight. Later, when we were in bed, I rolled him over onto his back.

"First you lubricate your middle finger," I said, mimicking his instructions. "Then you insert it slowly," I added, doing so. "Eventually you will find a little bump in there. That will be your partner's prostate. He'll let you know when you find it."

I was, in fact, massaging the heck out of Philip's little bump at that point. He levitated for a moment and said, "You found it, you found it."

"When your partner is comfortable with one finger, gently insert a second finger," I said, continuing the lecture as I followed my own instructions.

When I got to the part about the third finger, he said, "Enough already. Shut up and fuck me like you really love me."

I did so.

We were already on the deck taking in the sun when the boys

turned up the next morning. They had bowls of cereal in hand, and they both looked somewhat the worse for wear.

I sat up on my lounge chair and said, "Looks like somebody had a night of wild sex."

"You know we did," Steve said.

"It was great," Roger said. "I've never felt anything like it."

"Me neither. We did each other, and it was awesome," Steve said.

"I forgot to mention one thing last night," Philip said.

"What?" Steve said.

"If you guys ever have the urge to try rimming, be sure that you wash your butts out thoroughly with soap and water."

"Rimming?" Roger said. "What's that?"

"Sticking your tongue up your partner's anus," I said.

"Ugh, that's disgusting," Steve said, making a face.

"It might sound like it," Philip said, "but one of these days you might get carried away and try it."

"You can get hepatitis from ingesting fecal matter," I said, "hence the need for extreme cleanliness."

The boys joined us on the deck, and later we all donned running shorts and went for a run down the beach with Lance at our heels.

Tuesday morning came all too soon. We spent the first part of the morning on the deck. Later, when the boys were preparing to go down to the beach with Lance, I said, "When you come back, don't march into the house naked. Remember, we're expecting Mason and Angela to be here by lunchtime."

We showered, dressed, and began to prepare lunch while we waited for our guests to arrive. When the doorbell rang, I left Philip in the kitchen and went down to let the Cartwrights in. I showed them their bedroom and gave them a quick tour of the house. When we were back downstairs, Angela said, "Where are the boys?"

"Out on the beach being boys," I said. "Follow me."

We went out on the deck and looked down at the beach. The boys were throwing a Frisbee for Lance to catch, and Mason said, "They certainly seem to be enjoying themselves."

"They have done that," I said. "Hunger will bring them back inside shortly. Can I get you something to drink?"

We were settled at the kitchen counter, drinks in hand, when two boys and a dog emerged from the shower room. The boys had towels wrapped around their waists.

"Mom, Dad, hi," Roger said. "Give us a minute to go up and get dressed."

Without waiting for a reply, the boys ran upstairs. Lance went straight to his water bowl, drank deeply, and flopped down on his bed.

"What's the matter, boy?" I said. "Did the guys wear you out?"

Lance rolled over and closed his eyes in answer.

The boys came back into the kitchen area dressed in shorts and polo shirts. Roger hugged both his parents, and to my surprise, Steve hugged them as well.

"How about setting the table for us, guys?" I said before any other conversation could get underway.

Mason helped the boys carry plates, silverware, and other things to the deck, and Angela helped us carry the food outside.

As we ate, the boys filled the Cartwrights in on their long period of relaxation. When they finally wound down, Angela said, "This is really a lovely place. How long have you had it?"

"Nearly ten years," I said. "My former partner and I bought it not too long after I finished law school. After he died, I gave his half interest to his sister, and we take turns using the place. Actually, it hasn't been used very much lately. You and Mason should feel free to take advantage of it anytime. My secretary keeps a calendar of which holiday weekends are spoken for. Most of the rest of the time it just sits here."

"I haven't heard from the foundation lately," Philip said. "What's the latest word on the suit?"

"It'll be filed on Friday," Mason said.

"That's good timing," I said.

"Why?" Mason said.

"Because it will make a splash on the weekend news, and the

other side will pretty much have a weekend to stew over it before they can officially respond," I said. "If the foundation attorney is smart, he'll hold a press conference just in time to make the five o'clock news."

We sat around the table for a couple of hours, talking, before we carried the dishes into the kitchen. When I returned to the deck, I said, "We plan to grill steaks this evening, if that's okay with everyone."

"It's more than okay," Mason said, "but only if you let me do it."

"Right," Angela said. "Mason knows his way around a grill, and I would love to take care of the rest of the meal."

"You talked us into it," I said. "Steve, why don't you come for a run down the beach with Philip and me? That will give Roger some time alone with his folks."

The three of us went upstairs and put on running shorts. Somehow Lance sensed what was up and was waiting for us at the door. We ran at an easy pace down to our usual turning point.

We stopped for a minute to catch our breath, and Steve said, "Uncle Philip, do you think I should offer to go home with you guys tomorrow morning so that Roger's parents can have more time with him?"

"That's a nice thought, and it certainly wouldn't hurt to offer," Philip said. Then we ran back up the beach to the house.

When we came back downstairs from dressing, we found Roger and his parents on the deck right where we'd left them. After a minute or two of standing around making small talk, Steve said, "Mrs. Cartwright, I told Uncle Philip that I would go back to Atlanta tomorrow with him and Uncle Charles so you could have more time with Roger."

Angela got up, hugged Steve, and said, "Oh, honey, it's sweet of you to offer, but it's not necessary. You're part of the family now."

"Besides which," Mason said, "from the look on Roger's face, I don't think he'd appreciate being left behind without you for two or three days."

Roger stood up, walked over to Steve, put his arm around him, and said, "You've got that right."

"Is this your way of making an announcement?" Philip said.

"Yes, I guess it is," Roger said after he thought about it for a moment. "Steve and I are officially boyfriends."

"When did the two of you decide that it was official?" Charles said.

"This past weekend," Roger said.

"Next time you talk to your mom, Steve," Philip said, "you should tell her, okay?"

"I will, Uncle Philip," Steve said.

The boys took Lancelot down to the beach, and the rest of us sat around talking, catching up on things. Philip brought up a subject that he and I had discussed at length when he said, "We've been thinking about allowing Steve to have wine with dinner, but didn't want to do so unless you folks thought it was a good idea for Roger to learn such things."

"It's fine with us," Mason said. "We've talked about doing just that from time to time."

"Mason and I both learned an appreciation for wine and a respect for alcohol as we were growing up," Angela said, "and we want our sons to go the same route."

That evening, we learned that Mason did indeed know his way around a grill, as the steaks were done to perfection. Angela demonstrated that she, too, knew her way around a kitchen.

I opened a bottle of zinfandel for the adults and a bottle of Beaujolais for Roger and Steve. The two boys sipped the wine and made faces, and Steve summed it up, saying, "It's all right, I guess, but I'd just as soon have a Coke."

After dinner, I brought out a deck of cards, and we played hearts for a while. During a lull between hands, Steve said, "Uncle Charles, how do you go about setting up a scholarship?"

"It depends upon what kind of scholarship you're talking about," I said. "There are one-time scholarships, and there are annual scholarships funded by an endowment."

"Steve and I want to do something in memory of Jimmy," Roger said.

"He really got to you two, didn't he?" Mason said.

"Yes, Sir, he did," Steve said. "We wanted to think of some way that he would always be remembered, and came up with the idea for a memorial scholarship."

"To do a scholarship every year," I said, "you simply have to raise enough money in donations to pay for a year's tuition and books every year. If you wanted to make it a scholarship for a boarding student, you could add that amount as well. Or you have to raise enough money to create an endowment and have the return on the investment fund the annual scholarship."

"I think we can persuade the team to use some of this summer's car wash proceeds to fund a scholarship for one year," Steve said.

"After that we'll have to work something out," Roger said.

"Charles and I can contribute to the fund," Philip said.

"So can we," Mason said.

"Thanks," Steve said, "but we want to do this ourselves."

"You'll have to get permission from Jimmy's parents to use his name," I said.

"Can we have them over to lunch some weekend and ask them?" Steve said.

"That can be arranged," I said.

The next morning after breakfast, Philip and I packed our belongings and took them, along with Lance, to the rental car. As we were saying good-bye, I said, "Angela, don't even think about cleaning the house before you leave. The cleaning service will take care of it next week, and they won't charge any less if it's already clean."

"What about leftover perishable items?" she said.

"They'll carry them off. It's part of the perks of their job. If I know that the house will be occupied within the next couple of weeks, I leave them a note and they only take things that will have spoiled by the next time someone is here."

Friday afternoon when I returned, Mason and the boys were waiting for me at the airport. The boys each gave Mason a hug before they loaded their gear in the plane and settled into their seats.

Just before I entered the cockpit, I said, "Mason, there's a full moon tonight and tomorrow night."

"So?" he said.

"It's very romantic and a good time for skinny-dipping."

"Can you do that here?"

"Our end of the beach is isolated because of an inlet a few hundred yards up from the house, and the neighbors and I have an understanding," I said. "As long as it's not in broad daylight and not too noisy, everyone looks the other way. Late evening is best."

"I'll bear that in mind," he said.

I circled the field after takeoff and saw him still standing by the car, watching us. I had a feeling that he would take my advice.

The boys had called their crew chiefs just before we took off, and shortly after we got home, the crew chiefs arrived in the trucks. Steve and Roger left immediately to inspect all of the jobs that had been done in their absence.

Sure enough, the Integrity Foundation's attorney, Logan O'Neill, managed to make the evening news with his press conference, and the front page of Saturday's morning paper had a banner across the top reading "Preacher charged with corrupting minors." Below the banner, a subheading read "Parents also file lawsuit against Baptist church."

I scanned the article and handed the paper to Philip, saying, "The foundation is all over the paper this morning."

He finished the article and said, "That will give them something to think about."

"I should think so, what with all the high-profile cases the foundation has taken on and won."

We had a late lunch on Sunday, as we were expecting Roger's parents to join us a little after one. They arrived right on time, and we had lunch in the sunroom.

"The two of you are looking very well rested," Gran said.

"I suppose we are," Mason said. "The beach was nice, and the weather was perfect."

"The full moon was especially nice," Angela said.

Mason, who was sitting beside Angela, gave me a wink, and I smiled in acknowledgment. We finished our lunch, and Angela said,

"We hate to eat and run, but…."

"We have to go and meet the bus that's bringing the boys back from camp," Mason said as he handed me the keys to the beach house.

"I meant what I said about using the house anytime. Just call my secretary and have her pencil you in on the calendar."

"We just might do that," Mason said.

Roger walked his folks to their car while I waited on the veranda. When he came back to where I was standing, he said, "I've never seen my folks with such dopey expressions on their faces."

"Trust me, Roger, a couple of nights of romance in the moonlight does wonders for a relationship."

"What do you mean?" He thought about it for a moment, the lightbulb came on, and he actually blushed and said, "Oh."

"You never think about your parents actually doing the deed, do you?" I said.

"I guess not, but how did you know about it?"

"Because just before I climbed into the cockpit to fly you and Steve home, I told Mason that there was a full moon and that late-night skinny-dipping was all right on our little section of the beach."

"How did you know they followed your suggestion?"

"Because when your mom mentioned the full moon, your dad winked at me across the table."

"Oh," he said.

"Exactly. Even parents are entitled to some romantic moments, aren't they?"

"I guess they are," he said. "I just never thought about it before."

I put my arm around his shoulder, and we went back inside.

14

Philip

ON A Sunday afternoon two weeks after we returned from spring break at the beach, Charles and I invited the parents of Jimmy Anderson to lunch. Because spring flowers were blooming profusely in the garden, we ate in the sunroom, where the garden was in full view. Mason and Angela were unable to be with us due to a conflict. Gran was present, of course, and graciously accepted the usual comments about the house and grounds from our guests.

Patrick and Julia Anderson were in their late thirties, and over the course of lunch, we learned that Jimmy had been the oldest of their four children. After the dishes had been cleared away, we lifted Mark and Steven out of their high chairs, and Grace led them back upstairs. Then Charles said to Steve and Roger, "Okay, guys, you have the floor."

It took Steve a moment to find his voice before he began. "Mr. and Mrs. Anderson, Roger and I asked Uncle Philip to invite you to lunch because we want to ask your permission to do something."

"Steve and I want to establish a scholarship fund at Exeter Academy in memory of Jimmy," Roger said.

"The Cartwrights and I offered to fund it," I said, "but the boys want to do this themselves."

"We're going to persuade the swim team to use part of the proceeds from the car wash this summer to start an…. What's that word, Uncle Charles?"

"An endowment," Charles said.

"Right," Steve said, "an endowment. We want to set up a permanent fund, and when it grows big enough, the earnings from it will provide a scholarship every year."

"But we need your permission to do that," Roger said.

"Why would you want to do all that?" Mr. Anderson said.

"Because Jimmy never had a chance to make a name for himself," Roger said, "and we think that a scholarship would be a way to make certain that at least some people will always know who he was."

Mrs. Anderson was beginning to tear up and said to her husband, "Oh, Patrick, this is what we've been looking for."

"What my wife is referring to is the insurance money," Mr. Anderson said. "I'm a chartered life underwriter, and I believe in what I do. Because of that, as each of our children were born, I took out very large policies on them. Policies that could be cashed in when they became eighteen and used for their education."

"There's a huge amount of money in the bank right now," Mrs. Anderson said, "and we haven't felt right about using it for anything. It's just sitting there, earning interest."

"How much are you talking about?" Charles said.

"Half a million," Mr. Anderson said.

"With proper management, that's more than enough to fund two or three scholarships every year," Charles said.

"What would we have to do to set up an endowment?" Mr. Anderson said.

"I'll set up an appointment with the school administrator who handles that sort of thing," Charles said. "I'll also draw up an agreement that ensures that the fund will always be used for the purposes intended."

"Why do you need to do that?" I said.

"Because I won't be around forever, nor will the current administration of the school, nor, for that matter, will Mr. and Mrs. Anderson. We want to be very certain that decades from now, some future administrator at the school won't be able to decide that he or she has a better use for the funds."

"Does that sort of thing happen very often?" Mr. Anderson said.

"Not often, but it happens," Charles said. "I can think of one well-known local church whose governing board decided it was all right to deplete an endowment and use it for a new building project instead of the originally stated purpose of the fund. They didn't get away with it because the great-grandchildren of the man whose bequest set up the fund hired an attorney to stop them. If the endowment had been set up with proper safeguards, they wouldn't even have been able to contemplate such a thing."

"You're speaking from experience, aren't you?" I said.

"I was the attorney," he said.

Charles and Mr. Anderson discussed details for a few minutes, and Mr. Anderson said, "Great. Let's do it."

I noticed that Steve and Roger weren't exactly beaming with delight, so I said, "What's the matter, Steve? You should be happy about this."

"I am, Uncle Philip," he said. "It's just that Roger and I wanted to do this all by ourselves."

"My dear boy," Gran said, "as you grow older, you will learn that you can't always do everything yourself. You and Roger should be proud of the fact that you had a wonderful idea to commemorate the life of the young man and that others were able to carry your idea to completion."

"Right," Charles said. "If you guys hadn't come up with this idea, we wouldn't be having this conversation."

"Besides," I said, "there's no reason why you can't persuade the team to donate some or all of this summer's proceeds to the fund. The larger the endowment, the more scholarships there will be."

"I hadn't thought of it that way, Uncle Philip," Steve said.

"Well, think about it," I said. "Does the team have a particular goal in mind for this year's earnings?"

"We want to purchase a couple of whirlpools for the locker room," Roger said, "but that's all."

"Good. Then you and Steve can use your powers of persuasion to see to it that the rest of the car wash proceeds go to the new scholarship fund."

"We can do that," Steve said.

Later that week, I attended a pretrial conference concerning the lawsuit the foundation had brought on behalf of the Cartwrights and the other parents against Reverend Wilson and his church. I was present because it was, after all, my foundation. Also present were Logan O'Neill, the foundation's attorney, and Ted Savage, representing the defendants. Charles was there, as well.

There was a bit of conversation about nothing at all before the defense attorney finally said, "What will it take to make this case go away, Mr. O'Neill?"

Logan O'Neill slid a document across the table to Ted Savage, who picked it up, read it, and said, "This is basically what the original filing asked for."

"It's cheap compared to the alternative," Mr. O'Neill said.

"And that would be?"

"I would like nothing better than to put the Southern Baptist Church on trial, and I'm fully prepared to do so," Mr. O'Neill said as he slid another document across the table.

"What's this?" Savage said.

"A list of fifty Bible scholars, representing Episcopal, Methodist, Presbyterian, and Lutheran seminaries. I even have a couple of Jesuit scholars who have broken with Rome on the subject of homosexuality. These witnesses are ready to refute, point by point, all of the various things that the defendant taught the plaintiffs' children."

"You would actually call fifty people to testify?"

"Indeed, I would. Understand this—I have a blank check from the foundation and from the plaintiffs. The document you are looking at is merely my A list of witnesses. I also have a B list and a C list, both of which are equally long, if not longer. Needless to say, the press will have a field day."

Savage looked at Charles and said, "Mr. Barnett, what's your position on all of this?"

"I am here of counsel and to make the point that the full resources of Chandler, Todd, Woodward & Barnett are available to Mr. O'Neill, should he need them."

"Just so we understand each other," Mr. O'Neill said, "the plaintiffs want compensation in the amounts stated and a very public apology for what your client, and by extension, his church, did to those children. These parents are extremely angry, and there's very little wiggle room for negotiation."

Mr. Savage sighed and said, "Give me a few days, and I'll get back to you."

"We'll give you a week before we proceed," Mr. O'Neill said.

Savage returned his paperwork to his briefcase, closed it, and left the room.

"Well, Charles," O'Neill said, "what do you think?"

"It's hard to say, Logan. In the end, I suspect it will depend upon what price that church places on its pride. On the other hand, Mr. Savage is smart enough to explain to Mr. Wilson and his church that a lengthy trial will involve several weeks, perhaps even months, of negative publicity. He also has to be very much aware that the foundation hasn't lost a case yet."

"Then we'll just have to wait and see," O'Neill said.

Charles and I walked back to the parking lot together, and he said, "It's nearly eleven thirty. Want to have an early lunch?"

"You're on," I said.

We drove to a quiet little restaurant in the Virginia Highlands neighborhood and were seated at a table on the rear patio. Charles said, "You know, babe, I've been thinking."

"About?"

"With four boys and two more on the way, we need to think about enlarging the beach house."

"Should we expand up or out?"

"Whichever will be easier. I think there's enough room between the entrance of the house and the street to add a couple of rooms at the first-floor level."

"Will the setback restrictions allow that?" I said.

"Probably, but I'll have to check it out."

"Handle it, handle it."

"Consider it done."

"I guess great minds think alike," I said.

"Meaning?"

"I've been thinking about the Keep and whether or not it should be enlarged to accommodate our tribe."

"Handle it, handle it," he said, tossing my words back at me.

"You know I've been working with a Realtor in North Carolina, hoping to acquire more land in the valley?"

"I remember you telling me about it."

"As of this morning, I've tied up two adjacent tracts, with enough cleared land to create a grass landing strip."

"Will it be long enough?"

"About a hundred yards longer than you told me the plane required at that altitude."

"That should do it," Charles said.

"I've also had a few other thoughts."

"Are you going to keep them secret?"

"I'm a little worried about the direction in which the country is currently headed, so I'm thinking about making us considerably more liquid than we are."

"You're referring to the possibility of a huge tax increase?"

"I'm referring to the possibility of a confiscatory tax increase," I said.

"Can you achieve the desired amount of liquidity without incurring a lot of capital gains?"

"You know I'm days away from donating the Boston building to the foundation," I said.

"And?"

"I'm going to sell a number of stocks that aren't doing too well right now. The losses will be absorbed by the gain on the Boston building."

"That's your area of expertise, babe," he said. "Make it so."

"I'll set things in motion next week."

"Have you any specific plans for the proceeds from those stocks?"

"I haven't worked it out yet," I said, "but I'm thinking we should put at least a fourth of it in gold, and I think it's time we had a couple of offshore accounts."

"Are you referring to gold stocks?"

"No, I'm referring to coins, specifically Krugerrands."

"You're really serious about this, aren't you?" he said.

"Indeed I am. There are too many candidates running for office that believe they know what's best for everyone and are perfectly willing to confiscate our money and 'redistribute' it to accomplish their goals."

"There's something else we ought to do," he said.

"And that would be?"

"Shift a larger percentage of our investments into tax-exempt securities."

"Great minds again," I said. "Randolph and I have been working on a strategy to do just that."

"At the risk of seeming repetitious, handle it, babe, handle it," he said.

"You know I will."

"By the way, I keep forgetting to ask you about the new book. How's it coming?"

"Mostly by hand," I said.

"Very funny."

"You set 'em up, and I'll knock 'em down."

"I like what you said about our brood just now," he said.

"What did I say?"

"You referred to them as the tribe," he said.

"Oh yes, so I did."

"I think we need to remember that one and use it again," he said.

"Works for me."

"However did I get so lucky?" he said with a smile.

"Lucky?"

"Don't be coy. You know what I mean."

"Perhaps, but it's nice to hear it once in a while."

We finished our lunch and drove back to the parking lot where I'd left my car. I went straight home and changed into shorts and a knit shirt. As I walked down the hall to our office, I heard sounds from overhead, so I climbed to the third-floor playroom and found Gran and Grace sitting in easy chairs, watching Mark and Steven running about and J. J. and R. B. crawling around after them.

"It makes me tired to look at them," Gran said. "All that energy."

"Too bad we can't figure out a way to harness it."

I got down on the floor and played with the boys for a while until Grace announced that it was naptime. She and I each picked up one of the crawlers, and we led the other two down the stairs. After the kids were down for the count, I joined Gran downstairs in the sunroom for a cup of tea before I went up to the office and started writing.

I was still at it a few hours later, when I sensed a presence in the room just before I felt Charles's arms circling me from behind. "Are you at a stopping point?"

"Give me five minutes to wrap up this scene," I said.

"Just so you have your naked body in the bed by the time I get out of the shower," he said, and he left the room.

After we exercised our naked bodies on the bed, we showered together and then dressed to go downstairs for dinner. We escorted Steven and Mark down to the dining room. As soon as the two of them were able to sit in high chairs, we'd begun to make a point of having the entire family at dinner. Occasionally, Charles had to work late or Roger and Steve were delayed by either their business or some after-school activity, but we managed to have everyone at the dinner table roughly eight nights out of ten, at least on weeknights.

The boys were occasionally tempted to grab fast food on the way home, but we'd managed to persuade them not to do so. We'd discussed this with Mason and Angela, and they were in total agreement with the idea.

Our program wasn't rigid. We made exceptions on those nights when the gang came over with pizza, and Steve and Roger were allowed an occasional weekend night out to have dinner together and go to a movie.

After dinner, we took the little ones up to the playroom. Steve and Roger joined us and played with the boys for a while before they went to their room to do their homework. Later that evening, Charles and I were in the upstairs study, listening to music, when the teenagers joined us.

"What's up, guys?" Charles said.

"Can we invite Tom and Larry over for the weekend?" Steve said.

"Tom and Larry from the swim team?" I said, picturing the two very attractive blonds I'd met several times over the summer.

"Right," Steve said.

"They're a couple, aren't they?" Charles said.

"Yes, Sir, just like us," Roger said.

"Do their parents know about them?" I said. "And for that matter, do their parents know they'll be spending the weekend in a gay household?"

"Yes to all of the above, Uncle Philip," Steve said.

"In that case, no problem," Charles said.

"What about your customers?" I said.

"We'll be caught up by Friday afternoon," Steve said.

"The crew will handle the weekend, no problem," Roger said.

The two houseguests rode home from school with Steve and Roger. As soon as their guests had been shown their room, the four boys went out to the pool. Later, at the dinner table, they held their own, participating in the lively conversation that had become standard for our little family at the table. We learned, among other things, that both boys held black belts in karate. Steve and Roger had been taking lessons off and on but hadn't progressed that far with their training, mostly due to lack of time.

The four boys joined us in the upstairs study later, and I said, "Steve, what do you guys have on tap for tomorrow?"

"We want to go to a matinee at the multiplex out at the Mall of Georgia."

"That's a long way to drive just for a movie," Charles said.

"Yes, Sir," Roger said, "but the film we want to see isn't playing anywhere else in town."

"Randy Baldwin and his girlfriend are going to meet us there," Steve said.

"Why do I recognize that name?" I said.

"From our payroll," Steve said. "He's one of our crew leaders."

"Tom and Larry," Charles said, "are your parents okay with you going to a movie way out in the suburbs?"

"Probably," Tom said.

"Ditto," Larry said.

Charles handed Tom his cell phone and said, "Why don't you call them and make certain."

Following Charles's cue, I handed Larry my cell phone and asked him to do the same. We listened to the boys' ends of the calls and were satisfied at what we heard.

Steve had an extremely puzzled and hurt look on his face, and he said, "Was that necessary, Uncle Philip?"

"Yes, Steve," Charles said, answering for me, "it was. Tom and Larry are our guests for the weekend, and that makes us responsible. If we let the four of you go out to Gwinnett County without their parents' knowledge and you had an accident or something, we could be held legally liable."

"You didn't ask Roger to call his parents," Steve said.

"Of course not," Charles said. "When Roger moved in here, his parents signed documents allowing Philip and me to stand in loco parentis."

"What's that mean?"

"You've studied Latin," I said. "You tell me."

"Can you repeat what you said, Uncle Charles?"

"In loco parentis."

He thought about it for a minute and then said, "In the place of parents."

"Go to the head of the class, kiddo," I said. "You guys all watch television. How many programs have you seen involving a scenario where teenagers came to harm while the parents had no idea where they were or what they were doing?"

"Sorry, guys," Charles said, addressing our guests. "I'm a lawyer, and I don't believe in taking unnecessary risks."

"I understand," Tom said.

"So do I," Larry said. "I wish the parents of some of our other friends were interested enough to worry about such things."

I went to Steve, who was standing, and gave him a hug. "Steve, I promised my sister that you would never come to harm on my watch. That protection extends to your friends when they're under this roof. Do you understand?"

He hugged me back and said, "Yes, Uncle Philip, I understand. I'm sorry I got carried away."

The boys all said goodnight and headed down the hallway. Charles filled two wineglasses and handed one of them to me. "We've got a lot to look forward to," he said.

"You've got that right," I said as I raised my glass to his.

The next morning at breakfast, the four boys acted as though there'd been no tension the night before. They spent most of the morning around the pool, and after a late lunch, they left for the Mall of Georgia in my car, with Steve at the wheel.

Their movie was around three thirty, and they planned to eat afterward, promising to be home by eight.

We spent an hour in the playroom with the tribe, as we now

referred to them, and when naptime arrived, Charles and I went on a small shopping expedition, which included a visit to Lenox Square and a wine shop in Buckhead.

We were on the way back to the house when Charles said, "By the way, we have a wine tasting next week."

"I saw the flyer but didn't take time to look at it. Tell me about it."

"We are doing a horizontal tasting of Ravenswood zinfandel. It should be very interesting—same grape, same winemaker, fourteen different geographic locations."

"Geography makes that much difference?" I said.

"You bet," he said. "I can name a couple of vineyards on hillsides in Napa Valley that have three distinct microclimates, all within twenty or so acres. Each microclimate leaves its own distinct mark on the grapes."

"You're the expert."

"Hardly that, but I'm learning."

We arrived at home and took our purchases into the house. I carried the clothing we'd purchased upstairs while Charles took two cases of wine to the basement wine cellar.

We spent some time playing with the tribe; then we went to the master bedroom to unwind for a while. We'd just taken a shower and finished dressing when Charles's cell phone rang.

He answered and said, "Yes, I'll accept the charges."

He listened for a minute or two and then said, "Start from the beginning, and tell me everything."

Finally he said, "We're on our way," and he ended the call.

"What was that about?" I said.

"Steve and the others have been arrested in Gwinnett County, and we have to leave right now."

15

Charles

"ARRESTED?" Philip said. "Arrested as in jail?"

I gave it to him in twenty-five words or less and said, "Eavesdrop on my next three telephone calls and you'll know all there is to know. Meanwhile, we have to hit the road."

I grabbed my briefcase, put my PDA in my pocket, and headed downstairs. I stuck my head into the sunroom long enough to tell Gran that we were leaving and why, then dashed to the garage with Philip at my heels. As soon as I was behind the wheel of the car, I handed Philip my PDA and asked him to look up the telephone numbers of Tom's and Larry's parents. During the course of the previous summer, all of the parents of members of the swim team had become acquainted, and I'd compiled a database.

When we were on the way to the interstate, I dialed Mason, told him what had happened, and said, "Philip and I are on the way to Gwinnett County. Can you pick up Hayden and Lawrence and bring them out there?"

"Of course. Both families live nearby," he said.

"Good. I'll call both of them and tell them to expect you. Okay, babe," I said as I handed Philip my cell phone, "punch in the Lamberts' telephone number."

He did so and pushed Send. Lawrence Lambert reacted calmly to the news and agreed to wait for Mason to pick him up.

I ended the call and said, "Now enter the Hansens' number."

I made the second call with similar results. When the call ended, Philip said, "Are you sure you don't want me to drive? You know I drive a lot faster than you."

By way of answering, I pressed down on the accelerator, and the Jag shot forward. Traffic on I-85 was flowing at its usual rapid pace, and I maintained a steady seventy-five until we reached its intersection with I-285, known locally as Spaghetti Junction. I had to slow down a bit until we cleared the interchange; then I was able to accelerate once again.

Once we were off I-85 and on secondary roads, I had to slow down to a pace that was almost maddening, but we finally arrived at the facility where the boys were being held. In the parking lot, I put on my poker face. Then I marched into the building and up to the front desk and handed my card to the uniformed officer behind the desk.

"My name is Charles Barnett. I believe you're holding five of my clients here."

"Who are your clients?"

"Steven Cox, Roger Cartwright, Tom Hansen, Larry Lambert, and Randy Baldwin. They were arrested after a scuffle at the Mall of Georgia."

"Oh, you mean the queers," he said.

I looked at the uniform's nametag and said, "Sergeant Roberts, you are referring to five young men who were assaulted outside the Mall of Georgia—their sexual identity is not relevant. You will allow me to speak to my clients right now, or I will start climbing your chain of command. Do I make myself clear?"

"Yes, Sir," he said. "Please wait here."

Before he could pick up his telephone, I said, "I will also require a copy of the arrest report."

"Yes, Sir," he said as he picked up the telephone and pushed a button. After a slight pause, he said, "Hey, Joe, I got a lawyer out here. He wants to see the fags." He placed the receiver back in its cradle and looked at me. "Your clients will be in an interview room in a few minutes."

I was seething inside, but maintaining what I hoped was an icy exterior calm, I said, "And the arrest report?"

"By the time your clients are in the interview room, you'll have it," he said. He walked across the room and opened a file cabinet.

I surveyed the room for the first time and saw Philip talking to a young girl, so I walked over to them, and he said, "This is Randy's girlfriend."

The girl extended her hand and said, "Susan Myers."

"Charles Barnett," I said as I shook her hand. "Did you see what happened at the mall?"

"You bet I did. I even got most of it on my cell phone camera. The battery died right at the end of things and before the police arrived."

"Way to go, Susan. I want those pictures just as soon as you can get them to me." I pulled a small recorder out of my briefcase and turned it on, pointing the microphone in her direction. "While we wait, how about giving me your version of what happened?"

She gave me a clear and concise account of what had happened, and I said, "Thank you, Susan. That will be a great help when this case goes to court."

I heard my name being called, so I said, "Philip, you and Susan stay here and wait for Mason and the other parents while I go talk to the boys."

"We'll be right here," he said.

I walked back to the desk, and Sergeant Roberts led me down a corridor to an interview room, where I found the five boys waiting for me. They were quite a sight, and I did a quick visual inventory and spotted one black eye, a number of bruises, and some torn clothing.

"Uncle Charles," Steve said as he gave me a hug.

"Are you guys all right?" I said.

"You bet we are," Roger said.

"How about the rest of you?"

The other three boys indicated that they were okay.

"Does anybody need medical attention?"

They all indicated that they did not.

"Uncle Charles," Steve said, "they didn't arrest the guys that attacked us."

"Those bastards were let go with only a warning," Tom said.

"Okay, we'll deal with that later. Right now, I need to focus on getting you guys out of here," I said.

"Does my dad know about this?" Larry said.

"Yes. Roger's father is driving your father and Tom's father out here. You must be Randy," I said to the one boy I didn't know.

"Yes, Sir," he said.

"I'm sorry to have to meet you under these circumstances. Is there anyone I can call for you?"

"I'm pretty sure that Susan called my parents after I gave her my cell phone. She ran down her batteries filming the fight."

"She told me," I said. "She's one cool girl to think of doing that."

"She's pretty smart. I gave her my keys so she could drive my truck over here."

"Okay, this is what Susan told me happened." I told the boys what she'd said and added, "Do any of you have anything to add to her statement?"

"No, Sir," Roger said. "That's about it."

"Okay," I said. "You guys sit tight and stay cool. I'll have you out of here as quickly as I can. By the way, I need some information."

"What information?" Roger said.

"I want to go in there and tell the officers that none of you have ever been in trouble with the police before. But I want to make sure I don't get caught in a lie later." I looked at Tom and said, "How about you, Tom?"

"No, Sir, never."

"Larry?"

"Never."

"Randy?"

"No, Sir. I've never even had a speeding ticket."

"Good," I said. "I know that Steve and Roger are honor students. What about the rest of you?"

"Larry and I have straight As," Tom said.

"Randy?"

"All As and a couple of Bs," he said.

"Good," I said. "I'll go get this show on the road."

I knocked on the door, called the guard, and went back to the lobby area. Mason and the other two fathers were there waiting, along with a couple I didn't know who were introduced as Randy's parents.

After that, everyone started talking at once until I held up my hand for silence and said, "I just saw all five boys, and a few bruises and a black eye aside, they're fine. I'm going to get them out of here as quickly as I can."

I walked to the desk and said, "Sergeant Roberts, I would like you to release the boys into my custody."

"I can't do that," he said.

"Who can?"

"The sheriff."

"In that case, I suggest you call him and get him down here right now."

"I already did that. He'll be here in a few minutes."

"What about the arrest report?"

"Here it is," he said, and he handed me a few documents.

I scanned the pages quickly and turned to the sergeant. "It says here that the perpetrators weren't arrested."

"Right," he said. "The officers at the scene gave them a talking-to and sent them home."

"Yet he chose to arrest the victims," I said. "Why?"

"You'll have to ask Sheriff Barnes that," he said.

"You bet I will when he gets here."

Almost on cue, a man with a florid complexion and a huge beer gut came into the room through a back door and said, "What's going on, Sergeant?"

"Lawyer from Atlanta wants the fags released into his custody," the sergeant said.

"Does he?"

"Yes, I do," I said. "I want those five boys released, and I want the boys who started the fight arrested. I can't begin to believe that your people let them go at the scene."

"I'm not going to do that," the sheriff said.

"Then let's go to your office, and I'll call someone who can change your mind for you."

"This way," he said, and he pointed toward a door at the side of the room.

"Mason," I said, "I want you and one other parent along to witness this."

"Are these the parents?" the sheriff said.

"Yes."

"Bring 'em all along. I don't care."

The sheriff led us down another hallway, and we entered a large office. He walked around the desk, sat down, and looked up at me expectantly, so I pointed at the phone on his desk and said, "Can that telephone work as a speaker phone?"

"Yes."

"Then turn the speaker function on and dial this number." I gave him the numbers to dial.

While he punched the buttons on his telephone, I turned to Mason and the others and said, "We're calling the district attorney for this county."

After a few minutes, a voice said, "Angus Ferguson."

"Hello, Angus," I said. "Charles Barnett here."

"Charles," he said, "long time. What can I do for you?"

"I'm standing in the office of Sheriff Barnes in your county. With me are the sheriff and the parents and/or guardians of five boys who were arrested at the Mall of Georgia an hour or so ago."

"What happened?"

"The boys were at the movies this afternoon. Four of the boys are gay, and the fifth boy was there with his girlfriend. As they exited the theater, the boy with the girlfriend was holding hands with her. Two of the gay boys were also holding hands, which wasn't smart of them but hardly illegal. You can guess what happened next."

"Unfortunately, I can, but tell me anyway," Angus said.

"Four of your local tough boys took violent exception to the hand-holding. They followed the group out of the theater and began calling them names. My clients wisely ignored them, but the situation quickly escalated into pushing, shoving, and finally a full-fledged fight. As it happens, the two boys who were holding hands hold black belts in karate, and the other three boys aren't exactly slouches when it comes to self-defense, so they gave as good as they got. By the time the police got there, the four local boys were on their stomachs on the sidewalk, each with a gay boy sitting on them holding their hands behind their backs in some sort of wrestling hold."

"That works for me," Angus said. "Was anyone hurt?"

"My clients have a few bruises, at least one black eye, and some torn clothing, but otherwise no serious damage. I don't know about the perpetrators. All five of my clients are students at Exeter Academy, and four of them are on the swim team there and are honor students, as well. The fifth boy maintains an A and B average. To the best of my knowledge, none of them has ever been in trouble with the law, but I haven't verified that."

"My wife used the famous car wash a couple of times last summer when she was at Lenox," Angus said. "What's the problem and what can I do for you?"

"The problem is that the local deputies arrested the victims and let the perpetrators go. The problem is that Sheriff Barnes refuses to release the boys into my custody. I will, of course, be preferring charges against the officers involved, as well as the sheriff."

"Roscoe," Angus said, "does Mr. Barnett's account coincide with what you know of the event?"

"Pretty much," Roscoe said.

"Dammit, Roscoe, your people know better than to pull stunts like that, arresting the victims and letting the perpetrators go. What were they thinking?"

"We don't like that sort of thing here in this county," the sheriff said. "If fags are allowed to hold hands in public, where's it going to stop?"

"What you like, Roscoe, doesn't matter," Angus said. "You were elected to enforce the law, not your Pentecostal prejudices. For that matter, Roscoe, you may be sheriff, but as district attorney, I decide what gets prosecuted in this county, as well as what doesn't. You heard Mr. Barnett. He's in a position to cause a great deal of trouble for your people."

"I'm not afraid of a city lawyer."

"Well, you'd better be afraid of this one."

"Why?"

"Because he doesn't take prisoners."

"What the hell does that mean?" Roscoe said.

"Remember that big case in Atlanta a couple of years ago where the district attorney, a couple of cops, and a big-shot television preacher were busted?"

"I remember."

"That was Mr. Barnett's doing. He nailed them all and then sued them for millions and millions of dollars."

"Shit," Roscoe said.

"Just so," Angus said. "Now here's what you're going to do. You are going to release those boys into Mr. Barnett's custody right now. Got it?"

"Yes, Sir."

"And Roscoe, my wife and I are planning to attend an eight o'clock service at St. Andrew's Episcopal Church tomorrow morning. Then we're taking the kids up to Lake Lanier for the rest of the day. I'm going to call your office before I go to church, and I had better find out that the four boys who started this were picked up and formally charged and booked. They can be released to their parents afterwards, but I want them to go through the full process. Do I make myself clear?"

"Yes, Sir."

"Charles," Angus said, "is there anything else I can do for you tonight?"

"I don't think so, Angus," I said. "I'll have signed statements from the five boys and the girl in your hands Monday afternoon. By the way, the girl captured a great deal of the affair on her cell phone. I'll get you a copy of that, also."

"Isn't technology wonderful," Angus said.

"You've got that right," I said. "Thank you, Angus. Have a good weekend, or what's left of it. Next time you're in the wicked city, call me and I'll buy you lunch."

Angus broke the connection, and I looked at the sheriff. "Well?" I said.

He picked up the handset, dialed a number, and said, "Sergeant, have them bring those five boys to the front office." He replaced the handset and said, "It'll take a few minutes for them to retrieve their belongings."

"What happened to their car?" I said.

"We haven't gotten around to having it towed," he said. "It's most likely still at the mall parking lot where they left it."

"Thank you, Sheriff," I said, and I turned on my heel and left the room. Mason and the others followed me back to the lobby area.

When we were all standing around waiting, Mason said, "Damn, Charles, you put on quite a performance in there."

"It's what I do for a living, Mason," I said.

"It may be an everyday occurrence for you," Hayden Hansen said, "but it impressed the heck out of me."

"What do we do now?" Lawrence Lambert said.

"I would like everyone, parents included, to come to my house as soon as the boys are released."

"Why?" Lawrence said.

"Because I want to get statements from all five boys while everything is fresh in their minds. I'll have them transcribed by noon Monday so the boys can sign them. You heard me promise the district attorney that he'd have them on Monday."

"We don't know where you live," Randy's mother said.

"Susan, Randy knows where we live. Do you?"

"Yes, Sir. I've stopped by your house with him a couple of times when he was working for Steve and Roger."

"Good, then you can ride with his folks and direct them to the house."

A few minutes later, five very relieved-looking boys were led into the room, and there were hugs all around. I gave everyone a few minutes, then got their attention.

"Okay, folks," I said, "let's get out of here and do what we have to do. Mason, why don't you take Steve and Roger to the mall so they can retrieve Philip's car? We'll take the other two boys and be waiting for you at the house."

"Consider it done," he said.

"Steve," I said, "you guys never got a chance to have dinner, did you?"

"No, Sir."

"Not a problem. I'll call ahead and have Mrs. Goodman go into high gear. There'll be plenty of food at the house when you get there."

"Cool."

Tom and Larry followed Philip and me back to the car. "Want to drive us home, babe?" I said to Philip.

"Done."

Tom and Larry got in the backseat. Once I was settled in the passenger seat, I called Gran and brought her up to date, and I told her that we were bringing six hungry teenagers with us. She said that she'd take care of the preparations.

Charles

WHEN we arrived at the house, Philip went straight to the kitchen to see if Mrs. Goodman needed any assistance. I told Mr. Goodman that people would be arriving in groups of three or four, and the two boys and I settled down to wait. When all of our guests had assembled, I sent the kids to the dining room to eat. Then I invited the adults up to the study and offered them something to drink. When they were settled, glasses in hand, I took the floor.

"Here's how I suggest we proceed with this," I said. "As soon as the kids have eaten, I want to take them down the hall to my office one at a time and record their statements. My secretary will transcribe them first thing Monday morning, and we'll arrange to get them to your children for their signatures. I'd like to have a parent with me as I interview each of your sons."

"What else, Charles?" Mason said.

"It turns out that Randy's girlfriend caught most of the fight on her cell phone. I would like very much to make some of that public."

"How?" Tom's father said.

"I want to send a very clear message that this sort of thing isn't acceptable. I think if we make the video available for download on both YouTube and Facebook, the kids who did this will be very embarrassed. It might even discourage further attacks."

"That works for me," Larry's father said.

"I'd also like to get some of it on the news, perhaps even the eleven o'clock news tonight," I said, "but there isn't enough time to have a technician blur the faces of those involved."

"Charles," Mason said, "the boys are all minors, so their names can't be released. I don't see any problem showing their faces. It'll send a much stronger message, won't it?"

"It certainly will, provided everyone is in agreement."

Nobody objected, so I continued, "Let's see how clear the images are before we make a final decision."

Steve and Roger came into the study as I finished, and I said, "Did you get enough to eat?"

"Yes, Sir," Roger said. "The others will be done shortly."

"Good," I said. "I want the two of you to go get Susan's cell phone and download those pictures. I know it has a dead battery, but surely someone in the group has a similar model and can swap batteries with her. She might even have a charger in her purse. In any case, I want you to burn half a dozen or so DVDs with the images. Ask one of the others to come up here to make a statement. He can finish eating later."

"We can do that," Steve said, and the two boys went back downstairs.

A few minutes later, Tom appeared, and I led him down to the office, along with his dad. I dialed the office dictation system and took Tom's statement, after which I asked him a few questions.

"Okay, Tom," I said. "That was great. Now go back downstairs and send me someone else along with a parent."

Shortly after that, Larry and his dad appeared, and I repeated the process. It didn't take very long to interview all five boys. Since I already had Susan's statement, I didn't ask her to repeat herself.

We once again assembled in the study, and Steve set up a copy of the DVD to play for the group. We watched the fight in silent fascination. The images were a little blurred at times, but it was great theater.

"Okay," I said. "Do any of you participants have any objection to this video being uploaded to YouTube or Facebook or, for that matter, local television stations? I've already asked your parents."

"Why do you want to do that, Mr. Barnett?" Roger said.

"To make a point. To embarrass the attackers. To possibly discourage other kids from doing the same thing. Because all of you are minors, your names can't be released to anyone. The images are just fuzzy enough that it would be virtually impossible to identify you. Think about the impact it will have when the narrator says some rednecks tried to beat up several gay guys and wound up on the ground down for the count."

"I don't care if anyone identifies me," Steve said. "We're all 'out' at school, and nobody cares."

"What about you, Randy?" I said. "You're not gay."

"I'm not worried," he said.

"How about the rest of you?" I said.

The other three boys expressed sentiments similar to Steve's.

"That's all well and good, but the decision has to be made with the approval of your parents or guardians," I said. "Before we discuss that, there's something else I need to say. Tom, do you and Larry realize that holding hands in public wasn't the smartest thing you've ever done?"

"Yes, Sir," Tom said.

"It was kind of a spur of the moment thing, and we really didn't think anyone would mind," Larry said, "but looking back, it was kind of dumb."

"Good," I said, "then you've learned something today, haven't you?"

"Yes, Sir," both boys said.

"How are you going to proceed, Charles?" Mason said.

"First, with the help of my friend Angus Ferguson, I intend to make certain that the four boys who started this thing are prosecuted. They need to learn that certain kinds of behavior aren't acceptable. Second, I'm almost certain that I can get all charges against these five boys dismissed and probably get the arrest record expunged. Third, I will definitely file charges against the arresting officers and possibly the sheriff. I certainly didn't like the way the personnel in that office acted."

"In what way?" Lawrence said.

"When I went to the desk and asked to see my clients, the sergeant referred to them as 'that bunch of queers'. Then, when he called someone in the back to arrange for the interview, he told that person that a lawyer was there to see 'the fags'. That's not the kind of language I expect to hear from public servants."

"Uncle Charles?"

"Yes, Steve?"

"There was at least one deputy who didn't feel that way. He kind of went out of his way to be nice to us."

Roger said, "That's right. Maybe if you talked to him privately you might learn something about that office."

"That's good thinking," I said. "Do any of you remember his name?"

"I think his nametag said Higgs, or Biggs, or something like that," Steve said.

"It was Briggs," Larry said.

"Good. I'll look into it," I said. Then I added, almost as an afterthought, "I wish we had the names of a couple of the onlookers."

"I got a couple of names and telephone numbers," Susan said. "I guess in the excitement I forgot to mention it."

"Good girl," I said. "That will be extremely helpful."

"Do any of you parents have any problem going after these people?" I said.

One by one, Philip, Mason, and the others said no.

"Should we sue them?" Philip said.

"Absolutely. As soon as the dust has settled and the charges against these boys have been dropped, we should file suits alleging false arrest and a number of other things. We probably ought to sue the families of the boys who started this, as well. Winning a suit like that is more about making a point, and making it very publicly, than winning money."

"Good," Mason said. "Now, about that video. If Roger doesn't mind the uncensored version being released, I certainly don't."

Again, the other parents agreed one by one.

Eventually everyone ran out of things to say, and Randy and Susan left, followed by his parents.

Hayden Hansen said, "Ready to go home, Tom?"

"If it's okay, Dad," Tom said, "I'd rather stay here and finish the weekend. Mom will get a bit upset if she sees the way I look right now, and I'll look better tomorrow. Can't I stay?"

"Only if you call your mother right now and tell her what's going on."

"Why don't you and Lawrence bring your families over tomorrow afternoon, Hayden?" I said. "We can have an informal brunch around the pool, and everyone will have had some time to put the events of the evening in perspective."

"That goes for you and Angela as well, Mason," Philip said.

"Okay," Mason said. "We'll see you tomorrow, say around two o'clock?"

"That's fine," I said.

We saw the last of our guests out and returned to the study with the four boys.

"Uncle Philip," Steve said, "have you and Uncle Charles ever held hands in public?"

"To tell you the truth, Steve, Charles and I don't go in for public displays of affection," Philip said. "But to answer your question, yes, we did hold hands in public once."

"But it was on Castro Street in San Francisco, where we were absolutely certain that nobody would object," I said.

The four boys went down the hall, presumably to watch television. As soon as I was sure they were settled down for the night, I called Brian Scott, a reporter with one of the local television stations, and told him what I had to offer. Thirty minutes later, he appeared at our doors, accompanied by a cameraman.

I took them up to the study, where Philip was waiting, and introduced Brian and his cameraman to Philip. Then I played the DVD for them. I gave them a copy of the video; then we went back downstairs to the library, where Brian interviewed me. I pulled no punches in describing the prejudice of the sheriff and his deputies.

When I showed them to the door, Brian said, "This is great stuff, Mr. Barnett. I owe you one."

As soon as I was back upstairs, I knocked on Steve and Roger's door and told them that the video would be on the eleven o'clock news. After that, I went to the computer and e-mailed an account of the arrest to my contact at the newspaper, attaching a copy of the video.

I went back to the study, where I found Philip and Gran, glasses of wine in hand. I collapsed on the sofa and said, "Can I ask you to pour me one of those?"

Wordlessly, Philip complied. He also handed me a plate of sandwiches, saying, "We never got around to eating."

"I suppose Mrs. Goodman has retired by now," I said.

"Of course," Gran said. "Why do you ask?"

"I forgot to give her a heads-up about tomorrow afternoon."

"Been there, done that," Philip said.

"I hope you asked her politely not to try to do it all herself," I said.

"I did, but it was a waste of breath. You know how she is about feeding people, especially kids."

"Well, at the very least we'll get some steaks for the adults and hamburger for the kids, and we can grill the meat right there by the pool," I said.

"I, for one, am glad to know that our boys gave a good account of themselves," Gran said. "You know that I don't approve of fighting, but self-defense is another matter entirely."

"Oh, they certainly did that," I said. "The boys who started it will think twice before they pick on anybody else."

After Gran said goodnight and went to her quarters, Philip and I settled down in the study to wait for the news. It must have been a slow news day, because the station devoted nearly a third of the news portion of the broadcast to the story. The video was shown in its entirety, complete with a voice-over narration, and the interview I'd given ran virtually uncut.

When the newscast was over, I turned the television off and said, "It's time to climb the well-worn stairs, speaking metaphorically. Tomorrow will be a very busy day. By the way, did you pick up vibes from Brian Scott?"

"Oh, yes. He's definitely family."

I held out my hand. "Ready to go to bed?"

"Let's check on the tribe first," he said.

We did just that, then settled down in our comfortable bed for a well-deserved rest.

The first page of the local section of Sunday's paper featured the picture showing the four boys on their stomachs, each with another boy sitting on them. The headline was priceless—"Gays 4 - Bullies 0 in Mall of Georgia Incident." The article quoted me almost verbatim.

I showed it to Philip, who scanned the article and said, "Too bad we can't get that picture and article pinned on a few bulletin boards at whatever schools those boys attend."

"Who says we can't?"

"Handle it, babe, handle it."

"You bet I will."

The brunch/pool party Sunday was a success. In addition to Susan and the five boys, all of the parents were present, along with six or seven younger siblings.

We'd made an early run to Publix and acquired steaks, ground chuck, and hot dogs, along with soft drinks, paper plates, and cups. Mr. Goodman set up a number of folding tables, and Mrs. Goodman produced an amazing variety of dishes to complement the meat coming off the grill.

The kids spent most of the time in the pool. Grace brought Mark and Steven down for a while, and Steve and Roger took them into the pool. The toddlers wore protective diapers to keep any "accidents" from fouling the water. We'd started swimming lessons for them shortly before their first birthday. They were both comfortable in the water and protested loudly when Grace announced that it was time to go back to the house.

A point arrived at which things were quiet because nearly

everyone was eating. I stood up and tapped a knife on my glass and said, "Philip and I are pleased that all of you could join us today. But this isn't about us, this is about five boys. Belay that, this is about five young men who found themselves in a very difficult situation and handled themselves and the situation better than anyone could have expected. Let's raise our glasses to Steve, Roger, Tom, Larry, and Randy, as well as to Susan, who had the presence of mind to not only film the event but acquire the names of two eyewitnesses."

"Hear, hear," several adults said as we raised our glasses.

When things were quiet again, Steve said, "Thank you, Uncle Charles, for that and for getting us out of jail last night."

There was an embarrassingly long round of applause. Then I smiled and said, "Okay. Thanks. However, it isn't over until the fat lady sings, and right now she's just warming up in the wings. We still have to nail the bad guys, and by bad guys, I mean the boys who started things and the sheriff's department who handled it so poorly."

"We saw the newscast last night and the article in the paper this morning. However did you manage that?" Mason said.

"In cases like this, the media can be your best friend or your worst enemy, and I've had a fair amount of experience in keeping them on my side," I said.

"You just tell us what to do and when to do it," Hayden Hansen said.

"And send us a bill as you go," Mason said.

"Well, I'll certainly keep you posted, but as for a bill, I don't know. Nailing the bad guys in situations like this is so much fun I hate to charge anyone for it. Besides, Steve and Roger are family."

"Perhaps," Mason said, "but there will be expenses, won't there?"

"You bet, and I'll gladly accept your help in covering them. We have a great deal of research to do, and that will take time. The best thing to do now is to carry on as though nothing happened."

The group left things at that, and conversation switched to other topics, including the Speedos Car Wash, which was scheduled to resume on the first weekend in May.

Rosemary transcribed all of the statements early Monday

morning, and she and I took them out to the school after lunch. One by one, the boys were called to the dean's office, where we were waiting, and Rosemary notarized each statement as it was signed. Susan and Randy's school was nearby, so we stopped by so they could sign their statements as well. Once we were back in the office, Rosemary made a number of copies and sent one set to Angus Ferguson by courier, along with a copy of the DVD.

Meanwhile, I called Richard and engaged his services to interview Deputy Briggs at his home, if possible, so that he wouldn't get into trouble for talking to us.

We learned on Tuesday that the case against the Reverend Wilson and his church was about to be settled—the other side had blinked. Wilson had agreed to write an op-ed piece for the paper, the language of which had to be approved and agreed to by the plaintiffs. He'd also agreed to make a public statement from the pulpit.

Life resumed its normal pace for a couple of weeks until Steve and Roger came home from work late one afternoon. As it happened, I'd come home a little earlier than usual, and Philip and I were sitting in the study when the boys popped in.

"Uncle Charles," Steve said, "we need to talk to you as soon as we shower and change, okay?"

"I'm not planning to go anywhere," I said, and they went down the hall.

The two boys appeared some time later, fresh from the shower and, I suspected from the looks on their faces, a quickie.

I said, "Okay, guys, what's up?"

17

Charles

"EVERY time we go out to Gwinnett County to do a job, a deputy sheriff starts following us," Steve said.

"It's almost like they're watching for us," Roger said. "They even pulled us over a couple of times last week and again this week."

"They don't give us a ticket or anything, they just take a lot of time looking at our licenses, registration, and insurance. Then they inspect the truck and trailer to see if they can find anything wrong. They also make a few nasty comments about cocksuckers and stuff," Steve said.

"We always have one or two helpers with us who are earning ten dollars an hour while all this is going on, and it's costing us," Roger said.

"It costs even more when the truck is driven by our crew chief," Steve said.

I asked a few questions and listened to their answers. Finally, I said, "This is a job for super sleuth."

"Who?" Roger said.

"Who do we know that detects for a living?" Philip said.

"Richard Greene," Steve said.

"Bingo."

I got Richard on the phone and asked him to come over after dinner in an official capacity. We went downstairs for dinner with the family and were back in the study waiting when Richard and Bruce arrived.

"What's up, Charley?" Richard said without preamble as he entered the room.

"This involves the incident at the Mall of Georgia," I said. "Remember? You interviewed Deputy Briggs for me."

"Right."

"Steve and Roger are being harassed by deputies every time they go into Gwinnett County, and I want you to document it for us."

He nodded, and I continued, "The boys will give you their schedule for visits to customers in that county, and every time they get in their truck to head that way, I want someone discreetly following them. I want to document the fact that they're being followed and occasionally stopped and harassed, and I want them wired for audio and video. If you can't get the names of the officers on film, at the very least I want to be able to identify them and their county vehicles. Plus anything else you can think of that might help."

"You've got it, Charley," Richard said.

"I just had a great idea," I said.

"Are you going to keep it a secret?" Richard said.

"Let me run it by you," I said, and I did so.

"I like it," Richard said.

"Me too," Philip said.

"Steve, you and Roger can go do your homework while I call this guy and get him over here," I said. "If he agrees to do this, I'll introduce you after a bit."

The boys gave Richard a copy of their schedule and exchanged contact numbers with him. They said goodnight and went to their room to do their homework. I placed a call to Brian Scott and told him I had a part-time job for him, if he wanted it. I gave him just enough hints to entice him to come over right away. He said he would be over in half an hour.

We poured some wine for our guests and visited while we waited for Brian to arrive. True to his word, Brian was at our door thirty minutes later, and I led him upstairs to the study, where the others were waiting.

"Brian," I said, "this is Richard Greene and his partner Bruce Lawson. You already know my partner, Philip. Guys, this is Brian Scott, ace television reporter."

Philip gave Brian a glass of wine, and I gave him a few minutes to get acquainted with the others. Then I said, "Okay, Brian, here's the deal. You remember reporting on the incident at the Mall of Georgia?"

"Of course. I got a lot of brownie points with my boss out of that one."

"Two of the boys that were attacked operate a lawn care and landscaping service, and they have a number of clients in Gwinnett County. Ever since the Mall of Georgia incident, they've been harassed by deputies every time they enter that county."

"You sort of hinted at that on the phone, and I think it's terrible."

"So it is, and we're going to do something about it. Starting next week, one of Richard's investigators will be following the boys' truck every time they enter Gwinnett County. The boys are going to be wired for video and sound, and the investigator will be filming everything that happens. I'd like to have one of your cameramen with the investigator, and I'd like to have you in the jump seat of the boys' truck. You look young enough to pass as one of their employees, especially if you wear a baseball cap and kind of keep your head down. Are you interested?"

"Am I interested?" he said. "Of course I am. This is a chance to strike a blow for our side."

"I told you he was family," Philip said kind of smugly.

"My partner is justifiably proud of his 'gaydar'," I said. "That aside, the important thing in all of this is that you have to sit on this story for a while."

"How long?" Brian said.

"Until we have enough evidence to convince a judge to issue an injunction ordering the sheriff's office to cease and desist."

"How long do you think that will take?" Brian said.

"Two, possibly three weeks," I said.

"I don't have a problem with that," he said.

"What about your boss? Will he or she grant you that much leeway?"

"After the scoop you gave me last time, my boss will give me all the leeway I want."

"Good. I can promise you at least an hour of lead time after the judge issues an injunction. If you have your report ready to roll, that should give you a leg up over the competition."

"An hour is more than enough," he said. "We can headline it as a breaking news story."

"Let me introduce you to the boys."

"They're here?" he said.

"Steve is Philip's nephew," I said. "His boyfriend, Roger, lives here also."

"There must be a story behind that."

"True, but since they're minors, it can't be published without the respective parents' permission," I said. "Are you familiar with the recent lawsuit against that Baptist preacher and his church?"

"Yes, I am."

"Roger's parents let him live here with us because his younger brothers were two of the preacher's victims," I said. "After Roger came out to his family, his brothers were constantly telling him that he was going to Hell because he was gay."

"The bastard," Brian said.

"That about sums it up. Philip, why don't you ask the boys to join us?"

Philip went down the hall and returned a few minutes later with Steve and Roger. We introduced the boys to Brian and told them what we'd decided. "So, guys," I said, "want to take on a new and somewhat temporary employee?"

"You bet we do, Uncle Charles," Steve said.

"All right," I said. "Let's get this thing organized."

We spent another half an hour planning our little operation. The boys said goodnight a second time and went back to their room.

At our invitation, Brian hung around long enough to have another glass of wine. He left when Richard and Bruce did, and Philip and I went to the door to see them out.

Two weeks later, we had Mason, Angela, and their younger sons over to dinner. I noted with interest that the younger boys' attitude toward Roger appeared to be thawing just a bit. After dinner, Roger's brothers were picked up by their grandmother, and the rest of us retired to the upstairs study, where we were joined a little later by Brian Scott.

I introduced Brian to the Cartwrights, who already knew what we'd been up to, and gave him the floor, saying, "I understand you have something to show us, Brian."

"Two somethings, actually," he said. He handed me a DVD and asked me to play it, saying, "This is the piece that we're going to run on the early news next week, just as soon as you get your injunction and give me a heads-up."

We watched the DVD with interest. It was a clear and concise report detailing the harassment the boys had been experiencing. Brian had even concealed a tiny camera in his hat and had captured some very up close and personal shots of various deputies giving Steve and Roger a hard time, complete with crude or vulgar comments.

In his voice-over commentary, Brian managed to convey the fear he'd felt while sitting in the cab of the truck experiencing the harassment. The film ended with a summary of the legal action I'd taken, and included a reference to one deputy's sworn statement that they had been ordered to "have some fun with the fags."

The segment ended, and we all congratulated Brian on a job well done. Then I said, "What's the 'other something' you wanted to show us, Brian?"

"Well," he said, "Steve and Roger have probably told you that in addition to the trips to Gwinnett County, I've been following them around with a cameraman for the past week. I've put together a twenty-minute human-interest story on two teenagers who are working hard to pay for their education, even though they didn't have to do so. I'd like very much to obtain permission from you folks to run the piece."

"Let's have a look at it," I said.

Brian handed me another DVD, and I inserted it in the machine in place of the one we'd just seen.

The story was extremely well done. Brian had evidently interviewed the two boys at length before paring the interviews down to just enough details to get a sense of their lives, including the reason that Steve was living in Atlanta. They'd even been interviewed on the school campus, standing in front of the administration building, and some footage from the previous summer's car wash had been thrown in for good measure.

The camera picked up a typical day for them, beginning with practice with the swim team, which was their last school activity every day, and following them from school to several of their jobs. There was some amusing speeded-up footage of Steve, Roger, and two of their employees mowing, trimming, and edging, followed by a brief interview with the four boys in their sweat-soaked T-shirts after a hard afternoon's work. The story ended with a slightly longer version of the previous video we'd been shown.

When it ended, I turned off the television, and Philip broke the silence, saying, "Wow, that's prize-winning material."

"It certainly is," Mason said.

"The question is," Brian said, "can I use it? My boss wants to run it in four or five segments over several evenings."

"Mason, Angela, what do you think?" Philip said.

"I don't have a problem with it," Angela said.

"Neither do I," Mason said.

"Steve, are you and Roger okay with this?" I said.

"Yes, Sir," Steve said. "We think it's kind of cool."

"Especially since we got in a plug for this summer's car wash and the Jimmy Anderson Memorial Scholarship," Roger said.

"Then I say go for it," Philip said.

"Just one thing, Brian," I said.

"What?"

"I want some assurance that what will be aired is pretty much what we just saw. It would be very easy for someone to chop it up a bit and place the boys in a bad light."

"If you're worried about any rampant homophobia at the station," Brian said, "you needn't be. I have total editorial control over this story, and more importantly, my boss backs me completely."

Mason and Philip signed the necessary consent forms, and Brian left. When I came back upstairs, I said, "Mason, was it my imagination, or were your two younger boys just a little less uptight than before?"

"It's a subtle difference, but I think you're right."

"They've still got a very long way to go," Angela said.

18

Charles

THE following Friday I was in Gwinnett County, waiting to see Angus Ferguson. When I was shown into his office, Angus stood to greet me, and we shook hands. He was about my height with thinning blond hair, appeared to be fairly fit, and was still a year or so on the good side of forty. He said, "I saw your name on my appointment list, Charles, and I assumed it had something to do with the Mall of Georgia incident."

"It does, but not in the way you might think. I'm about to file some fairly serious charges against Sheriff Barnes. Take a quick look at these documents, and we'll talk."

I handed him a file folder and settled down to wait for him to peruse the documents it contained. It took a while for him to digest everything I'd placed in front of him, but finally, he put the file down and said, "That stupid son of a bitch."

"I couldn't have said it better myself. I'm going to file the suit, and then I'm going to ask Judge Hampton to grant a temporary injunction putting a stop to the harassment."

"Judge Hampton has a heavy schedule. Do you have an appointment?"

"Yes, I do, and I've scheduled a press conference on the courthouse steps for about an hour after that. Want to go with me?"

"You bet I do. Give me a minute to return two calls."

Angus went with me to the clerk's office and waited while I filed my paperwork and obtained some certified copies. From there, we went to Judge Hampton's office, where a plump middle-aged lady politely asked us to take a seat. After a short wait, we were ushered into the judge's chambers.

Judge William Hampton rose to greet us as we entered his office. He was a tall, distinguished-looking, and very thin black man. It was difficult to judge his age, but I guessed him to be pushing sixty. He greeted Angus warmly, and when Angus introduced me, the judge said, "I'm pleased to finally meet you, Mr. Barnett. I've watched your career with a great deal of interest, and I must say you've accomplished a lot in just a few years."

"It's mostly a case of being in the right place at the right time and knowing the right people," I said.

"Don't be modest, young man," he said. "Some of what you say may be true, but if you didn't have what it takes, you wouldn't be where you are today."

"Thank you, but I have to ask why you've been following my career."

"Because when your grandfather was first appointed to the federal bench, he saw potential in a young, wet-behind-the-ears colored boy from Augusta and made me his first law clerk. I'd just finished my first year of law school at the time and in a lot of ways, those two years with Judge Barnett were the best two years of my life. Your grandfather had one of the finest legal minds I've ever encountered. There were a lot of folks back then, myself included, who thought that, had he lived, Judge Barnett would have been on the Supreme Court in a few short years." The judge sat back in his chair, and there was a faraway look in his eyes for a moment or two.

When he came back to the present, he said, "Have you ever considered following in your grandfather's footsteps?"

"The thought has crossed my mind from time to time, but right now I enjoy what I'm doing too much to give it up. Ask me again in twenty years or so."

"If I'm still around in twenty years, I may do just that," he said. "Have a seat, gentlemen, and tell me what brings a prominent Atlanta attorney to our little corner of the world."

"Your Honor, I've just filed a lawsuit charging the sheriff of this county with misfeasance, malfeasance, and a few other things. I'm here to ask you to issue a temporary injunction in the matter."

"Those are serious charges. Please elaborate," Judge Hampton said.

"I'd be happy to, Your Honor. Are you familiar with an incident that took place at the Mall of Georgia a few weeks ago, where some local rednecks went after four gay boys and a straight friend of theirs?"

"I know a little bit about the case. Why don't you start at the beginning and fill me in?" he said.

I gave him a quick summary of the incident, and Angus said, "The deputies arrested the victims at the scene and allowed the instigators to walk. Later, when Mr. Barnett called me from the sheriff's office, I directed Roscoe to release the victims into Mr. Barnett's custody. I also directed Roscoe to have the instigators picked up, booked, and then released to their parents."

"The parents of the victims have pending actions against the families of the boys who started the fight, and I've filed charges against the sheriff and his department," I said. "Which brings us to the present problem."

"And that would be?" the judge said.

"Do you have a DVD player and a television set in your chamber?" I said.

"I do. Why do you ask?"

"If you have a few minutes, I can show you the reason for the suit," I said. "Two of the victims in that incident operate a lawn care and landscaping service. Ever since that incident, the boys have been harassed by deputies nearly every time they enter this county. I've had a reporter riding in the backseat every time one of the boys' trucks entered your county for a period of two weeks, and he's been working on a human-interest story about two teenagers running a business to pay for their education. The miniature camera he wore while in their trucks caught three different deputies in action."

I pulled a DVD out of my briefcase and handed it to him.

The judge went to one side of his chambers and opened what I'd taken to be an armoire, revealing a well-equipped media center. He picked up a remote control and turned the equipment on, placing the DVD in the player. After a couple of minutes, a menu displayed on the screen.

"Track one is a rough cut of the full story," I said. "Tracks two through seven contain raw footage taken in the cab of the truck on different days."

The three of us sat through the story and three of the other tracks before the judge turned the device off, saying, "Enough."

I said, "As mentioned in the piece we just watched, deputies have even interviewed some of the boys' customers, telling them that the boys are 'under investigation' for things unspecified."

"Are you certain that the sheriff is aware of what his people are doing?"

"Yes, Your Honor. I have affidavits from three of the boys' customers. I also have affidavits from two of the deputies to the effect that they were personally ordered by Sheriff Barnes to 'have a little fun with the fags' whenever they could."

"Oh, my sweet Jesus, the man has lost his mind," Judge Hampton said.

"Either that or he's living in the wrong century," I said.

"He's certainly totally out of control," Angus said. "I'm planning to launch a grand jury investigation of the sheriff and his department."

"I should certainly hope so," Judge Hampton said. "When will the story we just watched be aired?"

"The reporter agreed to sit on it until after I filed suit," I said. "I understand that it will be aired in four or five segments sometime next week."

"I trust you've given Mr. Ferguson a copy of these videos."

"Oh, yes, that and much more."

"Good. May I see your complaint?"

"Certainly," I said, and I handed him the file.

He quickly scanned the complaint and glanced at the attached affidavits. He put the file down after a few minutes and said, "Your writing style reminds me of your grandfather. Clearly you think like he did."

"I'm flattered that you think I'm anywhere close to being in his league."

"Oh, you are. I spent two years doing research for Judge Barnett, and during that time I became well acquainted with his thought processes, and those same processes show up in your pleadings. Let's have a look at that injunction."

I reached into my briefcase, pulled out the document, and handed it to him. He read the document, then took a pen from a holder on his desk and scratched through a few things on the page. He punched a button on his intercom and said, "May Belle, can you come in here for a minute?"

The middle-aged lady from the outer office came into the room and walked up to the judge's desk.

"May Belle, this is an order granting an injunction," he said. "I want you to retype it exactly as you see it, except those places where I have scratched through the word 'temporary'."

She took the document, said, "Yes, Sir," and she was about to leave the room when I stopped her.

"Excuse me, Ma'am," I said.

"Yes, Sir?"

"I have that document on a thumb drive. It will save you some work if you care to use it and you have access to WordPerfect."

"Is there any other word processing program?" she said with a smile.

"Not in my office," I said. I fished the thumb drive out of my briefcase and handed it to her.

"Thank you," she said, and she left the room.

The judge looked at us and said, "What those boys have been going through is frighteningly reminiscent of what my people used to go through back in the day."

"I totally agree," I said. "However, I'm not sure some of the more vocal black activists would concur."

"Those people," Judge Hampton said, and he snorted with contempt, "seem to think that they have a patent on suffering, and no other group's pain even comes close to theirs."

"You know, Judge, this whole situation is going to stir up the proverbial hornet's nest in this county," Angus said.

"I know," the judge said with a sigh, "but we'll just have to muddle our way through it."

Our conversation was interrupted by May Belle, who entered the office bearing a document, which she handed to the judge.

He read through it and handed it to me.

I looked it over and said, "That's fine with me."

"Good," he said. He signed it with a flourish and handed it back to his secretary. "You know what to do with this, May Belle. After you've processed it, bring Mr. Barnett two or three certified copies."

"Yes, Sir," she said, and she left the office once again.

"Wow," I said. "She's as efficient as my secretary."

"May Belle has been with me for a decade, and she's a treasure," he said.

We made small talk for a minute or two before May Belle returned with three certified copies of the injunction. She handed them to Judge Hampton, and he handed them to me.

"I expect you're going to hand this to the sheriff yourself," he said.

"I certainly am, and then Angus and I are going to hold a small press conference on the courthouse steps."

Judge Hampton told me again how pleased he was to have finally met me, and as Angus and I prepared to leave his office, he added, "Give my regards to your grandmother. I still remember her many kindnesses from all those years ago."

Angus led me across the judicial complex to a building I recognized as the one in which Steve and the others had been held. While we were walking, I called Brian on my cell phone. When he answered, I said, "We have our injunction. You may proceed when ready."

He thanked me and ended the call.

Angus and I entered the sheriff's office and found him at his desk. Angus didn't waste any time with preliminary chitchat. "Roscoe, you remember Mr. Barnett, don't you?" he said.

"How could I forget?" the sheriff said.

"He's just given me a batch of paperwork that involves your department," Angus said.

"What do you mean?"

"I mean that your deputies have been harassing two of the boys that were involved in that affair at the Mall of Georgia," Angus said. "They have a lawn care and landscaping business, and every time they come into Gwinnett County your deputies are following them, stopping them, and harassing them."

"Says who?" the sheriff said.

"Says the two boys. Says several of their employees. Says a firm of private investigators, who have been following them around for two weeks, taking video and some audio of your deputies' activities. What the hell were you thinking, Roscoe?" Angus said. "Your people have even interviewed several of the boys' customers, telling them that the boys are 'under investigation'."

Roscoe started to babble an explanation, but Angus cut him off, saying, "That was a rhetorical question, Roscoe. I told you not to mess with Mr. Barnett, and I know perfectly well what you've been up to. I even have sworn affidavits from two of your deputies, stating that they've been directed to harass the boys. I also have affidavits from the boys' customers."

"We were just having a bit of fun," Roscoe said.

"Fun!" Angus said. "Fun? Let me tell you what your 'fun' has accomplished. Mr. Barnett has just filed a lawsuit charging you with a list of crimes too long to mention. He also has an injunction signed by Judge Hampton, which orders you to stop harassing those boys. Your idea of 'fun' is going to wind up costing the taxpayers of this county millions of dollars."

I took that as my cue to toss a certified copy of the injunction on the sheriff's desk.

"Okay, you've made your point. I'll put a stop to it," Roscoe said.

"It's too late," I said. "Judge Hampton has already put a stop to it."

"If you're smart, you'll do more than that, Roscoe," Angus said. "I'm going to launch a grand jury investigation of your department, which will very likely end with your removal from office. You might possibly save your pension by resigning immediately, but even that won't stop the investigation."

Before the sheriff could reply, Angus turned to leave the room and said, "Let's go, Charles, before I really lose my temper."

We returned to the courthouse and were waiting on the steps when the first reporters began to arrive. When the appointed time came, I spoke up. "As many of you know, I'm Charles Barnett, senior partner of Chandler, Todd, Woodward & Barnett in Atlanta. With me is Angus Ferguson, district attorney for Gwinnett County."

Brian, who was in the front row of the assembled reporters, took this as his cue and said, "Why are we here, Mr. Barnett?"

I proceeded to tell them that Judge Hampton had just granted an injunction and why. Then I turned things over to Angus, who detailed his intention to launch a grand jury investigation of the sheriff's department. We entertained their questions for twenty minutes or so before things wound down.

The reporters left to send in their stories, and Angus walked with me back to where I was parked. As I was about to enter my car, I said, "Thank you, Angus. I owe you."

"I'm not sure who owes who at this point, but you're welcome," he said.

"I'll be in touch," I said, and I closed the door.

When I arrived at the house, Philip was waiting for me in the study and said, "I've got the breaking news story on disc for you, and you're going to love it. Our boy beat the competition by almost an hour."

"Give me ten minutes to shower and change."

Exactly ten minutes later, I was in the study with a glass of wine in my hand and said, "Okay, roll tape. Hmm, I wonder if there's a newer word to use when it's not really tape?"

He ignored me and pushed a button on the recorder. Then we sat back to watch the early news. The newscast started with a close-up of Brian Scott, who said, "This is Brian Scott reporting for Channel 2. I have spent nearly three weeks conducting an undercover investigation of the Gwinnett County Sheriff's Office."

He went into considerable detail, starting with the Mall of Georgia incident and ending with an account of his undercover experiences. The report switched to video excerpts of deputies stopping Steve and Roger's truck and audio of some of the things that the deputies had said.

"This reporter was sitting in the jump seat in the truck during several of the above encounters, and I can tell you that it was frightening in the extreme. These two boys and their employees have been subjected to harassment and verbal abuse of the worst sort for no reason at all other than that the two boys are gay.

"Earlier this afternoon, Judge William Hampton of Gwinnett County issued an injunction ordering the sheriff's office to cease the harassment. This reporter is reliably informed that a lawsuit has been filed, charging the sheriff with misfeasance, malfeasance, and numerous other crimes. We have also learned that a grand jury will be conducting an investigation of the sheriff's office."

Philip muted the sound at that point, and I said, "Way to go, Brian."

"The five o'clock news was pretty much a repeat of what we just watched, with the addition of a plug for the human-interest story next week," Philip said. "I recorded it, as well, in case you want to watch."

"Thanks, babe, but this one is enough."

It being "gang" night, we spent some time in the Jacuzzi, discussing the events of the day with the gang.

"So, Charley, I guess this means 'case closed' and we can stop the surveillance," Richard said.

"I'm not so sure about that," I said.

"Why, Uncle Charles?" Steve said.

"When the DA and I visited the sheriff and I handed him the

injunction, there was a lot of residual defiance in his attitude, and I saw something in his eyes that bothers me."

"Do you think he'll try something?" Philip said.

"I don't know. However, I prefer to err on the side of caution."

"Does that mean you want me to continue the surveillance?" Richard said.

"Yes. At least for another week or two. In addition, does anyone at the Georgia Bureau of Investigation owe you any favors?"

"Actually, one of the top guys over there owes me a big one," Richard said.

"Good. In that case, here's what I'd like you to do." I outlined a brief plan of action.

Richard thought about it for a full minute and said, "We can set that up, no problem."

Later, as we were all dressing, John said, "Don't forget tomorrow evening. Joe is going to pull out all the Italian food stops."

"That's right. I'm digging deeply into my grandmother's recipes," Joe said.

"Is this a special occasion?" Philip said.

"You might say that, but it's a secret for now," John said.

19

Philip

SATURDAY evening Charles and I arrived in midtown at the appointed time. It was the first time we'd been back to the townhouse since we'd sold the place to Richard and Bruce.

Bruce greeted us at the door and suggested that we go up to the study so we could all be convenient to the kitchen, where Joe was hard at work. We followed Bruce upstairs, where we found Joe at the counter, wearing an apron and stirring something on the stove. John, similarly attired, was nearby working on a salad.

Charles set four bottles of wine on the counter, saying, "We brought two each of a red and a white, just in case. All of the bottles are fresh from our wine cellar."

Joe examined the bottles and said, "Wow, Santa Margherita pinot grigio. That's the best, but I don't recognize the red wine."

"It's a Super Tuscan," Charles said. "Tenuta dell'Ornellia. I think you'll like it very much."

"Thanks," Joe said. "We're always willing to learn more about wine. Dinner will be on the table soon."

"Why don't you open the Santa Margherita and take it into the study?" John said, handing Charles a corkscrew.

Charles opened the wine and carried the bottle into the study as directed. Richard rose from his chair to greet us, and Charles handed him the bottle, making pouring motions. Bruce produced six glasses, and Richard carefully divided the contents of the bottle between them. Bruce carried two of the glasses to the kitchen before returning to the study.

We sipped our wine in silence. We'd all been together the evening before, so there wasn't a lot of catching up to do. I looked around at the study and saw that Richard and Bruce had added a few personal touches, but it was very much the same room it had been before Charles and I had vacated the premises.

Before any conversation could get underway, John joined us and said, "Dinner will be on the table in five minutes."

"What's on the menu?" Charles said.

"Ossobuco alla Milanese. It was one of Grandma Cacci's specialties. There will also be pasta and homemade garlic bread on the side."

"Sounds good to me, and I know Philip loves it," Charles said.

"The red wine will do it justice," I said.

"Too right, babe," Charles said.

We'd been talking about nothing in particular for a few minutes when Joe entered the study. He'd removed his apron, had one arm pressed to his stomach, and a white towel was neatly folded across his forearm. He intoned, "Dinner is served."

We followed him to the dining room, where we found the table set very formally, complete with place cards and napkin rings. Joe asked us to sit while he and John served. That being done, he and John took their places. The food was superb, and we all told Joe so at length.

The conversation at the table ranged freely over a number of subjects before it wound down. Finally, Charles said, "Okay, guys. What's the occasion?"

"We thought you'd never ask," John said.

"You know that John and I have been making do with just one car for more than a year now, right?" Joe said.

"Yes," I said.

"You won't believe how much money that has saved us, what with car payments, gas, insurance, and other things," John said.

"And both of us are pulling the occasional double shift," Joe said.

"The bottom line is we reached our goal with the nest egg, and we've found a house," John said.

"Great," Charles said. "Where?"

"Just around the corner. If you look out the back windows of this house, you can almost see it," Joe said.

"Right. It's a smaller town house one street over," John said.

"We almost didn't get it," Joe said. "The bank had approved us, but they wanted an obscene interest rate, which would have made the payments a bit out of our comfort zone, even with 10 percent down."

"We told the Realtor that, and he came back with an offer from the owners, something called Midtown Properties, LLC. They agreed to carry the mortgage themselves with a fixed interest rate at prime plus one point," John said.

"It turns out they're liquidating a lot of their holdings, and there are tax advantages for them to do what is called an installment sale," Joe said.

I said, "So, when do you close and when do we get to see the house?"

"On the tenth of next month, and as soon thereafter as we can furnish it," John said.

"We're very happy for you," Charles said. "I hope you'll let the rest of us throw you a housewarming."

"You're on," Joe said. "Now, who wants dessert? I made Grandma Cacci's famous tiramisu."

"That's the magic word," Charles said.

Now that their secret was out, John and Joe were beside themselves describing their plans, and conversation revolved around that subject for most of the rest of the evening. Finally, we reached a point at which we were ready to go home. We thanked John and Joe again and left them in the kitchen, cleaning up. Bruce stayed upstairs to help them while Richard walked us down to the car.

We were just about to get in the car when Richard said, "That was a good thing you guys did."

"Whatever do you mean?" Charles said.

"Come on, Charley, this is me you're talking to. When John and Joe told me about this deal, I checked into Midtown Properties, LLC."

"And?" Charles said.

"It's true that they've liquidated several properties in the midtown area, but it's also true that they haven't taken a mortgage back on any property they've sold. This will be the only one on which they're carrying the paper."

"So?"

"There were so many layers of ownership that even I couldn't pierce the corporate veil, as the saying goes."

"I hate to repeat myself, but so?" Charles said.

"I can't prove shit, but this deal has your fingerprints all over it."

"Don't look at me. Philip's the real estate tycoon."

"And Philip doesn't do anything that you don't know about, does he?"

"Philip and I have no secrets from each other, if that's what you mean."

"So, I'll repeat myself: that was a good thing that you guys did. Don't worry, I haven't told John and Joe or, for that matter, Bruce, what I suspect I know." He touched his finger to the side of his nose in the universal gesture for secrecy.

"We've had a lovely evening, Richard," Charles said, and he gave him a hug. "Why don't we let Philip and Bruce organize the housewarming?"

"You've got it, boyo." Richard returned the hug and went back into the house.

As we headed over to Peachtree, Charles said, "Sometimes Richard is just a little too clever."

"There are still three properties in various stages of negotiation. Maybe we need to offer to carry the paper on a couple of them."

"No problem. Like the man said, there are tax advantages."

"It was really sad listening to some of the stories Joe told about his experiences working the detox ward," I said.

"Did you ever try drugs, babe?" he said.

"In a word, no. Not even pot."

"Me neither. I guess that makes us the last two Boy Scouts, doesn't it?"

The following Monday I was sitting in the sunroom with Lancelot at my feet when Charles came home from work. I was watching Roger and Steve, who were working in the garden, planting some flowering plants. They were wearing running shorts and tennis shoes and were shirtless and covered with sweat.

Charles said, "Hi, babe, what's up?" He reached down to rub the bridge of Lance's nose. Lance leaned into the rubbing—next to a liver treat, it was his favorite thing.

"Not much. I took a break from writing, and I've been sitting here with a glass of iced tea watching the boys at work. It's kind of interesting, watching them interact."

"How so?"

"For one thing, if Roger bends over one more time, he's going to get royally fucked."

"What are you talking about?"

"I've been sitting here for twenty minutes. Every time Roger bends over to dig a hole for a plant, Steve sort of stops what he's doing and focuses on Roger's ass. I think one more display will trigger things."

"Surely you exaggerate."

"Just watch for a minute and you'll see what I'm talking about."

A minute or two later Roger got on his knees to use a trowel to dig another hole. When he leaned forward, Steve stopped working and stared at Roger's ass. A few short seconds later, he got up, placed his hand on Roger's butt, leaned down, and whispered something in his ear. Roger turned to face Steve with a grin on his face, and they got up and headed toward the pool house at a trot.

"I told you so."

"Very clever of you."

"Not really. As a writer I'm a careful observer of the human condition."

"In that case, why don't you come upstairs and carefully observe this human's condition?"

"I thought you'd never ask."

"You have to be asked?"

"Point taken."

After I'd finished observing and taking care of Charles's condition, we went up to the playroom, where we found Gran watching the older members of our tribe at play. She turned her attention from the kids when she saw us and said, "It wears me out, watching those two."

"I know what you mean," Charles said as he scooped up one of the boys. "It's too bad we can't find a way to put all of that energy to some use."

"Just wait until those two are big enough to join them," I said, picking up the other toddler and indicating the two younger boys, who were at the moment confined to a playpen.

"Speaking of energy," Charles said, "what were Steve and Roger planting when I came home?"

"They came to me the other day and suggested that they could make the garden even more colorful than it is," Gran said. "I didn't ask what they had in mind, I simply told them to go right ahead."

"Steve has been compiling a portfolio of the landscaping jobs they've done. It's quite impressive," I said.

"I've seen it," she said. "He's justifiably proud of the three projects that used his own ideas rather than the developer's."

"Good for him," Charles said. "I hope we can raise these four to be as hardworking as Roger and Steve."

"That, my boy," Gran said, "is entirely dependent upon the example set by the two of you."

Later that evening, while we were in the study listening to music,

Steve and Roger came and sat down quietly across the room from us.

"What's that, Uncle Philip?" Steve said.

"Fauré's *Requiem*," I said.

"It's nice," Roger said.

"Nice?" Charles said. "Nice? Is that the best you can do? It's sublimely beautiful."

"Yeah, that too," Steve said.

"And it's still kind of nice," Roger said.

Charles threw up his hands in surrender. I decided to change the subject and said, "You guys are going back to Gwinnett County tomorrow, aren't you?"

"Yes, Sir," Steve said, "and again on Thursday."

"Does Richard have everything set up to your satisfaction?" Charles said.

"You bet," Roger said. "We'll even have an officer from the GBI actually driving the truck, just in case."

"Richard said he was going to call in a marker. Good for him," Charles said.

"Are you nervous?" I said.

"Not really, but that doesn't mean we won't be careful," Steve said.

"Good for you. You guys have handled yourselves extremely well through this whole thing," Charles said.

Tuesday and Wednesday came and went without incident. Thursday evening, Charles arrived home somewhat earlier than usual. I glanced at my watch and said, "It's a bit early, isn't it?"

"Brian Scott is on the way to the house with some video footage for us to see."

"Something happened with the boys?"

"In a word, yes. But it's all been handled, and everything's cool."

"Aren't you going to tell me?"

"Give me a few minutes to shower and change, babe. By that

time, Brian will be here with the videos."

"Go ahead. I'll listen for the door."

Ten minutes or so later, I led Brian Scott upstairs to the study, arriving as Charles emerged from the master suite, his hair still looking a bit damp.

"Hi, Brian," Charles said. "Help yourself to the equipment." He pointed at the television and DVD player.

Without a word, Brian went to the entertainment center and inserted a disc into the player. I retrieved the remote control, turned the TV on, and handed the control to Brian.

While he brought the images up, he said, "This is all rough footage. We had two cameras running, one in the cab of the truck and one in a following vehicle. I've already done some editing to combine the two. My guys are editing it down to a short version for the six o'clock news; a longer version will be used for a later broadcast."

We watched in fascination as the screen showed Roger climbing into the jump seat and Steve getting into the passenger seat of one of the trucks, with an unidentified female taking the driver's seat. Brian sped up the player as the truck headed up I-85 toward the suburbs. They'd just turned off of I-85 onto a secondary highway when a voice could be heard saying, "Get ready, here they come."

A siren could be heard in the distance, and the truck pulled off the highway onto the shoulder. A county car with lights flashing pulled off the road ahead of the truck.

A female voice said, "Okay, guys, let me do the talking."

The camera shot shifted to the driver's window as a deputy sheriff came into view and said, "License and registration, please."

"We weren't speeding," the female could be clearly heard to say.

"License and registration, please," he said.

"Deputy, I must inform you that you are under court order to cease your harassment of these two young men and their crews," she said.

"Sheriff says not to worry about what that nigger judge says; we're doing the Lord's work," the deputy said. "What are you, another one of those faggot-loving reporters?"

"No, Deputy," she said, "I'm Captain Thelma Gamble of the Georgia Bureau of Investigation, and you are under arrest."

She flashed her badge and opened the door of the truck. As she did so, an unmarked car drove up to the scene, and two officers jumped out with their guns drawn. The deputy was cuffed and taken away in the unmarked car.

Brian turned the machine off at that point and said, "I've already taped my report for the six o'clock news. The sheriff has been arrested, and in addition to the one deputy who was arrested, two others have been placed on administrative leave pending further investigation."

"Just before I left the office," Charles said, "Richard called. He gave me a preliminary report on his investigation. It seems that the sheriff and several of his deputies belong to a very small fundamentalist sect that is virulently homophobic. Their whole theology is evidently built around their anti-gay beliefs."

"Does that mean the ordeal is over as far as Steve and Roger are concerned?" I said.

"I should think so," Charles said. "If these people have any sympathizers, they'll certainly think twice before attempting anything else."

"I guess I'd better call my sister and let her know what's happening with Steve," I said.

"Handle it, babe. Meanwhile, I'll call Mason and Angela."

We offered Brian a drink, but he declined, saying that he had to get back to the station to do some more polishing of his eleven o'clock report.

Saturday afternoon, we were sitting in the study, enjoying a glass of wine with Mason, when the boys came in from work.

"Hi, Dad," Roger said. "I saw your car in the driveway. Where's Mom?"

Mason stood to give Roger a hug. "She took your brothers to the mall. They're both going through growth spurts and needed clothes. She wants you to call her if you need anything."

"Thanks, Dad, but you know Steve and I have been buying our own clothes for quite a while."

"Roger, take my advice and call your mother. She's not quite ready to have you all grown up and independent. She needs to feel needed. Give her a call and let her buy you something, even if it's only socks, okay?"

"Sure, Dad," Roger said. He pulled out his cell phone and punched a speed-dial number. "Hi, Mom. Dad said to give you a call. … Oh, nothing really. … Well, if you insist, maybe some handkerchiefs and dress socks. Thanks, Mom. … Bye."

The boys settled on a sofa, and Steve said, "Uncle Charles, do you think we could build a small greenhouse somewhere at the back of the property?"

"I don't see why not," Charles said. "Why do you need a greenhouse?"

"We want to start rooting shrubs from cuttings. As soon as they're big enough, we can put them in containers. Mr. and Mrs. Johnson are willing to let us keep the containers on a part of their property that they're not using," Steve said.

"They said we can pay a small amount of rent for the use of the land," Roger said.

"What kind of greenhouse are you considering?" I said.

"We have a book that shows plans for building one using redwood lumber and sheets of corrugated fiberglass," Steve said.

"I don't have a problem with that," Charles said, "but let me run it by Gran first. This is her house too."

I was looking at the boys and detected something in Steve's expression, so I said, "Is there something else you guys need?"

Steve looked at Roger and nodded.

"Dad, do you know anybody that sells equipment?" Roger said.

"That depends on what kind of equipment you're talking about," Mason said. "What kind and why?"

"We need to buy a Ditch Witch trencher," Roger said.

"That's a huge, not to mention hugely expensive, piece of equipment," Mason said. "What possible use would you have for such a thing?"

"Not the big Ditch Witch, Dad," Roger said. "I'm talking about the little one that you walk along behind as you operate it. It's about the size of a rototiller, and it digs a trench about a foot deep."

"Let me guess," Charles said. "You guys are doing landscaping and have to install sprinkler systems."

"Right," Roger said. "It's easy to do, and we make a lot of money doing it. We've branched out a bit and are installing sprinkler systems in places that didn't already have them."

"We're spending a lot of money renting trenchers," Steve said. "I keep hearing you guys say that if someone can make money renting you something, you ought to be able to save money by owning it."

"Can you afford to pay for it?" I said.

"Yes, Sir," Steve said. "We've got more than enough set aside for equipment purchases."

"In that case," Mason said, "let me make a couple of calls and see if I can set up a time for you to go see a dealer."

"Thanks, Dad," Roger said. "Do you think you could find time to go with me when I do? You might be able to drive a better bargain than I could."

Roger turned his head so that Mason couldn't see his face, and winked at us as he said that. I looked at Charles and was barely able to suppress a smile. *Roger's a quick study*, I thought.

"Sure, son," Mason said as he set down his empty wine glass. He said good-bye, and Roger followed him downstairs to see him out.

"That little devil," Charles said.

"What do you mean?" Steve said.

"After what Mason said about his mom needing to feel needed, Roger decided that his dad need to feel needed also," I said.

"Oh," Steve said. "I get it." His expression grew a bit cloudy for a moment.

I walked over and gave him a hug. "I know, Steve. You don't have a dad, at least not in any real sense of the word. However, you've got a great mom, and you've got the two of us."

"I know. You and Uncle Charles have shown me more love and affection in the short time I've been here than my dad did in my entire life. You don't know how much I appreciate that."

"But you can't help but wonder sometimes what it would have been like if things had been different," Charles said.

"Yeah," Steve said softly.

"There's nothing wrong with that," I said, "as long as you keep things in perspective."

"I love you guys," Steve said, and he excused himself to go down the hallway.

20

Charles

SUNDAY evening Philip and I took Steve and Roger to an organ concert at St. Philip's Cathedral. The performer was a young man from Jacksonville named Tom Foster, and we'd heard great things about his playing from friends in that city. The boys hadn't been terribly excited about going with us, so I watched their reactions carefully from time to time during the performance, noting with satisfaction that they seemed to be deeply engrossed in the music.

We took them to a dessert restaurant afterward and talked about the performance over our sweets. Philip said, "Steve, which piece did you like best?"

"Gee, Uncle Philip," he said, "I liked it all, but I guess my favorite would have to be the 'Variations on America'."

"Good choice," I said. "Did you read in the program notes that Ives was only sixteen or so when he wrote that piece?"

"Yes, Sir, I did," Steve said. "It was so neat and even funny at times."

"No argument there," I said. "What about you, Roger?"

"I liked the 'Prelude et fugue sur le nom d'Alain'," Roger said. "It was so fantastic, especially when he turned the theme upside down near the end."

"Actually, the word you are looking for is 'inverted'," I said. "He inverted the theme."

"I also liked the way Duruflé worked the theme from Alain's

'Litanies' into the piece," Roger said, ignoring my minor correction. "It was neat that he performed Alain's work just before the 'Prelude et fugue sur le nom d'Alain'."

"It's kind of sad when you think about it," Philip said. "Jehan Alain was killed in World War II, just a couple of years after he wrote that piece. He was not yet thirty at the time."

"I don't understand how you can spell out A-L-A-I-N in music," Steve said. "I used to be in the band, and there aren't any notes for L, I, or N."

"He substituted other notes," I said, "which made his task somewhat easier, as it gave him more leeway. The note A is sung 'la', and the fugal theme was built around the phrase 'la re la, la fa la', and it went on from there. Duruflé, the composer, was a real craftsman in that he spent a lot of time polishing his work. He had a long life but a very small output, unlike Mozart, who is said to have had his works fully composed in his head before he ever wrote them down on paper. No drafts, no corrections. He simply set them down on paper."

"Duruflé's wife was also a gifted organist," Philip said. "She and her husband were in an automobile accident that ended his career and very nearly ended hers. Yet after his death, she went on tour playing his works and others'."

"How do you know all that stuff?" Roger said.

"Charles and I have two different recordings of the piece, and we were interested enough to do a little research," Philip said. "One of the CDs I purchased after the concert today has both pieces on it."

"Uncle Philip," Steve said, "which piece did you like best?"

"Well," Philip said, "don't laugh, but I liked the final encore." There had been three encores, each of which was an improvisation on a theme submitted by the audience.

"What?" I said. "Mary Had a Little Lamb?"

"Think about it," Philip said. "He took that little tune and ran with it for at least five minutes, turning it upside down, sideways, and every which way but loose, and never once was it boring. At one point, he actually had a marvelous little fugue going. I know they teach people to improvise, but this guy seems to have a natural talent for it."

"Point taken," I said. "Nobody asked me, but I agree with Roger. I've always loved the Duruflé piece."

"I guess this means that we'll be going to more recitals," Philip said.

"You bet," Roger said.

"Ditto that," Steve said.

We finished our desserts and headed home.

When I got home from work Monday, Philip was waiting for me in the study. I kissed him briefly and said, "From the look on your face, something has happened, hasn't it?"

"You could say that," he said. "Take a quick shower, and I'll fill you in afterwards."

I hurried through a quick shower, changed clothes, and went back to the study. Philip handed me a glass of wine.

"Okay, babe," I said. "What's up?"

"Marie called me about an hour ago."

"And?"

"Frank was stabbed to death earlier today by another inmate."

"Does Steve know?"

"Not yet. I didn't see any point in disturbing him until he and Roger get home. They only had two small jobs scheduled after school today, and both are in the neighborhood."

"Are you going to take Steve down to Louisiana?" I said.

"I think I should, although I'm not at all certain that Steve will want to go. You remember what he said after the trial?"

"True, but no matter how he feels about Frank, his mother will need him."

Steve and Roger arrived home with just enough time to shower and change before dinner. They talked about school and plans for the car wash, which was only a couple of weeks from starting for the summer. When everyone had finished, Philip asked Steve, Roger, and Gran to join us upstairs.

When we were all settled in the study, Philip told Steve about the phone call from Marie.

All Steve said was "They told us this might happen."

"I'm planning on flying down to spend a couple of days with your mother," Philip said. "Would you like to come with me?"

"Why?" Steve said. "She divorced the bastard, didn't she? His family will probably take care of any arrangements."

"I know, but your mother and sisters may need some moral support from the men in the family, and that's you and me, kiddo."

"What about Uncle Julien?" Steve said.

"He'll probably be there as well," Philip said.

"Okay," Steve said. "I'll go with you to visit Mom, but I won't be a hypocrite and go to the funeral."

"I've just had a brainwave," I said.

"Well?" Philip said.

"Why don't you bring Marie and the girls up here for a few days? There's bound to be a lot of publicity down there, and it might be better if they were out of sight for a while."

"That's not a bad idea," Philip said. "Things might even get unpleasant if Frank's family causes a stink, and they're just the kind of people who will."

"I think that's a splendid idea," Gran said.

"Then pick up the phone and call Marie right now," I said.

Philip picked up his phone and punched a couple of buttons. "Hi, sis. How's everything? … Listen, I know I told you that I'd come down there for a couple of days, but Charles has a better idea. … He thinks I should fly you and the girls up here for a few days, maybe a week or so, and I agree. … You do? … Good. I was afraid I'd have to argue with you. … Okay, I'll make the reservations and call you back. Bye."

"You're a genius," Philip said. "Marie has already received a couple of ugly telephone calls from her former in-laws, and she jumped at the chance to get away for a while. I need to go to the computer and check airline schedules."

"Go," I said.

Philip headed down the hall, and I looked at the boys and said, "Steve, how do your sisters feel about their father?"

"Well, they know how badly he treated Mom, having all those affairs, and they know what he did to me. We haven't really talked about it, but I don't think either one of them has much affection for him."

"Do either of the girls have any really close ties to anyone in your hometown?"

"Each of them has a best friend," Steve said, "but that's about it as far as I know. Why?"

"I was thinking that it might be a good idea for your mother to sell the business and relocate."

"If you mean to Atlanta, she doesn't particularly like big cities," Steve said. "On the other hand, she knows a lot of people in Alexandria from visiting Uncle Julien so often."

"That's interesting," I said. "Don't say anything about this conversation until I've had time to talk to Philip."

"Talk to Philip about what?" Philip said from the doorway.

"I was thinking that it would be a good thing if Marie and the girls were to relocate. Steve pointed out two things—his mother doesn't like big cities, and she knows a lot of people in Alexandria."

"Wow! You're on a roll tonight with all the bright ideas. I like it," he said.

"When will Mom and the girls get here?" Steve said.

"Just after midnight tonight. Why don't you and Roger meet them at the airport?"

"You can take the Jag," I said. "Philip's car is just a bit small for that many people and their luggage."

"We can do that," Steve said. "If you guys will excuse us, right now we've got a bit of homework to take care of first."

"I think it's time I headed down the hall myself," Gran said.

"After Gran had left the room I said, "Babe, didn't you tell me that Frank had some life insurance?"

"That he did, and Marie has made sure the premiums have been paid. There'll be more than enough to pay off her mortgage and any business obligations. As you know, I've already set up college funds for the girls, so Marie won't have to worry about their education."

"In that case, there isn't any reason why she shouldn't benefit from Frank's death. The insurance proceeds could give her a chance to make a new life somewhere else, away from all the bad memories."

"I think I'll call Julien right now and tell him what we're thinking. Maybe even invite him up here while Marie and the girls are here," Philip said.

"Gang up on her, you mean."

"I think we can be more subtle than that."

I left Philip to his telephone calling and went into the nursery to check on our two youngest, then down the hall to have a look at Mark and Steven. I went back to the study, poured two glasses of wine, and handed one of them to Philip as he was saying good-bye to Julien.

I looked a question at him, and he said, "Great minds follow the same path."

"Meaning?"

"I didn't know it, but evidently Julien has had more than one conversation with Marie on the subject of relocation."

"And?"

"He says that she's been thinking about it and that this latest development will probably tip the scales in favor of a move."

"Good for Julien. Is he coming here?"

"He and Sylvia will fly up Friday and stay until Monday morning."

"We're going to have a busy week," I said. "Don't forget that we're hosting the swim team Saturday so they can have a final planning session for the car wash."

"Actually, that had slipped my mind," he said. "By the way, I forgot to ask earlier—what's happening in Gwinnett County? Any developments?"

"Angus Ferguson called me just before I left the office. The sheriff has been arraigned and posted a rather high bond. It has been suggested to him that he should take early retirement, but right now all bets are off. The deputy was unable to post bond, so he remains in jail.

The other two deputies are still on administrative leave until everything has been resolved."

"Do you think the cases will go to trial?"

"I certainly hope so. A message needs to be sent, and a trial would do just that. In any case, nobody will dare mess with our boys after this."

"Good."

We stayed up until Steve and Roger returned from the airport with our guests. We gave Marie and the girls their usual rooms, and everyone went to bed.

21

Charles

When I arrived home from work the next evening, I found everyone in the attic playroom, watching the tribe. Well, the adults were watching, and Steve's sisters were on the floor playing with Mark and Steven. I said hello to everyone and then excused myself to go downstairs and change. Philip came into our bedroom as I finished dressing, and I said, "Hi, babe," and kissed him.

"Hi, yourself."

"What's happening?"

"Not much. Marie and the girls slept late, and we've all been sort of lazing around the house today. I decided not to talk about anything important until Julien gets here on Friday."

"That makes sense. How are the girls handling their father's death?"

"They don't seem to be fazed by it one way or the other."

"I don't like the sound of that," I said. "Maybe I'll call Lydia and pick her brain a bit."

"I think that would be a good idea. I'm planning to take everyone shopping tomorrow—you know how women love the malls."

"That should distract them a bit."

"I did find time this afternoon to show them the latest videos of the adventures of Steve and Roger. Marie knew about the events of last week, of course, but I hadn't gotten around to sending her a DVD."

"What did she say?"

"Not much, just that she was glad the whole sorry episode was about to be behind us."

"Ditto that for all of us. By the way, guess who I had lunch with today?"

"I give."

"Mason."

"Any particular reason?"

"We've been doing some work for one of his companies, and we needed to talk about it. He told me that when he went with Roger to buy the Ditch Witch, they stopped at a 7-Eleven. While Roger went in to purchase some bottles of water, Mason noticed a CD sticking out of the radio in the truck, so he pushed it in and was shocked to hear Bach coming out of the speakers."

"Let me guess. Glenn Gould?"

"You've got it. I told him that Roger and Steve had heard that disc playing in the study and had been somewhat taken with it. But I didn't know they'd bought a copy."

"I've often wondered about Mason," Philip said.

"What do you mean?"

"Well, he told us about having a jack-off buddy when he was a teenager."

"Right."

"I sometimes wonder if there wasn't more to it than that."

"Why? Do you get vibes from him?"

"Not really, but I have this feeling that at some point in his young life he made a conscious decision to play it straight."

"Based on what?"

"Based on nothing more than his complete and total acceptance of Roger and Steve, and maybe a tiny gut feeling."

"I'll defer to your superior instincts in that respect. In any case, we'll never know, and it wouldn't matter if we did."

"True."

Steve and Roger got home, as usual, just in time for dinner. Everyone seemed to be determined to steer clear of the reason for Marie and the girls being with us. In fact, they'd been our guests often enough that we were comfortable leaving them to their own devices. Philip had given Marie the keys to his car so she could be free to come and go as she pleased.

By Friday afternoon everyone was relaxed and rested. Philip and Marie went to the airport to pick up Julien and Sylvia and arrived at the house just as I got home. I'd never met Julien's wife, so Philip made the introductions while we were still in the driveway. Sylvia d'Autremont was a stunning woman in her early forties and was in very good shape for a woman who'd given birth to several children. I found myself instinctively liking her.

Philip and Marie showed them to their room while I went to shower and change. Since our lives more or less revolved around the tribe's playtime, we assembled upstairs with Gran and the kids. Sylvia immediately figured out which two members of the tribe were Philip's. *What is this thing women have with infants and kids? Babies all look alike to me.*

After dinner we gathered upstairs, wineglasses in hand, and Julien brought up the subject we'd been avoiding for the past few days. Steve and Roger had taken the girls to a movie, so only the adults were present.

"I guess you all know that I attended Frank's funeral yesterday," Julien said. "I sort of represented our family."

"How was it?" Philip said.

"Just a simple graveside ceremony," Julien said. "Frank's family was there, and a couple of reporters."

"Did anyone give you a hard time?" Philip said.

"I think the Cox family had enough of me during the divorce and didn't want to mess with me."

"Marie got some ugly phone calls from them," Philip said.

"And some more messages were left after I came here," Marie said.

"I know," Julien said. "Frankly, I think you should seriously consider what we've been talking about for the past three months."

"What? Move to Alexandria?" Marie said.

"Exactly," Julien said. "There's ample insurance to pay off your mortgage, what little business debts there are, and give you a fresh start. You could sell the business or have someone run it for you and collect the profit."

"Sis," Philip said, "there can't be many happy memories for you in that town, and the situation with the Cox family will take a long time, perhaps years, to blow over."

"Put your house on the market and come stay with us," Sylvia said. "That way you can take your time finding a home. Besides, you've been with us so often over the years that you already know a great many people in Alexandria."

"What about the girls?" Marie said. "They have friends."

"They're young and will adjust," Philip said. "They might not think so now, but it will happen."

"Speaking of the girls," I said, "I'm sort of concerned that they don't seem to have processed their father's death completely, or if they have they aren't talking about it."

"I know," Marie said. "I've tried to talk to them, but they sort of shut down when I try."

"Summer is almost here," I said. "Why don't you send them to us for a few weeks while you get settled in Alexandria? I'll talk to Lydia and arrange for her to see them."

"Lydia?" Julien said.

"Lydia Brannon," I said. "A very old friend of mine who happens to be a prominent child psychologist. She helped Steve a great deal when he was dealing with the trauma Frank inflicted on him."

"You all make it sound so easy," Marie said.

"Of course it's not easy, my dear," Gran said. "Uprooting yourself after all those years in one place is never easy, but you have a chance to wipe the slate clean, so to speak, and start over."

"I'll think about it," Marie said.

"Good," I said. "Changing the subject, I don't think Julien and

Sylvia are up to date on the adventures of Steve and Roger. Why don't you cue up a couple of those DVDs, Philip?"

While Philip went to do just that, I continued, "Of course, you know about the situation in Gwinnett County, but we have the whole thing on film, starting with the altercation at the Mall of Georgia—you might find it interesting."

Philip first played the brief film of the fight, and then the first pieces done by Brian Scott, followed by the human-interest story, and finishing with the events of the previous week.

When the last images had faded, there was silence until Julien said, "Wow! I would expect that sort of crap in our neck of the woods, but here in the Atlanta area?"

"It's everywhere, Julien," I said. "Mostly just below the surface, where it fortunately stays most of the time. These people are an aberration because they belong to a bizarre little cult that hates homosexuals above all things."

"Do you really think it's over?" Marie said.

"Yes, I do," I said, and I filled them in on the legal situation.

"What impresses me the most," Philip said, "is how well Steve and Roger have handled themselves throughout all of this."

"Absolutely," I said. "I give both of them full marks for dealing with this whole sorry business in an extremely mature and adult manner."

"Aren't they both going to Georgia Tech?" Sylvia said.

"Indeed they are, and sooner than we thought," Philip said. "They both have so many AP credits that they're going to take some courses at Tech next year while finishing up their senior year at Exeter Academy. They'll start at Tech full time the following year, technically as juniors."

"How's their business doing?" Marie said. "Steve doesn't tell me a whole lot on the phone."

"Those two are young capitalists at heart," I said. "They already have two trucks and crews working, and now that they've expanded into installing sprinkler systems, it wouldn't surprise me if they have a third crew very soon. In fact, they just purchased a small Ditch Witch to dig the trenches for the irrigation pipe. Their justification was that they'd been paying too much to rent similar equipment."

"Are they able to pay for all that equipment?" Julien said.

"You bet," Philip said. "Roger's father and I financed the first truck and trailer, and the boys paid it off in record time, so we financed a second truck and trailer. They've very nearly paid that debt off, as well, and they paid cash for the latest equipment."

"Not to mention the fact that they've been buying their own clothes for nearly a year and will be paying their own way to Tech," I said.

"Good for them," Sylvia said. "They also make a really cute couple."

"Yes, they do," Gran said. "I've watched them closely, and each of them always seems to know what the other is thinking. If they've ever had an argument, it certainly doesn't show."

"I think they trust Philip and me enough that they would come to us if there was ever a problem," I said.

"I don't know about Roger," Marie said, "but my son thinks you and Philip walk on water. He's made that quite clear to me."

"Sis," Philip said, "all we've done is be there for him."

"Thank God for that," she said. "If Jeff and his brother hadn't brought Steve here that night, I don't know what might have happened."

"So," I said to change the subject, "have you decided to take Julien and Sylvia up on their offer?"

"Yes," she said, "I guess I've done just that."

"Good," I said. "That calls for a toast."

Philip refilled everyone's glasses, and we raised them to Marie's new life.

"By the way," I said, "we have a small crowd coming over tomorrow."

"Right," Philip said. "The entire swim team from Exeter Academy will be gathering at the pool to swim and later finalize plans for this year's Speedos Car Wash."

"There will mostly be fathers present at the pool, but Roger's mother and the dean's wife will be here as well," I said.

"The dean's wife?" Sylvia said.

"Dean Mangrum is dean of St. Philip's Cathedral. His wife is a charming woman," Gran said. "Their son is on the swim team with our boys."

"The boys will amuse themselves in the pool; then we'll have a cookout," Philip said. "After that, they'll conduct a business session and get things rolling."

"Do you know how much money they raised last year?" I said.

"No," Sylvia said.

"Over $100,000."

"That much?" Julien said.

"You bet," I said. "They spent part of it on a steam room for the team's locker room, donated $50,000 to the Aflac Cancer Center at Children's Health Care, and made the balance available for scholarships."

"This year they have a couple of small goals for the school," Philip said, "but Roger and Steve have persuaded the team to donate the rest to a scholarship fund."

"A scholarship fund?" Sylvia said.

"The boys were donating some time at the children's hospital and were teaching an eleven-year-old cancer patient to swim," I said. "The little boy died unexpectedly, and Roger and Steve took it to heart. The team is going to endow scholarships in the boy's name."

"They even met with the boy's parents," Philip said. "It turns out that the father is a CLU, and there was a large insurance policy on the kid. The parents donated a cool half million to start the endowment going."

"Steve never told me anything about that," Marie said.

"We're supposed to do good works, my dear," Gran said, "but bragging about them isn't good form."

"I see what you mean," Marie said, "but he could at least have told me about it."

"Sis," Philip said, "look at it this way. You raised Steve to have certain values, and he's demonstrating them quite clearly."

"I give up," she said.

The conversation turned to more general subjects, and by the time most of us were on our third glass of wine, Marie said, "Shouldn't the kids be home by now?"

I looked at my watch and said, "Just about now, I should think, based on the movie schedule Steve showed me. They went to the multiplex at Lenox Square, which isn't too far from here."

Just then Lance, who had been curled up on the floor beside my chair, raised his head and cocked an ear for a minute. Then he got up and trotted toward the stairs.

"Lance always seems to know when the boys drive up in the driveway," I said. "I think it has something to do with the fact that they're always munching on something and are very generous with the handouts."

A few minutes went by, and Marie said, "Shouldn't the kids be up here by now?"

"They probably went straight to the kitchen," I said. "Mrs. Goodman keeps the freezer well stocked with ice cream, and I think she was baking cookies this afternoon."

I was interrupted when the intercom rang. Philip answered it and listened for a minute. "Be sure you leave the kitchen as you found it," he said, "and don't give Lance anything containing chocolate." Then he hung up.

"They're in the sunroom with cookies and ice cream," he said.

Around ten o'clock the next morning, team members and their dads began to arrive. By eleven, the pool was full of boys, and a dozen men were sitting around visiting. Philip and I fired up the gas grill and began preparing hot dogs, hamburger patties, and chicken breasts.

Goodman started setting up folding tables, and Mrs. Goodman appeared, accompanied by several of the ladies. All of them were carrying platters and bowls of food. When we were ready, Philip blew a whistle to get the boys' attention. He didn't have to say anything—he merely pointed at the food.

When the boys had toweled themselves dry and assembled around the tables, Dean Mangrum said grace, and we watched the food disappear.

When everyone had eaten their fill, the ladies retired to the house, and Steve and Roger called the meeting to order. The boys quickly elected Sammy Mangrum and a boy named Buster Marshall to be cochairmen of this year's car wash. The group also agreed to an expanded schedule and once again opened up participation to younger brothers. They selected the various committees who would be handling the details and adjourned.

After the group had departed, Roger's brothers walked up to where we were talking with Julien and Mason. Steve and Roger were sitting with us, and Jack said, "Roger, would it be all right if I participated in the car wash this year? I meet the age requirement."

"Sure you can," Roger said. "The more bodies the better."

"That was good of you to offer, Jack," Mason said. "Why don't you and Harry go find your mother and tell her that we're ready to go home?"

After Jack and Harry were out of the pool enclosure, I said, "That was certainly a shot out of the blue. Did you know Jack was going to do that, Mason?"

"I hadn't a clue."

"Steve," Philip said, "were you and Roger planning to do anything this evening with your sisters?"

"We were talking about going to see the latest Harry Potter film."

"Why don't you ask Jack and Harry if they'd like to go with you?"

"Sure, Uncle Philip, we don't mind."

I noticed something in Roger's expression, so I said, "I'm not sure Roger agrees with you, Steve."

Steve looked at Roger and said, "Is that true?"

"Well, I don't exactly feel wonderful about it," Roger said.

"I know, son," Mason said, "but look at it this way—your brothers were brainwashed by an adult whom they had every reason to trust and respect. In that sense, they weren't totally responsible for what they did."

"And you're older and more mature," I said. "Surely you can be man enough to deal with it."

"I can do that, but it's hard," Roger said.

"Of course it is, son," Mason said. "Life can be hard sometimes, but you learn to deal with things."

"Okay," Roger said, "I give up." He took Steve's hand and said, "Come on, let's go talk to the kids."

When they were out of earshot, Philip said, "You know, Mason, our boys aren't boys anymore."

"No, they're not," Mason said, "but they're not quite men, either."

"No argument there," I said.

We followed the boys back to the house, where we found everyone in the sunroom. We visited for a few minutes before Steve and Roger excused themselves to change into their work clothes, saying that they had several jobs to take care of.

Mason, Angela, and the two younger boys left shortly after that, but not before accepting an invitation to dine with us Sunday evening. Jack and Harry had thanked Steve and Roger for the movie invitation but had politely declined.

22

Philip

WE WENT to St. Philip's in two cars Sunday morning. Steve and Roger took the girls in my car, and Charles drove the five adults in Gran's Town Car, Gran having decided to remain at home.

After lunch, the boys went to the back of the property to begin constructing the new greenhouse. They'd purchased a do-it-yourself book at Home Depot and selected a design that pleased everyone. The girls elected to go with them and serve as gofers for the project. Lance, as usual, followed the boys.

We spent most of the afternoon in the sunroom visiting with our guests. At one point, Grace brought the two toddlers downstairs and left them with us while she went back upstairs to care for the younger two.

"Did I understand from someone that you guys are planning to have two more children?" Sylvia said.

"There will be two final additions to our tribe sometime in July," I said.

"Well, I've never known you to do anything halfway," Julien said.

Sylvia, who had been gazing at the grounds beyond the sunroom, said, "Your garden is lovely, Mrs. Barnett."

"Thank you, my dear," Gran said. "Steve and Roger are responsible for much of what you see."

"Good for them," Marie said.

Gran said, "Charles, did you know that Steve has presented me with a grand plan for revamping all of the plantings in front of the house?"

"No, I didn't," Charles said.

"Neither did I," I said, "but knowing him, I'll bet he wants to include a modest little sign at the entrance to the driveway announcing that the landscaping is by R & S."

"I told him that I would think about it after I consulted with the two of you," Gran said.

"What are they going to use the new greenhouse for?" Julien said.

"To root cuttings, which they can later sell," I said. "They buy nearly all of their plants from an old couple who live outside of Atlanta. They have several greenhouses and a good deal of acreage, some of which is not being used by their nursery operation. After the cuttings take root, the boys will transfer them into pots and take them to the nursery."

"Where will they get the cuttings to root?" Marie said.

"I asked Steve that," Charles said. "It was a dumb question, although he was polite enough not to say so. What he did say was 'Uncle Charles, every time we do a job that includes hedges or shrubbery, we accumulate tons of clippings of all kinds.'"

"Actually," I said, "I'm 99 percent certain that Mr. and Mrs. Johnson, who own the nursery, are going to want to retire and sell out in a couple of years. Mason and I are planning to help the boys acquire the property if and when the time comes."

"They probably won't need any help," Charles said.

"What do you mean?" I said.

"After you, Mason, and the other parents settle your suits against Gwinnett County," Charles said, "you'll all be in a position to set up trust funds for the kids."

"I hadn't thought about that," I said, "but if we do that and structure it properly, the boys will have all the capital they need to expand their business."

"You wouldn't just turn huge sums of money over to them, would you?" Julien said.

"Of course not," I said. "I'll set up a trust that won't allow Steve access to the capital until he's twenty-five or so, but there's no reason that the trust couldn't buy the property for him."

"When you come down to it," Charles said, "neither Steve nor Roger has shown any tendency toward extravagance."

"True," I said. "I help them with their accounting and monitor their bank accounts. They're very careful with their money."

"They work hard to earn it," Charles said, "and they can be reluctant to part with it."

23

Philip

MONDAY morning was more than a little hectic. Marie and the girls had a nine o'clock flight, but Julien and Sylvia weren't scheduled to leave until noon. In the end, Julien and I drove Marie and the girls to the airport and saw them off. An hour later, I drove Julien and Sylvia to Hartsfield so they could catch their flight. I arrived home in time to have a late lunch with Gran, over which the two of us revisited the events of the weekend.

When Steve and Roger got home that evening, I went looking for them and found them in their room, doing their homework. The door was open, so I said, "Hi, guys."

"What's up?" Steve said.

"Not much," I said, "except I have two envelopes from Georgia Tech that came today. One for each of you."

I handed them the envelopes, and they tore them open eagerly. I waited a minute for them to examine the contents and then said, "Well?"

"These letters say that we're both eligible to take courses in the summer term," Roger said.

"Yeah," Steve said. "Look at this. We could take beginning drafting in the summer term and intermediate drafting in the fall."

"Why not?" I said. "As I recall, you'll both need those courses. What's the deadline for registration?"

"The end of this month," Roger said.

"Yeah," Steve said, "but if we want to get in, we'd better do it now."

"Can you register online?" I said.

"It says here that we can," Steve said.

"Can you handle the fees and tuition?" I said.

"No problem," Roger said. "We're good for it."

"Then I'll leave you to it," I said, and I left the room.

Before I went back to the office, I took a look at the room we'd begun to call "the little room under the stairs." It wasn't really a little room, but enlarging the stairway to the attic had narrowed it somewhat. Surveying the room confirmed what I'd been thinking about for some time, so I went to the office and made a telephone call. Several days later, when the boys got home, Angela and I were waiting for them.

"Mom," Roger said, "what's happening?"

She gave him a hug and said, "You and Steve come down the hall. Philip and I have a surprise for you."

We led the boys down to the little room and opened the door. I let Angela do the talking, and she said, "We decided that since you're starting college, you need a better place to study, so we fixed this room up for you."

The room now contained a pair of easy chairs in one corner with a reading lamp between them. Two decent-size desks were on the opposite wall, and a good-quality drafting table was in another corner. Freestanding bookcases had been placed under the stairway.

The boys were overwhelmed, and Steve said, "Wow, you guys didn't have to do this."

"Steve, nobody has to do anything," I said, "but we wanted to. You and Roger have gotten so independent, paying your own way and such, that we decided it was time we did something for you."

"Gee, Mom," Roger said, "I don't know what to say, except thanks a bunch."

"A hug would be good," Angela said.

"You got it," Roger said.

Steve grabbed me in a bear hug and said, "Thanks, Uncle Philip."

"You've earned it and you deserve it. Set the room up any way you like. There's plenty of room for your computers and printer, and I'm pretty sure this room is in range of the wireless router in the office. There's also room for your filing cabinet under the stairs."

"All right," Roger said. "Let's do it."

The boys hurried out of the room, presumably to start moving. Angela looked at me, smiled, and said, "It's good to know we can still surprise them."

"That's true. Can I offer you a glass of wine?"

"Thanks, but I have to get home and look after the rest of my family."

"Any change in attitude there?" I said.

"Not much."

"I really thought when Jack asked Roger to participate in the car wash that we were seeing the beginnings of a thaw."

"Without coming right out and asking, I've done a little probing about Jack's motive. It turns out that his best friend has an older brother on the team, and the friend was planning to participate."

"That would explain it," I said. I saw her to the door, then went to the sunroom, where Gran was sitting with a book in her lap.

"Well?" she said.

"They were overwhelmed," I said.

"Good. They work hard and deserve something special once in a while. It was very clever of you to involve Angela in your little project."

"I did it for a reason. She has to feel somewhat left out of Roger's life, and I thought bringing her in on fixing up the room would help."

"As I said, it was very clever of you."

"By the way," I said, "I'm going to be gone a couple of days next week. I have to run up to North Carolina to handle some real estate matters."

"Don't worry about it, my boy. This household is like a well-oiled machine and pretty much runs itself."

"Before I leave, I'll give you and Grace my hotel number and the number of the Realtor I'm meeting. The boys will have the numbers also."

Gran knew about the mountain hideaway and asked, "Are you increasing your existing holdings or purchasing somewhere else?"

"This will be an expansion. We already own a couple of tracts in the same valley, and I'm closing on an abandoned farm property."

"What are you going to do with it, if I may ask?"

"The plan is to renovate the farmhouse and install a married couple as caretakers," I said. "Then I'm going to establish a grass landing strip so that we can fly in when we wish to do so."

"Does Charles have much experience landing on grass strips?"

"He says he does, and I have no reason to doubt him. He told me how long the strip needed to be, and I've allowed for that length plus an extra hundred yards or so."

"It sounds as though you have things well in hand," she said.

"Perhaps, but I may have a surprise or two in store for him by the time the project is finished."

Mason stopped by after dinner to look at the new room. After Roger had given his father the tour, Mason joined us in the study for a glass of wine, and he said, "I can't thank you enough for involving Angela in that little project. It meant a lot to her."

"I thought it might," I said. "That's why I did it."

"Mason," Charles said, "have you given any thought to a graduation present for Roger next year?"

"Not really," Mason said, "but obviously you have something in mind."

"We've been talking about taking the boys to Europe for ten days or so," I said.

"So far, it's just talk," Charles said, "but we might fly into Paris for a couple of days and then take the Chunnel train to London."

"If you like the idea," I said, "why don't you and Angela come along?"

"You could even bring Jack and Harry with you," Charles said.

"Have you and Angela been to Europe?" I said.

"We went to Paris on our honeymoon," Mason said, "but somehow we've never gotten around to going back."

"Think about it and talk it over with Angela," Charles said. "It's too early to do anything now, but I'd like to start making reservations at least by fall."

"Will do," Mason said.

Our conversation was ended by the arrival of Steve and Roger, who had some paperwork in their hands.

"While you're here, Dad," Roger said, "we want to show you the latest operating statement on the business." He handed Mason a document, and Steve handed one to me.

I examined my copy carefully, gave it to Charles, and said, "You guys are really going full tilt, and summer isn't even here."

"We know," Steve said, "and we're ready to buy a third truck and trailer to be used for the irrigation side of things."

"Yeah," Roger said, "and the trailer needs to be longer, so it can carry twenty-foot-long sections of PVC pipe."

"Either that," Steve said, "or we need some sort of steel frame that can allow the pipe to be carried on the truck."

"I've seen that sort of thing," Mason said, "and it looks a little more practical than an extra-long trailer."

"Welding shops fabricate rigs like that all the time using angle iron," I said.

"Then let's do it," Mason said. "Same terms as last time?"

"Yes, Sir," Roger said.

"Uncle Philip," Steve said, "do you have time to go with us next week?"

"If we can do it on Monday, I can," I said. "I'm going to be gone Tuesday and most of Wednesday."

"What's wrong with Saturday?" Charles said. "Car dealers are open seven days a week."

"If Steve and Roger don't have any jobs scheduled, we can find a truck Saturday morning," I said.

"For that matter," Charles said, "call the salesman who sold you the last two trucks and ask him to find one and bring it to you."

"Now why didn't I think of that?" I said.

"Because you don't have a trained legal mind?" Charles said and grinned.

"I wouldn't touch that one if I were you," Mason said. "Anyhow, I've got to run along home. Let me know when you have a deal and I'll get you a check for my share."

Roger went to the door with his dad, and Steve retrieved the business card of the truck salesman. I called the man, told him what we wanted, said thanks, and ended the call.

"Well?" Steve said.

"He has just what you're looking for and will be here in half an hour," I said.

"Greed is a powerful motivator, isn't it?" Charles said.

"Especially when you're a commissioned salesman," I said.

Jasper Leone, the salesman, arrived at our door almost exactly a half hour later. He was driving a Ranger almost identical to the two trucks the boys already had, except that it was almost new and had very low mileage.

The boys looked it over and took it for a test drive with the salesman sitting in one of the jump seats. When they returned, I asked Jasper to join us in the house. We offered him a drink, which he politely declined, accepting iced tea instead. We haggled for quite a while before he finally accepted my offer, but not before he called his boss for approval.

I went online to the credit union and transferred funds from an account Charles and I maintained into the boys' corporate account, and Steve and Roger wrote a check for the truck.

The dealership faxed some paperwork to us, and everything was signed to Jasper's satisfaction. Steve and Roger drove him back to his office in the truck and picked up the temporary tag and other paperwork.

"Well, that's half the battle," I said after they'd left.

"It may have been a mistake, inviting him here," Charles said.

"Why?"

"I think he took one look at his surroundings and decided he had an easy sale."

"You may be right, but it didn't work out quite that way, did it?"

It was a rhetorical question, and he didn't bother to answer. When the boys returned with the paperwork, I called our insurance agent at home and asked him to verbally bind the company for the necessary coverages.

"Okay, guys," I said, "do you need me to go with you to buy the trailer tomorrow?"

"I think we can do that, Uncle Philip," Steve said.

"And there's a welding shop out near the nursery," Roger said. "We'll go out there in the morning and talk to them about racks for the pipe."

"Good," I said. "Just don't let them talk you into buying more than you need."

"What do you mean, Uncle Philip?" Steve said.

We were still in the office, so I took a yellow pad out, made a rough sketch, and said, "All you need, I think, is something simple like this."

"They might try to convince you to do something much more elaborate and expensive," Charles said.

"Maybe you should come with us," Roger said.

"No," I said, "you've got to learn to deal with this sort of thing. Just trust your instincts. If they try to make it too elaborate or complicated, trust your gut and walk away from it."

"That's good advice," Charles said. "There are lots of welding shops in the area."

Charles and I returned to the study, and the boys went to their room. We settled down with a glass of wine.

24

Charles

WEDNESDAY afternoon while I was at my desk studying a deposition, my private line rang. Somewhat annoyed that my concentration had been broken, I picked up the telephone and snapped, "Yes."

"Well, if that's the kind of greeting I get," Philip said from the other end of the line, "maybe I'd better stay in North Carolina."

"Sorry, it's been a rough day."

"How rough?"

"Babe, any day that begins with me waking up in an empty bed is already off to a bad start."

"Flattery will get you anything," he said.

"What's up?"

"I just wanted to let you know that I'm just about to head toward home."

"Good," I said. "Please try to curb your impulse to speed."

"Yes, Sir," he said. "Love you, bye."

"Me too," I said, and I hung up.

Before I could get back into my deposition, the other line rang. When I picked it up, Rosemary said, "Do you want to speak to the attorney representing Gwinnett County?"

"You bet I do."

When that call ended, I buzzed Rosemary and asked her to set up a conference call with the affected parents. "Don't bother calling Mason Cartwright or Philip," I said. "I already have carte blanche from both of them."

All of the parents agreed to the settlement that had been offered, and to my surprise, they also agreed to follow my advice concerning setting up trusts for their respective children. After the conference call was over, I called Mason to tell him the good news.

"They caved in rather quickly, didn't they?" Mason said.

"I think the county wants this behind them before the sheriff goes on trial. I get the impression from the county attorney that they just want the whole thing to blow over and be forgotten."

"I sincerely hope we aren't going to allow that to happen," Mason said.

"Not on your life. We still have litigation underway against the sheriff and two deputies individually. That, plus separate trials for the bad guys, will keep this whole thing in the public eye for quite a while."

"Good," he said.

When I got home, Philip was waiting for me upstairs. He followed me into the bedroom, shutting the door behind him. By the time I had my suit safely hanging in the closet, he was naked in the bed.

"I guess you don't want to wait for me to shower?" I said.

"I was never into sweaty field hands, but how sweaty can you get riding a desk all day?"

I pulled off the rest of my clothes and pounced on him. Later we showered together, and while we were dressing, I told him about the settlement offer from the county.

"That sounds good to me," he said.

"Right. Everybody has agreed to accept the offer, and they've all agreed to set up trusts for their children."

"Good for them. I was afraid one or more of them might want to take the money and run. What about you?"

"What do you mean?"

"Are you getting a nice fee out of this?"

"Not really," I said. "The settlement included court costs and attorney fees, so I settled for an hourly rate instead of a percentage. As you know, babe, this one comes under the heading of 'fun'."

"Did you have to agree to keep the settlement quiet?"

"We've agreed to let the media know that the case has been settled for an undisclosed amount."

"I'll have documents ready for you and Mason to sign tomorrow," I said. "Rosemary is making appointments for the other parents to stop by the office."

"You expect to have the money that quickly?"

"Babe, the county is so anxious to put this behind them they offered to send a check over to my office by courier tomorrow morning."

"Why are they so anxious to settle?" he said.

"Probably because the sheriff goes on trial a couple of weeks before Spring Break begins at Exeter Academy, and there'll be a media circus."

"I thought he'd have accepted some sort of deal by now; everyone else involved has done so."

"That's true—the boys who started the fight at the Mall of Georgia have entered guilty pleas and are on probation, and their families have settled the civil suits."

"Everyone but the sheriff has given in."

"Everyone but him, and according to Angus, he's been offered several opportunities to enter a plea bargain, and his attorney has urged him to take all of them."

"What's the problem, then?" he said.

"Unlike the deputy who accepted a deal and is already in prison, the sheriff not only wants to have his day in court, he's looking forward to it."

"Shit."

"I'm not so sure I agree with that assessment of the situation," I said.

"Why?"

"Think about it for a minute or two. We both agree that Steve and Roger need to have this whole thing over. A trial and conviction will be good for them in terms of putting the whole sorry episode to rest."

"I can see that," he said. "Maybe another round of publicity will give their business a boost."

"Stranger things have happened."

"We haven't talked about North Carolina," he said.

"I knew you'd get around to it in your own good time."

"Well, the bottom line is that we now own a somewhat larger chunk of the valley than we did."

"And?"

"You have a decision to make."

"What kind of decision?" I said.

"Wouldn't you rather have an asphalt or concrete runway?"

"Instead of grass?"

"Yes," he said. "Frankly, the idea of a grass strip makes me nervous."

"How about gravel?" I said. "It would be a lot less expensive, and gravel strips are good."

"Okay."

"You gave up too easily on that, babe."

"You got me there."

"All right, if you must, make it concrete."

"Okay."

"Let's go upstairs," I said. "I'm pretty sure I hear the tribe at play."

Saturday morning Philip and I made good use of the running track, as we'd done almost daily since I was fully recovered from my injuries. After we'd showered and had our breakfast, he asked me to go for a ride with him. We got in his car, and he drove seemingly at random but in a generally westward direction until we arrived in the area of the Johnsons' nursery operation. He pulled over on the shoulder of the road and stopped.

"Okay, babe," I said, "what are you up to?"

"Take a look at the parcels of land surrounding the Johnsons' property and tell me what you see."

"A number of shabby-looking houses, each with a small amount of land."

"Nine somewhat rundown houses with a total of almost thirty acres, to be exact," he said.

"And?"

"We have contracts to purchase all nine of them."

"Your plan being that when the Johnsons offer Steve and Roger their property, you'll combine all these parcels?"

"Right you are," he said. "Combined, they'll represent the largest single tract of undeveloped land within a ten-mile radius. What do you think?"

"It's a good idea. You do realize that you may have raised the probable selling price of the Johnsons' property with all these purchases?"

"Maybe, maybe not. The offers I've made have all been through different Realtors and from different entities. I don't think anyone will guess that someone is accumulating parcels, at least not for quite a while. I intend to renovate the houses and place solid tenants in each one."

"If I know you, you already have some plan in mind for the ultimate use of the property."

"Not precisely a plan," he said, "but I do have a vision."

"And that would be?"

"A shopping center, perhaps, with a good-sized nursery and garden center as its anchor," he said. "Maybe with an Ace or True Value hardware franchise tied into it somehow. The possibilities are limitless."

"Have you a timetable for all this?"

"I don't know. Perhaps sometime between now and the beginning of the next real estate boom. My crystal ball is a bit vague on that. In the meantime, the boys will have ample room for their nursery operation."

"You're that sure the Johnsons will ultimately wish to sell?"

"Based on my conversation with Mrs. Johnson, there isn't a doubt in my mind," he said. "It's only a matter of time."

"It sounds as though I need to generate some more corporate names for us. You must be running out of them after all this."

"Getting there."

"By the way," I said, "what's our total investment going to be in this little project?"

He told me and added, "You know we've been liquidating, so we're flush with cash at the moment."

"Okay, babe, it looks good to me. Can we go home now?"

Life in our household settled back into a routine. The car wash started on weekends only, then, as soon as school was out, became a seven-day-per-week operation. Steve and Roger were working their butts off, what with their expanded business, their drafting class at Tech, and participating in the car wash.

Marie brought the girls up at the beginning of June for an extended stay. She returned home the next day to close up and sell her house and begin the process of searching for a new home in Alexandria.

Lydia came by to see the girls two or three times a week. As it turned out, they were dealing with their father's death better than we'd suspected. A couple of their cousins on the Cox side of the family had been giving them a very rough time at school, and they weren't at all upset at the prospect of moving to Alexandria.

Marie came to collect them on the same weekend that Philip and I arrived home from Boston with Paul George Barnett in our arms. Two weeks later, we flew back to Boston to pick up Raymond James Barnett, and the tribe was complete.

25

Charles

THE arrival of two more little ones in our household required some changes. We moved the two middle boys into a small bedroom next to that of Mark and Steven, thus making room in the nursery for Paul and Raymond. As Grace's responsibilities increased, so did her salary. In addition, the young woman who'd been helping Grace part time agreed to work full time. Even with that much help, the logistics of having six children all in diapers at the same time dictated that all of us, including Roger and Steve, got involved at one time or another. The boys' reaction to their first hands-on experience with very dirty diapers was priceless.

Despite the myriad of things going on in our lives, we managed to find time to go to the beach for a couple of long weekends during the summer. The gang made use of the house several times as well, but without our presence. We had the two new arrivals christened at the beginning of August, and, as before, we sent invitations to all of Philip's siblings. This time, all of them accepted, and we had a house full of guests. For once, there were no empty bedrooms upstairs.

Our guests included Julien and his wife Sylvia, the middle brothers and their wives, and Marie and the girls, the latter of whom had to double up and share a room with their mother this time. Philip told me it was the first time all of his siblings had been together since their parents had died, so it was a very special occasion.

After the ceremony at St. Philip's, we had the usual gathering at the house, with only the family and very close friends present. Richard and the gang had once again been pressed into service as godfathers, with Lydia and Marie as godmothers.

Andrew and Emily were also with us; it was the first time I'd seen Andrew in quite a while. He told me privately that Emily had finally had enough of travel and they were content to settle down into retirement in their Decatur home. Andrew promised to have lunch with me from time to time now that his travels were at an end, and I was looking forward to that. I'd truly missed his input and guidance during the months he'd been away.

I worked my way through the crowd to where Philip was deep in conversation with Bruce, and said, "I can guess what the two of you are up to."

"You probably can, since the housewarming is next weekend," Bruce said.

"It's about time, after having been postponed two or three times," I said. "In any case, I'll leave you to it while I mingle with our other guests."

As I wandered from room to room, I noted that Gran had settled in the sunroom with Andrew and Emily, while Richard was on a sofa at the other end of the room, deep in conversation with Steve and Roger. I sat down with them for a couple of minutes and said, "Where are John and Joe?"

"The last time I saw them," Richard said, "they were headed up to the playroom. Steve's sisters were with them."

"That's probably a good thing, since Bruce and Philip are busy talking about final plans for next weekend," I said.

"I, for one, will be glad when that shindig is behind us," Richard said. "Bruce is so wrapped up in it that he doesn't have time for anything else."

"Feeling neglected, are we?"

"In a word, yes," Richard said. "Bruce is absolutely obsessed with getting every little detail just right."

"I'll bet you're missing Joe's cooking, also," I said.

"Damn straight," Richard said. "Bruce and I know our way around a kitchen, but we aren't in Joe's league."

"I guess the house seems a bit empty with them gone."

"That too," Richard said, "but we're going to make use of some of the space."

"How?"

"Bruce is setting up an office upstairs so he can telecommute at least part of the time," Richard said. "In addition to that, I'll be handling some of my agency's back-office functions at home."

"Big changes all around," I said. "More power to you. I guess I don't have to remind you about the tax advantages of having a home office."

"We've got that all worked out and calculated."

I excused myself and worked my way back to the library, where Philip and Bruce were still engrossed in their conversation, so I said, "Philip, we need to circulate a bit. After all, we *are* the hosts of this affair."

"Okay, I'll let him go for now," Bruce said. "Have you seen Richard?"

"He's out in the sunroom talking to the boys," I said. "I think he's feeling a bit neglected and might need some TLC."

Bruce headed toward the sunroom, and Philip and I began to seriously circulate, working our way through the house until we'd managed to have a conversation, however brief, with everyone present. People eventually began to ease their way toward the front door, and finally we were left with just family present.

Philip and his siblings were in the sunroom when I came back from seeing the last guest out. I'd just settled down in a chair when Steve and Roger appeared, so I said, "What's up, guys?"

"We're headed to Lenox to fill in for two guys at the car wash who have to leave early," Roger said.

"Have fun," Philip said. "Don't forget we're grilling steaks by the pool this evening."

"Save a couple for us, Uncle Philip," Steve said, and they exited the room.

"Where's Gran?" I said. "And for that matter, where are the girls?"

"The girls are in their room watching television, and Mrs. Barnett went to her room," Marie said. "She said she needed a nap, but I think she just wanted us to have some time together."

"That would be totally in character for her," I said. "Maybe I should go take a nap."

"Not on your life," Philip said. "Like it or not, you're part of this family."

"What time will the boys be home?" Marie said.

"On Sundays, the car wash shuts down when the mall closes," I said. "It takes them a while to finish the last customers, but no later than seven, I should think."

"Steve told me that he and Roger really enjoyed their classes at Georgia Tech this summer," Marie said.

"Yes, they did," I said, "and they're looking forward to taking a couple of classes at Tech in the mornings and then going to Exeter in the afternoons this year."

"Were they able to get on the same schedule?" Julien asked.

"For the next year they'll be finishing up the basic college courses," I said. "As I understand it, they're both in the same classes for the next two semesters. How are you adjusting to life in Alexandria, Marie?"

"Just fine, and the girls are looking forward to being in new schools. As you know, they had a pretty bad time of it during the weeks before school was out—courtesy of their Cox cousins."

"Have you decided to sell the business?"

"I'm still thinking that one over," she said. "I have a competent crew running things for me, and it's doing well enough to pay a manager and support me, so there's no urgency. I drive up there once a week to check on things, and that's about it."

Our cookout by the pool went very well that evening, and we managed to get all of our guests to the airport in time to catch their flights the next morning.

The week sped by uneventfully. Early Saturday evening, Philip went over to Richard and Bruce's to help Bruce begin the final preparations for the housewarming. My assigned task was to join them half an hour ahead of the event, at which time Richard and I were expected to assist in transporting all sorts of things to the party.

The four of us arrived at John and Joe's new home some fifteen minutes before the rest of the guests were expected to arrive. Not having been in their house before, I looked around with interest. John saw me doing so and offered to give me a quick tour. The living room furnishings were serviceable but not new. It wasn't a matched suite of chairs and sofas, but the guys had done a credible job of matching disparate pieces of furniture.

"We call it thrift shop chic," John said in answer to my query.

Joe happened to be nearby, heard that, and said, "We both learned a huge lesson about debt with all of those student loans, so we've decided to wait and buy good furniture one room at a time—when we can pay cash for it."

By the time my tour was over, Bruce and Philip had everything set up to their satisfaction, everything being a table full of finger foods and a small bar.

During the months that John and Joe had lived with Richard and Bruce, Bruce had become at least casually acquainted with a number of John and Joe's friends, and vice versa. This had enabled Bruce to compile a guest list of about twenty people, all of whom arrived bearing gifts. Philip and Bruce had spent a lot of time on the telephone making certain that no two of the guests arrived carrying the same gift item. By the time everyone was present, the gift table was loaded with an impressive array of small appliances and other useful household items.

Philip and I stayed until the last guest had departed so that we could assist in the cleaning up. John and Joe were profuse in their praise of the effort that had been put into the affair.

"It was our pleasure," Bruce said.

"Ditto," Philip said.

"Now can I get some attention from you?" Richard said.

This produced a laugh, as we all realized that Richard had felt somewhat neglected while the party was being planned.

26

Philip

THE rest of the year flew by in a rush of activity, not least of which was a huge gathering at Christmas. Charles insisted that I invite all of my siblings, but only Julien and Marie were able to come to Atlanta, as my other brothers had already made commitments to celebrate Christmas with their wives' families.

Mark and Steven were old enough to appreciate that something special was happening, and we had a huge tree set up in the library. In the basement, Charles found a number of boxes of old decorations that we'd overlooked on previous Christmases and added them to the decorations we already had. The tree as well as the house was decorated to the hilt.

Steve and Roger celebrated Christmas morning opening gifts with us, then went to the Cartwrights' for Christmas dinner. They later reported that Jack and Harry had been on their best behavior and everyone seemed to have a good time.

Mason and Angela decided to participate in our proposed graduation trip for the boys. They were, however, going to leave Jack and Harry behind with their maternal grandparents. Angela said it would give Mason and her some real vacation time for themselves, whereas with the two younger boys along they would be spending most of the time parenting.

The four of us had held many brainstorming sessions during the fall and settled on an itinerary that pleased everyone. We were going to spring the trip on the boys as a total surprise, and thanks to a school trip to Canada, both boys already had passports.

The airline seats had been booked, as had the seats on the Eurostar Chunnel train from Paris to London. By the end of October, we'd nailed down all of our hotel and/or bed-and-breakfast reservations, and all that remained was to select at least one show in London on our final weekend abroad. Angela had some ideas on that score, so we left it to her to handle the arrangements.

I'd been busy finalizing my own surprise for Charles, and in late March I suggested that we drive to the mountains to inspect the new airstrip. I'd thought that he might wish to drive there on this trip so that he could view it from the ground first, but he decided to fly straight there instead.

We took off early on a Saturday morning. Charles had checked his maps and used his latest toy—a GPS navigation system for the plane—to take us in pretty much a straight line to the valley. He circled the valley a few times, then made a couple of low-level passes over the field, expressing pleasure with the wind sock we could see flying from a pole high above what looked very much like a barn.

"What do you think?" I said.

"I think you did a clever job with the runway. What is that, camouflage paint?"

"Not exactly. I did some research and learned that they can mix latex paint in with the concrete to achieve color. In fact, they replace a certain percent of the water with the latex. The camouflage effect was achieved by using different colors in the various batches of concrete they mixed. The idea was to minimize the visibility of the runway from the air."

"Well, they certainly did that. As you know, I had a hard time spotting it."

"I guess that means that you like it."

"Yes, I do. It looks good, babe. I especially like that long strip of grass that extends from each end of the runway. I'm going to set her down."

We circled the field one more time. Then he put the plane down very gently onto the new concrete runway. Near one end of the runway was a concrete strip leading at an angle to the runway and ending at a wide concrete pad at the side of the barn. Our landing roll ended where the side strip began, and we taxied up to the barn. Before he could shut down the engines, I said, "Pull up to within ten feet from the side of the barn."

"Why?"

"Humor me and you'll see," I said.

He did as instructed, pulling the plane up so close that the nose was only about a dozen feet from the wall of the barn.

From the air, the barn had appeared to be old and weathered. On the ground and up close, however, you could see that it was a new structure with exterior walls of metal. The apparent age and weathering had been achieved by a very clever paint job.

"Wow," he said. "This isn't an old barn after all, is it?"

"Not on your life, and you haven't seen the best part."

I took a small device out of my pocket, pointed it at the wall of the barn, and pressed a button. The entire wall of the barn began to fold up, back, and out of sight, revealing the interior of the barn to be a small hangar constructed of steel beams and metal siding. Inside the barn/hangar, there was a two-year-old Jeep Cherokee parked in one corner.

"You can ease her right into the barn or use that little piece of equipment behind the Cherokee," I said.

"What about the prop wash?"

"The contractor assures me that the building is designed to withstand more prop wash than this plane generates."

"What piece of equipment?"

"It's called a Nose-Dragger. I've heard you talk about them."

"You think of everything, don't you?"

"I try."

He shut the engines down and we exited the plane. As we were walking to where the Nose-Dragger was stored, an older couple walked up to us, and the man said, "Show me how to use that thing and I'll give you a hand."

"You bet," I said.

We used the device to get the plane into the hangar and pointed back at the runway, and Charles chocked the wheels. Then I introduced him to Mr. and Mrs. Hall, whom I'd put in place as caretakers of the property, and we chatted with them for a few minutes before taking our leave.

As I was driving us to the Keep, which was about a half mile up the valley, Charles said, "You outdid yourself this time, babe. Thanks."

"You're very welcome."

"Tell me about the old couple."

"He's retired. She's semiretired and works from time to time as a substitute teacher. Mr. Hall is going to plant corn on both sides of the runway, leaving a five-foot strip of grass clear on each side."

"What's he going to do with the corn?"

"He has a few head of cattle in an adjacent field," I said. "He plans to turn it into silage for the cattle."

"The runway looks more like an extra-wide driveway than a runway," he said. "I guess that wasn't an accident, was it?"

"Was that a rhetorical question?"

He laughed and said, "Yes, I suppose it was."

"It may look like a driveway, but the real driveway actually runs in the other direction. Mr. and Mrs. Hall are under strict instructions to keep the runway clear of obstructions at all time."

"Good."

"Actually, since the stream is between the property and the highway and there's a strip of undergrowth and tall trees between the stream and the highway, it's kind of hard to see the runway at all until you get way up the mountain."

We'd pulled around to the back of the Keep as I said that. The additions, all of which were at the rear of the building, had been carefully tailored to match the original building in every respect. A casual observer would be hard put to notice that the entire structure hadn't always been there in its present state.

Charles was inspecting the building and said, "Good job here, as well."

"Wait 'til you see the rest of it."

I parked the Jeep in the garage and pushed the appropriate button to close the garage door. When it had closed behind us, I said, "On the ground floor, the addition is given over to more storage space, as well as a bathroom." We walked up the stairs, and I showed him the next two floors of the addition, both of which contained two small bedrooms and a shared bath. The top floor of the addition contained a slightly larger bedroom and an ample bathroom.

"There's enough room in each of the bedrooms for two beds," he said.

"That or bunk beds, as needed."

"You seem to have thought of everything."

"I tried. You will note that there are, as yet, no furnishings. It'll be a while before they're needed."

"True, but we might want to consider putting a bed in the last bedroom in case you decide to bring Steve and Roger up here." He paused for a moment before he continued, "We've talked about this, babe, and it's entirely up to you. This has always been your private retreat."

I interrupted him, saying, "That was back in the days when I never expected to partner up with anyone. Now, it's *our* private retreat."

"No argument there. But the decision concerning whether or not to allow Steve and Roger to invade that privacy, so to speak, is and must be yours. Our children are one thing, but Steve and Roger don't quite qualify."

"I sort of think of them in that way," I said. "Don't you?"

"Babe, you know I do. Still, it's your decision."

"Okay. We'll talk about it again, but not right now."

We spent a leisurely afternoon in the top-floor great room and allowed the sounds from the waterfall to lull us to sleep. Then we had a long session in bed, followed by a shower.

While Charles was dressing, I descended to the kitchen. There were no perishables on hand, but the freezer was full of meats and vegetables. Charles came up behind me as I was taking inventory of the food supply. He put his arms around me from behind and said, "Why don't I take you to that little restaurant in Waynesville that you're so fond of?"

"Meaning you're not fond of it?"

"You know better than that, babe. I was merely trying to make it sound special for you."

"Ready when you are," I said, and we were off.

Sunday we slept late, made a quick breakfast using the contents of the freezer, and were on the way back to Atlanta by midafternoon. I'd been worried about our takeoff, but Charles assured me that the climbing rate of the Cessna was more than adequate to clear the ridges, especially at the lower end of the valley.

"That certainly beats the heck out of driving to the mountains," Charles said as he taxied the plane up to the hangar in Marietta.

"No argument there," I said.

Mason and Angela came over after dinner that evening, and we gathered in the upstairs study. We'd decided it was time to spring the European trip on the boys, so we asked them to join us. Steve and Roger settled into chairs and looked inquiringly at us. Nobody said anything for a minute or two until Roger finally said, "What's up?"

Mason said, "You boys will be on spring break in two or three weeks, and we've decided to give you an early graduation present."

Angela said, "We, that is, the four of us, are going to take you and Steve to Europe for ten days or so."

"Cool," Roger said.

"I don't know what to say, except thanks," Steve said.

"The two of you certainly deserve it," I said. "We're telling you now so you'll have some time to schedule your crews."

"Where exactly will we be going?" Roger said.

"We're flying to Paris, where we'll see the basic tourist things,"

Charles said. "Then we'll take the Chunnel train to London. We'll visit a few places in the English countryside and then wind up with a weekend in London."

Angela handed each of the boys a sheet of paper and said, "This is our itinerary."

"What kind of clothes do we need to take?" Roger said without looking up from his perusal of the itinerary.

"It will be cool and possibly damp in some places," Charles said, "so you'll need jeans, sneakers, and long-sleeved shirts. Add a couple of pullover sweaters and at least one light windbreaker."

"Don't forget a coat and tie," I said. "We're having high tea at the Dorchester Hotel, and we need to dress for that. Your school blazers will do just fine."

Both boys looked up at that, and their faces clearly reflected what they thought of the idea, so I said, "Steve, have we ever taken you to a function of any kind that you didn't really enjoy?"

"No, Sir, I guess not."

"Good," Angela said. "Then follow his advice."

"What about Jack and Harry?" Roger said.

"We're leaving them with your grandparents," Mason said. "Your mother and I intend to find some time for just the two of us during this trip."

"I look at it as a sort of mini second honeymoon," Angela said with a sly smile.

"Who's going to look after things here at home?" Steve said.

"This household pretty much runs itself," I said, "and your mother is flying up to lend a hand while we're gone."

"The girls too?"

"They don't have spring break at the same time you do," I said, "so they're staying with Julien and Sylvia. Steve, didn't your mother teach you some French when you were younger?"

"Some," Steve said, "but I don't know how much of it I remember."

"I guess you'll find out in Paris," I said.

"I just thought of something," Roger said.

"What?" his mother said.

"We only have overnight bags, and that won't be enough for ten days."

"Angela and Philip have taken care of that," Charles said. "Go look behind the easy chairs in the master bedroom. You'll find what you need hidden there."

The boys did as instructed and emerged a couple of minutes later pulling hard-sided roll-around suitcases behind them, and Angela said, "Make sure each case has a luggage tag with your name, address, and telephone number on it. You'll find a supply inside each case."

"Thanks, Mom," Roger said.

"Thanks, Uncle Philip," Steve echoed.

"We're going to rent a minivan in England," Charles said. "The operative word being mini—cars over there tend to be somewhat smaller than we're accustomed to. We'll have to fit all six of us and our luggage into it."

"In other words," Mason said, "only one large bag and one carry-on bag per traveler."

"I think we can make an exception for the lady of the group," I said, smiling at Angela.

"Thanks," she said.

"Uncle Philip, what do we do for money?" Steve said.

"I'm glad you asked," I said. "Your debit cards from the credit union will work just fine over there, and the best and cheapest way to get foreign currency is from an ATM machine while you're over there, provided your bank doesn't hit you with huge fees, and the credit union doesn't. That being said, we're going to get a small amount of currency to carry with us."

"How do you do that?" Steve said.

"One of the major banks downtown can obtain it for us," I said, "or I can order it from a large bank in New York and it will be sent to us in a FedEx overnight envelope."

"Cool," Roger said.

27

Charles

AFTER several delays and postponements, the date of the sheriff's trial was fast approaching, and everyone involved had received notices to appear in court at the appointed time. Philip and I were keeping an eye on Steve and Roger, and we were poised to talk to them if they showed any signs of nervousness. However, if they were at all nervous, they were doing a very good job of concealing their feelings.

The case had originally been assigned to Judge Hampton, but due to his having issued the original injunction, he'd recused himself.

When I heard about the judge, I called Angus to express my concern, and he said, "Don't worry about having a different judge handle the case. Everyone in the legal system in this county wants to have this whole sorry business become nothing more than a distant memory. Even the most redneck judge will be unlikely to cause any problems. Besides, after my grand jury investigation was complete and they handed down several indictments of Sheriff Barnes, I filed a formal petition with the courts to have him removed from office. It's just too bad that we had to do it the hard way just because he didn't have the decency to resign."

I said, "I can assure you that the participants want this business buried in the distant past as well."

"Good," he said. "See you in court."

Just a few short days later, Mason and Angela came over to the house and we all drove to the courthouse in Lawrenceville in one vehicle.

"This is a big car," Angela said as she was about to climb into the second row of seats. Steve and Roger were already in the third row.

"We decided we needed a larger vehicle now that our tribe has grown," Philip said, "so I bought an Expedition to use on family occasions."

We headed out of Atlanta and Angus called me just as we exited I-85. When the call had ended, Philip said, "What was that about?"

"That was Angus," I said. "He wanted to let us know that some of the sheriff's coreligionists are holding a rally in his support."

"That doesn't sound good."

"It could be a lot worse. The sheriff's little cult is small but vocal, and—like that group in Kansas that travels around the country demonstrating at the funerals of soldiers—its members consist mostly of the sheriff's extended family and a few friends. Angus also said that there are a couple of gay groups on hand and the situation could very easily get out of control."

"Which would explain why I heard you say 'we'll meet you there.'"

"Precisely. Angus told me to go an area of the parking lot near his office, and one of his people will meet us and take us through a back entrance to the courtroom area."

We arrived at the courthouse complex and saw that the circus had begun. Even from the side street we could read the typical "God hates fags" signs being carried by the religious nuts, and the gay groups present were waving their rainbow flags.

"Why can't people just let us go about our business quietly?" Angela said.

"Because these hate-driven groups thrive on publicity, and there's absolutely no way to prevent it," I said.

An assistant district attorney whom I'd met on a previous visit to Angus's office met us in the back parking lot and led us inside the building. At the appointed time, we seated ourselves in a back row in the courtroom and waited for things to get under way. Angus had decided to handle the case personally, as I'd suspected he would. It took him most of the morning to select twelve jurors and four alternates, and he had to use all of his peremptory challenges in the process of weeding homophobes out of the jury pool. After that, the judge laid down a few ground rules for the trial, and court was adjourned for lunch.

Over lunch in a nearby restaurant, Steve said, "Uncle Charles, why didn't that sheriff just plead guilty and take his punishment like everyone else?"

"That's hard to narrow down to just one reason, Steve. The office of sheriff is a fairly powerful one in county politics, and he's been in office for more than twenty years. During that time, he's become accustomed to using his power as he sees fit, so it's safe to say that he either doesn't want to back down or perhaps he doesn't know how to do so. When this is over, he'll probably wish he had, because the grand jury investigation uncovered a laundry list of questionable activities from over the past few years, which explains why he's already been removed from office."

"So the sheriff is gonna have his dirty laundry flapping in the wind for all the world to see, isn't he," Philip said.

"Pretty much, and not for the first time," I said. "The grand jury investigation received a great deal of publicity in this county, so most of his dirty little secrets are already a matter of public record. Angus says there's been a lot of behind-the-scenes discussions, during which the defense attorney tried and failed to get the sheriff's history of abuses of power kept out of this case."

"Sounds like it's going to be an interesting afternoon," Philip said.

"You could say that again," I said.

When the trial resumed after lunch, both sides made their opening statements and Angus called his first witness. He'd discussed his strategy with me at length and had finally elected to call Steve and Roger as his first two witnesses. He led first Steve, then Roger through the entire chain of events, beginning with the incident at the Mall of Georgia and ending with the arrest of the last deputy sheriff who'd stopped one of their trucks. The two boys did well under the cross-examination by the sheriff's attorney. He did his best to throw them off-guard and upset them, but they rather steadfastly refused to take the bait.

I was called next, and Angus walked me carefully through my experience with the case, starting with my first visit to the sheriff's office after the boys had been arrested at the Mall of Georgia. During my testimony, I had an opportunity to observe the sheriff for the first time, and I noted that his complexion was even more florid than it had been the last time I'd seen him. He was doing his best to look confident and defiant, but he wasn't succeeding very well.

The defense attorney tried to delve into the subject of entrapment and said, "Mr. Barnett, as a prominent Atlanta attorney and senior partner of one of the oldest and most respected firms in that city, aren't you just a little bit ashamed at having been involved in what amounts to entrapment?"

"Entrapment?" I said. "I hardly think so, because entrapment only occurs when a defendant is *enticed* into committing an illegal activity. In the present case, a pattern of behavior had already begun before it was reported to me. All I did was arrange for the deputies in question to be caught in the act of committing the same crimes in which they were already engaged."

We sparred back and forth for several minutes until the defense attorney gave up and said, "No more questions."

Angus then showed the jury two DVDs of the harassment and arrest incidents caught on camera. When the scene showing the deputy quoting what the sheriff had said about Judge Hampton's order, there was an audible gasp among the spectators in the courtroom. That came as a surprise to me, because I'd have thought that everyone would have seen the videos by now; they had certainly been broadcast and rebroadcast enough times. After the videos had been presented to the jury, Angus called several deputies from the sheriff's department, including the ones who had been directly involved with harassing the boys. Without exception, they testified that they'd been ordered to "have a little fun with the fags" whenever possible.

The collective impact of the testimony was damning, and Angus finally rested his case a little before five. Court was adjourned until the following morning, and we filed out of the building with the other spectators.

On the drive home, Mason said, "There's no way he's going to get out of this, is there?"

"Not a chance," I said.

"Do we need to come back tomorrow?" Steve said.

"Angus told me that he had no plans to recall any of us as witnesses," I said.

"In that case, there's no need for you guys to miss another day of school," Philip said.

"Absolutely," Angela said. "You should go to school tomorrow and put this whole experience behind you."

"Uncle Charles," Steve said, "do you think the jury will hand down a verdict tomorrow?"

"I'm told that the defense attorney has a very short list of defense witnesses, and it's not a capital case, so a unanimous verdict isn't required. All of the above being the case, I don't see why the trial won't be over by this time tomorrow."

"Then if you and Uncle Philip don't mind, I'd like to be there when that happens."

"Me too," Roger said.

"Is that okay with your parents?" Philip said.

"Absolutely," Mason said. "It won't hurt the boys to see the justice system at work."

Angela added her agreement, so I said, "Okay, then. We'll come back tomorrow."

"So will we," Angela said. "I'd like to see this thing through."

Which is why we were once again in the Expedition the next morning and on our way to Lawrenceville. I'd arranged to be met by one of Angus's people as we had the previous day, and we were seated in the same back row of spectators when the trial resumed. The defense attorney focused on producing character witnesses, most of whom appeared to be members of the sheriff's cult. Then the sheriff was called to the stand and sworn in.

The defense attorney devoted most of his time to questions about the sheriff's years of service to the county and, in doing so, made it appear as though he was some sort of local hero. Then the questions focused on the problem at hand, and the defense attorney carefully walked the sheriff through his motivation and reasoning for the actions he'd taken, starting with the incident at the Mall of Georgia. The sheriff's answers to the questions were hardly surprising and boiled down to the fact that he felt he was doing the Lord's work in exposing the evils of homosexuality, etcetera. In fact, he was allowed to launch into several lengthy diatribes on the subject, so much so that I was surprised when Angus didn't object to them. Each time he began to rant anew he worked himself into such a feverish state that his face grew even redder than usual, until at one point, I thought his eyes were going to pop out of his head. The defense attorney finally said, "Your witness."

Angus stood, walked up to a spot in front of the witness box where the sheriff sat glowering at him belligerently, and said, "Mr. Barnes, you testified that—"

"That's Sheriff Barnes to you."

"Not anymore, it isn't," Angus said.

The sheriff's face got redder as he said, "It's a courtesy title for life, and I expect people to use it."

"Mr. Barnes, so-called 'courtesy titles' have to be earned, and elected officials who've been removed from office in disgrace forfeit all claim to them—"

Angus was once again cut off midstatement when the sheriff said, "You did that to me, you son of a bitch."

"No, Mr. Barnes,"—Angus stressed the "Mr."—"you did it to yourself. When the incident at the Mall of Georgia was called to my attention, I warned you at the time not to pursue the matter."

"I do what I want to do."

"Yes, you do, and look where it's gotten you."

"I just do the Lord's work," the sheriff said.

"He talks to you personally, does he?"

"It's all in the book."

"No, Sir. That's where you're wrong," Angus said. He walked back to the prosecution's table, found a document, and returned to his spot in front of the witness box with it in hand.

"What's that?" the sheriff said.

"A list of fifty prominent Bible scholars representing every major Protestant denomination in the country who are prepared to testify as to the incorrectness of your interpretation of the Bible."

Philip leaned over and whispered in my ear, "He got that from you, didn't he?"

I nodded and put a finger to my lips.

"Those guys don't know anything," the sheriff said scornfully.

"So you say, but they have something that you don't have."

"What would that be?"

"Credentials and credibility."

The sheriff's face got redder still, and he said, "I don't need that stuff. I've got the Bible on my side."

"Do you, really?"

"Of course. It says right there in the Old Testament that thou shalt not lie with mankind, as with womankind: it is abomination."

"And your whole theology is built around that, isn't it?" Angus said.

"Of course."

"Just like the snake-handling cults in the hills of Tennessee built their entire faith around a passage in Mark, correct?"

"Don't put me in the same category with those idiots," the sheriff said.

"But that's just the problem, Mr. Barnes," Angus said. "As far as mainstream Christianity is concerned, and for that matter, most people in this country, that's precisely the category in which you belong. But let's move on. Didn't you understand that if you broke the law and harassed those young men, you'd be violating your oath of office?"

"What oath?"

"The oath you took the first time you were elected, and at every re-election since then. You swore to uphold the law, did you not?"

"Yes."

"And yet, you ordered your deputies to deliberately break it," Angus said.

"So?"

"Was it worth it? Was it worth the price you paid?"

"What price?"

"Don't be disingenuous, Mr. Barnes. As a direct result of the unlawful orders you issued, you've been removed from office in disgrace; the county has been sued for a huge amount in damages, as have you yourself; and last but not least, there's every reason to believe that your pension rights will be forfeited. I'll repeat the question: you took a deliberate action, one that you knew was illegal, and you've paid a heavy price—was it worth it?"

"You bet it was, and I'd do it again."

I couldn't see Angus's face as he made his final statement, but his body language suggested complete and utter contempt as he said, "So be it. Your Honor, the prosecution rests."

The judge called Angus and the defense attorney up to the bench, and after a brief conversation, they returned to their seats. The judge said, "Counsel for both sides have assured the court that their closing arguments will be brief, so we'll hear them before we adjourn for lunch."

The closing arguments from both sides were indeed brief, and then we accepted Angus's offer to join him for sandwiches and soft drinks in the conference room at his office. We sat around a table and helped ourselves to the food, and I'd barely had time to take a bite of my sandwich when Angus's receptionist rushed into the room, said, "You've got to see this," and turned on a television set.

She changed channels until she found the one she wanted and turned up the volume in time for us to hear the former sheriff ranting and raving. The barely contained rage that had expressed itself in his increasingly reddening complexion in court was exploding all over the place. The camera switched to the crowd in front of him and focused for a minute on the "God hates fags" sign and other similar placards. Then as the cameraman panned the crowd, we saw two groups of gays carrying rainbow flags.

"I hope the jury can't see this, Angus," I said.

"Not a chance. Because of all the demonstrators, we've had the jury sequestered and they're deliberating while they eat."

"Good. Any predictions as to how long it will take them to reach a verdict?" Philip said.

"Not long, I should think," Angus said. "You heard what the judge said when he gave the jury their instructions. He did everything but direct them to find a verdict of guilty."

"Don't forget that since this isn't a capital case, the verdict doesn't have to be unanimous," I said.

One of the reporters had just shoved a microphone in the sheriff's face and said, "You seem to be pretty sure of the jury's verdict, Sheriff."

"The people in this county haven't kept re-electing me because they don't like me," the sheriff said.

"Yet you were forcibly removed from office."

"That was the doing of that faggot-loving DA and a nigger judge."

"Are you saying that the district attorney and a judge manipulated the grand jury?" the reporter said.

"You bet I am. This courthouse is full of officials that don't like me, but the people will prevail." He paused and then added with considerable bravado, "And I fully expect to be acquitted."

Someone walked up to the reporter and whispered in his ear. Then the reporter turned back to the camera and said, "I've just been informed that the jury is on its way back to the courtroom, so we'll learn the outcome of this trial soon enough. Stay tuned."

We were still processing that bit of information when one of Angus's people hurried into the room and said, "The jury's coming back."

"We're on our way," Angus said, "let's get this show on the road."

We were on our way back to the courtroom before we had time for any conversation, but once we were in our seats, Philip said, "That was quick."

"Yeah," I said.

"Is that good or bad?" Mason said.

"That's hard to say, but I'm guessing that it's good."

A bailiff in the front of the courtroom said, "All rise," and conversation ceased.

The judge entered from a rear door and took his seat on the bench, and we sat as instructed while the jury filed back into the room and resumed their seats.

"Ladies and gentlemen of the jury, have you reached a verdict?" the judge said.

The jury foreman stood and said, "Yes, Your Honor," and handed a folded piece of paper to a bailiff.

The defendant and his attorney stood while the judge unfolded the slip of paper, glanced at it briefly before handing it back to the bailiff, and said, "What say you, Madame Foreman?"

The foreman, a fortysomething woman, took the piece of paper when the bailiff handed it back to her, opened it, and in a clear alto voice read, "We the jury, in a unanimous decision, find the defendant guilty on all counts."

The chaos in the courtroom was immediate and loud, and when order was finally restored, the judge looked at the defendant and said, "Mr. Barnes, have you anything to say before this court pronounces its sentence?"

The sheriff said, "You bet I do, you faggot-loving son of a bitch," and began to rant and rave with even more vehemence than he'd shown in front of the cameras earlier. He got louder and totally incoherent until finally he made a gurgling sound and fell face forward across the defense table.

We sat in stunned silence, as did most of the spectators, and watched as the sheriff was laid out on the floor and someone attempted to revive him. Eventually, Angus directed his assistant to make his way back to us with a message.

"Mr. Barnett," he said, "Mr. Ferguson said to let you know that Mr. Barnes is dead. One of the spectators is a retired doctor, and he seems to think the former sheriff had a stroke or some sort of seizure."

"Please thank him for letting me know," I said. He nodded and headed back to the front of the room.

"Well. That was certainly interesting," Philip said.

"Yeah. Is everybody ready to head for the car?" I said.

We reached the rear entrance we'd been using and found Brian Scott and his cameraman waiting for us.

"Hello, Brian," I said. "Were you inside the courtroom just now?"

"You bet I was. Mr. Barnett, would you folks like to comment on the events of the morning?"

"Only if you'll turn that microphone off and give us a minute to discuss this among ourselves," I said, and he made a show of pointing the microphone in another direction.

I turned my back on him for a moment and said, "It's up to you folks. Do you want to be interviewed?"

"Not particularly," Mason said. "Why don't you make a brief statement on our behalf?"

I looked at Philip and he nodded in agreement.

"Okay, then." I turned back to Brian and said, "I've been asked to speak on everyone else's behalf, if that will do."

"Sure, Mr. Barnett," Brian said. He pointed the microphone at me, said "Let's roll" to his cameraman, and conducted a very thorough interview. Then he thanked us and went on his way.

When we were back in the car, Angela said, "Can we stop somewhere and get something to drink?"

"Yeah, Uncle Philip," Steve said, "we rushed out of that conference room so quickly that I never finished eating my sandwich."

"Find us a chain restaurant," I said to Philip, who was driving. "Anything but fast food will do."

"There's an Applebee's not too far from here," Roger said. "We passed right by it on the way to the courthouse."

Once we were in the restaurant and had placed our orders, everyone seemed to find a need to use the facilities. The boys ordered a full lunch, and the adults settled for salads. Nobody seemed to want to talk about the trial until I said, "Steve, Roger, what do you think about what just happened in that courtroom?"

"It was wild, Uncle Charles," Steve said.

"I'm just glad this whole thing is behind us," Roger said.

"Amen to that," Angela said.

"Yeah," Steve said, "and I'm glad we're getting on an airplane in a few days."

"No argument there," Philip said. "We all need to get away for a while."

28

Philip

A FEW days before we flew to Europe, we were all packed and ready. In fact, four suitcases had been stacked in the foyer for a couple of days. Charles and I had each packed a small carry-on bag with shaving kits and a change of clothes in case our bags didn't arrive in Paris with us, and we'd seen to it that the boys had done the same.

Marie flew in two days before we were to leave and was brought up to speed on the operation of the household. On the eve of our departure, we were all in the upstairs study.

"Steve," Marie said, "is there anything I need to do for your business?"

"Like what, Mom?"

"Collecting the money, depositing it in the bank, that sort of thing," she said.

"It's under control," Steve said. "This time of the year, most of our business is from customers who pay a flat monthly fee for year-round services."

"Yeah," Roger said. "It's only during the summer that we get a lot of cash customers."

"How do you actually collect the fees?" she said.

"We invoice them, and most of them mail us a check," Steve said. "Once in a while a customer will hand a check to a crew chief."

"Right," Roger said. "All three crew chiefs have a supply of deposit slips, and they'll run through the drive-up teller and handle it."

"I'll leave a key with you in case anything lands in the post office box," Steve said. "The post office branch is right down the street in Buckhead, and deposit slips are in the top drawer of our filing cabinet in front of the file folders. I'll show you where they are before we go to bed tonight. The credit union is just a few doors down from the post office. Anyhow, we'll be in touch by e-mail, no matter where we are."

"Don't worry about a thing," she said. "This trip is a wonderful opportunity for you, and I want you to be able to enjoy it."

Our Delta flight was scheduled to leave around six o'clock, and we'd arranged to meet Mason and Angela at the airport. Luck and timing were with us, and we were settled in a lounge in the international terminal a little over an hour before the flight. The boys were in high states of excitement, bouncing around the room, taking it all in, and the rest of us were settled in comfortable chairs, drinks in hand.

Mason was watching Roger and Steve and said, "It's good to see that they still have the capacity to get excited over something new and different."

"I agree," I said. "Kids today are exposed to so much so quickly that all too many of them are or seem to be totally jaded by the time they're in high school."

"I think we did the right thing planning to stay in small hotels most of the time," Angela said. "The boys will experience more local color that way."

"No argument there," Charles said.

The boys returned to where we were seated and settled on a sofa, and I said, "Steve, remember what I told you about the flight? If you're smart, you'll go to sleep after dinner is served, or at least after the movie has finished. That way you will wake up in Paris tomorrow morning and won't suffer quite so much from jet lag."

"I'll try, Uncle Philip," he said.

"The fact that our flight is supposed to have the new seats in first class that recline almost fully should be helpful in that respect," Charles said.

"Also," I said, "as soon as we're on the plane, set your watches to Paris time. It will help you adjust your thinking."

We landed in Paris and made our way through customs without incident, finally arriving at a long queue of taxicabs, where I said, "I think we'll have to take two cabs, Mason. None of these look big enough to accommodate all of us."

"You take the boys in your cab," Charles said, "and I'll go with Angela and Mason." He said that because we had determined that neither of the Cartwrights knew any French.

The boys and I worked our way to the head of the line, and I said to the driver of the first available taxi, "*Hotel St. Germaine du Pres, s'il vous plaît, quarante-six rue Jacob.*"

I was rewarded with a huge smile, presumably because I had spoken to him in French. We loaded our suitcases in the taxi and were off. The driver became quite voluble during the ride, and I was hard-pressed to keep up with his conversation. The boys were too busy rubbernecking to pay any attention to the driver or me.

We arrived at the hotel about five minutes ahead of the other taxi. After both taxis were unloaded, we sorted ourselves out in the hotel lobby and checked in. We'd already established a plan of action, so we went to our respective rooms to shower and change and were back in the lobby at the appointed time.

We walked around the corner to Les Deux Magots, a café on Boulevard Saint-Germaine, and settled down at an outdoor table for an early lunch. Charles played tour guide and said, "This is a famous café, guys. The name Deux Magots refers to the two large statues just inside the door. In the thirties or thereabouts, some pretty famous members of the literary set used to hang out here."

We placed our orders and had a nice lunch, during which we found time to call home and check on the tribe, even though it was fairly early in the morning in Atlanta. From the café, we strolled over to the church of Saint-Sulpice and went inside the sanctuary. Evidently, we'd arrived at the tail end of a wedding, because the newlyweds were on their way down the aisle toward the rear of the church, and we could hear organ music.

Steve perked up at the music and said, "I know that music. Didn't the organist play it at St. Philip's a couple of weeks ago?"

"Yeah," Roger said. "But I can't remember the name of it."

"It's the Toccata from the *Fifth Organ Symphony* by Widor," Charles said. "Arguably one of the most recognized organ works in the world, and most appropriate for this church."

"Why is that, Uncle Charles?" Steve said.

"Because Charles-Marie Widor, the composer, was appointed organist of this church in 1870, when he was twenty-six years old," Charles said. "Widor stayed at that post for an amazing sixty-three years. He was something of a Renaissance man and held a salon in the choir loft after Sunday services. The writers and thinkers of the day met there regularly. At the time of his appointment, Saint-Sulpice was deemed to be the most important post in Paris for an organist, partly because of the organ, which was considered to be the masterwork of organ builder Aristide Cavaillé-Coll, who is widely regarded to be the greatest French organ builder of the nineteenth century."

"Wow," I said, "you're a fountain of knowledge. What else do you know about him?"

"Well," Charles said, "along with Dr. Albert Schweitzer, he edited and produced the Widor-Schweitzer edition of Bach's organ works, which was published almost one hundred years ago and has been used to train several generations of organists."

"Sixty-three years," Roger said. "That would have made him almost ninety when he retired."

"Do you see how high up that choir loft is?" Charles said.

"I see," Roger said.

"The story goes that Widor retired at the age of eighty-nine because he could no longer climb up the steps to the loft."

"That's kind of sad," Steve said.

"Do you guys know what is meant by the term Renaissance man?" I said.

"Yes, Sir, we do," Roger said. "Our English teacher talked about it a lot last year."

"I'm impressed by that recitation, Charles," Mason said.

"What can I say," Charles said. "I've spent a lot of time studying the lives of my favorite composers, and I've been here before."

We finished our tour of Saint-Sulpice and walked through the nearby Luxembourg Gardens, which were bursting with spring flowers. From there, we strolled along the Seine, across a bridge to the Louvre, and spent the rest of the afternoon marveling at the art on display.

Because we were all getting a little tired, we took a taxi back to the Left Bank and on to Restaurant Polidor, which both Angela and Charles had wanted to try, having seen it featured on a Rick Steves program.

The restaurant had been a neighborhood fixture since the mid-nineteenth century. Seating was more or less family style at long tables that accommodated twelve people comfortably. We'd just about finished eating when Roger excused himself to go to the restroom.

He came back a few minutes later with an astonished look on his face and said, "You're not going to believe this."

"Believe what?" Steve said.

"The restroom. There's no toilet, just a hole in the floor with an outline painted to show you where to place your feet."

"That would be old-style Mediterranean squat plumbing," Charles said, "so named for obvious reasons."

"This I gotta see," Steve said, and he left the table. He returned a few minutes later wearing the same expression as Roger. "Wow," he said, "you weren't kidding, were you?"

We walked back to the hotel, enjoying the ambience of a Paris Left Bank neighborhood. We were all tired and happy, and after having consumed a couple of bottles of wine, at least four of us were very mellow. The boys had been limited to two small glasses of wine each, but even they were showing signs of wear. Before we went up to our rooms, we agreed to meet at eight for breakfast.

After breakfast the next morning, Angela and Mason left to do their thing, which included a day of activities culminating in a romantic dinner cruise on the Seine. Charles and I took the boys to Notre Dame, where we climbed to the top of one of the towers and enjoyed the view. After that, we went to the Eiffel Tower for more sightseeing.

After lunch, we toured the Musée d'Orsay to pay our respects to *Whistler's Mother* and other works of art. We spent the rest of the afternoon strolling along the Seine, enjoying the weather, the view, and each other's company.

We walked down a street of very nice shops, and the boys purchased gifts for various family members. Before we headed back to the hotel, we stopped at an outdoor café to have a glass of wine and a plate of cheese and fruit. While there, we called Marie and managed to say a few words to Mark and Steven.

That evening, while Angela and Mason were having their romantic dinner on the riverboat, we took the boys to the Moulin Rouge. They were suitably impressed and said so at length during the taxi ride back to the hotel.

"Wow," Steve said, "I thought it was just going to be tits and ass."

"Me too," Roger said. "I sure didn't expect all those acrobats and stuff."

The next morning we took the boys out to Versailles, after which we met Angela and Mason for an early lunch at Les Deux Magots.

"So, Angela," I said, "how was Paris the second time around?"

"Very nice," she said with a little sigh of contentment.

"Did you do any shopping?" Charles said.

"We walked through a lot of stores on Boulevard Haussmann," Mason said, "but she managed to resist temptation."

"I didn't find all that much to tempt me," Angela said. "The large stores were interesting, and one of them was gorgeous, but I didn't see anything I wanted or needed. Besides which, most of the fun is in looking, not buying."

As soon as we'd finished lunch, we checked out of the hotel and took a pair of taxis to the Gare du Nord, where we had a wait of about forty-five minutes before we could board our Eurostar train to London.

Steve went to the restroom off the main waiting area and came back with his own tale. "Uncle Philip," he said, "you have to pay a fee to use the restroom, and when you get inside, the urinals are in a direct line of sight of the old lady who sits in the booth collecting money."

"I wouldn't worry about that," I said. "I would imagine her attitude is 'seen one, seen 'em all'."

Steve was visibly not amused, but before he could say anything else, we were called to board the train.

"Roger," Mason said, "what did you guys think of Paris?"

"We liked it," Roger said.

"Yeah," Steve said, "and we want to come back someday and see more of it."

"That's good," Charles said. "What you got this trip was a quick once-over of the high spots. When you decide to come back, plan on spending several half days in the Louvre."

"Yeah," Roger said, "the paintings did kind of blur after a while. You can only take in so much at a time."

I took a nap shortly after that and woke up just in time to hear the announcement that we were entering the Chunnel. *That's nice*, I thought as I drifted off to sleep again.

I woke up again somewhere between Dover and London. We disembarked at the St. Pancras International Station, where we walked through an underground corridor, finally arriving at a sign announcing that drug-sniffing dogs were on duty. After we rounded a corner and traveled a few yards further on, there was a sign with a picture of a black Labrador announcing that the drug-sniffing dog of the day was Rupert. A few yards further, we came face to face with Rupert and his handler, but Rupert showed no interest in us as we walked by him.

Leaving the station, we found a line of taxis and took two of them to a rental car office in the Marble Arch area near Hyde Park. We picked up our minivan, loaded it, and headed out of London.

29

Charles

AFTER we had the rental van loaded, we climbed in and were on our way. I was driving and Philip was in the passenger seat. Mason and Angela were in the seats behind us, and the boys occupied the third bench seat. To my surprise, we weren't particularly cramped.

I handed Philip the map and said, "Navigate, please," and I drove cautiously out of London.

"Have you driven on the wrong side of the road before this?" Angela said.

"Two or three times in the past few years," I said. "After a while you sort of get used to it. The only time I've ever had a problem has been when I let myself get panicked. When that happens, old habits kick in and you find yourself driving as though you were back home."

"Then don't let yourself get panicked," Philip said.

"Just don't distract me and I'll be okay."

It took a while, but we finally gained access to the M4 motorway, which led west toward Wales. Once we were on the limited-access M4, I relaxed enough to enjoy the scenery, which was wonderful.

Angela was enjoying it too. "This is gorgeous," she said.

"Isn't it?" I said. "This is my favorite time of the year to visit the UK. It's so green and so many things are blooming."

"What are those fields full of yellow blossoms?" Mason said.

"The plants are oilseed rape," I said. "Some part of them, the seeds, I think, is used in the production of canola oil, which is used in the making of margarine, biofuels, and other things. They grow them in the Dakotas at home, I believe."

"Is it my imagination," Philip said, "or are things a slightly different shade of green here?"

"I have no idea," I said, "but I almost always get that impression when I'm here at this time of year."

We left the M4 at the A46, and ten miles later we were in Bath. With Philip's help, I found the Redcar Hotel, which occupied a Georgian townhouse in the heart of Bath.

The hotel was superbly appointed. Angela, in particular, was overwhelmed by the elegance of our surroundings. As we'd done in Paris, we checked in, went to our rooms, and freshened up. We met in the lobby and decided to walk toward the city center, which was only a couple of blocks away.

Two or three blocks from the hotel, I spotted a restaurant across the street from us. The sign said "No. 5 Bistro." "See that restaurant across the street?" I said. "I've heard about it from friends who've eaten there. They gave it rave reviews."

"I'm game," Angela said.

Roger said, "I'm hungry. Can we stop now?"

"Why not?" Mason said.

We walked across to the restaurant and studied the menu posted in the window until Philip said, "Is everyone okay with this?"

Everyone said yes, so we went inside, and it proved to be a wonderful choice. Even the two boys were impressed.

The menu was very interesting and featured a number of dishes that most of us had read about but not experienced. I was pleased to see that even the boys got a little bit adventuresome with their selections. For an appetizer, I selected a mushroom soufflé. It was presented in the shape of a flan—the gray color wasn't particularly attractive, but the flavors were superb. I raved about it until everyone else was tempted to, and actually did, sample it.

By the time we'd finished our meal and two bottles of wine, we were ready to call it an evening, so we headed back to the hotel. We met in the hotel dining room the next morning and were more than pleased with the available breakfast choices.

Looking at the menu, Steve said, "Uncle Charles, what does it mean by 'full English breakfast'?"

"Do you remember the movie *Four Weddings and a Funeral*?"

"Sure," Steve said. "It was cool."

"Do you remember at the very beginning, where the guy who later became the subject of the funeral had a skillet in his hand containing his breakfast?"

"Sort of."

"That skillet contained a full English breakfast," I said. "Everything was fried and swimming in grease."

"I think I'll pass," Steve said.

"Good idea," Philip said.

We spent the rest of the morning walking around Bath, and just before lunch, we toured the ruins of the Roman baths for which the city was named. We had a nice lunch at Sally Lunn's and tried the well-known Bath Buns. After lunch, we took a bus tour of the town, which included stops at a couple of the more popular attractions, including the famous Royal Crescent.

Angela and Mason selected a restaurant in which to have dinner, and it proved a good choice. After breakfast the next morning, we checked out of the hotel and drove to Longleat, which is an English country house and the home of the Marquess of Bath. Lord Bath had turned his ancestral home into a major tourist destination featuring a safari park and other attractions. The house is considered to be a fine example of high Elizabethan architecture. The current Lord Bath, a wonderfully eccentric man, has been seen on numerous travel programs.

From Longleat we drove to Salisbury, stopping at Stonehenge on the way. As we walked around the famous circle of stones, everyone had the same first impression: "I thought it would be bigger." That being said, we were suitably impressed. We spent the night in Salisbury and took time to visit Salisbury Cathedral before driving on to Sussex County.

We arrived in the village of Amberley in the late afternoon and checked in at Amberley Castle. To enter the castle, we drove through an actual working portcullis. Parts of the castle dated back to the thirteenth century. The oldest portions of the castle were ruins, but the main sections were two or three hundred years newer and had been converted into a luxury hotel.

We had a first-class dinner in the castle's dining room. The boys couldn't stop talking about their room, which had a door leading from the bathroom to a private stairway that led to the top of the castle walls. We walked around the castle grounds before breakfast the next morning and were fascinated by the pair of white peacocks strutting around the garden.

A few miles down the road, we rounded a curve and saw the walls of Arundel Castle rising above and behind the town of Arundel. The castle was the home of the Duke of Norfolk, and the village below it was picture-postcard perfect in every respect.

We toured the castle and the village. Then we had lunch in a local tea room. We wanted to linger in Arundel, but we had to stay more or less on schedule, so we got back in the minivan and headed toward our next stop.

We arrived in Rye in the late afternoon. Rye is a medieval walled city, one of the original Cinque Ports. To gain access to the heart of the town, we had to drive through one of the original city gates. We checked into the Rye Lodge in time to have a memorable meal in the hotel dining room.

We explored the town's high street first thing the next morning. Angela was more than a bit taken with the shops, so we left her to it and went up a side street to the parish church. For a small fee, we were allowed to climb to the top of the church's tower, from which we had a splendid view of the marshland between the town and the English Channel.

Rye was an important port in medieval times, and some say it was a major center for smugglers. The harbor had silted up sometime in the past three hundred years, leaving only a small river channel.

We met Angela back at the hotel and drove over to nearby Battle, which derived its name from the Battle of Hastings, which occurred there in 1066. We toured the battle site and what was left of Battle Abbey and had lunch in a local pub.

Our next stop was Bodiam Castle, which was just a few miles from Battle. The boys were totally taken by it, as were the adults.

"I've always thought that Bodiam is the prettiest castle in England," I said as we walked across the bridge to the entrance.

Surrounded on all four sides by a moat, Bodiam represents the image that first comes to mind when one thinks of a castle.

"It's certainly picturesque," Angela said.

We explored the castle thoroughly and ended up in the top floor of one of the towers, looking at a small anteroom where what was clearly a wooden toilet seat was firmly affixed to a ledge of stone. There was a sheet of plastic, or more likely Plexiglas, under the seat, and you could see rough rock walls going all the way down and out of sight.

"I wonder what they used for toilet paper in those days?" Steve said.

"Well," Philip began to recite, "the ancient Romans kept a sponge on a stick in a jug of salt water for that purpose, but most people in medieval Europe used moss or leaves or whatever they had that was handy. In some parts of the Middle East, people simply cleaned themselves with their left hands, which is why the left hand is considered unclean in some cultures today—"

"Whoa, babe," I said, cutting him off. "That's almost TMI."

The boys giggled, and Angela looked puzzled. "What's TMI?" she said.

"TMI means too much information, Mom," Roger said.

"Oh," she said. "I get it."

"How do you know all this stuff, Uncle Philip?" Steve said.

"I've written a couple of books set in medieval times," Philip said, "and I always thoroughly research any period I'm going to write about."

"What happened to all the accumulated crap at the bottom of this shaft?" Roger said, looking down.

"Most likely there was some sort of opening that allowed water from the moat in and out to carry it off," I said.

"I wonder if they swam in the moat back then?" Steve said.

"I certainly hope not," Angela said.

We finished touring the castle and drove back to Rye, where we again had a great meal in the hotel restaurant.

"This is such a quaint little town," Angela said.

"Yes, it is," I said. "Did you notice the little park on the other side of the high street just up from the hotel?"

"Yes, I did," she said. "Why?"

"There's a plaque in the park which memorializes E. F. Benson," I said. "He was mayor of Rye at one time, but he is better known as the author of the Mapp and Lucia series of books, which involve two middle-aged ladies vying for social supremacy in a small English seaside town in the 1920s and 1930s."

"I saw that series on PBS," she said. "It was wonderful."

"Yes, it was," I said. "The series starred Prunella Scales as Miss Mapp and Geraldine McEwen as Lucia. Ms. Scales is best known in the USA for portraying the long-suffering Sybil Fawlty in *Fawlty Towers*, and Ms. McEwen most recently portrayed Miss Marple in a PBS Mystery series. The exterior location shots for *Mapp & Lucia* were filmed right here in Rye."

"I could spend another day or two exploring the shops here," Angela said.

"In that case, I'm glad we're leaving tomorrow," Mason said.

We left for London first thing the next morning, and within an hour we were approaching the outskirts. After that, it was slow going, as the signage on the outskirts of the city was less than wonderful, but we eventually found our way to the Dorchester Hotel.

At the hotel, we unloaded the car, and I took it to the rental car place while the rest of the group checked into the hotel.

By the end of the day, we were exhausted, having been to the Tower of London, St. Paul's Cathedral, Trafalgar Square, and points in between. We used the London Underground frequently, and the boys were both taken with the recorded announcements that were played every time we boarded a subway car. They walked along with us, intoning "mind the gap" and giggling every time they did. We had dinner in the hotel, mainly because we didn't feel like going anywhere else.

Over dessert, I said, "By the way, Angela, you were handling our theater tickets. Are you ready to tell us what we're seeing?"

"Yes, I am," she said. "I did an extensive search, but the bottom line is that there aren't any blockbuster musicals playing in London right now that we either haven't seen or would want to see."

"Did you come up with a plan B?" Mason said.

"It came down to the Agatha Christie play *The Mousetrap*, which has been running continuously for decades, or a performance at Covent Garden."

"So what did you choose?" Philip said.

"Both," she said. "We have a matinee of *The Mousetrap* tomorrow, and we're attending a performance of *Tosca* tomorrow night at Covent Garden."

"Well done, Angela," I said.

We all thoroughly enjoyed *The Mousetrap* and arrived back at the hotel just in time to have high tea in the promenade. Angela seemed especially taken with the experience, and the boys enjoyed it as well.

Our seats for *Tosca* were in an excellent location, and the performance was first rate. The title role was sung by a Russian soprano with whom I wasn't familiar, but who was more than adequate to the task. Her "Vissi d'arte" earned a standing ovation.

Afterward, in the taxi, I asked the boys what they had thought of the performance.

Steve summed it up, saying, "It was great, but they all died."

"Yeah," Roger said.

"That's grand opera for you," I said. "Happy endings aren't the norm, and *Tosca* is the ultimate in grand opera. In fact, the Italians have a saying: *C'è un solo Dio e c'è una sola Tosca*, which translates as 'there is one God, and there is one *Tosca*.'"

At the hotel, we went to the bar to have a nightcap. We talked about the opera for a while, and then Angela decided to change the subject. "Roger," she said, "are you and Steve going to the prom?"

"We haven't quite decided, Mom," Roger said.

"We've been talking about it," Steve said, "and so have Tom and Larry."

"If Tom and Larry decide to go," Roger said, "then Steve and I will too."

"I think you should go," Angela said. "The senior prom is a big event in your life."

"What do you think, Uncle Philip?" Steve said.

"I agree with Angela," Philip said, "but it has to be your decision."

"Do you have any idea how the school will react to a same-sex couple attending the prom?" I said.

"No, Sir," Steve said, "but we know somebody on the board who might be able to find out for us."

"I guess I walked right into that one," I said.

"That you did," Philip said.

"When we get home, I'll make a few calls," I said.

"What time do we leave in the morning?" Mason said.

"You and I are catching a train to Windsor at nine," Angela said.

"And we're taking the boys on a train to Cambridge at about the same time but from a different station," I said.

"Then I think it's time we all retired," Mason said.

"No argument," I said, and we left the bar and went back up to our rooms.

Philip and I and the boys arrived in Cambridge around ten and caught the sightseeing bus that circles the city, allowing you to get off and back on again as often as you wish.

We paid our entry fee and entered the King's College Chapel, where we sat in awe, looking at what is arguably the most beautiful ceiling in the world.

"Wow," Steve said as he stared up at the ceiling, "that's amazing. What do they call it?"

"It's called fan vaulting," Philip said, "and it's all the more amazing because it's almost five hundred years old."

"This whole place is amazing," Roger said, "and the architecture is wonderful."

"There speaks the would-be architect," I said, "but you're absolutely right. They really knew how to design and build beautiful things back then."

We somewhat reluctantly parted company with the beauty of the chapel and made our way back to London, arriving in time to meet Mason and Angela for lunch at Harrods. After lunch, Angela intended to do some serious shopping while the rest of us toured the famous food court, marveling at the variety of foods and treats on display.

We eventually caught up with Angela downstairs in the tax department, where she was completing the paperwork to claim a refund for the VAT that had been included in her purchases. They gave her a completed form that she was to drop in a special drop box at the airport, and would result in a refund to her credit card of the total VAT taxes paid.

That evening we were back in the vicinity of Harrods and had a great dinner at Turner's Restaurant, our last dinner in the UK. We made an early evening of it, as we had to get back to the hotel and pack for the trip home.

We were at the airport by nine the next morning, and our eleven o'clock flight left pretty much on time. We arrived in Atlanta a little after three thirty that afternoon and were home an hour later. The tribe were all napping, which gave us time to catch up on things with Gran, Marie, and Grace.

We'd called home every day and had even talked to Steven and

Mark a couple of times, but firsthand information is always best. The boys went to their room to unpack, and Philip and I did the same. When we assembled downstairs for dinner, Philip and I presented the three ladies with various little gifts we had purchased. We also had gifts for the fourth lady, Mrs. Goodman. It took a couple of days for us to get firmly settled back into our normal routine.

30

Charles

I KEPT my promise to the boys and called the headmaster at Exeter Academy and one or two members of the board. None of them expressed any displeasure at the prospect of two same-sex couples attending the prom. In point of fact, and to my surprise, one of them thought it would be very good for the school's image and wondered if some positive publicity might be derived. I passed that information along to Steve and Roger, who said they would pass it along to the other two boys.

The night of the prom arrived, and Philip and I attended as chaperones. As high school proms go it was a fairly tame affair, but the boys seemed to have a good time. Steve and Roger danced with each other, as did Tom and Larry; then the two couples changed partners and Steve danced with Tom while Roger danced with Larry. I was keeping a careful watch on the other kids as well as the adults that were present, and I was unable to spot any overt looks of disapproval. It probably helped that all four boys had been out at the school for most of the past two years and were well liked by all of their classmates. Philip and I even managed to dance together a couple of times, something we almost never had an opportunity to do, given that we were not particularly inclined to go clubbing.

After the excitement of the prom, the actual graduation was almost an anticlimax. Steve and Roger were heavily involved in the Speedos Car Wash that summer, to the extent they were able to be, given that they were carrying a full load of summer courses at Tech.

We had a summer full of birthday celebrations, as R. B. and J. J. turned two in May and July respectively, and Paul and Raymond had a joint birthday party for their first birthday in August. Steve and Roger had a highly successful summer with their business, as well. Philip and I marveled at the energy the two of them seemed to have as they dashed from one responsibility to another, juggling school, work, and the car wash. Oh, to be eighteen again.

Steve and Roger finished their summer at Tech and began the fall term with enough credits to be technically considered juniors, although some obscure rule prevented them from being officially labeled as such.

In October, Philip got a call from Mrs. Johnson at the nursery. Her husband had suffered a stroke, and they were going to have to sell everything and move to Florida, where they had family to help take care of Mr. Johnson. Philip immediately went to see the Johnsons and made a firm offer on the property, which they accepted.

That evening we gathered in the upstairs study. Steve and Roger were present, as were Mason and Angela. Philip had called Mason to give him a heads-up as to the reason for the meeting.

"I've made an offer on behalf of the boys," Philip said, "and the Johnsons have accepted it."

"How much did you have to offer?" Mason said.

Philip told him, adding that the terms were $100,000 down and the Johnsons would hold a five-year mortgage for the balance.

"That's not a bad price for their going business and the house and twenty acres," Mason said. "Too bad we can't snap up the surrounding properties, as well."

"Why would we want to do that, Dad?" Roger said.

"Because the twenty acres the Johnsons own is the largest undeveloped tract of land in that area," Mason said, "and with just a little more acreage, we could put in a nice strip center anchored by the nursery."

"Why would we do that?" Steve said.

"Because the nursery alone wouldn't bring in enough revenue to carry the mortgage on the property," I said. "Rental income from a strip center would take up the slack quite nicely. The Johnsons didn't have a problem keeping things going because they've owned the property for twenty years or more and didn't have high carrying costs. Their sale alone will trigger an increase in the assessed value for real estate taxes."

"He's right," Mason said. "I've been quietly looking into the surrounding parcels for some time, but they've all been acquired by different purchasers over the past two years, and I haven't been able to track any of them down. I think some son of a bitch of a developer has been quietly buying up those parcels, but whoever he is, he's got a clever lawyer, and he's hidden behind many more layers of holding companies than I've been able to penetrate."

Philip was grinning from ear to ear. Mason noticed the grin and said, "What?"

Philip held up a finger and said, "Give me a minute."

He disappeared down the hall. A few minutes later, he returned with a large roll of paper, which he spread out on the coffee table.

"Are these the parcels to which you're referring, Mason?" Philip said.

The paper was a sketch of all the properties surrounding the Johnson's twenty acres.

"Those are the ones," Mason said.

I couldn't help myself, and I began to grin as well.

"Okay, you two," Mason said. "What's the joke?"

"There's no joke," Philip said. "I'm the son of a bitch of a developer, and Charles is the clever lawyer who's hidden my purchases behind layers of holding companies. What you see is a sketch of all the properties around the Johnsons' acreage. Over the past two years, I've acquired a total of nine properties. The total acreage is thirty, not counting the twenty acres owned by the Johnsons."

"You sly dog," Mason said. "I'm impressed."

"You should apologize to Philip," Angela said.

"Why?" Mason said.

"For calling him a son of a bitch."

"Don't worry, Angela," I said. "Mason was speaking out of jealousy because he didn't get there first, and I'm absolutely certain that Philip took it as a compliment."

"That I did," Philip said. "After my initial conversation with Mrs. Johnson back when Steve and Roger first started buying plants from them, I started looking into the surrounding properties. Charles and I were liquidating a lot of assets at the time, so there was plenty of ready cash for the purchases."

"What do you propose doing?" Mason said.

"My idea is to transfer the excess acreage to a new entity, with Steve and Roger as the principal shareholders," Philip said. "That will give them enough acreage to keep the nursery operation going, although they'll have to move some of the plants away from their current location, thereby freeing up some of the property near the road for the development. I'll keep the residences for the time being, but if the boys' operation needs more cash flow, I'll transfer some of the rental property as well."

"He neglected to mention that he'll do the transfers at cost," I said. "There will be no profit involved."

"Okay," Mason said, "now we're talking business."

"How much cash will it take to get the property developed?" I said.

"Give me some time to put together a plan," Mason said, "and I'll come up with some numbers."

"Meanwhile," Philip said, "if you and the boys agree, we can use the cash in those two trust funds to close the purchase with the Johnsons."

"Absolutely," Mason said. "This is what you and I have been waiting for."

"Steve," I said, "you and Roger have been mighty quiet through all of this. What do you guys think?"

"I think it sounds good," Steve said, "even if I don't quite understand all of it."

"Me too," Roger said.

"To put things in the simplest terms possible," Philip said, "you and Roger will have a nice little nursery operation attached to some sort of garden center, probably including an Ace Hardware or True Value hardware franchise. It will generate income for you, and it will provide you with a very inexpensive source of shrubs and trees for your landscaping business."

"Right," Mason said, "and the income from the strip center will be more than enough to pay for the whole operation."

"Are you sure?" Roger said.

"Roger," Mason said, "this is what I do for a living. Developing small shopping centers is what has kept you and your brothers housed and fed most of your lives."

"Okay, Dad," Roger said. "We'll rely on your expertise."

"Can I take this sketch with me?" Mason said.

"Sure," Philip said. "I have two more copies."

"Give me a week," Mason said, "and I'll come back with a couple of proposals."

"I still think you should apologize to Philip," Angela said.

"Sure," Mason said. "For what it's worth, I apologize for calling the son of a bitch a son of a bitch."

"Apology accepted," Philip said, laughing.

Angela threw her hands in the air and said, "I give up. Sometimes I just don't understand guy talk."

"This calls for a toast," I said. "Give me a minute to go downstairs and select something suitable."

I went to the small wine cooler downstairs and selected a first growth Bordeaux that I felt would be worthy of the occasion. Back in the study, I opened it and split the bottle between the six of us.

"Oh, my," Angela said after she'd taken a sip, "that's wonderful. What is it?"

"It's a Chateau Margaux 1994," I said. "One of the first growth Bordeaux wines."

"What do you mean by first growth Bordeaux?" Steve said.

"It refers to what is known as the Bordeaux Wine Official Classification of 1855," I said. "For an exposition in 1855, the Emperor Napoleon III requested that Bordeaux wines be classified as to quality because they were going to be on display to visitors from around the world. The wines were ranked from first growth down to fifth growth. Originally, there were only four first growth wines, but in 1973, Chateau Mouton Rothschild was elevated from second growth to first growth status. This wine is one of five wines considered to be the best of the best that Bordeaux has to offer."

"Do you like it, Steve?" Philip said.

"Oh, yes," Steve said. "It's tasty."

I raised my glass and said, "To the success of the new venture."

Everyone else followed suit.

"It just hit me," Philip said. "We need a clever name for the shopping center."

"I think that's Mason's area of expertise," I said.

"You're right," Philip said, "but maybe Steve and Roger can come up with some ideas as well."

Ten days later, we met in the study once again. Mason presented a detailed proposal for a strip center with a sizeable garden center and hardware store as the anchor tenants. The proposal included space for a dozen other stores and still set aside thirty acres for the nursery operation. He'd also designated a few choice parcels close to the road as out parcels, which would be ideal for fast food operations.

"This looks good," I said. "Now let's see some numbers."

Mason was on top of it and handed each of us a proposal detailing construction costs, financing costs, and a multitude of other necessary components.

Philip was particularly interested in the financing and asked more questions than I would have thought possible. Mason fielded them one by one until Philip ran out of things to ask.

There was a long pause, and Mason finally asked, "Well, what do you think?"

"I like it," I said, "but I defer to the expert in the family."

"Can we really accomplish all of this with the amount of financing proposed?" Philip said.

"Without a doubt," Mason said. "Even if you add an additional 10 percent for contingencies, there isn't a banker in this city who won't jump at the opportunity."

"At what interest rate?" Philip said.

"Prime plus one or two points," Mason said.

"Charles and I will underwrite the project for prime plus one point," Philip said, giving me a look that told me not to object.

"Why would you do that?" Angela said.

"To keep it in the family," Philip said. "If it's a good deal for a bank, it's an even better deal for us, and it will save a ton of fees."

"I'm amazed," Mason said. "I had no idea you guys had that kind of liquidity."

"At the moment we do," Philip said. "As I mentioned at our last meeting, Charles and I have been liquidating a great deal of late, and the money is just sitting there earning a pitiful amount of interest, waiting for us to decide what to invest in next."

"As long as you're not putting all your eggs in one basket," Mason said.

"Don't worry," I said, "that's not the case. Philip is probably the most talented investor I've ever known, and even with all that liquidating, we're still more diversified than I would have thought possible."

"Mason," Philip said, "do you think it'll be possible to complete this project by spring?"

"Perhaps not the entire center," Mason said, "but certainly the nursery/hardware operation could be up and running by then."

"Good," Philip said. "I'd like to see at least that portion of the project operating by then so it can take full advantage of all those homeowners looking for plants and shrubs at that time of the year."

"We'll make the garden center phase one," Mason said, "and

focus on completing it before we even start phase two."

"That sounds like a plan," I said. "Make it so."

The decisions having been made, the proposed project shifted into high gear. It was Mason and Philip's area of expertise, so I left them to it and concentrated on what I knew best.

We had special guests on a Saturday evening in mid-November, as Judge William Hampton and his wife, Alma, had accepted an invitation to dinner. We'd planned to have them on a number of occasions since the incident at the Mall of Georgia, but schedules had kept conflicting.

Mrs. Hampton was a tiny woman and very dignified. She made me think of Cicely Tyson playing Miss Jane Pittman. Gran was genuinely glad to see both of them and apologized for not having contacted them long before.

"When my husband died," Gran said by way of explanation, "I withdrew from life for a while. Then this young man's parents were killed and I suddenly had a child to raise once again. After that, the years simply got away from me."

We were sitting in the library, and Judge Hampton looked up at my grandfather's portrait and said, "You have nothing for which to apologize, Mrs. Barnett. You know how much that man meant to me, and I've never forgotten your many kindnesses back then, either."

"We appreciate the way you helped us when my nephew and his friends were arrested at the Mall of Georgia," Philip said.

"I only did what was right and proper," Judge Hampton said, "not to mention what was fully within the law. I have good reason to concern myself with poor treatment of gays."

"What my husband means," Mrs. Hampton said, "is that we have personal reasons to feel that way. Our youngest son was homosexual. His siblings didn't handle it very well when he told them about it. Nor, I'm ashamed to say, did my husband and I. To make a long story short, he eventually killed himself rather than have to come to terms with who he was."

"My dear," Gran said, "I'm so sorry to hear that. Losing a child for any reason is tragic enough, but to have one be driven by circumstance to an ultimate act such as that must have been dreadful."

"It was a long time ago," Mrs. Hampton said, "but some things are never quite fully laid to rest."

Roger and Steve came into the library, and Steve said, "Mrs. Goodman says dinner is ready."

I introduced the boys to Judge and Mrs. Hampton, and the boys thanked the judge for his help. The dinner conversation centered around the boys, their schooling, and their ultimate plans. After that, Gran, with her usual skill, extracted a great deal of information from the Hamptons. We learned that their two surviving sons were both lawyers, one in Chicago and one in Washington, and that they had five grandchildren.

The boys excused themselves to go do their homework, and the rest of us retired to the sunroom.

"This is such a beautiful room," Mrs. Hampton said.

"You must come and see the garden in the spring, my dear," Gran said. "It was always lovely, but those two young men have worked their magic on it for the last two seasons, and I am looking forward to spring with anticipation."

"They seem to be very ambitious," the judge said.

"They're hard workers," Philip said, "and budding capitalists. We, that is, Roger's father and I, lent them the money to buy their first truck, trailer, and equipment, and they repaid us in a very short period. Then we provided funds for a second truck and equipment, and their business took off."

"It's reassuring to see two young men their age willing to work that hard," the judge said. "All the more so when it's fairly obvious that they needn't have done so."

"The really interesting thing," I said, "is how truly tight-fisted they are with their hard-earned money. On the other hand, they can be incredibly generous." I related the story of Jimmy Anderson and the scholarship that had been established on his behalf.

"I read some of that in the paper when the current school year began," Mrs. Hampton said. "Didn't they raise a lot of money for that scholarship fund from the famous car wash last summer?"

"Absolutely," I said. "Exeter Academy has several new students this term courtesy of that scholarship fund, all of them from the poorest backgrounds you can imagine. The scholarships are awarded strictly on merit so that kids with promise will have a chance to realize their full potential."

The Hamptons left, but not without promising to visit again in the near future.

We celebrated Mark and Steven's third birthday in November and had a small party for them. They'd begun to attend a new kindergarten program for three-year-olds at the school, so a few of their classmates were at the party.

Philip and I flew to the Keep Thanksgiving afternoon, planning to spend the weekend in the mountains. We were up early the next morning and decided to drive over to Maggie Valley. Near the end of the valley, immediately past Ghost Town, we saw a sign pointing to Cataloochee Ranch.

"Ever been up that road?" I said.

"No."

"Then let's check it out." We drove slowly up the road, and I could tell by the way my ears were popping that we were climbing steadily, despite the ups and downs of the road.

"Look up ahead," Philip said. "There are two guys jogging up the road with an Irish Setter."

We cruised slowly by the two men and their dog. I was driving, but Philip turned to look as closely at them as he could while I passed them.

"Definitely family," he said.

"How can you tell without interacting with them?" I said.

"Body language."

We reached the top of the mountain and saw a large complex of cabins and buildings. A sign pointed the way to a ski area to our left. I pulled over, and we got out of the Jeep. We walked over to a log at the side of the road and sat for a long while, enjoying the air and the scenery. When the two men and the dog drew abreast of us, we got up and walked over to them.

We learned that the blond was George Martin and the brunet was Mike Foster. Their dog was Thorin Oakenshield, aka Thor, and they owned a cabin a couple of miles back down the road. They invited us to lunch, and we accepted, so they and the dog climbed into the Jeep, and I drove us back down the mountain.

George instructed me to turn into a driveway on the right-hand side of the road, and I stopped at a keypad that obviously controlled the gate across their driveway. He gave me the combination, and I pressed the buttons. The gate opened, and we drove down a concrete driveway to their cabin.

It was a great place. There was a ground floor containing a garage, a couple of storerooms, a laundry room, and a huge recreation area. The second story was a modified A-frame design with a huge great room, a small kitchen and breakfast nook, two bedrooms, and a nice master bath. There was a loft above the bedrooms.

We learned that George was with the sheriff's department down in Jacksonville and that Mike ran his own computer business.

We also discovered a mutual interest in running, and Philip and I accepted an invitation to visit them in Jacksonville in order to participate in the next River Run, a 15K event that was reported to be one of the best in the country.

After a nice lunch, we headed back to the other side of Waynesville and up the mountain to the Keep. We spent the rest of the weekend doing as little as possible and flew back to Atlanta Sunday afternoon.

Christmas was a really big affair, given the ages of the various members of the tribe, and the house was filled with the noise of small boys having a great time.

AS SOON as the decision had been made to go ahead with the garden center and adjacent strip shopping center, we went into high gear. Rather than wait for surveyors, we had a fencing contractor fence in the acreage behind all of the rental houses, as well as that part of the former Johnson acreage that was to be set aside for nursery operations.

While the fence was being installed, Steve and Roger put their crews to work. The timing was perfect, given that fall was a slow season for them. The entire nursery operation was relocated, including the greenhouses, which were dismantled and moved to the edge of the designated nursery area. By the time the contractor was ready to begin actual on-site operations, the nursery was up and running in its new setting, and plans were underway to significantly expand its selection of plants, shrubs, and trees.

The boys also constructed two greenhouses specifically for the propagation of cuttings. They were similar to but significantly larger than the greenhouse they'd built on the grounds of our house.

Philip and Mason had worded the contract very carefully, giving the contractor plenty of incentives for early completion and some significant penalties should the work not be done in the time specified. A small miracle was accomplished and phase one was completed by mid-March. When ground was broken for phase two, the strip center, Mason used his contacts to secure deals for two out parcels with McDonald's and a branch of a regional bank.

Steve and Roger had hired Mr. Goodman to oversee their sprinkler system crews. As Gran had put it, "With four men in the house, Mr. Goodman has less and less to do," so he jumped at the chance to work for the boys and, as he put it, "to once again feel useful."

The hiring of Mr. Goodman had come about mostly by accident. The boys had received a call from a customer about a jet of water squirting out of his lawn in the wrong place. Roger was dealing with a bout of the flu, so Mr. Goodman had volunteered to accompany Steve to fix the problem. When they returned from fixing the problem, a lengthy conversation ensued between all of us—and Mr. Goodman went to work for the boys.

Mason's luck ran out when he tried to find an anchor tenant for phase two of the shopping center. He and Angela had come over after dinner one evening, and we were in the study discussing the situation.

"I don't know why you can't get Publix to open a store there,"

Angela said. "They don't have a store anywhere near that area."

"Honey," Mason said, "I've tried, but they're worried about the economy."

"Nonsense," she said. "People have to eat."

"True," he said, "but when people start tightening their belts, they're looking for Walmart prices."

"So talk to Walmart."

"Been there, done that," he said. "They don't put stores in strip centers anymore—they prefer stand-alone sites. Beyond that, they don't want to be next door to a nursery/hardware operation that would compete with two of their departments."

"Mason," Philip said, "what kind of sweetheart deal would it take to get a decision-maker's attention at Publix?"

"I'm not sure, but give me a range of options and I'll have a go at it."

Philip tossed a few ideas out, and he and Mason kicked them around for a while, eventually agreeing upon a series of three choices with a rock-bottom price as the final offer.

"Uncle Philip," Steve said, "why can't we offer that kind of deal to all the tenants?"

"You could, I suppose," Philip said, "if you didn't want to see any return on your investment at all for ten or fifteen years."

"However," Mason said, "once you get Publix on board, you won't have to work so hard to sign up smaller tenants—they're smart enough to know that Publix will generate the traffic."

So phase two was set in motion. By the time we returned from participating in the River Run down in Jacksonville, leases had been signed with Publix and several smaller tenants.

A couple of weeks later, Philip and I were in the upstairs study having a glass of wine and reflecting on the previous few years.

"We've come a long way from where we began, haven't we?" he said.

"Yeah. Who would have thought it? Being responsible for a pair of teenagers, raising our own kids, the whole nine yards."

Lance padded into the study, walked up to where I sat, and placed his head in my lap.

"And here's the biggest and most lovable kid of all. Aren't you, Lance?"

"Woof," Lance replied, looking at me with his big brown eyes.

ETIENNE lives in central Florida, very near the hamlet in which he grew up. He always wanted to write but didn't find his muse until a few years ago, when he started posting stories online. These days he spends most of his time battling with her, as she is a capricious bitch who, when she isn't hiding from him, often rides him mercilessly, digging her spurs into his sides and forcing the flow of words from a trickle to a flood.

Visit Etienne at http://www.etiennestories.blogspot.com. You can contact him at Etienne.Reynard@comcast.net.

The APPEARANCES Trilogy: Book 1

http://www.dreamspinnerpress.com

The APPEARANCES Trilogy: Book 2

http://www.dreamspinnerpress.com

The APPEARANCES Trilogy: Book 3

http://www.dreamspinnerpress.com

The Avondale Stories

http://www.dreamspinnerpress.com

Also by ETIENNE

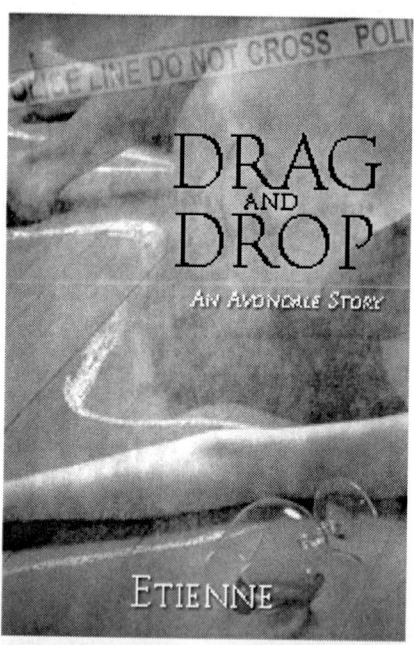

http://www.dreamspinnerpress.com

More Avondale Stories

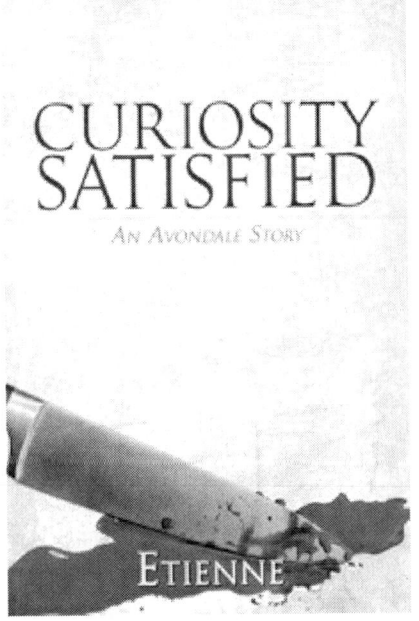

http://www.dreamspinnerpress.com

Also from ETIENNE

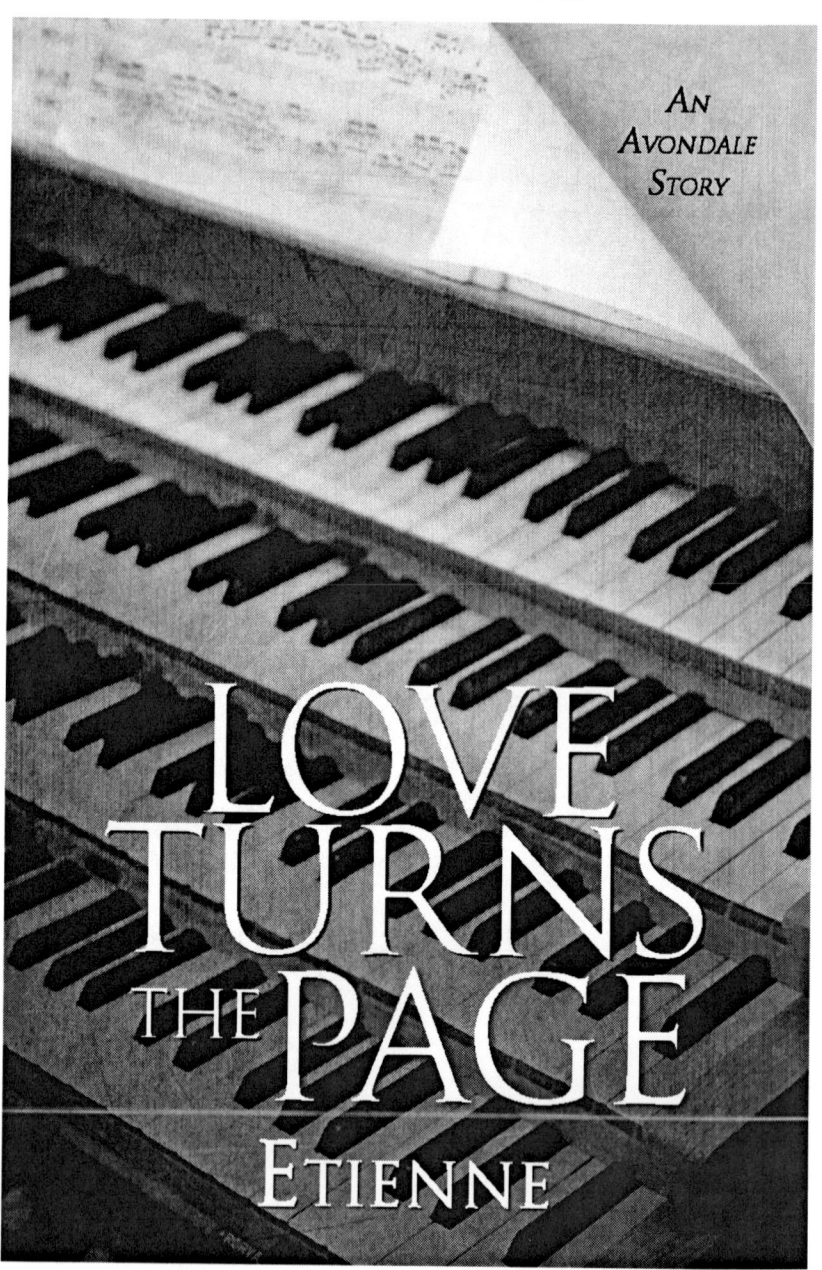

http://www.dreamspinnerpress.com

Also from ETIENNE

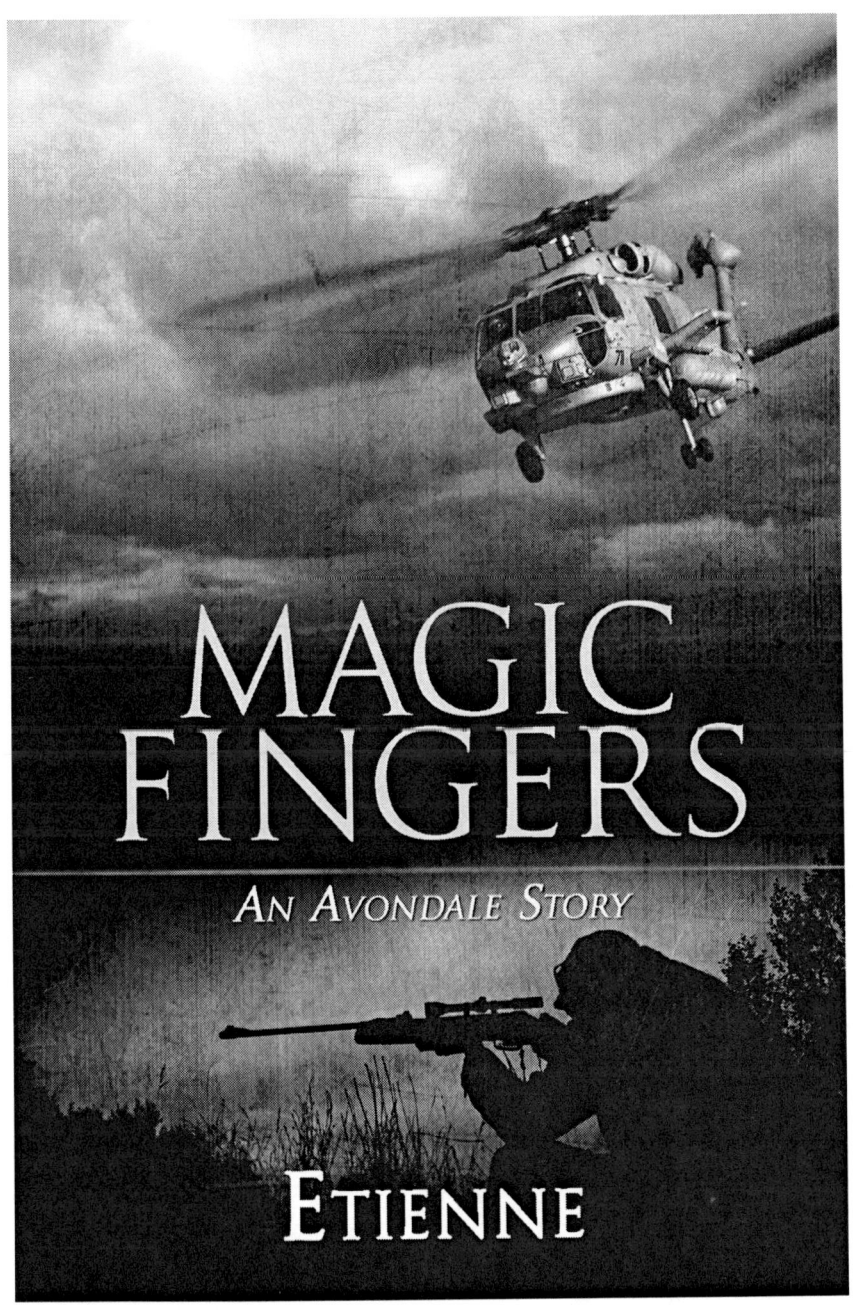

http://www.dreamspinnerpress.com

Also by Etienne

http://www.dreamspinnerpress.com

CPSIA information can be obtained at www.ICGtesting.com
Printed in the USA
BVOW080853071212

307476BV00007BA/199/P